AS ABOVE...

MARROW CHARM

...SO BELOW

Marrow Charm

Kristin Jacques

Book One

The Gate Cycle

THE PARLIAMENT HOUSE

To Mom, for shaping a mind capable of wonder.

PART I
PATHWAYS

The Wolf in the Web

❧

The gap between the blacksmith and Morgan's Drink House was just wide enough for Azzy and her pickaxe to squeeze through. The soot-covered apprentices and hungover patrons paid little attention to the lone girl sneaking off between the buildings. None of them would snitch on her—they hated the Elder as much as she did.

The damp air outside the Heap belied the dangers of the dark. She kept a sharp ear out for the ever-present threat of grimwerms, trailing her fingers along the slick wall of the main tunnel to guide her. A light would be discovered by the watchers at the gate, and Azzy found her way better in the dark. Light made too many shadows, made her miss things. She would have missed this opening if she relied on so simple a sense as sight.

The chill caught her attention, that teasing hint of air so cold it nipped her trailing fingers. She crouched down, tentatively dipping her hand into the hole, holding her breath as she waited for another gust of air to reach her. *There!*

No guarantee that the crevice wouldn't peter out into a dead end or narrow too much for her to crawl through. The massive grimwerms constantly burrowed through, where their maggot-pale bulk upset and collapsed the earth into new configurations. The walls were snug against her shoulders as she crawled inside, but she pressed on, goaded by the whisper of icy air. She reached for a jut of rock to pull herself forward and stopped, marveling at the faint glow of her skin. There was light ahead, weak and gray, but pure— nothing like the filmy luminescence of the day lamps.

Eager, she scrambled forward, blinded by the sudden influx of light as she tumbled into wet, white powder. She gasped at the sensation and squeezed her eyes shut until the light didn't scald her closed lids. Blinking rapidly, she forced them to adjust, opening them wide at last. The numbness in her fingers and penetrating chill that seeped up from her knees were forgotten at the sight before her.

Azzy could count on one hand the number of times she'd ventured to the Above. Each time left her breathless. Stars sparked like trapped gems in a swirling mass of velvety purple and deep blue. Their light reflected off the white blanketing the ground, revealing snow, chips of diamond that covered every inch of the land. She rose to her feet, laughing as she spun, head flung back to the heavens.

The stars felt physically close, as if she could reach up and skim her fingers against the underbelly of that endless velvet dark. Her mama told her stories of how people once rode through the sky on metal wings. She wondered if they could touch the stars. Azzy stopped her spinning abruptly as she thought of her mother. Her reason for risking this little excursion weighed on her anew, draining away her elation. Time to get to work.

The moon hung low and full, either rising or setting

over the horizon, she couldn't be sure. The solitary howl of some animal sounded in the distance, low and mournful and a firm reminder to be swift with her task. If the tunnels were dangerous, the Above was worse by a hundredfold. "Grab anything green, grab any plants you can find"—those were her goals.

Azzy unhooked the scraper blade strapped to her leg and knelt to peel the moss and lichen clinging to the rocks. "Moss for rashes, lichen to strengthen the body's defenses." She continued her mental recitation as she wrapped each individual sample in separating cloth. The necessity of speed and meticulous care sent a tremor through her arms. Biting the inside of her cheek, she ripped the bark from the surrounding trees. Strip, wrap, strip, wrap. She could hear the familiar lecture on cross-contamination droning on in her head, steadying her movements. This was too important to muck up. Azzy knelt and scraped back the snow to dig out the dried shoots of sleeping plants, anything and everything she could think of to restock the Apothecary's supplies. Someone had to; the Foragers had been gone for nearly two months. Their supplies were perilously low. She couldn't procure the more exotic ingredients to refill all that had run out but having nothing on hand was a dangerous position for an apothecary, especially after her brother's episode last night...

Another howl cut through the air, much closer than before, choked at the end. Azzy looked up, staring through the dark columns of snow-covered trees. A high-pitched whine emanated from within, filled with pain and fear. The sound stroked her skin like the point of a blade, made the hair rise on her arms. Exchanging the scraper for her pick-axe, she moved forward, scanning her surroundings for the danger.

A rough-barked tree snagged on her clothing.

Azzy looked down, puzzled by the translucent threads trailing from her sleeve, catching on the bark. She pulled away. The threads went taut. The bark ripped away, so suddenly that Azzy rocked on her heels. She froze, her breath caught in her throat, following the threads to denser strands of gauzy white that laced through the higher branches. Not threads—web. The sparse canopy of trees was interconnected with swaths of webs, twisting in the wind with a soft clicking sound. They were entangled with bones, hung like macabre wind chimes. Broken skulls leered down at her.

She swallowed hard. Screams were for fools and food; Azzy refused to be either. Of course, she was a fool for blithely wandering into a winnowrook's web. A grotesque melding of crow and spider far larger than either, winnowrooks were an all too common predator. Every time she ventured to the Above, their infestation of the area seemed to spread. but she wasn't caught, not yet. She took a step back. Movement thrashed in the corner of her eye. She bit her tongue bloody to keep from crying out. A pitiful whine reached her ears, wrapping around her better judgment as her traitorous gaze followed the sound to its source.

A massive wolf dangled a foot off the ground from the thick gray cords, his twisted position giving her an eyeful of his anatomy. He wrenched against the web, painting it red. The threads were so tight around his body they cut through the thick pelt of mottled black and gray fur. He was killing himself. The more he fought, the tighter the web would constrict until it cut off his air or he bled to death. He jerked into a halting spin, half facing her. His pale yellow eyes were sightless and wild, so panicked he didn't see her standing there.

His dying movements would draw them out, and soon, with the delectable promise of fresh meat. Azzy had to flee, run for the safety of the caves before the winnowrooks descended from the treetops like spidery angels of death. She holstered her axe and bent her knees, prepared to run away. The wolf's choking whimper made her pause. Her breath shuddered with her hesitation, her body vibrating on the edge of indecision. Her thoughts bordered on madness.

Don't be stupid, Azzy, he's already dead, he just can't accept it yet.

She chewed on her lip, listening hard for the telltale skitter-skatter of claws on silk as she tapped the scraper knife strapped to her thigh. It went against every instinct, every inner voice that screamed at her to run except one— one tiny niggling voice that made her spin around in the snow. She palmed her blade as she rushed for the wolf.

Death smelled sweet, of warm sucrose against the clean wet snow.

A devious weapon—the cloying scent of the winnowrooks, evoking memories of hearth and home, and the sweet treats of childhood. It teased her nostrils as her blade snagged against the strands binding the wolf's rear flank. She gritted her teeth and sawed, the blade not made for this sort of cut. She would leave his jaw for last—sensible, as he lashed out blindly at her presence, brushing against her hard enough she nearly lost her footing. She spread her legs to ground herself and hewed at the webs. There was no room for error, not when the bones began to click and rattle overhead.

Snap. One hind leg free, the severed web released enough weight to drop the wolf back to the ground. The beast startled and lunged forward. A thread nearly sliced off his ear. Azzy grabbed his entrapped jaw, breathing hard as she tried to hold him steady, mentally begging for him to

7

calm. She sawed at the next thick strand. The bones sang their *click clack* warning song from the high branches, reaching a desperate crescendo that ended with eerie silence. She shuddered and kept sawing.

The smell enveloped her, curling around her like cooling sweet cakes fresh from the fire at first light strike. Azzy didn't dare turn around. She knew what crept toward her, watching for its shadow out of the corner of her eye. *Snap,* another thread cut. She doubled her efforts, hacking at the last stubborn mass of webbing. The wolf went still, his yellow eyes focused, settling on her briefly before shifting over her shoulder. A low growl rumbled from his chest as a spindly shadow stretched across the snow at her feet. Her muscles tensed. Azzy changed her grip on the blade.

She pivoted, jumping back as the winnowrook's claw-tipped leg descended. It wasn't far enough. Hooked claws sliced through her layers of clothing to draw a long burning line between her breasts. She yelped and slashed wildly in return. It was pure luck she caught the winnowrook across one of its eyes, distracting it with pain. It reared with a screech, limbs flailing. Its feathery lower body slammed into her and pinned her against the wolf. The winnowrook's blood smoked on her skin, not hot but cold, ice searing her flesh. She had no breath to gasp, her lungs pinched between her ribs. Her grip was slicked by blood, both from the wolf and the winnowrook, but she managed to twist her arm back and cut the last knot of web with a desperate yank.

Azzy and the wolf tumbled away from the scrabbling winnowrook. The consequence was the loss of her knife, flung away into the snow. She rolled to her knees, pulling her pickaxe from the holster on her back as the winnowrook shook off its injury and set its remaining seven eyes on her. Its beak opened to emit a crackling hiss, dead leaves over stone. The pinfeather ruff that crowned its head stood on end. It lifted the upper half of its segmented body, legs splayed in a gesture of pure aggression.

Azzy braced herself and clenched her pickaxe tight in front of her. No time for regrets and thoughts of unkept promises—she'd go down fighting. The wolf flew over her head, a streak of gray and red. He latched his bloodied jaws on the monster's exposed underbelly and tore into it. The winnowrook was massive, but it was no match for the injured beast. With a snarl, the wolf whipped his head, taking a chunk of the monster with it. Dark blood spilled over the muddied snow, sending plumes of sweet-smelling smoke into the air. Its rattling scream numbed her ears and made her molars ache. She watched—terrified, transfixed— as the wolf tore into it, again and again, ripping away a piece each time until the winnowrook collapsed to the ground in a pool of black fluid. Its eyes paled, milky at the moment of its death.

She released a shaky breath. The cut between her breasts throbbed. The wolf cleaned his muzzle in a snow-drift, wiping off the winnowrook's icy blood. Azzy attempted to stand, but her legs were too wobbly to support her weight. She needed to leave, to clear the area before the wolf's attention fell to her.

His head snapped up at her movement. She froze, calling herself all kinds of stupid for freeing the damn thing. What was she thinking? Of course, he was going to turn on her, he was a wild creature, half-mad from the winnowrook's death trap. Her knuckles turned white on the axe handle. Had she freed the wolf only to kill him now? It felt wrong. Her palms itched. Wrong, this was wrong.

The wolf's lip curled in a sneer, lowering into a hunter's crouch. Azzy's senses fizzed with awareness. The axe slipped from her hands, landing with a thud at her feet. There it was, the same niggling voice, a whisper at the back

9

of her thoughts. She listened, reaching through the torn layers of her shirt to dip a hand in her own blood. The wolf's ears swiveled forward as she lifted her red painted fingertips for him to see.

He padded toward her with hesitant steps, his head tilted. He towered over her kneeling form. His torn nose drew closer, inhaling her scent. Azzy closed the distance, and gently swabbed her blood across his muzzle. Her thumb swept down, through his red slicked fur. She pulled back, drawing her thumb across her forehead, like a ritual, a binding gesture. The wolf drew back with a huff, shaking himself. He leaned in to sniff her again, closer, his great head nuzzling the cut across her chest. A pink tongue darted out, leaving a trail of warmth as he lapped her wound clean. Azzy kept perfectly still until he finished and drew back to stare at her with stunning mead-colored eyes. For a moment, she saw something flicker like lightning in his pupils, before the wolf turned and slunk away.

Azzy remained where she was, too shocked by her survival and her odd impulsive actions to move. Her knees were numb in the snow, the cut between her breasts tingled, and her blood-stained fingers kept curling open and closed. When the cold wet crept up her thighs, she finally forced herself to stand, her legs steady at last. Surveying the carcass of the winnowrook, she gave a strained laugh. She was alive. Azzy retrieved her weapons, thinking of grisly necessities as she cleaned her knife. Her foot nudged one of the winnowrook's severed legs. This was a treasure trove of exotic ingredients to take home.

Setting her jaw, Azzy crouched down and used her axe to dismantle the pieces she needed. Her brother's face slipped into her thoughts, his skin pale and bruised, and the voice—that terrible voice that drove her into the tunnels this morning. That voice she'd risk the dangers of Above and the wrath of the Elder to never hear again. Even now, as the adrenaline of her encounter drained away, she felt the return of urgency, the impulse to run home with everything she'd so painstakingly gathered. The words chased one another in her mind, nagging her faster and faster.

The Rot is coming.

City of Shadow and Stone

✤

Azzy tied up as much as she could carry in the thin dropcloth she used to gather supplies, tucking the scraps of vegetation into her belt to avoid cross-contamination.

It was a tense flight from clearing to cave, digging her heels into the snow to throw herself forward with each step. The very parts she'd fought for might still get her killed. Any blood that leaked through the cloth left a trail of smoke, a flare for predators to follow. By the time she hit the mouth of the tunnel, it clouded around her, pricked at her eyes, and left an acrid taste at the back of her throat.

The tunnel was hell to maneuver. She held onto the memory of Armin shuddering in her arms. The terrible voice echoed in her ears. She kept going, falling into the pattern of her labor, stopping every few inches to pull and push the bulky pieces she collected through the narrowest gaps. The carcass seared her skin white and numb through the cloth. It was a relief to finally stagger into the main tunnels and the warm welcoming dark that caressed her frost-nipped skin.

Bone-weary, she made her way to the Heap. There was no way she could squeeze herself through the alehouse alley. She pushed her exhausted mind to concoct a lie. Luck was on her side as she approached the gates. Cale was on guard, and he was wonderfully drunk.

He blinked at her bloodied appearance, pursing his lips and squinting his eyes in the dim light like a cave mole.

"Azzy? Wha'r'ya doin' out thar?" Judging by the slur in his voice, Cale was already three flasks in for his shift on watch. She smiled and bowed her head. He still stood between her and the safety of the Heap. *Best to play respectfully.*

"Cale, would you open the gate for me?"

His long nose twitched at her. "What ya got thar?" he nodded at the oozing bundle at her feet. "Smells like bad pipe weed."

She shrugged. "Found a rook cobbled up in an offshoot tunnel. Pretty fresh, too, though I had trouble digging it out," she said as she gestured to her bloody clothing. "Scraped myself up pretty good."

Cale shuddered. The winnowrooks hunted and bred in the Above, but they came into the caves to die, entombing themselves in small hollows. Usually, their bodies made a meal for the scavenger grimwerms, who would knock them loose, though the Foragers would bring Brixby the leftover dregs. It made sense for her to find some, especially when they hadn't seen a hint of Windham and his crew in the tunnels for weeks. Nothing so fresh as what Azzy had bundled with her. Azzy shuffled nervously, wishing Cale would let her in before someone with sober eyes and nose came by.

The guard shook his head, hawking a lob of spit in the dirt. "Right mess you'ar. Get your arse in here, before Prast's men see ya."

Her smile turned genuine. Cale wedged open the gate long enough for her to drag her haul in, watching the streets instead of the tunnels. Azzy nodded to him, lifting the saturated cloth off the ground. She couldn't afford to leave a trail through the crumbling stone paths of the Heap to Brixby's door. Prast would throw a fit, probably have her in a cell before the lamps went out for the night. The streets were quiet, well past the morning grind; her scavenging must have lasted long past light strike. Armin was going to throttle her.

She made a hobbling dash for Brixby's shop, wincing each time the package slapped her thigh. Her leg was numb by the time she clambered up the stone steps of the Apothecary, easing through the doorway in case there were any patrons inside.

Two hands clamped down on her shoulders. Azzy yipped as they hauled her around to face fuming gray eyes. She groaned inwardly. She'd hoped to avoid a confrontation with Armin until after she'd cleaned up.

"Where have you been?" Her younger brother hissed. Despite the anger in his voice, his hands flitted down her arms, checking her over. His eyes darkened at the sight of her bloody torn shirt. "You're hurt."

Azzy dropped the bundle, lifting her arms to gently shove him off. "I'm fine. Just a scrape while scavenging," she lied, thankful the low lighting of the shop made it difficult for him to see her face. "Where's Brixby?"

Armin winced and looked away. "Nell went into labor this morning. The babe didn't make it. There's to be a Feast this eve."

She froze, her stomach pinching tight at his words. Part of her wished she'd further delayed her return, but then the Elder would surely have noticed her absence. The whole community would be present for the Feast. Her stomach felt hollow, twisting in on itself; she remembered she hadn't eaten since before light strike. A Feast was awful enough without an empty stomach.

The side door swung open, revealing Brixby, dressed in his finest. He paused at the sight of his two wards. His gaze shot to Azzy, fatherly concern evident in his perusal of her rough appearance. He sighed. The fall of his shoulders added a spike of guilt to the churning dread in her gut.

"Store it all in the dry cellar and wash up. We will discuss this later."

"I brought you—"

"Azure," Brixby spoke over her, his green eyes dull, dark as cave moss, surrounded by smudges of exhaustion. She swallowed her words, and the last dregs of exaltation over her successful haul evaporated at his weary expression. She nodded once, carefully gathering what she'd worked so hard to bring home. The dry cellar was behind the shop's counter, connected directly to Brixby's laboratory. She lingered in the quiet room, fighting the pull of exhaustion on her limbs.

She'd waited too long. It had taken one of Armin's episodes—and that *voice*—to drive her to the Above. Perhaps if she'd gone sooner, her guardian could've saved Nell's newborn.

But you saved the wolf.

The whisper of thought made her stiffen. She'd saved a monster Above while a child died Below, far from an equal exchange. Tears welled as she reached up to touch the puckered scab over her chest. It would scar.

Far from equal.

*W*e fear magic and those who are tainted by it. So quick to exile these doomed souls, be they innocent youths or beloved spouses. We expel those who fall prey to their own blood and yet use the castoffs, the remnants of twisted fauna and corrupted flora, to cure our ills. Survival has made hypocrites of us all.

Her fingers skimmed the page, her gaze unfocused. She didn't need to read the words, having memorized them long ago. Her mind was elsewhere, dredging up last night, how her brother had thrashed, helpless, as the words poured from his mouth. *The Rot is coming,*

"You're stalling," Armin spoke from the doorway. She snapped the journal shut. Her brother pursed his lips. "That is Brixby's, Azzy."

"No, it's Mother's. Brixby keeps it safe and I merely borrow it," she said, the back of her neck hot. "If Elder Prast ever saw these pages, he'd have an apoplexy."

"Probably why it's normally kept in a locked drawer, sister mine." Armin took the book from her and tucked it back under her pillow where she'd kept it hidden the past few days. The little bother likely knew it was there the whole time. He turned her to face him, clucking his tongue against his teeth.

"We can't present you like this," he said, frowning at her rumpled skirt and blouse. "Did you pull these out of the bottom of your clothes chest?"

That was exactly what she'd done. "I doubt anyone will mind a few wrinkles on such a somber occasion."

"Least let me fix your hair."

"What's wrong with my hair?" She twined her fingers through an errant strand. Armin wore a pained expression, his features a comical grimace. She glanced sideways at her looking glass. Normally Azzy wore the length in a tight braid or bun at her nape—practical for her activities

—but she'd let it down for the Feast. It spilled in a haphazard tumble down her back, full of snarls, and frizzed at the top like a crown of spare white-blonde filaments.

She winced, fishing her comb from the assortment of trinkets cluttering her bedside table. "Right, fix it."

Her brother smirked as his long fingers set to work on the snarled mass. "Don't know why you wear it so long. Preparing to dazzle your future suitors?"

His tone was gently teasing, but it didn't lessen the acute ache in her chest. "I think we both know there are no suitors in my future."

There was a pause before his fingers resumed their delicate work, separating her hair into even sections. "Do you say that because of me or because of Mother?"

Azzy bit her tongue, cursing to herself. Touching upon either subject typically descended into bitter spats between them. Armin never divulged how much memory he possessed of the episodes. It was too frightening, too stressful, especially when Elder Prast kept such a watchful eye on their household. They'd already lost so much.

Armin deftly twisted and twined her hair into a cluster of braids. He was tying the ends when she found her voice again. "Is Brixby furious with me?"

His eyes met hers in the looking glass, so similar to hers in shape but in her brother's, there were storms. Mother used to say Armin was the rain to Azzy's sun.

"He could never stay mad at you. He's angry about many things, but not you. We need to help him get through this, Azzy. Everyone will be looking for someone to blame," said Armin.

She felt a flare of fire behind her eyes. "Blame never touches the one who truly deserves it."

Armin closed his eyes, squeezing her shoulders. "Do try

to keep a civil tongue in your head. No matter what that oaf says."

A low knock interrupted their exchange. Brixby poked his graying head through the door. "Time, you two."

Her brother released her, moving to join their guardian. She hesitated.

"Be right there," she said with a reassuring smile. The moment they were out of sight, she retrieved her mother's journal from beneath her pillow and returned it to its locked desk drawer on her way out. It felt safer, keeping such words under lock and key.

⁂

Another bout of the Rot will break us, thought Azzy. Her eyes wandered the pitted hollows that stretched up the stone walls of the Heap, high overhead. People had lived there once, carving homes in the rock. Now they were abandoned, deeper pools of shadow within shadows, untouched by the feeble light of the grit-clouded street lamps.

It hadn't always been called the Heap. Haven, the great stone city, was a refuge for the dwindling human populace. Once upon a time, Haven had contained over a hundred thousand human souls, one of six underground cities loosely clustered beneath a mountain range. Not all monsters existed Above. The grimwerms, the cave moles, and wailing natters made travel risky, but doable in large groups. The real enemy was one they could not see.

The first wave of Rot had decimated Haven. Entire quadrants of the city went dark. It wasn't the only city to suffer. Caletum, their nearest neighbor, shut their doors to all but the Foragers when the sickness first reached Haven, determined to keep it out. Salvation, to the south, was lost.

They hadn't heard a whisper from the others, Sospes, Tutis, and Sanctum, in years. When the Rot finally released its choking grip, only five cities were left, and Haven's population had been halved.

The Rot resurfaced every few decades, whittling down the population, breaking its vitality and spirit until Haven had crumbled to the Heap: a broken city, dwindled down to crumbling stones, with an ever-present layer of grime and hollow-eyed citizens. A city succumbing to the shadows that spilled from its dead spaces. The occasional air current made the derelict spaces moan their loss, a city full of ghosts.

The dim lamplight gave way to blooms of open flame, flickering blossoms in bowls placed in even intervals on the long tables that filled the town square. Except for the guards on duty, the greater population of the Heap was already present, speaking in hushed voices and furtive glances at the head table. Nell, the grieving mother, sat with her head bowed beside Elder Prast, and the remainder of her family occupied one side of the table. Pale and wan, she should have been resting, but according to Brixby, she had insisted she attend. The other half held figures of importance—tradesmen and politicians—with three empty seats on the end for the Apothecary and his wards. They were among the stragglers. Eyes fell on Brixby as they passed, the voices stuttering to a halt.

Armin's hand found hers, clasping her fingers in a tight nervous hold. It grounded her, kept her from lashing out at those hostile stares. For his part, their guardian remained stoic, his shoulders held back as he led them to their place of 'honor'. She tucked in her skirts beside him, squelching the urge to wrap her arms around Brixby. The next wave of the Rot, they would be the first to come begging for the Apothecary's aid.

Nell's eyes remained focused on her lap, ignoring them. When it was clear there would be no confrontation, conversation slowly revived as servers set out bundles of loam bread and mushroom cake. Azzy kept her hands clenched beneath the table and tried not to stare at the empty bowl before her. She wished the woman had made a scene. Anything to avoid the rest of the Feast. Azzy's palms grew slick, sweat seeping through her blouse until the cloth clung to her skin. Guilt writhed in her gut. It was possible Brixby could have made the salve to revive the newborn. *If* it could have been saved. *If* the Elder hadn't refused to look for the Foragers and the supplies the Heap needed. Such caustic truth would banish her from the Feast and leave Armin and Brixby to soak up the backlash. Better to fume to herself.

Her knuckles turned white as the cauldrons made their rounds. The servers wore hoods, to conceal their faces. No one wanted to know who handled the stew. No one wanted to see the dark knowledge in their eyes. They already knew what went into the Feast. A dull silver ladle tipped a portion into her bowl. The stew gave off the rich scent of cooked meat and herbs. Saliva filled her mouth even as she grew nauseous.

Don't think about it, force it down. She hated the Feasts, hated what was expected. There were few who held her reservations, most digging in with vigor. A Feast guaranteed a hearty meal, which was something too many people rarely saw. It was a ceremony born from necessity when meat was scarce. There were no burial grounds in the Heap. It was difficult to dig into the bedrock, and a shallow grave would attract grimwerms. Most bodies were burned, but some were used for the Feasts. Her mother had told her that, long ago, the practice was considered an abomination. Yet here they sat, expected to at least take a sip as a sign of respect to the grieving parties.

Elder Prast ate with audible slurping sounds. The hair rose on the back of Azzy's neck. Nell brought a spoonful to her lips, tipping it down her throat, the mother who gave the flesh, cycling it back into herself. Did the monsters of the Above consume their own dead? The more reluctant participants took a small quick sip, their due diligence acknowledged by Nell's nod.

The churn of bile in her stomach grew worse, sending a tingle that ran through her fingertips. A whisper tugged at the back of her mind. Armin dipped his spoon, the swirl of liquid tunneling to her sole focus. The whispers gained ground, trembling through her limbs. Something oily and foul nipped at the underside of her tongue. *No, no, no, don't drink, don't swallow it down.* Brixby's arm rose in the corner of her vision, bringing the stew to his lips. Her arms darted out on either side, snatching up their hands, knocking the spoons from their hold. The clatter of metal on wood echoed through the silence.

The Apothecary's Wardship

❧❀❧

A cacophony of whispers sifted through her ears. Azzy swayed, the hands holding Armin and Brixby the only things keeping her upright. Her skin grew clammy, her vision unfocused. The taste on the back of her tongue intensified, coating the inside of her mouth.

"What is the meaning of this?" Elder Prast hissed at them, rising from his seat. Brixby beat him to it, sending his own chair clacking along the cobbled stones. His pulled Azzy into the crux of his arm, fingers wrapping around her bicep in a tense, bruising grip.

"Forgive us, Azure is still ill from this morning. If you will excuse us, I will escort her to bed." Her guardian's word was respected, no matter what blame the people placed on his shoulders. Azzy did not have to fake sick, certain if Brixby didn't escort her away from the crowd, she would retch all over the Elder's fine shoes.

Prast's scrutiny was palpable. He flapped his hand in a gesture of dismissal. "Take the girl home. I will visit on the morrow to see how she fares."

Brixby stiffened beside her, his only response to the

veiled threat in the Elder's words. No doubt Prast would bring that infernal rod with him.

Armin appeared at her other side, taking half her weight as they made their way through the gauntlet of whispers and stares. The further she moved away from the bowls, the better she felt. Nell rose as they left. It couldn't be helped. By the time they reached the open street, the foul taste abated, letting her breathe again. She shook out of her companions' hold as Nell stepped in front of her.

Azzy closed her eyes for the slap, the blow hard enough to snap her head to the left. Nell raised her hand for another strike. Brixby surged forward and caught the mourning mother's arm as Armin shielded his sister. Nell fought Brixby's hold. The woman jerked around him to spit at Azzy's feet.

"Selfish, stupid girl! This is your fault. It's your fault!" Nell's choking sobs stung far more than her slap. Azzy buried her face in Armin's shoulder.

Brixby brought his mouth to the woman's ear, his voice low and urgent. "What madness do you speak? Azure had no hand in your child's fate. Do not destroy another in your grief." His wary gaze darted to the shadows around them, certain Prast's men would slip out of the cracks in the stone.

"Liar! Where was she this morning when I came begging at your door? Where was your ward, Apothecary?" Nell sneered into his face. "Do you even know?"

Azzy peered at the grieving woman, the soft cloth of her brother's shirt a protective barrier against the acid of the words. The failed birth of her child had left its mark etched into Nell's gaunt features, her fingers like claws plucking at Brixby's sleeves. Her pasty skin was coated in perspiration; her unwashed scent tinged with the coppery tang of dried blood and the hint of some fragrant flower that teased

Azzy's memory. Despite the bitterness in her words, Nell's eyes were full of agony. This was the third child she'd lost, her young daughter and son both fallen to the last wave of Rot four years prior. Brixby and Azzy had sat with her to their last breaths.

"I'm sorry," Azzy whispered. Separating from Armin, she reached out and wrapped Nell's thin fingers with her own. The contact jolted the woman. Their eyes met, passing a thread of unspoken words between them.

The sneer dropped off Nell's face as she swallowed, her dark eyes brimming until tears traced the sharp angles of her face. Her grip briefly tightened on Azzy's fingers. "Go, go before Prast comes looking for me," said Nell. Her hand slipped away, dropping limply at her side. Brixby nodded and wrapped a protective arm around his ward's shoulders to pull her past the hollow-eyed Nell. Azzy kept gazing back at the woman's still form, as a memory slowly sifted through the fog of the past, gaining clarity the closer they drew to home.

"I know that scent." She didn't realize she'd said it out loud.

"What was that?" said Armin. His sober expression accented the worry in his eyes. That he should be so concerned for her broke her heart.

"Nell, she wore a perfumed oil, some sort of flower," she said. Brixby's forearm twitched against her shoulders. "Mother had the same scent."

೭⁑ನ

I n the temporary safety of the shop's front hall, Brixby pulled both siblings into a fierce embrace, cupping the backs of their heads in his large brown hands.

"I shouldn't have dragged you with me. I could have

made an excuse for you," he murmured against Azzy's hair. His voice wavered, betraying how scared their guardian was.

"This isn't the first time the Elder has scrutinized us," Azzy said. She smoothed her fingers along the rigid line of his shoulders.

Armin gave a muffled snort and pulled back to give her a sardonic look. "Nor will it be the last. He will keep 'visiting' until the damn device goes off. Then we'll be tossed out on our backsides to the Above." He stifled a yawn with one hand.

Brixby frowned at his younger ward. "Perhaps, but it will not be this time. Now, if you will excuse me, I have a haul to sort." He squeezed Azzy's shoulder as he passed.

Armin nudged her as soon as their guardian was out of earshot. "What happened tonight?"

She shuddered at the memory of that foul oily taste on her tongue. "I don't know, everything felt wrong." Her brother rolled his eyes, reaching up to gently cup her swollen cheek.

"Not that, it's no secret you hate the Feasts. That hit, sister mine. I've seen you dodge stones from snotty children. Why did you let her strike you?" His brows drew together. "If you really think this is your fault, I might slap you myself."

Azzy smiled against his palm, holding his hand to her face. She knew there were many factors to Nell's loss. Her guilt was her own to deal with, no matter how misplaced. "She needed to."

Her brother scowled at her. "That's a terrible reason." He pinched her chin, hard enough to make her wince. "You can't keep taking everyone's pain for your own. Including mine." He leaned in to brush his lips across her forehead. "I know you're exhausted, Azzy. Go lie down. We'll deal with Prast on the morrow."

She retired to her room to appease Armin; aware his storm-ridden eyes followed her progress until she shut the door. She lay there, staring at the smooth pitted stone above her bed long after the street lamps went out.

Azzy was still awake when Brixby opened her door, deep in the night. She turned toward his sigh.

"Why don't you come join me in the shop?"

She stopped to listen at Armin's door, to his heavy breaths of deep slumber, before she crept onward. The lantern in Brixby's shop nearly blinded her when she came down the stairs. She followed the familiar thwack of metal on wood. Brixby was making use of the cutting board her brother had carved for him last year, begging the Foragers for a scrap of the firewood they carried in their carts. Armin had hacked and sanded it into a smooth block, which Azzy had partnered with a gift of fresh blades. She'd traded them for a dozen hours working the bellows for the blacksmith. Such simple gifts, but their guardian treasured both.

The workspace smelled like charcoal and the dozens of intertwining musty scents from dried mosses and herbs, all overlaid by the new smell of burnt sucrose. Brixby paused mid-chop, gesturing to the hooks by the door with his cleaver.

"Tie on a cloth, Azure," he said, resuming his work with a deft flick that separated the carapace of the winnowrook from the flesh beneath. His dark hands were bare as he set each piece on the block, switching to the grater. He'd already drained what he could of the rook's caustic blood, set to cure in bottles at the end of the table; the blood needed to be aged for safe use. Azzy settled on a nearby stool, observing as he shaved down the grisly chunks she'd brought him into thin strips.

Dried out, like jerky, the flesh neutralized toxins in the body. The carapace, crushed into a fine powder, could be added to a salve to clear the lungs and open the airways. The blood was the real prize. Aged properly, it was a key ingredient in the cure for the Rot.

The bark, roots, and other materials she'd gathered were stopgaps—they made treatments to soothe the sickness that plagued the Heap but were not strong enough to stop it. Only the flesh of monsters could cure diseases borne of magic. The terrible irony was the chance that the cure could worsen the effects of the disease. There was only so much magic the body could absorb without contamination. It had been so with her mother.

Her gaze shifted from the block to the man who had opened his doors to them so many years ago.

Oswin Brixby wasn't from Haven. He'd arrived with the Foragers over twenty years ago, filling the desperate need for a competent apothecary. She wasn't sure what city he hailed from, but his features were exotic among the local fare. His dark skin, the rich brown of soft shale, coupled with his green eyes to make him stand out in a town of pale skin. The only one who had stood out more was Azzy's mother, with hair like fire—the one who knew too many deep secrets. Their mutual oddness had brought them together, kindling a friendship that gained him acceptance with the others. Years later, after Brixby had watched his dear friend succumb to the taint of magic in her blood, he'd opened his home to her children. A lesser man might have balked at taking in two strays with no blood ties to himself, but Azzy never felt anything but love from their guardian, a love as fierce as their mother's.

"I can feel you staring," said Brixby. Those cool green eyes held hers, the worry evident in their depths.

Mother had once told her Brixby's eyes were the color of the summer sea, a vast body of water that stretched farther than the eye could focus. Azzy could barely imagine what that must look like. It wasn't until Azzy was older that she questioned how a woman who had lived her entire life underground could know about the sea, or how people used to fly in the sky. Her mother had known and seen many things she shouldn't have.

"I was thinking about the past," Azzy answered truthfully, picking at her nails. She grimaced at a dried bit of winnowrook under her thumbnail.

"You mean you were fretting over things you can't change." Brixby flashed her a grin, his teeth like square pearls against his dark skin.

"Am I that obvious?" At his too-serious nod, she stuck her tongue out at him. Her tone shifted as memory tugged at her, bringing her full circle to the tumble of thoughts that kept her awake this eve. "It wasn't a perfume I smelled was it?"

Brixby set the grater down, bracing his forearms on the block as he sighed. "I was waiting for you to make the connection."

A jolt of dread pierced her chest as pieces began to fall into place. "Mother had the same smell while she was sick, right before...they took her away. What is that scent?"

Pain ghosted over his face at the mention of his lost friend. Brixby looked up at her, his face creased with deep sadness. "I would've protected you from this forever if I could have, but your brother's nightmares grow worse—"

"You and I both know what they are."

He nodded, clearing his throat. "His *visions* grow stronger. If the neighbors ever broke their silence, Prast would cast him out in the space of a breath."

Azzy swallowed through the fear squeezing her throat. The walls were too thin and the night too quiet for their neighbors not to hear the shrieking voice that spewed from Armin's mouth. Their saving grace was that the tradesmen quarter was filled with secrets. No one mentioned how the blacksmith handled glowing red iron with his bare hands. Not a word was spoken of how plants grew around Widow Hester's door, even without light. They failed to mention how the baker's pastries evoked passionate feelings in their recipients when given as gifts by young suitors. And they ignored the Apothecary's ward who could see the future.

Feared as magic was, many of the Heap's citizens bore a spark of it in their families. As long as their spark didn't ignite, the inhabitants of the quarter protected one another's odd quirks with their silence.

Brixby recaptured her attention as he rummaged through his cabinets. He turned back to her with a small worn wooden box, placing it with reverent care between them.

"Open it slowly, the contents are fragile," he said, taking up the grater to resume his task. He watched her from the corner of his eye.

As instructed, she opened it with all the care it would take to disarm a trap, wondering how accurate a comparison this was as she unwrapped a layer of yellowed cotton to reveal a dried flower.

In her few excursions to the Above, she'd glimpsed few flowers, and none like this one. Age made the head of thin clustered petals a brittle brownish yellow, while the leaves curled in on themselves, like the Widow Hester's ancient wrinkled hands.

She didn't dare pick it up—it was far too fragile to be handled—but shifting its cotton bed sent a waft of musty fragrance into her face. Beneath the scent of dust was the one that matched her memory.

"What is it?"

"Before the world changed, it was a common weed. It

grew everywhere. When magic began its destructive crawl across the land, it changed as well."

Azzy peered up at him, mystified by his explanation. "Magic doesn't affect plants the way it does animals or people. How did it change?"

Her guardian looked thoughtful. "You're right, change is not the right word. Magic simply elevated its innate qualities. The witches knew better—they used dandelions for many purposes."

She frowned at him. "Dandelions? What do they have to do with magic?"

Brixby slid the box away from her, gently folding the cotton back with one hand. "That name has been all but forgotten. Now they call it the Rustic Oracle."

No wonder he'd dragged the box away from her. The name evoked such a flood of emotions, Azzy might have crushed the flower in her anger. She never saw it intact before, in its complete innocuous form, only as a vial of powder dangling from the end of Prast's sensing rod, when it glowed for those who would be cast out to the Above.

"It senses magic." She hissed through her teeth, her gaze inexorably drawn to the ceiling, where Armin slept above.

"Why do you think I kept it?" Brixby's question made her chest ache.

"How close do you think he is?" She asked in little more than a whisper.

"I'm afraid any incident that puts his body under extreme stress will trigger it." He kept shaving the flesh of the winnowrook with quick, vigorous strokes, belying the calm tone of his voice. "Why did you stop us from partaking in the Feast, Azure?"

She was wondering when he would toss the question between them. No answer readily rolled off her tongue.

"Have I ever smelled like dandelions?" She blurted out.

It was Brixby's turn to frown as he considered her. "No, not once in all the years you've lived under my roof." His brow creased. "That does not answer the question."

"I—"

Screams erupted from above, the hollow echo of dozens of voices speaking at once. Azzy scrambled from her seat, bolting for the stairs with Brixby on her heels.

"—it's here, it's here, the Rot, the Rot, the Rot is here—"

She fought the urge to sink to her knees and cover her ears. Her brother needed her; beneath the boom of those terrible voices, she could hear his pain. She threw open his door, her steps faltering at the sight of Armin on his feet beside the bed. His head lolled against his chest, his arms hung limp at his sides. His body balanced on the very tips of his toes, but the effort caused them to bleed. Horrified, she tore her gaze from his bleeding feet and ran to him, ignoring Brixby's shout.

Heat shot through her palms the second she touched him, so intense she yelped. Armin's dangling hands shot up and wrapped around her biceps. His head lifted, the dim light more than enough to reveal the swirling mass of gray in his eyes.

"The cure, the cure waits in the nattering tunnels." The voices were different, a voluminous whisper pounding against her temples. Armin collapsed against her, dragging her to the floor with his unexpected weight.

Brixby pulled him off, hauling her pale sweat-soaked brother back onto the bed. Their guardian looked ashen himself, scanning Azzy for signs of injury as he cradled the unconscious boy in his arms.

"I'm okay," she said, grabbing the bedpost to heave herself up. "I'm okay." A faint flowery scent hit her, undoubtedly rising off her brother.

They both started at the frantic pounding on the front door.

"I'll go," said Azzy, her legs shaky but stable. "See if you can wake him."

Her steps carried her down the stairs to the shopfront with no small amount of trepidation. The moment her fingers closed around the door handle, the oily foul taste soaked her tongue once again. Swallowing the wave of nausea, she opened the door to the panting messenger. She recognized him, one of the wall guards who didn't attend the Feast. Dread solidified in the pit of her stomach.

"The Apothecary," he gasped, clutching his chest for breath, "we need the Apothecary! The Rot hit in the night."

Azzy's fingers tightened on the door handle. "Which household? Who is affected?"

The guard looked up at her with wild eyes. "Everyone."

Silence and Sacrifice

✦❦✦

B rixby rustled through the ingredient drawers as he muttered to himself. Azzy watched him, twisting a bottle of the winnowrook blood over and over in her hands. It still gave off a faint chill that gradually numbed her fingers. The Apothecary stopped in the middle of the room and ran both hands through his tightly cropped hair.

"It's bad, isn't it?" said Azzy, her voice soft. He'd gone to assess the extent of the Rot a scant two hours ago while she kept vigil by Armin's bedside. Her brother slept, wracked by chills. They couldn't wake him, even when Brixby pricked a needle against the vulnerable skin of his wrist. She'd washed and bandaged his bloody feet. She'd placed a poultice on his chest to ease his shakes, though she could do little more than wipe the sweat from his brow. The words of the voice spun in her head. She knew it was bad, and the knowledge sat heavy on her shoulders.

The bottle continued to turn end over end in her hands. Brixby stared at the other containers lined up on the work table. Too fresh, too caustic to be used for the lifesaving syrup. He cursed under his breath.

"There is enough here to cure over two-thirds of the city but not enough time," he said. A visible weariness settled over him. He sank onto a stool, kneading his forehead. "This is too sudden, too widespread, there are too many infected for this to be a normal resurgence of the Rot."

"The guard told the truth, it hit everyone," Azzy whispered. Her hands began to shake.

"Azure." She looked up at her name, gazing into the shadowed depths of the summer sea. "It's rooted in their mouths, all of them. Every single person has a Rot blossom on their tongue."

The hair rose on her arms. "The Feast."

Brixby nodded. "Nell was unaffected. The guards threw her in the cells this morning."

Azzy set the bottle down before she shattered it in her fingers. "She couldn't do this."

"Are you so sure?"

No, but she needed her guardian to believe her excuse. He needed to work unhindered by worry, keeping as many people alive as possible until her return.

"I can find out," she said, tying up the knotted tangle of her hair. "Who's guarding her?"

Brixby pursued his lips, looking thoughtful. He leapt to his feet, retrieved a corked flask from the locked drawer of his desk, and tossed it to her. "Cale. That should be enough to bribe your way past."

She tucked the flask into her hip pocket, praying her tight smile didn't give away the lie. "I'll check on Armin before I go."

Her steps dragged on the stairs. She stalled to a stop in

the hallway outside their bedrooms. It wouldn't matter what truth or lies left Nell's mouth. Prast would still cast her out in the Above, if he survived. Even the mild cases of the Rot could be deadly. That it was rooted in their mouths...the very idea made her shudder. The pain alone would kill some of them. It was worst among the children. Their young bodies couldn't handle the symptoms for long. The fever, the heat, as if their skin would crack apart. *The cure waits in the nattering tunnels...*

For a moment, she couldn't move. Squeezing her eyes tight, she leaned into the wall, hugging her elbows as a shudder ran through her frame. She could do this. She had to do this. No matter what waited for her.

Armin leaned his forehead against hers and slipped his hands under her own. The contact with his feverishly hot skin startled her. She opened her eyes, meeting his storm-shrouded gaze.

"What are you doing out of bed?" she whispered to him, gently squeezing his fingertips.

"You will not do this," he said, his voice cracked and hoarse. That answered her question. He clearly remembered what he'd said during his episode and knew her intention. Worried enough to come after her in this condition. Sweat clung to his skin, highlighting the bruised flesh spreading from the corners of his mouth, as if he had the Rot as well. His breath feathered against her cheek, cool compared to the heat coming off him. "You owe them nothing."

She reared back at his words. "This isn't about debts or favors owed."

"They killed our mother," said Armin. "Let the Rot take Prast, take all of them."

"You know what happened to her," Azzy countered,

reaching up to cup the back of his neck. "Our mother was gone long before they put her body to rest. The blame for her death does not fall on our neighbors or their children. Prast is as sick as the rest of them. He is not long for this world."

"Then tell one of his men. Let them risk their hides for the bloody cure!" Armin struggled to keep his voice low, unwilling to bring their guardian into the conversation.

"They wouldn't believe me, not without asking questions that I would refuse to answer," said Azzy. Her unwavering calm drew out his anger.

"You don't need to protect me!" he rasped. He might have shouted at her if he could. Her brother broke down with a sob. "I can't lose you, too." His trembling arms wrapped around her. He pressed his face against her shoulder. She could feel his tears saturating the worn fabric of her shirt, seeping straight down to her nerves.

"You won't lose me," she said, all bravado, but if it somehow convinced him, she would lie till her tongue fell out of her head.

"That's because I'm coming with you."

"You most certainly are not," Azzy hissed, resisting the urge to smack some sense into her fever-mad brother.

"I can help you," Armin insisted. The muscles in his chin tensed. She knew that look. They could argue for hours on end and her brother would still find a way to follow her into danger. She hesitated, her eyes searching his face, trailing over every curve and angle, committing it to memory. The moment swelled, gaining importance as Azzy weighed the decision on internal scales.

If we don't go, far too many people will die.

If we do go, I will lose him.

She bit the inside of her cheek until she tasted blood.

What could she live with? What could she possibly change? *If I leave him, I won't survive.*

"Get dressed," she told him. His expression lit up with relief as he followed her instruction. Azzy watched his retreating figure, her fingers curling and uncurling in the empty air.

❁

T he first time the voices had shattered the nighttime quiet of the tradesmen quarter, they'd made Hester a widow. Only hours before, the house had been filled with laughter. It was Armin's twelfth birthday, and the last night she slept at ease in her own bed.

At the first roaring swell of sound, she and Brixby had rushed from their rooms, unprepared for the sight of Armin's limp body channeling those powerful screams. They had listened, stunned, unable to react, as the voices spewed a warning of falling rock and crushed bone. When the power had finally relinquished her brother, his body had collapsed to the floor, and his muscles had seized. Both Azzy and their guardian had kept vigil for the remainder of the night, unable to wake the sleeping boy. They had tried to puzzle out the vague words, shaken and beyond exhausted when Armin finally opened his eyes at dawn.

Long after the day lamps were lit, they'd learned a hanging rock had come loose from the high ceiling and struck Hester's husband during his shift on guard duty. His skull had shattered on impact.

Armin had never spoken of the episode, dismissing it as a strong nightmare. They couldn't bring themselves to tell him the truth, not then. As more nights had passed without incident, Azzy thought they could all dismiss the episode as a fluke, a passing echo of their mother.

Until the voices had shrilled the coming of the Rot, the very plague that stole Nell's children. After that, Azzy had known it was only a matter of time. The episodes were infrequent, spanning months from one to the next, but each time they grew louder, clearer, as magic gained a foothold within her brother. She dreaded Elder Prast's visits, waving the sensing rod in front of their faces, lingering over Armin each time. Four years, countless visits, and not once had the dangling vial of the Rustic Oracle glowed in her brother's face.

Now, Armin threaded his fingers through hers, sensing her disquiet. She let him, thankful he couldn't see her expression in the dim light of the tunnels.

Leaving the Heap was simple. The Rot was everywhere, and too few were healthy enough to care for those already deep in the throes. Death clung to the air. It was a relief to reach the abandoned gates of the city. The two of them simply walked, unhindered, through the doors, closing in the sickness behind them.

Now they walked hand in hand in near darkness. These were the pathways the Foragers took between the cities, lit by the luminescent moss carpeting the floor and creeping up the walls. It muffled their footsteps as they reached a branch off the main route. This was a far different tunnel than the one Azzy had followed to the Above. Everyone knew about it, because it led to a place no one wanted to go.

She stopped where the moss ended. The tunnel before them was in complete darkness, a gaping maw waiting to swallow them up.

"Azzy?" Armin's uncertain whisper cut through the quiet, so soft she could barely hear it until it reverberated off the walls back to her. She turned to him, pressing a finger to her lips. The gesture came too late. A shrill chitter sounded in the dark, answered further on by the haunting calls that earned them their name. The wailing natters knew they were coming.

Armin peered, wide-eyed, into the darkness, a bitter reminder of how unprepared her brother was for this encounter. Her warning for silence dripped away like the first curls of winter frost. The wails subsided to chattering mutters as the natters passed gossip like old women on street corners.

"How do we do this?" he whispered. The noise picked up. Azzy glared at him and ripped the hem from her shirt. "What's that for?"

"I told you silence was a necessity," Azzy spat, flinging her harsh words into the tunnel. The natters went quiet for a moment, resuming their calls in soft chirps. Vicious when they clustered together, they were also cowards, down to the largest male. She yanked the flask from her waistband.

Her brother had the grace to look sheepish. "You didn't tell me why," he mumbled, pulling at his long fingers. "Or for how long."

Azzy sighed through her nose. "You shouldn't have come."

He flinched. "I know I'm not like you, sister mine, but we both know you need me. Otherwise, you'd have left me behind, no matter what I said."

The truth ground on her nerves. She opened Brixby's flask, certain it was the musky odor of mushroom brandy that made her eyes water. She fed the strip from her shirt into the opening on her fifth try.

"I've never seen one before," said Armin, continuing his vigil at the edge.

"You won't see one. They avoid the light," she retorted,

kneeling to spark the wick with a bit of flint against the head of her pickaxe. Squinting through the first flare of light, she waited until it coalesced to a wavering blue-tipped flame. The brandy was strong, and it should sustain a burn long enough for them to find what they needed.

"I thought we were going to feel our way through?" Armin squinted at her over his shoulder. The light threw the shadows of his face into sharp contrast, deepening the bruises at the seams of his mouth and beneath his eyes. He looked more like a wandering specter than her brother. Azzy swallowed the thought down, clasping his hand as she placed a foot into the tunnel.

The natters stopped, the silence akin to a fearfully held breath before a scream. Her brother's hand trembled in her grip. Azzy held the burning flask up high in front of her, barely illuminating the ground before them.

The absence of any sound made the soft scrape of their footsteps unbearably loud. Worse were the half-heard noises in the echo of their footfalls, the whisper of scales on stone, the muted scratch of claws, and the pause between breaths.

Twice in her life, Azzy had set foot in the nattering tunnels, exactly one foot, before she lost her nerve and fled for the safety of the main tunnel. They were in the thick of it now, the glow of the luminescent moss swallowed up by endless dark. The air was damp, thick with mold and ammonia that burned her nostrils, covering the pungent odor of decay. There were dead things in here.

A crunch shattered the silence, causing both siblings to jump. In the quivering light of her flask, Azzy caught sight of the floor.

"Don't look down," she whispered, jerking Armin forward when she felt him shift to do just that. She held the light higher, straining her muscles. It caught the flare of watching eyes. "Don't look up either."

"Where...where am I supposed to look?" She didn't miss the raised octave of her brother's voice.

"Watch my back," she said simply, scuffing her foot forward to clear a path through the bones. Hundreds and hundreds of bones littered the floor, brown with age, animal and human.

"Azzy," Armin stopped moving, jerking her back. She swung around to urge him on when the flame flashed on metal far to the side, back toward the tunnel wall. The attention of those watching eyes swung with her. She let go of him, unlatching her axe.

"Hold onto my shoulders," she said, sliding forward armed with axe and flask. The shades of a dozen pill bugs ran along her spine as the flash of metal expanded, revealing the unmistakable shape of a cart harness. The light fell over dark-stained cloth.

The harness was still attached to the person who bore it, or what was left of them. Armin released her as the flask lit the shredded stump of a neck. Its ribcage had flared open, mimicking the gore-stained teeth of a waiting trap. Armin fell to his rump, landing in the crusted trails of blood and viscera that spread out from the cart. A whimper escaped his throat as Azzy dropped to her knees, placing her axe on the floor to clap a hand over his mouth.

"Don't yell," she hissed through gritted teeth. Her face was slick with sweat as she scanned the room around them. "You must get up." She felt his muscles tense when he saw them, crouched in the corner of their vision. The siblings supported one another to their feet. Armin held her forearms until he brought down the shaking of his body.

When he nodded, she turned back to the remains,

following the harness to the intact cart. The missing Foragers, Windham and his crew, found at last. Her pulse hummed. Inside the cart, there would be a worn leather case of apothecary supplies. Complete with a hearty stock of aged winnowrook blood. Azzy shoved the flask into Armin's hands, scrambling up the side of worn wooden slats to paw through the overflowing contents. Where was it? It had to be here.

"Not in there." Armin's voice was curiously flat. She turned to find him facing the gruesome remains of the Forager, the flask held out before him to show a trail through the blood-soaked dirt where something skidded away from the wreck.

Or was dragged off.

"Stay several steps behind me. Keep the light on my back," said Azzy, hefting the axe in front of her as she crept forward. Within a couple yards, the metal clasp winked back at her from the shadowy indent along the wall. The air grew heavy, taut, hungry.

This was the moment.

"Armin," she whispered, "when I tell you, you will run back the way we came. Do you understand?" Her words fell flat in the weighted silence.

"Why are you talking like that?" She saw the shadow of his hand extend toward her. If he touched her now, her resolve would evaporate like so much smoke.

"Do you understand?"

His arm dropped. "Yes."

She approached alone, halting a few feet from the case. The shadows breathed behind it.

The muscles of her jaw creaked as she leaned forward, hooking her pickaxe on the edge of the case, dragging it back toward her. The blade end turned, showing her the reflection of needle-sharp teeth grinning at her from within the hollow.

Azzy locked her stance and grabbed the frayed handle. She turned just enough to toss it to Armin.

"Run!" she screamed. The light fell away. Her brother listened. She would not lose him here, no matter what it cost. Though she braced for it, the natter rammed the wind out of her.

They crashed backward onto the bone-littered floor, her axe buried in its side. She coughed for air, frantically shoving the twitching body off her. Natters never attacked alone. The second one caught the back of her head as she rose. It raked shallow cuts along her scalp. The blow made her stagger, but she kept her feet, barely dodging the third one so its claws merely grazed her skin.

A cry distracted her, the hard thud of a body on stone. She jerked, not quite avoiding her latest attacker. A talon sliced through her eyebrow, sending a gush of blood down the side of her face. She ignored it, throwing herself onto the graveyard of bones to avoid their swooping attacks.

"Armin!" Blind and bleeding, she belly-crawled, scraping her fingers on shards of bone. Listening to the tug and pull of her gut, she pitched and rolled away from the harrying natters; she reached for the sputtering flask on the cave floor.

"Armin, where are you?" she yelled to be heard above the chittering yips of the natters. One gripped her arm, flipping her over, yanking the joint from the socket before she wildly batted it off with her axe. She choked on the pain, using the axe to pull her forward with her remaining good arm. The natter attacks tapered off when she grabbed the flask, singeing her fingertips as she scooped it up. The tunnel vibrated with their affronted shrieks.

Armin lay slumped against the wall, the case at his side. Blood poured from his mouth, pooling into his hands, cradled slack on his lap.

"No," she sobbed, struggling to reach him. Her dislocated shoulder pulsed spots of dark red in her vision. She heaved herself beside him, using the wall to slam the joint back in place. Everything went fuzzy for a moment before her head cleared with the aftertaste of copper. She breathed again when her shaking fingers felt her brother's pulse, frantic beneath his clammy skin.

The flame snickered, burning low in the purest blue. The flask was far too light. The shadowy shapes of the natters converged around them, only the glint of their claws and flash of their eyes visible. Another dying sputter, but it was enough light to see Armin's eyes snap open. The swirling storms stared back at her.

This is how I live.

Power fizzed and snapped through the air, the cruel puppeteer wrenching her brother to his feet. He balanced on the tips of his toes. She could hear the rush of wings beating the air as he spread his arms. The calls of the natters pitched high, the keening cries of a predator turned prey. They scrambled away, but it was far too late. Armin opened his mouth.

"Perish." The howling voices condensed into one absolute command. She felt it squeeze her heart, tugging at her veins. Her ears popped from the pressure. The word swept outward. The screams of the natters cut off, followed by the collective thump of bodies hitting the ground.

Her vision wavered. She fought it, sitting upright as Armin sank to the ground, catching himself when he toppled forward. The flame sputtered out.

"Azzy?" A thousand voices tentatively called her name.

Her chin quivered, the first pent-up tear stealing down her face.

She grabbed his questing hand, letting him haul her

against him. They held each other, shaking, crying. Neither flinched when the ground cracked around them.

"It won't go away." The voices wept from her brother's mouth. Beneath them she heard the rasp of growing things surrounding them, sealing his fate. In a puff of brilliance, the tufted heads of the Rustic Oracle bloomed in the dark, a ring of dandelions circling them in a golden glow.

This is how I lose him.

Brother's Keeper

The cracked leather handles were a tenuous bridge linking brother and sister through the now silent tunnel, the leather case couched between them. They picked their way by feel; the distant glow of the main passage gradually drew closer. The ring of dandelions lost their light as Armin drew away. Azzy fought the urge to glance over her shoulder at those accusing tufted heads. It was all she could do not to crawl. Pain blossomed in dull rust-colored patches over her vision. Her brother remained silent, unwilling to release the wretched cascade of voices from his mouth.

This was her fault. She'd known the cost, she'd known the possible consequences. Guilt crusted over her soul. He'd saved her life and forfeited his own.

The twisted limbs of the fallen natters created pitfalls and traps for their feet. She was grateful for the blind dark, had never wished to see one of the beastly creatures, dead or alive. The dead tugged at her ankles, dragging her down. She released her grip on the case, trying to break her fall. Her palms skidded along cooling scales and sparse patches of coarse fur. She landed hard on a body of unnatural angles, the stench of sulfur and musk filling her mouth. Scrambling away, she gagged, and spat on the ground, trying to rid herself of the eye-watering smell. Armin found her, hauled her up, and held her steady until her legs could support her again.

She heard herself wheezing, her senses fuzzed out. It was so hard to listen to the internal nudging when pain spiraled through her like a flame. Urgency tugged at her beneath a fog of hurt and exhaustion. There was no time to recover her breath.

"Come on," she panted, fumbling for the case. They couldn't stop here, surrounded by death, old and new. Lives weighed on her—those waiting in the Heap, the lost ones at her feet, and Armin's. His weighed the heaviest of all. Each step toward home was another step toward a future without him. It was a truth she couldn't dwell on, one that threatened to drain everything she had left. It made her want to lie down on the floor amid the crumbling bones and dead natters and never rise again.

The rust stains in her vision flickered. For a moment she saw a mirage—a woman—the familiar spill of curls and dancing fingers stealing her breath anew. *Oh Mom, I've failed you so much.*

Armin sensed her faltering. He drew closer, cradling the box between their hips to slip an arm around her waist. He pulled her forward, kept her moving until they emerged into the main tunnel and sank down on the plush moss to find their second wind. The faint light stung their eyes and exposed the extent of their injuries. Her brother's stare turned bleak at the sight of her. He grasped her chin, gently tilting her head to examine the cuts on her face.

"It's nothing," she murmured, brushing him off. His injuries were far more worrisome. The blood had dried to a flaking crust on his skin that revealed the bruising at the corners of his mouth, forking over his face in a malevolent tattoo. She brushed her fingers along one, snatching her hand back at the heat of his skin.

"Come on. We need to keep moving." Azzy struggled to her feet, bracing herself on the smooth stone walls. Her mutinous legs wobbled on the verge of collapse. Armin gave her an exasperated huff, taking far more of her weight than she deserved.

The gesture choked her. She rested her head on his shoulder, allowing the swell of tears to spill down her cheeks, taking her weaknesses with them. One good cry, now, for her brother, before she locked them up tight. There would be no tears for Armin in the Heap, only fear.

They would turn on him, people he'd known all his life, the same as they did to Mother. That was the way. The tainted were too dangerous, too unpredictable as magic snaked through their veins, warping what they once were. The fear was so much that they declared their mother too far gone for banishment to the Above. Her fate was easy by comparison. Armin was newly tainted. He would be led out, thrown to the mercy of a world crawling with monsters until he became one. Alone. Azzy gritted her teeth, pushing her tears and sobs away. Not if they left first, though.

The Heap, the tradesmen quarter, Brixby—she'd give up everything. They could leave on their terms. The thought rose, throbbing and swollen, as they rounded a bend in the tunnel, revealing the abandoned gates of the Heap. She halted their steps, drawing back to examine him. Ignoring her brother's inquisitive expression, she studied his features, searching for differences, for anything strange beyond the bruises at his mouth. He would pass for now. They'd seen such bruises before.

. . .

"When we go through the gate, don't open your mouth for any reason," she said, pressing her thumb to his chin to stifle his protest. "Any reason."

She watched Armin's stricken expression, his thoughts turning behind his eyes. Questions etched themselves in the lines of his face, but his mouth remained shut. She took the case from him, carrying its full weight on her hip so she could clasp his hand. The voices terrified her. What he could do left her cold, but he was her brother, her Armin. The future bore down on them like a hungry beast. She would not fear him. She refused to fear him, no matter what he became.

The Reward of Heroes

❦

Nothing and no one hindered their progress through the city. No sight of an errant guard. The streets were empty, the houses quiet; their shuffling steps echoed off the buildings. The bordering hollows answered in whistling moans high overhead, all too reminiscent of their encounter in the nattering tunnels. It pushed Azzy to go faster, tightening her grip on Armin's hand, the edge of the case digging into her hip.

As they approached their home, they found half the population of Haven clustered around the shop. The Apothecary's door was flung wide open, emitting a slumped and shambling line of the desperate sick. They gathered in loose groups outside—white-faced men, the veins of their throats blackened as the Rot took root deep inside their bodies. Sobbing women held unconscious children to their breasts. The sight of them made her waver. Azzy fixed her gaze in front of her as they entered the gauntlet, unwilling to see how many of those children were too silent and still.

She felt it when their eyes fell on her, the sudden hush dragging over her skin like dull nails.

Shoving her way through, case first, she gained entry into the shop, Armin close behind her. They were met with the sight of sustained chaos, Brixby at its center. He was a flurry of limbs, shredding and crushing, turning out poultices and herbal mixes to a group of guards, who in turn doled out the medicine to the overwhelming mass of people. His dark face was streaked with sweat, his features haggard. He paused to wipe his forehead, leaving a clay-like green smear on his skin.

He looked up at her intake of breath. Relief flashed through his exhausted face but was quickly replaced by anger. "Where have you been?" he hissed through his teeth, bracing himself against the herb-stained counter. His anger failed to hide his assessing gaze, noting each scratch and cut on their persons. Azzy plunked the case down in front of him.

"We went to fetch you something," she said, unclasping the lid to reveal their hard-won prize. The supply case's contents were a mess, but miraculously intact. On the second tier was a row of vials filled with the unmistakable liquid they needed. Their guardian's eyes widened. He reached over, laying his hands on top of hers.

"Where did you get this?" Brixby whispered, glancing at the confused men surrounding their table.

"It's not important right now," said Azzy, easing her fingers from beneath his. "Tell us what to do."

The Apothecary wrestled with a flicker of indecision before pulling the case to himself. "I'll need the bowls from the top shelf, second cabinet." He pointed to one of the young guards. "You, fetch the packets of red moss from the third drawer of that chest in the corner. Get a fire lit under the cauldron and someone fetch me the quicksilver!" He rounded on his wards. "Armin."

Her brother started at his name, tucking his head against her shoulder to hide his mouth. Brixby frowned at him. "Take your sister upstairs and sew up those cuts—"

"We can help," Azzy protested, ignoring Armin's tug at the back of her bloodied shirt.

"You did help, Azure. You are also swaying on your feet." Brixby's quiet voice soothed the tremble in her limbs. "Go, rest, and stop bleeding on my floor."

She made to retort, but was stifled by Armin's hand tugging her arm. Her brother nodded to their guardian, forcing her toward the stairs. Normally, he would be coaxing her along, teasing her as Brixby had, but his lips remained sealed. The fight went out of her. He caught her when her legs gave out, nearly carrying her for the final steps to her room. She let him maneuver her to her bed, staring blindly at her folded hands in her lap as Armin fetched needle and thread. She continued to stare at her hands as he pulled up a chair across from her, staring at the dirty torn ends of her nails. Her hands were filthy.

"This is all my fault," she said. It was becoming a mantra. Her brother seized her chin, forcing her to meet his glare. He raised an eyebrow at her, waiting to see if she would clarify. Her red-rimmed eyes offered nothing. Sighing through his nose, he dabbed at the dried blood on the side of her face. Azzy sat pliant for his ministrations, drooping where she sat. Truly, she hadn't slept in two days. She was afraid if did she'd wake to find Armin gone. Exhaustion numbed the sting of the needle sewing the cut above her eye. It barely registered when her brother eased her legs up onto the bed and tilted her back onto her pillow.

S he sat up in a panic to silence. The sobs and cries downstairs had vanished. The street lamps were out, a sign of deep night. Too dark, but there was some illumination. The wall lantern outside her room still cast a faint light. It was enough to remind her she was home. She wheezed through the pressure in her chest, the vise-like grip easing when Armin snored, sprawled at the foot of her bed. The shift of cloth alerted her to Brixby's presence, his bulk stretched out across the chair by her window. She didn't think he was awake until he spoke.

"I wondered if that would be enough light to chase away your nightmares."

Azzy wrapped an arm around her legs, resting her cheek on her knees. Awake, all the little aches and injuries came to call. The cut in her eyebrow pinched at the movement. "How many were lost?"

Brixby sighed. "Less than I thought would be. Even our distinguished Elder survived. Word spread about what you did, though no one knows how. They want to hold a celebration to honor the two of you." A beat of silence passed as he waited for her to respond. "Where did you go?" His voice broke, lashing over her skin. "Armin refused to speak. Where did you take him, Azure?"

"The nattering tunnels," she whispered, rocking on her heels. "Windham's crew are dead." The Forager had been a friend of the family, before her mother died. They continued to be friendly to her and Armin, but there was a difference to their warmth. The knowledge of their death was a distant second to what was happening to her brother.

Brixby sucked in a breath. "Azzy—"

"No, no, I messed up," she said, swallowing hard. Tears threatened, pricking at the back of her eyes. She swiped them away. She didn't deserve to cry. "I think I let him follow me because I knew I wouldn't make it out alive without him. I knew what it could cost him, but I brought him anyway."

The moment dragged, thick with tension until Brixby finally asked. "What happened to him?"

Azzy dug her nails into her arms, wishing she could tear her guilt off like dead skin. "Hopefully he never speaks again."

"Tainted." The word quivered in the air between them. "I wondered which of you it was."

She looked up at the glow. Brixby held the wooden box open in his hands. The shriveled dandelion unfurled as she watched, regaining vitality, nourished by Armin's magic. Their guardian shut the box with a snap. She twitched, closing her eyes. The afterimage of the Rustic Oracle burned against her lids. "I think I'm a monster."

Brixby yanked her off the bed, enveloping her in a fierce hug. "You listen to me. You are not the same as your brother or your mother. You cannot see the future. You couldn't have known it would turn out this way."

"But I see something," said Azzy. Her hands curled as she thought how Prast tested her over and over after her mother succumbed. How he watched them both, expectant, but she never triggered the Rustic Oracle. She dismissed that inner voice over and over as nothing more than instinct and intuition. "Maybe not the future, but I know more than I should. It was my choice to bring him."

"It was also his choice to go along with you." Brixby stroked her hair. It was the same comforting gesture he'd used on the long nights after her mother's passing. "What will you do now?"

"I won't let them cast him to the Above alone," said Azzy.

Her guardian chuckled, the small laugh laced with

sadness. "In some ways, you are so much like your mother."

"If I was like my mother, I would have gone to the tunnels alone."

A fist thumped between her shoulder blades. Her brother gripped her shoulders, resting his forehead against the back of her head.

"I don't think he agrees with you," said Brixby. "There is still some time before they light the lamps. Let's—"

The front door to the shop crashed open. Brixby shoved his charges behind him as footsteps thundered up the stairs. The guards poured into her room, armed with lanterns, clubs, and chains.

"What is the meaning of this?" Brixby shouted, spreading his arms to shield his wards.

Dread infused itself into her pulse as another light entered the room. Elder Prast swung the sense rod toward them. The dangling vial flared, painting the room with its damning golden glow.

"Take her."

"What? No! You can't do this!" Brixby's cries fell on deaf ears as the guards surged forward. Azzy gasped as rough hands grabbed her bruised limbs, ripping her away from the others. They ignored the furious Apothecary, wrapping her arms in chains. "She saved you. She saved all of you."

"Do you think me blind, Oswin?" Prast sneered. "She is her mother's daughter. You think I missed her actions at the feast? Miraculously producing the ingredients for the cure? Probably poisoned us herself. And this," he brandished the rod at her. "Proof that she's tainted."

"You foolish bastard, you know she didn't do this," Brixby snarled, his arms around her brother. Armin strained to break free. Azzy stared at her brother, only her brother. Sweat beaded on his forehead. His pupils were blown.

"No," she said, ignoring the flinch of the guards

surrounding her. The tainted were dangerous. They expected her to fight them. Fear soured the air. So focused on her sibling, Azzy didn't see Prast's hand as it swung. It slammed across her cheek and snapped her head to the left. Pain lanced through her sinuses, but it was nothing compared to her brother's scream.

"Don't you touch her!"

The guards dropped her chains, clapping their hands over their ears. Prast sank to the floor, his eyes bulging in his pasty face. Armin shook off Brixby's hold like drops of water. His shadow seemed to spread behind him. A rush of wings beat the air. Azzy could feel the pressure building. She struggled to free herself from the weight of the chains.

"Per-"

Azzy slapped her hand over his mouth. "Not like this," she said. Her bleak expression grounded him.

"I'm sorry." His lips moved against her palm, the voices cowed.

"Take him! Take him!" Prast shrieked, rallying the guard into action. Armin stepped away from her and let them force him to the ground. He didn't fight them as they cocooned him in metal, or when a gag was forced into his mouth. Azzy held his gaze through it all, gripping her elbows to stop herself from making it worse for him. Prast could make this so much worse. The guard pulled the chains tight, forcing Armin to stand.

"Take him to the Hole. We'll bring them both to the tunnel mouth at first light." Prast directed his men to lead their prisoner away. The glowing vial dimmed the second her brother left the room. The elder turned toward her, his expression murderous. "Post a guard at the door. No one leaves until I say."

It wasn't until the Elder closed the front door that Azzy sank to the floor and finally allowed herself to cry. Brixby kneeled beside her and held her until the tears ebbed. She exhaled a long breath.

"Does the hatch still work?"

Into the Above

❧✿❧

"**N**o matter what you say, no matter what you do,
they will still cast him out." Brixby nipped at
Azzy's heels as she stalked from room to
room, accumulating odds and ends. A future at her brother's side stretched before her on a gossamer thread, so delicate, so very easy to snap. This wasn't a time for her rational
side, or her guardian's spoken truth. She dove into the thick
of the small, tugging, whispering voice she'd half listened to
for years. Now it led every step she took and decided each
object her fingers seized.

"Azure are you listening to me?" Brixby's calloused palm
wrapped around her wrist, halting her progress. "These are
trimming scissors. Do you plan to give the Elder a haircut?"

"What?" Azzy glanced down at the tarnished silver. The
ancient tool was something Brixby had brought with him to
the Heap, painstakingly sharpening the edge after each use.
He'd cut their hair, his own, even the threadlike mosses
with it over the years. Easing from his grip, she added them
to the growing cluster of objects on her bed. Her guardian
truly noticed the pile for the first time.

"You don't intend to stop them at all. You're not going alone." He spun on his heel, heading for his own room. It was her turn to follow.

Azzy exhaled. Aside from her brother, there was only one person in the Heap she truly loved. Brixby was respected and useful, a vital element of the community.

"Do you remember where I stored my traveling satchel?"

"You can't come with me," she said, clutching the frame of his bed. Her guardian drew up short at her words. "Everyone here needs you too much."

"Yes, well, I'm not as noble as you are Azure, I never have been." Brixby tugged a threadbare sack from the bottom of his clothes chest, stuffing a few shirts and underclothes in it before looking up at her incredulous expression. "I've raised you and your brother for years. You have the same selfless temperament as your mother. I watched her die doing what she thought was best for everyone else. The Heap can fall to the Rot; I will follow my children."

There were no words to counter such a statement. Azzy did not wish to try. She wrapped her arms around him, tucking her chin against his shoulder. Brixby was wrong.

She was very selfish.

❧

At the first strike of light, they stood by the open windows on the second floor, awaiting the procession below. Like the Feast, the casting out of individuals to the Above was a ritual developed over time. At dawn, the march began from the confines of the Hole, through the winding streets to the front gates. Their path would take them directly through the tradesmen quarter, likely why Prast demanded guards at their door. It did not matter—

this would not be the last time she looked upon her brother, but it would be the most painful.

Azzy could feel the tremor in her legs as the first swinging lanterns emerged around the bend. The occupants of the quarter stood in their open doorways or perched at their windows, watching like her, silent, eyes on the group passing through. Prast strode into view, the picture of rumpled pomp, his official tunic stained and wrinkled from sleeping in it. The smug satisfaction on his face made her fingers curl into fists against her thighs, but it was the sight of Armin that made her nearly leap from the window sill to throttle the Elder.

Her guardian sensed her distress, the shelter of his arm around her as her brother drew near.

Chains encircled Armin, wrapping tight around his arms, jangling at his ankles. Dried blood painted his mouth where Prast's men had sewn it shut. Azzy clenched her jaw, digging her nails into her palms. The shriek built and died in her throat and left her lungs burning, unable to get enough air. Nell was an afterthought—her hands tied behind her back with common rope, a simple cloth gag in her mouth. It was clear to all who Prast had deemed the real threat to the city.

Her brother's expression was vacant. He did not even lift his head as they hauled him by the Apothecary shop.

"Watch for me," Azzy whispered, her voice lost in the shuffle of feet and clank of chains. His head tilted to the side. Some part of him captured her words. Nell stumbled, unable to catch herself. She landed on her side, glancing up at the gathered crowd with haunted eyes. They met Azzy's for a brief moment. The connection crackled and fizzed.

Azzy's breath caught in her throat.

The guards dragged the woman to her feet, ignoring her pained groans as they shoved her back in line. The procession moved on, flowing around the bend out of the quarter. She waited until the last guard was out of sight before she spoke.

"I was wrong, Brixby."

He frowned at her. "About what?"

"Nell did cause the Rot."

❧

Azzy paced the length of the halls, running her fingers along the wall. This would be the last time the familiar wood would creak beneath her feet. She memorized every squeak and groan, the mingling herbal smell of her home, the grooves in the stone walls, each crack and stain—every detail she could think of she tucked away for later. When she needed it, she'd call up home.

Brixby ascended the stairwell, shouldering his woven satchel, wrapped in a thick traveling cloak. He carried one for her as well. He raised a brow at her puzzled expression. "It's winter in the mountains. Or do you mean to freeze at night?"

Azzy bit her lip. It was Brixby who had taught her everything she knew of the Above. If Prast hadn't so foolishly forbidden it, he would have gone there to gather supplies himself. Now, he was too singular to go unnoticed, his frame too large to use the scrape routes, so they would use another route, a dangerous one.

"Are you sure this way is still useable? What if part of it has collapsed? We will be well and truly trapped."

"You mean I'll be trapped," said Brixby, helping her slip on her pack. He handed her an odd-looking pair of goggles, the lenses blacked out.

"What are these for?" she slipped them over her neck, letting them rest on her chest.

"Honestly, girl, how did you manage to slip to the Above as often as you did? It will be daylight by the time we reach the surface. If you wish to avoid going blind, you will wear these until you can adjust."

"It was always dark when I got up there," grumbled Azzy as she followed her guardian to the end of the hall.

"Yes, well, we shifted our day to counter the Above for a reason," said Brixby, tapping his fingers against the wall. It echoed hollow from the other side until he hit something solid. Soft clay gave way as he dug his fingers into the disguised part of the wall. He scraped away the excess until he was able to pull back the latch, bracing his legs apart as he leaned back.

The wall swung open with a crumbling scrape, dust and shards of stone raining down as a gust of musty air pushed its way to freedom, caressing their faces with the stale, moldering scent of secrets and time.

The hidden hatch was already in place when Azzy and Armin came to live with their guardian. He'd showed it to them after their first visit from Prast. If Azzy had realized how little time they had after their return from the tunnels, she would have dragged Armin through it that very night. Failed foresight did her little good, but it would be their way past Prast's men now.

Brixby ushered her inside, using the opposite side of the latch to pull the entrance closed behind them. She reached out, dragging her fingers along the rough-hewn wall to guide her steps. A dozen steps in, they hit cool metal. Her fingers curled over the vertical rod to discover a ladder. Pulling close, Azzy lifted her foot, feeling for the first rung.

"I'm right behind you," Brixby murmured, brushing a hand down her back. Despite her earlier resolve to go alone, she was grateful for his presence. The sightless upward climb threaded tension through every muscle.

Each step was a nerve-wracking process, the mold-covered metal slowing their ascent to a crawl. More than once, her foot slid on the slick rungs, forcing her to cling hard and fast with her hands to avoid crashing down onto her mentor. When they finally reached the apex of their climb, Azzy's arms burned, her palms bruised by the repeated abuse. Gasping for breath, she crawled on her knees along sanded stone, taking in her surroundings as Brixby heaved himself up the final rungs. The ladder deposited them in the upper level of the city, a dead city that fell to the Rot years ago.

The distant street lamps of the Heap were just enough the throw the contents of the room into eerie relief. The long-abandoned bed sagged in on itself, mercifully empty. A chest at the foot of the bed was slowly succumbing to the elements, quietly crumbling away. Dust sat thick on the rotting vanity, still standing despite its advanced decay. It was a warped image of her own room, its occupant long lost to the unforgiving grip of the Rot. Azzy turned away, glancing through the open-air windows to the Heap far below. She could almost see what the Heap used to be from its tarnished edges. Wind ruffled her hair, chilling the sweat on her face. The wind carried the song of the forgotten dead. The ghosts of Haven moaned around her, singing the sorrowful song of their fallen city in the gaps between crumbling stones.

"Come, Azure, we can't rest here." Brixby grabbed her hand, pulling her through sagging doorways, past a table set for a meal never eaten, into the main hall of Haven's upper level. Deep within the city, once they were well hidden from prying eyes below, Brixby brought out a small lantern from his pack. The glow was immediate, casting shadows around them. Rather than rely on fuel and fire, he'd stuffed it full of the luminescent moss.

Hooking an arm through hers, he held the lantern high. "Run, and don't stop until we reach the end."

◈

They ran in silence. Brixby's warning soon made sense as the clicks and hoots of wailing natters drifted through the air. The beasties stayed well away from the light, but she could feel their eyes; their forms darted at the edges of her vision. The natters did not give chase. There were worse things lurking here, unseen.

They ran through areas where the air went cold, cold enough to cloud their harsh breaths into white steam. The echo of their footsteps abruptly vanished. The only sound Azzy could hear was the frantic pounding of her own heartbeat. These spots of silence were far worse than a cadre of natters at her back. Here the air felt truly haunted, the chill playing along the back of her neck like a specter's seeking fingers. Her guardian tightened his hold on her through these zones, as if afraid something would snatch her away, and grimly charged on.

Azzy couldn't track how long they ran. Time unwound itself as she pushed past her known physical limits. Her legs continued to carry her despite each muscle seizing. Her lungs continued to draw in another gasping breath through the knifelike pinch between her ribs. When Brixby finally let them stop, she fell to all fours, dry heaving until he forced a waterskin to her lips.

"Drink."

The simple command reached her. Azzy drank deep. The water worked its way through her system, tingling through her veins. Her limbs still felt full of sand, but she wasn't in danger of collapse. The tunnel around them was lit by more than just Brixby's lantern. She could just make out the distant mouth spilling into the Above, where the light was far brighter, smarting her eyes even at this distance. She'd never seen sunlight. She tapped the goggles at her throat.

"I know you're tired. We can stop here if you need to rest."

She looked up at him. He was winded but moved with far more ease than she did. Brixby possessed greater stamina than she had realized.

"I'll be fine if we walk for a bit," she said, taking his proffered hand to stand. Her legs felt liquid and wobbled at the knees. The image of her brother's sewn mouth played through her mind. It bothered her beyond the pain it caused him—the fact that it left him helpless. And just like that, she found her second wind.

Their pace was slow but steady, the light growing painfully bright the closer they got. Brixby slipped on his goggles, gesturing for her to do the same. They colored the world in shades of gray but she could look out without squinting.

At the mouth of the tunnel, she paused, stunned by the contrast of light and dark flowing before them. The sky was an endless stretch of scalloped gray clouds, covering the sun. It was still bright, dazzlingly so; the white snow glowed, leeching any surrounding color to a wet black. Armin was out here somewhere. She would find him. Brixby nudged her, reminding her of his presence. They stepped into the Above, their boots breaking through the thin crust of frozen snow.

Neither looked back.

The Snatchers

❧❦❧

This time, Azzy did not have a sense of wonder or adrenaline to keep her blood warm. The cold sank its claws into her skin, seeping into her bones. Without Brixby's cloak, she would have frozen through in the first hour. Even with the insulating layer, her teeth chattered, nipping at chunks of steaming air from her lungs. Brixby found a weathered stick, wrapping it in spare cloth to protect her fingers, which she used to balance on the uneven frozen ground. Beneath the snow lurked treacherous pitfalls, dips, and pockmarks that caught at their feet. More than once, Azzy pitched forward, scraping her palms raw and bloody on the icy crust.

Brixby fared no better. They stopped every few steps to bury their blood deep in the snow. He used a spare shirt to wrap their hands in ragged bandages. Messy but effective, the cloth kept her fingers somewhat warm and padded their landings. Their progress was slow, far slower than she wished, but it had direction. They cut a path parallel to the cave system, making for the opening the Heap used to deposit their cast-outs.

They passed a few openings that boasted markers, constructed of whatever scrap material was handy—dead wood, stone, and strips of leather.

"Passages for the Foragers," Brixby remarked quietly. It was the longest string of words he'd spoken to her since they left the caves, sticking to one- and two-word commands. Azzy couldn't blame him—both of them had their senses wide open, straining to catch the odd noise, a flash of movement, a scent on the air, anything to alert them to the presence of the Above's numerous predators. Winnowrooks were not the only creatures to lurk close to the caves hoping to catch a free meal.

The goggles bothered her—a necessary evil but they blacked out the corners of her vision. She itched to be rid of them, wondering if her sight could adjust in a timely fashion. Each minute dragged on her conscience. It didn't matter that Armin's days were numbered—she felt responsible for igniting the magic in his veins. She should have tied him to his bed and gone into the nattering tunnels alone, should have fetched the cure herself.

You would be dead, and then no one would be there to go after him.

Her inner logic was sound, but did little to ease the guilt lashing at her, spurring her onward. Brixby came to a sudden halt, extending an arm to catch her.

He held a finger to his lips, and jerked his head toward a break in the trees a few yards away. Leaning down, he put his mouth to her ear, the warmth of his breath painful on her numb skin. "The banish point should be up ahead. Go no further than the tree line." She shivered at the warning. There were stories, always there were stories, of nightmares waiting to snatch those unlucky banished souls, carting them to fates unknown. There were reasons the cast-outs never made their way back to the Heap. She prayed they weren't too late for Armin, that they would save him from the Snatchers. If they were too late, well, then she would track them. To hell, to lands' end—wherever they stole him away, she would find her brother again.

Her guardian crept forward on his toes, breaking through the thin crust of ice with deliberate care, his steps completely muffled. She followed in his wake, placing her feet in his passage. Brixby was almost to the tree line.

Her nerves screamed in warning, a pitch that echoed through her head. She wobbled on her feet as something plucked at her senses, the warning of danger so overwhelming she clenched her teeth to keep from making a sound. She struggled forward, trying to catch the back of Brixby's cloak. Her fingers brushed the roughly woven cloth, closing on air. She could see through the trees now, and the scene seared into her mind.

Figures surrounded a cart. They were large, bow-legged, and heavily muscled. Where they human? Chains extended off each of the cart's corner posts, tethering men clothed in rags by a collar around their necks. Their heads were bowed, concealing their faces behind dirty, matted hair.

Armin was on his knees in the low-slung cart. Wire binding cut into his wrists. Nell was loosely bound beside him, a simple rope around her waist, staring into the trees. Staring right at them. Something was wrong with her eyes. They were uncovered, wide open, focused on them.

In the pause, the moment before chaos, the two women locked gazes. It was long enough for Azzy to see the secondary translucent eyelid flick over Nell's eyes.

Nell opened her mouth. "Theeeeeerrrreeeee!" she screamed, her voice the drawn-out rasp of nails on metal. Her hand rose, pointing to their location. The surrounding figures turned, and even the chained ones snapped to attention with eyes that flared in the light—nocturnal eyes, predatorial eyes. They were nothing compared to the Snatchers, features warped and mashed together in a poor semblance of human.

"Fresh meat boys!" called the tallest of them, one eye dropping far below the other, framing a grinning crooked mouth filled with jagged teeth. His misshapen nostrils flared. "I smell female!" He roared as he brought down his sledgehammer of a fist onto the nearest post. The chain collapsed, allowing a collared man with wild eyes to spring forward.

All in the space of a few breathless moments, their world shifted. Azzy broke away from Nell's abnormal gaze, her breath caught in her throat. Armin struggled against his bonds, jerking his head around. She could hear his muffled screams through all the grunts and barks of the Snatchers. Brixby slid in front of her, blocking her view.

"Run!" her guardian yelled, a moment before the chained man leapt on him, driving him to the ground.

It wasn't simple self-preservation that moved her, nor Brixby's final command. The secret voice seized her, flooded her veins with a sizzling awareness. She spun and sprinted off into the wilderness. Another echoing clank of metal signaled the release of a second wild man, snapping and growling in her wake. This flight was different from their unending run through the haunted city. It was the breathless run of desperation. Azzy flew over the snow, her feet kissing the ground so fast she left the crust unbroken in her path. She veered off into the hollows and shadows of the tree-choked forest, praying the treacherous ground was as great a hindrance to her pursuer as it was to her. A dip snatched at her toes, threatening to twist her ankle out from under her. Low branches left searing lines on her cheeks and neck, tearing at her cloak. Azzy pushed through it all, refusing to look back. She could sense danger gaining on her, the panting low growls of the feral male closing the distance between them.

Her only warning was the sudden absence of his pounding footsteps as he went airborne. She closed her mouth to keep from biting through her tongue. He plowed into her midsection. Her chin hit the ground with a jarring thud, ice tearing at her skin. The right lens of her goggles cracked. The rest of her fared no better; she landed with bruising force. She couldn't breathe through the iron grip that wrapped around her chest and waist. Her disorientation had no time to abate as her captor flipped her over and snarled in her face.

Through the distorted vision of her goggles she caught sight of tangled curls that obscured part of the man's face. There were scars, fresh angry red welts marring the bare skin of his thickly muscled arms—arms that were caging her in before his hand swept upward and ripped her goggles off. Azzy hissed. The thick growth of the forest filtered the light, but it still made her eyes water. Tears spilled across her temples. A trickle of blood ran down her neck from the gash on her chin. The man paused as he inhaled.

Her senses buzzed. The inner voice stirred, straining for her attention. Through her watery vision she could see the collar around his neck, studded with inward facing spikes that dug into his skin. A chain trailed down at the dip between his collar bones, the clasp etched with block-like archaic symbols.

Release him. The whispers sang out to her, guiding her fingertips to the blood running down her neck. The action was familiar, a ritual played out once before, calling on power older and stronger than the crudely carved symbols. The wild man shifted over her, bending closer to her face, to her wound, inhaling deeply. Through tears, she caught sight of his eyes, liquid amber, startlingly beautiful beneath the fall of his dirty hair. Her blood-stained fingertips brushed over the collar. The metal hummed at her touch, a pulse of something vile and dark, that broke under at the contact with her blood.

The metal collar fell heavy on her chest as the air sizzled and popped. The man's form shimmered, replaced by a beast in the blurry blink of an eye. On top of her now perched a wolf, his open jaws inches from her face.

Azzy held her breath as she stared into his teeth. In the corner of her painful vision she saw the scar, the deep nick in his ear where a winnowrook's web nearly cut it off. Through the adrenaline and panic, she recognized him. The wolf—*her wolf*—hovered over her. He dipped low to sniff her neck. His tongue darted out, lapping over the wound on her chin. Her skin tingled.

The wolf leapt off her with a yip and sprinted away to freedom.

She stayed put for a moment, swallowing huge gulps of air, blinking furiously to clear her vision. The dim light of the forest hurt but after a few minutes of burning tears, she could see if she squinted. If he'd caught her in the open, she would be blind. The wolf who'd been a man...

Her fingers gingerly brushed her chin as her mind tried to process what had happened. She touched tender sealed skin between her breasts instead of an open cut. Memory crashed over her, the bloody encounter with the winnowrook, their exchange of blood, his ministrations to the wound on her chest. In the aftermath she'd forgotten it. Her hand trailed down to the cut now, nothing more than a faint pink scar. She released a shuddering breath as she slowly sat up.

The wolf was long gone, nothing more than a trail of paw prints in the snow. Should she follow him? Did he mean for her to follow? She glanced back at her haphazard flight through the trees. Her path was clear, too easy to trace. The Snatchers had three other wild men to chase her down. She couldn't stay here. She had to circle around, find a way back to rescue her brother and Brixby.

Snowflakes drifted through the gaps in the trees. She frowned, squinting through the gloom. Beyond the tree line, the snow poured from the sky, growing thicker by the second. The wind picked up, pulling on the high branches until they creaked in protest. Azzy wrapped her hands around her knees. Her pickaxe was missing, flung off somewhere when she crashed to the ground. She was alone, bruised, exhausted, and lost.

The snow fell harder, devouring her path as she watched.

The Bone Eater

Azzy forced herself to her feet. Sitting like a lump in the snow would accomplish nothing but freezing to death. Her legs trembled under her from her flight. She leaned against a tree, listening to the complaints of her body. The gash on her chin was sealed, but a riot of aches and bruises sang through her limbs. Taking a breath, she bent her arms and legs, testing, wincing at the sharp stab in her left thigh. Had she pulled a muscle? Her pack was still on her back, flattened but intact. Brixby had carried the bulk of their supplies, but she wasn't completely stripped of resources. She had to forge on. There was no shelter and no guarantee the Snatchers wouldn't send another wild man after her. The fallen collar lay in the snow at her feet, the carved runes blackened and blown out. She'd seen similar symbols before in her mother's workroom, though not quite the same. She didn't know their purpose, though she could guess. Did the Snatchers sense the runes breaking in the wolf's collar when she freed him?

That thought sent another finger of dread trailing down her back. If they caught her, they'd want to know how she'd broken their runes, and she couldn't tell them. She wasn't sure how she'd done it. Not that the knowledge would save her. If the Snatchers caught her, her life was forfeit. There were many stories about the Snatchers, but no one knew what happened to those captured. Not even the Foragers who'd crossed their paths more than once knew their destination. It made no difference if their quarry was tainted or not, the Snatchers bundled them off to parts unknown—for food, for trade, or for enslavement, no one knew. Those taken never returned.

Azzy gritted her teeth and pushed off the tree. It was time to change that. She refused to give up on Armin or Brixby. Her last sight of her guardian pricked at her conscience as she limped through the trees. Snow continued to fall in thick fluffy globs. Already, her path into the wood was nothing more than a line of indents beneath the fresh layer of powder. She cut a wide arc parallel to the vanishing path, hoping to circle around and pick up the Snatcher's trail. If she failed—well, she couldn't think of that now.

The snowfall muffled everything, even her own panting breaths. She could feel the weakness in her limbs gaining ground. Each step pulled on her watery muscles, as if bags of sand dragged on her ankles. The trees became necessary as she used them to push off, propelling herself forward; she had to continue.

Warnings whispered in her head.

Azzy stopped, half wrapped around a tree to keep upright. Her arced path had brought her to the mouth of a darkened copse. The tree growth was so thick in this part of the woods that the snow couldn't penetrate it. It was nothing but a dusting on the ground. The light was too dim to hurt her eyes, allowing her to peer, puzzled, through the gloom. Warning bells continued to ring between her ears.

She couldn't pinpoint the sensation at first, not until she took another tentative step forward into the shadows. There it was, like thousands of tiny needle-like legs crawling over her skin. The sensation swarmed her. Azzy rocked on her heels. She could smell it now, the staleness of the air. The thick growth should have been marginally warmer—so heavily sheltered from the wind and snow—but it was frigid, the cold of the frozen ground seeping up through the soles of her boots.

The ground sloped inward, the angle greater than she first thought. She could feel the way her toes pointed downward. The whole area sloped down to a shadowy center, invisible through the trees. Whatever waited there, Azzy preferred not to chance an encounter, easing her foot back out of the shadows.

The trap was a clever one, extending beyond the sloping pit beneath the safer flat ground, whittled down to nothing more than a thin crust designed to give way at the right amount of weight. Her foot punched through, tipping her off balance. Her arms grabbed for the trees and missed as she slid down the incline on her side. Azzy grabbed for roots, rocks, anything to halt her descent. The slope was sharper than it looked, causing her to barrel toward the center. Or did the ground tilt under her? The fall was disorienting. Her fingernails caught and tore on roots, but each slid from her grip. The speed of her fall was impossible, escalating the further she slid. She caught herself briefly on a tree. A tug pulled on her ankles.

Something had a hold of her. She glanced downward, unable to see anything wrapped around her legs. The tug came again, harder this time, ripping her away from the tree. She burst through a circle of trees, the trunks so tight she scraped and squeezed through them. Her trailing hair snagged on their bark and tore from her scalp in eye-watering chunks. She stopped in a clearing, and the tugging released her. Azzy lifted her head with care, slowly turning to look around.

The ground beneath her was smooth as glass and so cold her skin soon grew numb on contact. The circle of trees rose overhead, branches knitting together in a natural ceiling. At the center of the clearing, down by her feet, was a pool of black sand. All around her were piles of cloth, littered with pieces of frozen hair and chunks of bone. Azzy focused on the pile closest to her, staring into the empty eye sockets of half a skull, the jaw missing, scalp still attached. She could see teeth marks along the ridges of the cheekbones. Leftovers, she was surrounded by leftovers.

The pool of black sand came to life at her feet, rippling and writhing as something rose from beneath. It knew she was here. She tried to crawl away but was brought up short by the invisible hold on her legs. She was trapped the moment she set foot at the edge of the pit. Azzy closed her eyes, resignation crushing the air from her lungs. The Above had beaten her. There were too many unknown dangers, too many lurking horrors for her instincts to keep track of. Her small forays to gather roots and berries had done nothing to prepare her for the unrelenting danger of this world. She'd failed Armin, lost him the moment she'd set foot on the snowy ground. She would die here, unable to save her family or herself. Her heart ached with guilt, wondering how long Armin would wait for her to come rescue him before hope failed him.

Sounds slithered behind her, the rustling scrape of claws over the frozen ground. The entity inhaled, sniffed the air in great wet huffs that made Azzy cringe and hug the ground.

A voice warbled through the air, filled with teeth, gristle, and flying spittle.

"What schweet marrow hasssh come to my den?"

Azzy flinched at the voice. It crept over her skin, imbuing her with the knowledge that her death would not be a pleasant one. Unsteady steps shuffled toward her. It paused, breathing in her scent again with terrible wet sounds. It moaned. Her hands curled into fists. The invisible snare held her fast as her sense of self-preservation tried to force its way through the chokehold of despair. Her inner voice was silent. She couldn't see the point of a struggle. She went limp on her side and pressed her cheek to the icy ground as she waited for the end.

Armin's face filled her mind's eye. Not the bleak final expression he'd given her when she'd fled the Snatchers or the terrifying empty expression he'd worn as the echoing voice poured from his mouth. No, it was one where his lips parted in a feckless grin, crinkling the corners of his eyes. Their normal shroud of stormy gray was lit from within with mirth as he tugged on one of her loose strands of hair. *What trouble have you got yourself into, sister mine?*

A tear slipped over the bridge of her nose, stinging as it slid along the edge of her other eye. What would Armin think of her now? Waiting quietly for death? She'd failed him...

Listen.

Azzy tilted her head, shuddering as her despair rose. A physical thing wrapped gossamer threads around her, cocooning her in doubt and misery. She could actually see them now, glistening on her skin, translucent ropes that thickened as she watched. Her eyes followed the threads, swallowing hard. The threads trailed from the creature's maw, a malformed crease in the fleshy folds of its face, lined with serrated teeth.

How could such a thing exist? It was a construct of flesh and bone. Black sand clung to layer upon layer of rotting flesh that hung in loose folds on a broken skeleton. Its hind legs dangled uselessly as it dragged itself forward on curved boney scythes nearly her height in length. There were no eyes or apparent nose in the twisted mess of flesh covering its knobby skull, only the misshapen slit of a mouth. A pale mottled tongue unfurled, tasting the air.

It twitched as if it sensed her eyes on it.

"Mussst tassssste the schweet marrow." Its ragged maw gasped the words. The viscous threads tightened. Despair rose to smother her, to make her roll over and die.

"No." Azzy bared her teeth and dug her nails into her palms. Pain lanced the fog clouding her mind, allowing her inner voice to gain a foothold at last. Anger burned through her veins, until it seared away the creature's mutinous hold on her. She rolled to her knees and kicked away the oozing strands as she crawled for the edge of the clearing. The trees surrounded it like the crooked bars of a cell. Behind her, the creature shrieked, chasing after her with a tottering gait. It moved faster than she anticipated on those spindly appendages, quickly gaining on her. Azzy reached for a low hanging branch. Its mottled tongue lashed out, wrapping around her ankle to yank her down. The fall stole her breath, but her forearms caught her, absorbing the impact. She sucked in air, reaching desperately for something, anything, to use as a weapon. The tongue jerked her back as the creature lifted a scythe-like arm. This left it balanced on one unsteady blade tip. Azzy shifted, ready to roll, kick, anything to knock the monster off kilter.

The other leg came down and pierced her thigh to the bone.

A scream tore from her throat, the hollow echo of her pain muffled by the cage of trees. Agony scrambled her senses, throbbing in time to the frantic pounding of her heart. She bit down on a second scream as the creature dragged her closer. Tears blinded her but she could feel it looming over her. Its tongue swept along the back of her neck, leaving a trail of thick saliva that burned. Azzy couldn't help the sob that slipped out.

"Ssssalt and a hint of ssssomething..."

Azzy tensed as the tongue slid across her thigh, probing the torn flesh where the bony scythe had pierced her. It lapped at her blood, moaning with pleasure. A fresh wave of pain made her shake as its acidic saliva seared her skin. She cried out through her teeth, blinking the tears from her vision. To her left, just out of reach, a broken femur protruded from a heap of rags.

"Maaaaagic...maaaaagic deep in the marrow. Delissshioussss."

This was the moment to act or die. She stretched out her trembling hand, straining through the pain and the teasing distance. Her fingertips brushed the bone, jostling it but failing to gain purchase.

She sucked in a breath, shoving down the pain and fear. The creature leaned over her, moving in for the killing blow. The window was closing. Not enough time. It had her, ready to feast.

A growl rolled through the clearing.

The monster froze with a high keening whimper. Azzy threw herself forward and grabbed the bone. She twisted and plunged the jagged end into the spongy flesh of the creature's chest. Dark fluid gushed over her fist. Its scythe of an arm was still buried in her thigh, gouging her further as it reared back. A choked shriek bubbled from its maw, now dripping black blood, dead blood. Azzy shoved the bone deeper. Her vision grayed as its tongue wrapped around her windpipe.

The wolf slammed into the creature.

Azzy fell back, ripped free. Her head smacked the

ground hard, a minor annoyance as blood flowed from her torn leg. The creature's piercing shrieks fell silent with a thunderous crack. Her head lolled to the side, observing the shredded remains of the monster with distant interest. Cold was settling over her, numbing the advance of the pain. She didn't realize the wolf stood over her until his warm nose pressed into her cheek. His breaths soothed her, gently chasing the cold from her bones. Azzy started to float off, feeling a tentative lick at her wounded leg. The experience was far different from the foul tongue of the dead creature.

The wolf pulled back with a snarl, scraping his mouth against his foreleg. Azzy remembered how the creature's saliva had burned her. She lifted a hand toward him, alarmed by the weakness in her limbs.

"You tried," she whispered. The wolf cocked his head at her and sneezed. There was no fight left in her when his jaws closed on her good leg, dragging her back toward the pit of black sand. He dropped her at the edge and jumped in. Azzy watched him, exhausted and confused as he scooped the sand into his jaws. She didn't understand until he spat a mouthful onto her wound. The wet sand coated her leg like a plaster salve, it stopped the blood flow. Warmth flushed through her as a tingling sensation seized her nerves. She felt her consciousness slipping. The heat grew more intense, surrounding her, cushioning her.

Azzy embraced it, drifting off with her fingers entangled in thick gray fur.

Breathe

※❦※

A rmin laughed as he ran through the streets. He ducked behind people on their morning business, slipped in the cracks between buildings, and skipped through the open doors of their neighbors. It was their favorite game, one they played often over the years. Her brother slipped in and out of hiding spaces but no matter how clever the location, she always found him. Of course, he did make it easy, giggling whenever she drew near.

"Azure?"

She turned to the woman, her blurred features framed by untamed red curls. The woman's hands lifted toward her, fingertips stained black. Mother?

"Time to find your brother, love."

She could always find her brother...

In her dream their connection was a faint white thread, the ends falling away into darkness.

Azzy spun around, listening hard for the laugh she'd chased all her life. She wandered through the crowd of faceless strangers, reaching out, blindly searching for him.

"Armin?" she whispered, her voice small and scared. She could feel the faint ghost of their connection but couldn't follow it. The sensation of loss pierced her, causing her heart to contract painfully in her chest. She pressed her palm over her sternum, noticing the black stain on her fingertips for the first time. Ink on her skin.

The sudden awareness of eyes on her. Her skin prickled and the fine hairs on her arm stood on end. She glanced up through the crowd.

A man watched her, the intensity of his gaze like a physical caress. Scars twined up the lean muscles of his arms and bare chest—some old, some new, the account of a lifetime of pain. He cocked his head as he looked at her, studying her with interest, the sole focus of his attention.

From the frenzied whispers of her thoughts, she felt she should recognize him...

The insides of her eyelids felt coated in sand. They scraped over her eyes as she struggled to open them, wincing at the stab of filtered daylight. Her body was a mass of aches and twinges, throbbing straight through to the ends of her hair. Despite the pain, she was warm. Icy air kissed her face, but warmth cocooned her, chasing away the worst of the chill. She carefully rolled onto her side, gritting her teeth through a groan as a sharp stab flared from her thigh.

Her cheek met fur.

Azzy froze as memory stole through her sleep-fogged brain. Flashes flickered through her mind: of her breathless flight from the Snatchers, of the cold bite of snow numbing her skin, and of the searing agony as a monster pinned her to the ground, its misshapen maw hovering over her. She opened her eyes and met a deep umber gaze that studied her from mere inches away. This close, she could see the varying shades of his irises, how a light shade of honeyed brown lined his pupil like a starburst. His pupils contracted as she observed him.

The wolf had come back for her.

Armin was lost to her.

Her brother and guardian were in the hands of the Snatchers. The trail would be impossible to follow now, swallowed up by the passage of time and falling snow. Azzy was alone in the wilderness of the Above, wholly unprepared for its dangers. She curled inward, loss tearing into her like a physical wound. She pressed her palms hard against her chest, trying to dull the painful twist of her muscles.

A warm nose pressed into her hair. She lifted her face. The wolf rubbed his snout along her jawline, pulling away with a small lick on her chin. The knot in her chest began to unwind. The wolf was still here. She leaned into him, so his massive head rested over her shoulder. Snowflakes began to drift through the thick canopy of tree branches. Azzy wondered if winter lasted forever in the Above. She couldn't recall a time when she'd visited the surface without the sting of the cold. Would the Snatchers protect their cargo from the cold, or leave them to the punishing elements? The thought threatened another wave of sadness.

She shifted out from under the wolf and attempted to stand. Her injured leg refused to support her weight. The healing skin cracked at her efforts, released a fresh trickle of blood down her leg while the pain made her gasp. A growl vibrated through the ground. The wolf nipped the back of her shirt. Azzy stared at him as he sneezed his disapproval at her, grumbling as he cleaned her reopened wound.

"I can't stay here," she said. The dryness of her throat scraped the strength from her voice so it was nothing but a raspy croak. She kept her focus solely on the wolf until the sour note of decay stung her nose. Her gaze was inexorably drawn to the broken corpse of the creature spoiling within its own lair. It lay in a pool of blackish brown blood, the discolored flesh of its throat torn out. She remembered how it had paused above her, terrified of the wolf's presence. The garbled shrieks as it died were still fresh in her ears.

How had the Snatchers trapped a being as powerful as the wolf? In the guise of a human, no less. The symbols on the collar brushed across her thoughts.

The wolf surged to his feet, nudging her shoulder until she cautiously wrapped an arm around him. He held still as she pulled herself up, taking the bulk of her weight as her weak limbs mutinied beneath her. Azzy locked her knees at the burning rush of blood through her healing wound until her legs grudgingly held her up. Together, the two of them slowly made for the edge of the clearing. The wolf kept pace with her hobbling steps, pausing to let her regain her breath and strength until they reached the outer circle of trees.

The world was a swirl of white. The snow blew through the canopy of tangled branches in stinging currents, pelting against her as they stood in the gap of two trunks. Azzy sank down, wrapping her arms around the wolf's neck to stay upright. Her mind emptied, spinning out into the fury of the storm, blinding and impassable. What would she do now? How would she survive in this world?

She drew a deep breath and smelled the musk of the wolf tangling with the smell of the snow-choked wind. Her inner voice began to whisper to her.

I always find my brother.

The Failings of Tooth and Claw

❦

D aylight seeped away with the oncoming dusk. The refracted glow of the whiteout was enough to see without irritating her eyes. Azzy stared out at the storm through the tree trunks, falling restless amid the twinges of her healing body. The wolf settled against her back until her fidgeting got the better of her. She pulled herself to her feet with a frost-covered branch, regretting the loss of her companion's warmth. The need to move was too strong. The monster's body was settling into a gelled mass as rapid decay took hold, coating the air with the tang of rusted metal. She gave the dead creature a wide berth as she tried to circle the clearing without limping. Twice, three times. On the fourth time around, she knew she was simply trying to outrun her thoughts.

The storm showed no sign of abating. The wolf opened one eye when she settled next to him, digging through the meager supplies of her pack. The majority of the items were intact. Her one decent weapon was already gone, lost to the elements. Her thoughts churned in an ugly current as she took stock of her possessions. Silver scissors, a vial of ink, one of Armin's shirts, a small collection of medicinal herbs, a pack of jerky, a crushed waterskin, a handful of odd colored stones, and soap.

A seemingly impractical collection on the whole. She sighed through her nose, wondering what possible purpose half these items would serve her. None would help against the Snatchers, if she could ever find their trail. The inner voice, her secret voice, continued to whisper of things her exhausted self couldn't decipher. She once thought the voice was instinct, but the now dead creature raised questions she spent a lifetime avoiding.

Azzy nibbled on a strip of dried meat. How would she acquire food when everything in the Above sought to make a meal of her? How would she find safe sleeping ground with monsters at every turn? Her injuries were already a hindrance. The deep furrows the Snatchers created in their wake would be long gone by the time the snow stopped. Her doubts circled in her head over and over, her lips a thin white line, pressed so tight her teeth cut against the inside of her cheeks. Her breath came in short, sharp pants. Those deep instincts and inner voice she used to guide her had landed her in a monster's maw. It was only the wolf's interference that had saved her. Her eyes strayed over his sleeping form. Twice now, they'd exchanged blood. They'd saved one another. What did that mean to an animal like him?

She picked through the piles of bone chips and rags to distract the endless loop of her thoughts, placing a few bits and pieces into her pack as she went. Eventually, the wolf rolled to his feet and trotted over to her. His massive head nudged aside her arms as he pressed his nose to her thigh, sniffing her wound. He pulled back, his burnished yellow eyes meeting hers for a moment before he turned and made for the edge of the clearing. The storm had ceased.

The wolf was going to leave her again.

Dust filled her mouth as her throat pinched tight in panic. He'd saved her and healed her. They were even. He owed her nothing. Azzy closed her eyes and drew her knees up to her chest. She could do this alone. She would find a way.

A snarl startled her. Azzy looked up, ashamed at the chill of tears on her cheeks. The wolf waited, watching her. She scrubbed her face, shocked by the strength of her relief as she shouldered her pack. Whatever bond lay between them was tenuous, one without set boundaries or commitment. She followed with reservations, wondering when the wolf would turn on her like a wild thing once again. It wasn't until he brushed against her, supporting her injured side, she remembered the scarred man that had pinned her to the ground.

He hadn't always been a wolf. But had he ever truly been a man?

The two exited the monster's lair. Moonlight poured over the snow coated land in puddles of blue-white light. Azzy's breath curled through the air in silvery streams while the wolf puffed great clouds of steam that warmed her skin. Their progress was slowed by her hobbling gait, but the wolf remained fastened to her side. His ears swiveled back and forth, perking up at small noises in the surrounding shadows.

He stopped so suddenly she had to clutch him for balance. His chest rumbled beneath her hands. Azzy followed the path of his gaze. A set of eyes glowed from the trees to their left, three of them, focused on them, on her. The wolf's rumble deepened, his lips curling over large teeth. The sight of them caused the eyes to retreat into the darkness with a fearful screech.

He resumed their pace. Azzy thought that was far too

short a distance from the clearing before she caught the attention of another monster. How had Brixby expected them to survive out here? Neither of them had known the full extent of the dangers they faced. Her fingers threaded through the wolf's coarse fur. Thinking of her guardian was painful but there were many things he had taught her in late night discussions at his worktable. Lessons learned while peeling roots and crushing leaves she never thought she would need. Pieces of information she'd gleaned reading his journal in secret.

Magic didn't contaminate the flora, but it did twist human and animal alike. If an amalgamation maintained the ability of speech, it was likely once human. The thought was disturbing. It meant the dead creature in the clearing had begun life as a man before the corruption of magic stripped its humanity away. What was the wolf? Was he an animal forced into a human form, or had he been born a man? Could he turn at will? She longed to test the limits of his understanding, but around them the night breathed with unseen threats. They stopped twice more for predators she couldn't see. The wolf proved to be the greater contender both times. What would happen when they encountered something nastier? Azzy shuddered and kept her eyes trained for the hint of webs or worse things. A rush of water was close by, reminding her of the now empty waterskin in her pack. Their progress was slow but exhausting through calf-deep snow. Weariness hooked into her limbs, dragging on her. She longed to wash the grit from her wounds as the black sand abraded her skin with each step. Menial things, things she couldn't bring herself to say aloud. She could suffer a while longer if it meant putting more distance between her and the clearing.

The wolf dropped to a crouch and pulled her with him. There was no warning growl or dominant show of teeth. It was a fully defensive position. Snarls ripped from his throat. The foliage stirred, a large shape gliding through the darkness. Adrenaline shot through her as saw what approached them, not the least bit intimidated by a lone wolf.

Sleek feline muscles coiled and bunched, easily moving through the thick packed snow. She caught a glimpse of wicked claws curving out from its paws as it picked its way nimbly over the terrain. Scales shimmered through dark fur. The animal paused, considering them. Its tail thrashed as it tasted the air with a forked tongue. Its orange eyes held the luminous flicker of an open flame. Its stare was fixed on them, pupils little more than slits. She'd seen this creature before, but only on the pages of her guardian's journal. Those charcoal sketches did little to illustrate the raw beauty and coiled power of the animal. In the flesh, she knew without the warning bells of her instincts the pyguara was more than a match for the wolf.

Azzy cocked her head, listening to the splash of water over stone. *A river,* whispered the inner voice. There was a chance, a slim one. She prayed he would listen to her.

The pyguara began to circle them, looking for an opening. The whispers grew louder in her head as she squatted down, reaching into the snow. She tightened her other hand on the wolf, tugging on his fur.

"Run for the river." His ear flicked, the only sign he gave of listening. It had to be enough. Her fingers closed on a buried rock.

The moment flared wide open, her choices and paths diverging before her. Azzy acted without hesitation. Her wrist snapped forward, sending the rock into the creature's face. She took off as the pyguara reared back with a hiss. She feared the wolf would try to press the seeming advantage. After a breath, the wolf turned with a yip and loped along beside her.

She could see the glimmer of moonlight on water through the thinning trees. A raspy roar rose behind her. Death gave chase as Azzy and the wolf hurtled toward the churning dark water.

The wolf reached the water's edge first, skidding to a hard stop with a high-pitched whine. The river stretched before them in a wide frothing mass of black water, silvered by moonlight. Steam rose off the water's surface, further obscuring the depth and contents of the river, but there was no time for considerations, no time for strategy, only action. Azzy siphoned all her focus into a single thought, tuned to the guiding whispers in her mind. Her bad leg was forgotten as she leapt from the riverbank.

The river was deep, far deeper than she'd anticipated. She dropped into the water which was well over her head, the temperature curiously warm. She kicked off the river bottom of slime-covered rocks. The cold air nipped her skin when she broke the surface. The wolf hovered at the water's edge, the infuriated pyguara rapidly closing the distance behind him.

Azzy grabbed his front legs and yanked hard enough to upset his balance and send him tumbling forward. Claws swiped the air, catching the feathery ruff of his tail in passing. She kicked off a larger stone at her feet, hauling them both into a swirling eddy as the creature paced the shore. The opportunity to observe their pursuer was lost as the wolf whimpered and thrashed in the water beside her, clearly unable to stay aloft in the turbulent waters. His muzzle dipped under the surface, making him frantic. Azzy pulled him against her, sidelong to avoid his scrabbling paws, and tucked his head onto her shoulder as she treaded water for them both. She could not keep this up for long. Despite the present threat of the feline creature, her body was far too injured to push itself on adrenaline alone and the wolf was heavy, far too heavy for her. The water may have been warmer than the air, but it was chill enough to make her teeth chatter as her legs kicked to keep them afloat. Oils and foam swirled around them from the soap in her submerged pack, creating a spiral of bubbles that distracted her, drawing her gaze over and over. The significance of the foam was lost on her as the pyguara took a tentative step into the water.

"No," Azzy whispered, tightening her hold on the wolf. They were supposed to be safe here. The water was supposed to be a deterrent for their kind. Other than a hiss of malevolent intent in their direction, the feline evinced little reaction to the rushing water, wading in after them. Azzy wracked her brains for another solution, looking around for protruding branches in the water.

No branches, no larger rocks to gain purchase on, but there was a long fin that was gliding toward them.

Azzy dipped her head back, a tangled riot of emotions stinging the corners of her eyes. She blinked to clear her vision, tears mingling with the water on her face as she stared up into the sky. It was no less amazing than the last time she'd beheld it, though the stars seemed brighter, revealing a night sky of shifting shades of violet and blue. It was a beautiful last sight before she died.

The fin circled them, a hint of a much larger creature beneath the surface. The wolf whined in her ear. She reached up, stroking the wet fur between his ears.

"Shh, it's okay. It's okay," she said. The lie and comfort were all she could give him. Her instincts were far outmatched by this world. No matter which path she chose, it led to death.

Live, Armin, live for me. The words choked on her tongue into a silent prayer to the stars above.

The fin continued to weave around them. She saw

glimpses of a massive serpentine form, wider than the tree trunks lining the bank. Wider than the circle of her arms. It continued to weave around them, until her awareness prickled. The unseen arrival hesitated, and the pyguara continued to close in on them, unaware or careless of the lurking creature beneath the surface. Azzy watched the water around her, biting her tongue hard when a hand rose up through the dark water. Webbed skin connected the long spindly fingers that dipped through a spinning patch of soap suds. The pads of its fingertips rubbed together, sampling the filmy texture before slipping back underwater.

A crown of dark fibrous hair broke the surface a few feet from Azzy. She bit her tongue bloody as lambent yellow eyes stared back at her. The rest of the face crested the water, one that retained the barest features of its former humanity. It was a woman's face, sharp cheekbones overshadowed by the sharper points of her teeth. Her gaze was rife with curiosity and disbelief before she re-submerged, leaving Azzy baffled by the sight of her.

A greater problem presented itself as the pyguara splashed closer. The fin slipped away completely, the eel woman vanishing from sight. Azzy cursed, attempting to swim into deeper waters, dragging the wolf with her.

The water erupted.

A massive coil of wet charcoal-colored flesh wrapped itself around the middle of the pyguara, before both vanished, the water boiling and bubbling with the battle below. Azzy held her breath until her head swam, her lungs burning in protest as the water smoothed over. The eel woman's head rose above the water once again, the pyguara's tail dangling from her mouth.

A tremor rose through the muscles of Azzy's legs as shards of ice flooded her veins. Her eyes widened, fixed on the eel woman's face as she swallowed, the tail vanishing between her gray lips with a sodden pop. Her mouth stretched in a wide smile, revealing rows of triangular teeth in dark gray gums.

"Thank you, for the meal."

The voice sounded human, so very human. A noise grew and died in Azzy's throat. Her body shook, the tremor in her legs making it impossible to stay afloat. She waited for the strike, for the seizing coil of flesh to wrap itself around her and the wolf. The eel woman tilted her head, frowning at her.

"What are you waiting for?" Azzy whispered. The muscles in her leg seized, locking in place. She released the wolf as she sank, sensing him thrash next to her as her body dropped.

It wasn't a coil of slick flesh that seized her but an arm, looping around her waist. Azzy slid against skin the texture of wet sand. She went limp, her muscles strained and useless. Water rushed around her and pulled on her dangling limbs. Was the wolf with them? Was he left struggling downstream? Her lungs seized on the first kiss of air, inhaling in gulps as the eel woman set her down on smooth stones in shallow water. The wolf landed beside her, sneezing and spitting water as he wrapped himself around her. He growled at the hovering figure, defiant to the last.

The eel woman rose out of the water, revealing a distended midsection that still rippled with the protests of her dying prey. Belying the grotesque sight, the yellow eyes that peered down at them held a note of sympathy and warmth. Azzy swallowed her preconceptions, listening hard to the hum of her inner instincts.

"You saved us," she said in undisguised awe. She wrapped her fingers around her companion's snout, silencing his growls. "Why?"

The eel woman shrugged one shoulder and dipped her

upper body to lounge in the pool beside them. "It was a scent in the water." She nodded to the waterlogged pack on Azzy's back. "It reminded me."

The nerves along Azzy's spine sizzled at the eel woman's words.

"Reminded you?"

"Yes," said the eel woman, her expression a mixture of wistfulness and mourning. "I've all but forgotten what it was like to be human."

The Worth of Small Gifts

The flames licked the air with tongues of violet and green. The eel woman said the beached wood floated in from the ocean mouth upstream, saturated by salt. The colors dazzled Azzy while the fire chased away the clinging chill and dried her soaked clothing. The wolf curled his bulky frame around her back. His head rested on her thigh. Between fur and fire, she felt the first moment of comfort since stepping into the Above.

Their odd rescuer had brought them to a small shoal upriver. Located at the bottom of a sheer rock face, the area was a relative safe zone. The washed-up bracken and branches were dry enough for Azzy to conjure a fire with the flint from her pack. It was one of the few items sealed in wax cloth that had survived her dip in the river. Everything else in her pack was a wet mess, wafting trails of steam next to the open flames. Once girl and wolf were settled, their hostess had left them to hunt, intent on feeding her charges. The thought made Azzy shudder, the sight of the tail disappearing through the woman's lips still fresh in her mind. She turned her thoughts to her current companion.

She studied the mottled gray fur on the top of his head, running her fingers through the ruff on his neck. She hadn't expected him to stay with her once their feet were back on solid ground, but the wolf stuck to her like a burr. His golden amber eyes tracked every movement of the eel woman, placing himself between her and Azzy. She didn't know what to think of such gestures, they didn't fit the system of favors between them. The bond between them was shifting into something new, something undefined. She felt an unwanted crush of relief at his presence, one she refused to rely on. The wolf was a creature of the Above, one whose secrets were still largely unknown. She stared into the flames, like burning amethysts, recalling the metal collar with spikes turned inward, digging into his neck, the collar that made him human. What magic did the Snatchers use on him? Her fingers absently traced symbols in the dried silt.

The nearby water roiled. Azzy tensed, the wolf rising behind her, until a familiar form rose from the water. A growl rumbled in his chest. The eel woman ignored him, dropping her prize beside the fire. The fish was enormous, half as long as Azzy, with a wide mouth that kept gasping for air.

"Thank you," she said, watching their rescuer. Aside from the wolf, the eel woman was the first creature that didn't want to devour her. The reasoning behind their extended company spooked her. *"I've all but forgotten what it was like,"* the eel woman had said. Was that what would happen to her brother?

She dug her nails into the palms of her hands, trying to stifle the surge of panic gnawing at her nerves. The eel woman joined them on the small beachhead, drawing close to Azzy, an unreadable expression on her face. Her proximity should have been cause for alarm. The wolf remained tense and wary behind her, but nothing rose the warning bells of her instincts.

"Could I—could I touch your hair?" The eel woman's voice was low, full of sadness and longing. The wolf's growl tapered off.

Azzy nodded and held still as long fingers lifted a strand, holding it up to the violet firelight. Pain flared in the woman's yellow eyes, so intense it made Azzy's heartache for her.

"What's your name?" The eel woman's gaze lingered on her hair. The excuse she'd given Azzy for the rescue unraveled. The scent of soap in the water might have caught her attention, but Azzy remembered how the woman's eyes had widened at the sight of her.

"Azure. What's yours?"

"I don't remember anymore."

"Do you remember anything?"

"Pieces. Memories that melt like flakes of snow." Her voice was strained. For a moment, the resonance stopped. The eel woman blinked. "A daughter. I used to braid her hair. So fine. Could never tame it." She released Azzy's hair and brought both hands to her chest. "I can no longer recall her name either."

Azzy could feel her sorrow, the jagged texture of it. She sat forward, digging her fingers into damp silt beneath her. Her last sight of Armin haunted her—his sewn lips, the fear in his eyes. The eel woman grabbed her wrists, gently prying her hands from the earth.

"You left someone behind?"

She looked at the webbed fingers holding her, wondered

if the eel woman's daughter ever searched for her lost mother. She wondered if she and Armin would have gone looking for their mother if she'd been banished rather than killed.

"I am searching for someone," she admitted, meeting the eel woman's luminous eyes. "My brother."

The woman's gray lips parted. "You left your home for him?"

"He's my family," said Azzy. She released a shuddering breath. "The Snatchers have him, and our guardian."

"The misshapen ones," murmured the eel woman. Her eyes flicked to the wolf. "You're tracking them?"

"I don't know how," said Azzy, tugging her hands free. She grabbed a piece of wood, stabbing at the fire. "I don't think I am going to survive long enough to find them." Silence fell between them at her admission.

The truth of it weighed on her. There was no going back to the Heap. Even if she desired to, they would never let her back through the gate. Tracking the Snatchers seemed an impossible task. She didn't know where to begin. Now Azzy wondered if her brother would recognize her if she did find him. Or if her guardian still lived.

She clenched her jaw. She would find him, both of them. One problem at a time.

"There may be someone who can help," said the eel woman. Azzy glanced up at the hesitation in her voice. There was fear in the woman's eyes, but she continued. "The price for their favor is high."

"I'll find a way to pay it," said Azzy.

"It is settled then." The eel woman nodded to the fish. "Eat something. You will need your strength."

Her long body slipped back into the water until only her head was visible. "I'll return for you soon. Rest."

Azzy stared at the ripple of water in her wake. It was

difficult to accept the eel woman's willingness to help her, but she was grateful for it. It gave her a small measure of hope that no matter what state she found him in, she might be able to tap into Armin's humanity.

Moonlight shone off the wet scales of the fish. She'd never had one so fresh and was at a bit of a loss as to how to prepare it for consumption. Whatever fish made it to the Heap was cured and salted, prepared by the Foragers. She dug through the contents of her pack, hoping for something to hack into it. Her fingers met bone.

She'd forgotten it, the splintered leg that had saved her. The wolf's arrival may have heralded the death of the Bone Eater, but she had also fought back, she had chosen to live. The broken edges were still stained from her encounter. What little appetite she had left her. This was a piece of someone, another casualty of the Above. Someone's child, someone's brother or sister, devoured by a monster. It was a reminder of how close she'd come to death, how ill-prepared she was for the dangers of this world.

Azzy knelt at the water's edge, using handfuls of sandy river silt to scour the blood from the bone. She nabbed one of the current-tumbled stones and began to smooth the femur's rough edges. Her thoughts drifted, exhaustion causing her vision to waver through the mindless task. For a moment, her fingers appeared stained with ink. She blinked. Dirt crusted under her fingernails and traced the lines of her skin, but no ink. Azzy swallowed, forcing herself to focus on her task until her vision blurred. Hunger she could ignore, but her body demanded rest. Dragging herself away from the water's edge, she settled beside the wolf, staring into the guttering flames of the fire until her eyelids succumbed to their own weight and the weight of her dreams.

Azzy ran through a forest. The land contradicted itself.

The frozen ground bit into her bare feet. Snow numbed her toes while slivers of ice cut her soles. Blood bloomed in her footprints, gory roses that traced her flight. But the air that caressed her face and teased her hair was warm. A delicate perfume filled her nose, the smell of things she couldn't name or picture, spiked by the sour scent of decay and death. Tree branches brushed her face as she passed, laden with leaves like patches of green velvet. It was beautiful, but she could feel the danger of the thing that pursued her through the pillars of dark wood. It made the shadows deeper.

Red flared in the corner of her vision, a tendril of wildfire. Azzy stumbled, catching herself on a nearby tree. The howl of a wolf filled the air, warbling and twisting mid-note into a man's hoarse scream.

She looked up, searching for the source. She had to find him. Instead, she saw her hand pressed against the tree trunk. Ink stained her fingers, dripping down the bark.

She felt rather than saw the figure behind her. Felt a hot breath on the back of her neck as it leaned in to whisper in her ear.

"What will you choose?"

She startled awake, sitting up so fast the world spun. *Breathe.* Her heartbeat a furious rhythm against her ribs. Azzy dug her fingers into the cold earth, bracing herself as everything slowly came to a standstill. Her fingers emerged from the earth free of ink.

The fire had burnt down to smoldering coals that still gave off heat. Beside the pit was a large chunk of meat, coated in ash. Cooked meat. Her stomach clenched as hunger caught up to her and made her mouth water. She tugged a small piece free, tasting it. The fish flaked on her tongue, sweet and smoky to the taste. It wasn't movement that caught her attention but stillness.

The wolf was watching her, the bones of the fish picked clean between his paws. She nibbled at her portion, considering him. Had he dragged it through the flames for her? An animal wouldn't do that, no matter how well-trained. It was far too human a gesture.

"What are you?" she said, more to herself than the wolf. There was no forthcoming answer, but the honey-colored eyes broke off, peering through the lightening gloom at their surroundings. Azzy looked away from him, remembering the broken howl in her dream, how it changed. How anguished the man sounded. She shivered, forcing herself to eat. The wolf had left her a sizable portion. More than she needed. She carefully tucked the remaining fish into her pack, wrapped in the waterproof cloth.

The eel woman still hadn't returned. Azzy began to fear she wouldn't but she had no way to gauge how much time had passed. Any time felt like too much, widening the distance between her and her brother. She continued her task, polishing and smoothing the bone, honing its rough edges to a sharper finish. When she was satisfied with the results, her hands continued to itch for distraction. She fished through the contents of her pack.

She brushed aside the assorted rags and packets of herbs, pausing at the bottle of ink. Her dream continued to flick through her thoughts, now hazy and surreal, its meaning beyond her grasp. Azzy clenched her jaw and pushed the bottle to the side. At the bottom of her pack were the colored stones. Ribbons of deep turquoise scrolled through the rich browns in intricate swirling patterns. When her mother was still alive, Azzy used to gather pretty ones with the other girls, crafting jewelry from nothing but stones and strips of cloth. Her mother wore a pendant Azzy had made for her till the day she died. Once her mother was gone, there were no more gatherings with her peers, and she stopped making pretty, useless, things. Now, she turned the stones over in her fingers, finding the holes Brixby had once carefully drilled through them.

They were such a random addition to her bag, but she'd stopped questioning the whispered nudges in her thoughts long ago, convinced they were instinct, the same sort of nudges anyone would feel. The rustic oracle never once reacted to her.

Azzy pulled a scrap of cloth from her pack, using the scissors to reduce it to strips. Her hands worked, remembering a craft never truly forgotten. It was a small gift, another useless pretty thing. It was a reminder too, of a life lost and not merely left behind in the Heap.

A wooden raft bumped the shoreline. The wolf leapt to his feet with a snarl. Long webbed fingers curled over the top of it, followed by the stunning face of the eel woman. The tension released from Azzy's chest.

"My apologies," said the eel woman. "It took longer to find a suitable craft than I anticipated."

The raft was constructed of rough-hewn logs, tied together with leather rope. It was simple but sturdy and large enough to support girl and beast.

"Did you make this?"

The eel woman shook her head. "There are many who travel this river. There are abandoned skiffs and broken boats littering the shore. This one will get us to your destination." She paused. The sharp angles of her face made her distress all the more evident. "Are you sure you still wish to pursue this?"

Azzy's dream echoed through her consciousness. She could feel the pull, the guiding whispers leading her. There were no other options.

"Yes," said Azzy.

"Then climb aboard. I will take you as far as I can." The eel woman held the raft steady as Azzy climbed on. The wolf took more coaxing, his visible distrust of their companion warring with his desire to follow Azzy.

She held her arms out to him, guiding him aboard through hesitant steps until he rested his bulk next to her. The raft dipped low but took his weight. When the two of them were settled, the eel woman shoved them off the shore, swimming upstream, against the current.

The trip was brief but tense. The eel woman strained to maneuver their craft through the deep gullet of the river while the wolf shook beside her. Azzy kept her silence, stroking his fur until his shaking stilled. The first strains of daylight were lightening the sky when the eel woman steered their raft to shore amid the thick cover of trees. A worn path cut through the forest, untouched by bracken. Azzy could make out the stones that lined it, painted with black ink.

"Follow the path to its end," said the eel woman. "I don't know what will be asked of you, but I hope the price is not too high."

"Wait," said Azzy, grasping the eel woman's hand. She leaned over, carefully tying her gift to the woman's wrist. "Thank you. For everything."

The eel woman pulled back. Her lips parted as she stroked the stone-laced bracelet. An array of emotions played over her face before a sad smile creased her features.

"I remember," she said, her voice whisper-soft. "Her name was Rose."

"Your daughter?" asked Azzy.

The eel woman nodded, her expression a mixture of sorrow and gratitude. "Fare thee well, Azure. Be careful in these woods. Don't give up."

Azzy released her, watching as the eel woman slipped beneath the water and swam away on the current. The wolf clambered ashore after her.

The wood awaited them.

The Witch of the Wood

❧

The change was gradual. A teasing wisp of warmth on the tail end of a chill breeze. A flash of green among the snow-plastered trees. There was a constant sense of otherness to the air. Azzy could feel it, kept trying to find its source. The surrounding wood grew denser as they followed the path. The thick trunks grew wider, the gnarled twisting roots spilling into the walkway. The wolf constantly brushed against her side as they picked their way over the treacherous ground. He paused often, sniffing the air, his ears flat against his skull. A flash of red sped past her nose, landing on a low-slung tree branch. Azzy startled, following the movement, and stared.

It was another creature lifted from the pages of her mother's books. The sleek red feathers of its body fluffed as she watched. It cocked its crested head, bright black eyes studying her. The bird gave a sweet high chirp before launching from the branch, fluttering off along the path. A feather floated down in its wake. Its slow descent ended at Azzy's feet, a stain in the snow. She picked it up, twirling it in her fingers with a sense of wonder. The bird was so simple, a natural creature untainted by magic. How could it still exist?

She could see the bird further down the path, flitting from branch to branch. There were other things she noticed now, multiple strains of birdsong flaring through the woods. She could hear the rustle and crackle of living creatures moving and while her companion was wary, he hadn't sensed danger yet. The wood continued to exude a pervasive sense of peace. Azzy's pace quickened, driven by curiosity and the whispered spur of her instincts.

The wolf loped beside her, grumbling as he matched her stride. There were more flashes of color now, more birds passing through her field of vision in streaks of blue and white, russet browns and orange bellies. A cluster of them scattered in a chorus of chirps and affronted trills as she passed. The birds weren't the only change. Snow continued beneath her feet but Azzy could see it beginning to recede from the trees, the snow-covered branches giving way to bursting fragrant blooms. The air grew warmer against her skin as the smell hit her, a rich bouquet of wild sunshine and new growth. Beneath the cloying smell was the hint of decaying wood and rotting flesh, the raw earthy scent of compost. The similarities to her dream spooked her, but her sense of danger remained muted. She continued forward with slower, cautious steps, wrapping her fingers in the wolf's scruff for courage.

The path reached an abrupt end, depositing them before the trunk of a massive tree, nearly twice as wide as her room back in the Heap. The bark was burnt black, riddled with cracks. Its dead branches were bare of leaves and blossoms, but they were far from empty. The canopy was a collection of gruesome odds and ends to rival any winnowrook's nest.

She spotted a row of grinning skulls, runes painted on their bony foreheads.

More than one dead monster hung suspended by woven rope, lazily spinning in the warm breeze. There were winnowrooks, their legs plucked free from their bloated bodies. Their dark blood drained into a waiting vat nestled amid the branches. A pyguara hung by its hind limbs, without its skin. There were twisted shapes she didn't recognize, dissected, sliced apart, and left to rot in the golden sunlight. The display of death was an ill fit for the idyllic scenery. It sent chills spiraling down her arms.

Azzy untangled her fingers from the wolf's fur and swallowed past the dry coating of fear in her throat. There were worse things driving her. For Armin and Brixby, she took a step forward, wondering how to proceed.

"Brave, and more than a little foolish. Though the two attributes often walk hand in hand."

She jumped at the voice. Her eyes darted around the clearing until she spotted the woman. How had Azzy not seen her before?

The woman leaned against the blackened trunk, arms folded under her chest. The ragged gown she wore did little to hide a voluptuous figure, the cloth smeared with dirt and darker, more sinister stains. It fell to the tops of her bare feet, the hem dry despite the snow on the ground. Her skin was like fire-baked clay, a smooth dark brown that contrasted with the unruly mane of coppery fire that spilled to her waist. There were bits of bone, dried flowers, and feathers braided into her hair and a woven crown of vines atop her head. Eyes the shade of dark honey observed them, lit with a sharp intensity. Azzy felt them pierce through her, crawling around inside her skull.

The red bird perched on the woman's bare shoulder, chirping in her ear. The woman nodded, detaching from the

KRISTIN JACQUES

trunk to move toward them. The wolf dropped low, a cautious rumble rising through his tensed form. Azzy didn't have the heart to shush him, not when she felt the same. Quiet power radiated off the strange woman, brushing over Azzy's skin. It struck a chord of ambivalence, neither evil nor good. Neutrality could swing either way, unpredictably so. Azzy held her ground as the woman approached.

The woman completely ignored the wolf's presence, halting less than a foot away from Azzy. She began to circle the girl, studying her from all angles. She remained silent until the wolf refused to move from her path, pressing against Azzy's legs as the woman inspected her.

"Interesting," she murmured. Azzy turned as the woman squatted down next to the wolf, studying him with the same intensity until he broke her gaze with a shake of his great head. He whined, sinking to his belly on the ground. The sight compelled Azzy to insert herself in the scant space between the woman and the wolf so that her fearsome gaze broke off to look up at Azzy.

"Please don't hurt him," Azzy whispered.

The woman's eyes flared. "So, the bond is mutual. Very interesting indeed." She stood, several inches taller so that Azzy was staring at the column of her throat. Her hand snaked out, faster than Azzy could react. The woman caught her chin in a tight grip, this time forcing her to look up.

"You have shards of the sky in your eyes," said the woman. The grip softened as her hand stroked Azzy's cheek in an almost affectionate caress. "The sun-soaked day to your brother's storms."

Azzy shivered at her words. "I need to find him," she said. The words felt redundant as they left her mouth. This woman knew all, knew her inside and out, from her hopes and desires to the secrets she buried deep. Azzy wanted to scream at her to get out of her mind, but the woman leaned in close and breathed her in.

"My, my, that is a unique scent," she said, her dark lips parted. Her breath tasted of mint and metal, coating the inside of Azzy's mouth. She shied away from the woman's overbearing presence, flinching against the wolf. She wasn't alone here. Azzy set her jaw.

"Can you help me?" Azzy met the woman's burning gaze without flinching.

The intensity shattered as the woman laughed, rich and hearty, shaking her whole frame. "Yes, brave and foolish," she grinned at Azzy, revealing teeth with fine points. "Just my type. Come, my girl. Let's discuss terms."

The woman moved towards the massive tree, leaving Azzy awash in relief and confusion. She turned to follow, stumbling as the woman slid her hand along the tree trunk. The bark melted away, revealing a small well-lit chamber within.

"Come, come. Your wolf will have to wait outside," said the woman. A few birds emerged from within. Azzy hesitated, glancing down at her companion. "He will come to no harm in my forest," the woman called over her shoulder.

Azzy trailed her fingers through his fur as she followed, glancing over her shoulder more than once as she entered the tree. The opening closed behind her. She tried to banish the surge of panic at the thought of being trapped in close quarters with the woman, who observed her every reaction and gesture with a secretive smile on her lips.

The room contained the same strange mixture of odors as the air outside: crushed petals, drying meat, dead things, and fresh ink. A bed of clean scraped hides occupied one corner, far from the carefully constructed fire pit in the center. It was a clever contraption, the warmth of the flame contained and enhanced by a curved clay structure, complete with a fluted pipe that pumped smoke up to the natural openings of the dead tree. The fire was little more than coals now and gave off no smoke. Odd trophies decorated the walls, the preserved hollowed-out bodies of small strange animals, broken weapons, rusted squares of metal with printed numbers, and dented helmets from some long-ago conflict. There was even a set of spiked collars, carved with runes, like the one she'd unlatched on the wolf. The other side of the room was clearly a work station, one so familiar Azzy's chest ached at the sight of it.

"You're an apothecary?" Her fingers itched to touch the familiar implements, a sharp reminder it wasn't just Armin she sought. It was difficult to reconcile her guardian's peril with her brother's. Brixby contained such strength. He was the man who had protected and housed them for years. She hoped with every fiber of her being he'd survived their encounter with the Snatchers. He would do everything in his power to continue protecting Armin until Azzy found them again. A snort interrupted her sobering thoughts.

"Hardly," said the woman. She leaned a hip against the edge of her work station, the speculative gleam returned to her expression. "Now, you shall tell me what you seek, and I will tell you what you can do for me."

To find my family again. It was her one request, the motivation that had spurred her to this moment. Azzy opened her mouth—the words dangling like ripe fruit on the tip of her tongue—and stopped. Danger strummed a jangling alarm through her senses. Here was the ominous warning of her dream, the danger of deals and choices. The words withered away, leaving a bitter taste in her mouth. Azzy braced herself on the weathered wood of the workbench, digging her nails into the natural creases. She bit her lips to keep them closed, searching for the right words, the correct path to forge before she fell into a trap of her own making.

The bits and bobs of the room called to her attention over and over, spearing her concentration. Her eyes fell on the spines of ancient books, the cracked golden titles slowly flaking away. There were bottles of ink everywhere—capped, open, partially dried out—and ink spots spattered on the walls. Many of the bottles rested beside handmade dolls, where ink-stained needles had been used to tattoo runes in the cloth of their skin.

Below the collars with their cruel spikes was a shelf full of jars. These were all sealed shut. Mist swirled in some. Glowing liquid sloshed without aid in others. Other jars were quiet and dark, casting shadows where there was no light to cast them. Once she noticed them, Azzy found she couldn't look away from this odd collection of jars. She was reminded of another workshop, very different from Brixby's but no less familiar. She stared and stared until the woman's laughter broke the hold those vessels had on her. Azzy looked at her knowing smile. The woman's teeth no longer seemed so sharp.

That made them no less intimidating.

"I cannot find the right words," said Azzy. She lowered her gaze to the dirt-packed floor to evade the siren's song of the jars. Bare feet moved into her vision, a lighter shade than the earth beneath them. The woman's toenails were painted with elaborate scrolls of black ink.

"Look at me," said the woman, her voice forcing Azzy to obey before the thought processed. Her inner voices buzzed and thrashed, but following the order was a vital move too. *Don't show resistance.* Azzy let herself go blank, sinking deep within herself as those honey-colored eyes searched her face. "What are you really afraid of?"

Azzy could feel the lilting overlay in her words. Her voice possessed the same human quality as the eel woman's but with the power of her brother's echoing voice. She sank her nails deeper into the wood, slivers sinking into the tender flesh of her fingertips.

"Will your payment trap me here? Will it keep me from what I desire?"

The woman's lips parted, a soft sigh escaping that teased Azzy's hair with a touch of wonder.

She spun around—her fiery curls spilling down her back like a flash of wildfire—and took one of the dark quiet jars from her shelf. She turned back to Azzy, cupping it between her hands. This close, Azzy could see the ink that stained her fingertips as well. Her stomach knotted at a sight so familiar. She could remember the dark rivulets of liquid running across her mother's fair skin.

Witch.

"Do you know what these are?"

Azzy didn't have to look to know, but she did, riveted. "Your payments," she whispered.

"But do you know what this one is?" the witch repeated. Azzy finally tore her gaze away, lifting her shaking hands off the bench to clasp them behind her back.

Her tongue turned thick and sour. "Regrets."

The witch seemed pleased with her answer. She carefully set the jar back in place on the shelf, lifting another for Azzy's inspection. This one contained swirling mist, the powdery green color of crushed moss.

"Dreams," said Azzy.

The jar was returned to its proper place. The witch tapped the top of one jar filled with liquid, waiting for Azzy's answer.

Memory rose. Her mother's hands moved over her temples and drew the spinning thread of liquid forth.

"Don't worry, love, I'll give it back."

"Memories." Azzy closed her eyes, unwilling to show the witch her private sorrow. Her mother had kept that promise in a row of small sealed vials she left on her daughter's bed the day they took her away. They were small memories, tiny moments Azzy may have lost anyway without her mother's careful preservation. She could never bring herself to drink them down.

She opened her eyes to find the witch watching her. Azzy could see all the small resemblances now: the same shade of flame in their hair, the ink-flecked skin, and the collections of abstract substances. The taint of magic was strong in the witch, as it had been in her mother. The difference was that her mother had burned for it.

"Who was she?" the witch asked, reaching out and running her fingers down the side of Azzy's face.

"They killed her," said Azzy. The back of her throat burned with bottled anger and tears. "But I don't think she would have become a monster like—" She clipped her own words.

"Like the brother you seek?" The witch continued her exploration of Azzy's face, tracing the scar through her eyebrow, a memento from the nattering tunnels, and the one along her chin. "Do you think I am any less dangerous than your enamored wolf?"

"He is not my wolf," said Azzy, taking the witch's hand in her own. "And dangerous does not make you a monster." She studied the woman's inked palm. "My brother is not a monster."

Silence wove around them. The witch did not take her hand from Azzy's hold.

"He is dangerous," said the witch, stroking an absent finger over her own lips. "Are you certain you won't find a monster when you finally reach him?"

Azzy thought of the eel woman's face when she had tied the bracelet to her wrist. "No, but I will bring him back."

The witch curled her fingers over Azzy's hand. "Now, ask me what it is you really want."

Azzy sifted through the tangle of her fears and desires. Yes, she wanted to be reunited with her family, but she knew she'd only survived this long in the Above due to the wolf's interference. She could not continue to rely on his protection, no matter what the witch thought of the connection between them. "I want a path. One I can survive."

"There is risk, no matter what path I offer you." The witch's eyes moved toward the absent opening. The wolf waited on the other side. "There will be choices. The safest path is the one he cannot follow." She paused, releasing Azzy. "At least not as a wolf."

Azzy did not look at the spiked collars on the wall. She would never force such a nasty device on the wolf again. "Then he will go on his way."

The witch seemed about to say something, clearly holding back her words. "For payment, I require one memory. The more importance the memory has to you, the safer the path."

Ink-stained fingers touched against Azzy's temples, waiting for her permission. She nodded. She knew exactly what memory she needed to offer. It blossomed under the witch's touch. Armin, younger, happy, unburdened by the magic within him. The last night before the terrible voices appeared unwound through her thoughts, rising to the witch's touch. Her inner voice recoiled, flexing within her.

The fingers on her temples stiffened. A tremor ran up the witch's arm. "I can't take it from you."

"What?"

The witch stepped away, her expression unreadable. "Perhaps I could have taken it from you once, but not anymore." Her umber eyes darkened. "I don't think anyone can."

Panic threatened. She'd been willing to pay any price, willing to give up her most precious memory. If she could not complete her payment, where did that leave her? At the mercy of the wilds.

"There must be something else I can give," said Azzy, a note of desperation creeping into her voice. Her vision wavered, focusing on the more organic decorations adorning the witch's walls. "What about my hair? A piece of skin? A finger? Whatever you ask."

"I want no such trophies from you, dear girl," said the witch, her voice quiet. "They mean nothing to you."

Azzy would have fallen to her knees and begged if she thought it would get her anywhere with this woman. "Tell me what to offer you."

The witch considered her a moment. "A shard of sky."

Azzy touched the corner of her eye, right below her scarred brow. She wondered if her brother would recognize her when she finally reached him. It was worth the chance to find him again. Now she sank to her knees before the witch and lifted her face.

"Take it."

A Shard of Sky

The ceiling above the bed of furs was a constellation of cracked charcoal. The witch must have carved her home in the tree through awl and flame. Azzy traced the patterns. The world looked different and the same. Her left eye felt raw, coated in a dusting of powdered glass. Her fingers itched to touch it, to rub and press the pain away, but she'd learned the hard way that the lightest brush amplified the sensation to an unbearable level.

It had taken an hour for her to stop screaming. The wolf kept vigil outside, locked out, reinforcing his continued presence with an occasional scratch or whine. She was grateful for these small favors, grateful to the wolf who stayed with her through this misery.

The world looked different and the same. It hurt to swallow. Her shrieks had scraped her throat raw. A glance to her side found the water skin the witch had left her. *For when you recover.* Her touch was far too gentle for what she had inflicted on Azzy. A shard of sky proved far more abstract than she realized. She shuddered at the memory of a pain beyond anything physical she'd experienced in her life.

Water soothed the parched soreness of her throat, a balm to her cracked lips. Azzy drank until the skin was empty, surfacing for gasps of air. She'd raised herself up on her elbows to drink and her head spun from even that minor elevation. She closed her eyes until the disorientation passed, ignoring the feel of grit beneath her left lid. The witch's home had dredged up long buried and best forgotten memories, ones she'd pushed far down to survive. They'd clawed to the surface while she thrashed with pain, plaguing her as she lay there staring at the witch's charred ceiling.

They'd dragged it from the Above when Haven was first constructed, a monstrosity of cast iron, like a hollow metal grimwerm. They'd called it the burning room. The furnace had many uses over the years. At first, they fed it coal dug up from the earth and wood scavenged from the Above. Its warmth vented to the growing houses and hospital rooms. The first wave of Rot gave it new purpose. As Haven faded into the Heap, the burning room cremated its dead. Brixby's shop had kept a large stock of sage for those days and it was a scent one could not forget. Twice in Azzy's lifetime, it was used to cremate the living.

She rolled off the bed, landing hard on her knees. The dull throb chased away the cloud of memory fogging her thoughts. Dwelling on the past was pointless. The witch's fee was paid, it was time to collect. She swayed as she stood. The first step sent her pitching forward, catching herself on the work table. Herbs scattered, the leaves spiraling as they settled back down. Azzy braced herself on the worn wood, her pulse rushing in her ears. She used the wall, leaning against it as she circled to the knot of wood the witch had pointed out to her before the extraction. Sweat glazed her skin as she dragged herself forward. So focused on her destination, she stumbled into the shelf, jostling the jars and bottles. Disturbed dreams and regrets coalesced in a putrid glow on her sweat-slicked skin. The feeble light ground into her eyes. She squinted through the sickening swirl and caught her reflection in the warped glass of a trapped dream.

Azzy stared at herself. Her shaking fingers brushed the hollow shadow beneath her eye, as close as she dared venture. The memory of pain was still fresh, the unending tug and rip as the witch took her payment, but the organ was intact. The iris of her left eye was a crystalline white, like snow beneath moonlight, leeched of color, beautiful and chilling, clear evidence of her loss.

What's done is done. Azzy struggled back up, stumbling past the rack of jars, refusing to look at them again. Her appearance was of little consequence, she was far more grateful for retaining her vision through the altered organ. She slammed her fist against the knot of wood and the trunk revealed its hidden entrance. The initial brush of fresh air was bliss. Stars greeted her from a corona of shimmering dark blues and purples. The world looked different and the same. As she stared up into the breathtaking view, she swore she could see the fading ones, the individual dying stars, their light weakening through time. Azzy looked away, puzzled by the vision. Her gaze fell on the wolf. Her heart clenched at the sight of him, his perfect stillness as he waited for her. He didn't twitch a muscle until she lifted a hand toward him.

He was before her in a blink. The moment her fingers brushed his fur, she leaned into him, pressing her face into his ruff. The floral fragrance of the woods mixed with the wolf's musk was a balm for her nerves. She felt a brush of wet warmth ghost across her temple.

"You can't heal such a wound, wolf. The ache will ease with time."

A growl rumbled within his chest as the witch emerged from the shadows between the trees. She'd scrubbed the ink to a faint stain on her dusky skin; a stole of fine white fur graced her shoulders and thick leather boots with matching trim adorned her feet. Melting snow clung to her coppery curls. She must have ventured out beyond the wood. The witch paused before the two of them, her face almost mournful for a moment as it settled back into its aloof mask.

Round her neck hung a new ornament from a strip of cured leather, a thick circle of glass the exact hue of a cloudless, sun-drenched sky.

The witch's fingers grasped the jewel. She cast her gaze to the stars, aware of Azzy's fixed stare. "Do you see them now, Azure, the long deaths of the stars?" The words chipped away at Azzy's stolen moment of comfort. She glared at the witch over the wolf's shoulder to hide her confusion. The witch laughed, a hollow sound, full of unspoken words. The night sky flickered through the blue glass round her neck.

"You will see, girl, you will see so many wonders in this world. So many things you only glimpsed before, though you may not want to." The witch walked around them, entering her tree. "We leave at dawn." She moved to the covered pot simmering on her makeshift stove, removing the lid to unleash stew-flavored steam that made Azzy's mouth fill with saliva. Her hunger was so fierce she didn't track the witch's movements until a bowl was proffered, brimming with meat and vegetables.

She took it with trembling hands. The witch steadied her as she sat on the ground, going so far as to feed the first few bites to Azzy as strength returned to her limbs. When she could hold the bowl on her own, the witch turned away.

Azzy selected a large hunk of meat, holding it out in her palm for the wolf, who carefully lapped it up. The witch cleared her throat, winking at her as she slid a second bowl in front of him.

"Thank you," said Azzy, concentrating on her food.

"Our bargain was to set you on a safer path. I wouldn't be living up to my end if I sent you off weak with hunger, accompanied by a starving animal," said the witch.

The wolf snorted into his bowl at her words. His food disappeared in seconds. He settled himself at Azzy's side, dozing off while the women ate in companionable silence. This close to the witch's tree, the snow gave way to leaf-strewn dirt, comfortable with the addition of the wolf's heat. The air was cool this time of night but lacked the bite of winter. Between the atmosphere and a real meal in her belly, Azzy felt a moment of peace. The sentiment was dashed as thoughts of Armin crept over her.

Was he safe? Terrified? Was the magic twisting him into something unrecognizable the longer it took her to find him? The stew in her stomach churned. She set her bowl down half-finished, hugging her knees. If not for the dangers of the dark, she would have insisted the witch show her the path now.

"What is his name, this errant brother of yours?" The witch studied her between spoonfuls of stew.

"What is your name?" Azzy retorted. "Seems a fair exchange of information."

The witch raised a brow, flicking a bit of gristle into the fire. "You wish to go tit for tat?"

"I think if I asked you before now, you would have demanded another payment," said Azzy.

The witch smirked at that, running an absent finger along her newly acquired necklace. "Safiya."

"His name is Armin and he's not errant. He was taken," said Azzy. Her words earned another quirk of the witch's brow. Azzy sighed. "The Elder might have banished him, but the Snatchers have him now."

Safiya's eyes flitted to the wolf, a flicker of understanding in her gaze. Azzy didn't miss the look. "Why do you have those collars on your wall?"

The woman's eyes turned cool, flecks of frozen amber. "A live witch yields a high return in Avergard."

Azzy frowned, trying the strange word on her tongue. "What is Avergard?"

"Who was the witch your people killed?" Those hard eyes were on her, waiting for an answer.

The stew turned sour in her stomach. "My mother." Safiya softened at the admission.

Azzy's memories stirred like disturbed ashes, tossing sizzling sparks that burned her as they settled.

Her mother had known things no one could know of a world long gone. Her work table had been so much like Brixby's, but for the rows and rows of glass bottles. Another secret of the tradesmen quarter—the people came to her to forget, offering her memories too painful for them to bear. Days before they came for her, Azzy had watched her mother, her fingers on the blacksmith's temples, drawing out the memory of his dead first wife. The air had grown heavy. Her mother had gasped, yanking her hands away to clutch her wrist. The blacksmith had jumped when the bottles on the table shattered. Memories ran like ink, pooling onto the floor. Azzy had led the startled man away, returning to find her mother on her hands and knees, cupping the spilt memories as tears ran down her face.

"Too much," she'd whispered, "it's too much." Azzy had scrubbed the floor clean as her mother had sobbed.

"She sickened," said Azzy to the witch.

"We do not sicken," said the witch, her voice soft. "We are many things, but we do not suffer illness. And we do not change like the tainted. Your mother would look and age as a human."

The knowledge was a knife in her heart. Azzy clutched the spot, her eyes watering. The left one felt awash in acid. Safiya knelt next to her, gently swabbing her eyes with a cloth that reeked with a heavy floral scent. It ebbed the pain to a dull ache. She could not think of her mother now, or the events leading to her death.

"You never answered either of my questions," said Azzy. The witch sighed.

"Avergard is a city far from here," said Safiya, her expression darkening. "One of steel and smoke and towers of shining glass."

"A human city, above ground?"

The witch met her astonished gaze, her eyes haunted. "It is not a place for humans."

Azzy fell silent, turning over her words. She'd never heard of such a place, not even from the Foragers.

"The Snatchers occasionally set their dogs in here. They do not leave the wood and I collect their collars as payment for the inconvenience of disposing of them," said Safiya, staring at the slumbering wolf. She rose, lifting one of the collars from the wall. "I admit, I am curious how you took it off him." She presented it to Azzy with a flourish. "The Snatchers are reluctant to release their hounds. The runes are meant to unlock only upon death."

Azzy stared at the runes in fresh horror. Old blood stained the turned-in spikes. "Why make them human?"

Safiya shrugged one shoulder, pressing the ghastly collar

into Azzy's lap. "Easier to break them. Easier to handle. How did you free him of the collar?"

"I—I don't know," said Azzy, staring at the runes. She could feel their importance. She stared until each one etched itself into her memory before tossing it to the dirt. The wolf stirred in his slumber but did not waken. She watched the rise and fall of his chest. "Is he man or beast?"

"Both, neither. Are you so sure you can part from him now?"

Azzy scowled at the question. "It doesn't matter. If he can't follow where I am going, then we go our separate ways." She shifted, uncomfortable by how much the thought pained her. "It is odd he has lingered this long," she said.

"Not so odd," said Safiya, tracing the engravings of the collar. "I think your wolf will follow you into the bowels of the earth."

"He's not my wolf," Azzy insisted, a strange fear pricking at her. The underground would suffocate a creature like him.

A knowing smile played at the corners of Safiya's mouth. "We shall see."

The Unbroken Path

It was impossible to fixate on her worries or the trials ahead of her under the press of exhaustion. Azzy tucked her body against the wolf and fell into a dreamless sleep. Cold air at her back woke her. The wolf's warmth was absent. She shifted, looking for him. The quiet murmur of the witch's voice made her still, though no matter how hard she strained her ears, she could not comprehend the soft-spoken words. She saw their forms through the trees. Safiya knelt before the wolf, her hands slashing the air. The wolf answered with a sneeze, shaking his shaggy head. His muzzle turned toward Azzy, noticing she was awake. He trotted away from the witch, who rose with a huff, and rejoined them with a smooth expression. Azzy was beginning to recognize it now, an expression of stifled words and hidden warnings. What would two such beings argue in the long hours of the night?

The early morning sky was stained gray by thick cloud cover. The witch stood over Azzy, offering her a hand. Once she was on her feet, Safiya passed her a cake of nuts and fruit.

"Eat up, this could be your last decent meal for some time," said the witch.

The cake was sweet to the taste, with tangy bits of fruit. Fruit was rare in the Heap, brought in by the Foragers as dried, shriveled morsels. Now the flavors sizzled like sunspots in her mouth.

Azzy stared at the cake. The sensations were too sharp, too vivid. Safiya's hand floated into view, lifting her chin.

"You feel the differences? Tastes are sharper. You comprehend more than those surface sensations."

"Am...am I tainted?" Azzy's fingers tensed. Crumbs dripped from her clenched hand to the snow-dusted ground.

"If you were, those bothersome weeds would be sprouting at your feet."

"The Rustic Oracle?" She frowned at the witch. "Shouldn't they cover the ground beneath you?"

Safiya gave her a wry smile, scuffing her boot along the edge of the snow-covered ground, revealing the mud beneath. She pushed the snow back into place. "My presence isn't a strong enough pull, though you will see plenty of them on your path."

"Why wouldn't you draw them?" The answer was an important one. It was a doubt she'd carried for years, after Elder Prast's many inspections. She often wondered how her brother had escaped notice for so long, how the other secrets of her neighbors went unnoticed.

"The Rustic Oracle senses great bursts of magic. They are drawn to the impact of lightning, the erupting geyser, a predator's deadly strike—powerful moments, abrupt moments." Safiya waved her hand to the woods. "These woods are full of such moments, of strange and beautiful creatures birthed into this world. The constancy of my presence is not worth their notice."

Powerful moments, like the wave of death in the natter's tunnel. Was her brother still drawing them? Could she follow a path of scattered yellow blooms to him? The witch studied her, stroking the blue pendant round her neck.

"Come," said Safiya, "I will guide you to the beginning of the path. From there you will make your own way, for good or ill." She retrieved Azzy's pack from within the tree. It was notably heavier when Azzy set it on her shoulders. The witch flapped a hand at her questioning look. "It is nothing you haven't paid for."

The witch set off, expecting her to follow. Azzy spared one uncertain glance at the wolf and hurried after her. She concentrated on matching the witch's swift pace through the trees instead of the wolf's footfalls behind her.

⚜

Between witch and wolf, Azzy walked with an odd sense of safety. She could feel the eyes of the wood on her, the weak link in the chain, but nothing dared cross the teeth at her back and the vicious smile before her. It gave her the opportunity to observe the forest without the filter of fear.

Away from the witch's home and sphere of influence, the nip of winter regained its foothold on the wood. The sky lightened to a softer shade of gray as snow rained down in fat flakes that performed a drunken dance as they fell into the towering trees. The branches gathered them up until the weight became too much, the creak and crack of wood groaning over the wind. Amid the snow-covered trees were flashes of jewel-toned feathers—birds from Safiya's sanctuary—and the darting lithe forms of various predators.

Another pyguara watched them pass from a low hanging crook of thick branches. It didn't rise from its lazy sprawl, washing one of its curved paws with a forked tongue. The snow sprinkled into its odd mixed pelt of scales and fur, melting on contact. Azzy thought the pyguara a perfect summation of the Above: cold, beautiful, and dangerous.

Safiya came to an abrupt stop.

"This is where we part company, Azure," said the witch, turning to her with tight smile. She placed her brown hands on Azzy's shoulders. "Your path will be full of many difficult choices. There is nothing I can do to make that easier for you." Her eyes flitted to the silent wolf behind them, her expression full of conflict. "Daughter of a witch, but not a witch, you have powerful instincts. What you exchanged for this path has made them stronger." Safiya bent her head, touching her forehead to Azzy's. "Be careful to whom you reveal them."

The witch pulled away, her gaze distant, focused far beyond the snowy woods. "Follow this path to its end. Do not deviate from it, no matter where it brings you."

A flutter of panic rose in Azzy's chest. "How will I be sure it's the right one?" She thought of the underground roadways, full of splits and forks, of detours, pitfalls, and obstructions.

"You will know."

In all her observations of the surrounding forest, Azzy had failed to notice the very ground beneath her feet, bare of snow, fallen branches, and twisting roots. The packed dirt stretched further than she could see, cutting an unimpeded path through the trees.

"I shall keep an eye on you Azure. Remember to listen."

"But what—" Azzy stopped.

Safiya was gone, vanished.

The wolf pressed his nose into the slack hand hanging by her side. Azzy inhaled, grateful for his presence for however long she had it.

The two of them walked side by side, her fingers lightly brushing against his back. The path seemed outside the world around them, a tunnel through another realm untouched by the Above.

A herd of massive creatures made the ground shake, great shaggy beasts with coats like hanging moss, their heads crowned with horns like clawed hands. Despite their size, they nibbled strips of tree bark and the grounded wintergreen plants, unaware of the girl and the wolf who passed through their midst.

The two of them passed another section of the wood shrouded in webs. The wind whistled through dangling hollow bones. Azzy quickened her steps. The winnowrooks preferred their prey to come to them, but her last encounter with them still haunted her. The wolf pressed hard against her side as they passed, a soft whine the only sign of distress he displayed as they continued on. Still, the danger felt muted on the path.

True to Safiya's words, the Rustic Oracle appeared more than once. They circled the base of a lone tree, its branches heavily laden with strange pink-white fruits, like lumps of melting wax. They clustered in a spill of still-fresh blood staining the snow, a pool of red that refused to sink into the ground.

The flowers' appearance was jarring in the white landscape, but Azzy understood their purpose now.

They ambled along for hours until the sky darkened with the coming night, taking only brief stops for rest and food. Azzy found her pack filled with rations, a parting courtesy from the witch. She nibbled on one of the fruit-stuffed cakes, trying to stifle the rising sense of urgency that had weighed on her since waking. This was the way to her brother—she had only to follow it without overextending herself.

The storm-filled sky began to clear as night fell, the stars peering through jagged tears in the clouds, providing enough light to keep moving. But Azzy's footsteps faltered.

The unbroken path continued, unhindered, straight into the mouth of a cave. The entrance was small, far too narrow for one of them.

A chord of sorrow sang through her. She had thought she would have more time before this moment. The wolf stiffened beside her. His form remained tense as she shifted in front of him, bringing her forehead to his, a gesture that mirrored the witch's. Her breath broke with a shudder across his fur.

" Goodbye," Azzy whispered. She rose, trailing her hand along his fur until it met nothing but air. His whine made her pause, her throat tight, but she couldn't look back. She pressed on, entering the cave alone.

Ground Shaker

I t was the right choice. She recited it to herself, her lips reshaping the words in a soundless mantra as she descended into the earth. The walls cradled her in a stony embrace, brushing the slim width of her shoulders at points along the passage. It was far, far too tight for the bulk of the wolf. She'd made the right choice in leaving him behind.

Azzy could feel the lie on her face, tracking down her cheek from her good eye. The tear fell to her chest in a chilled drop that smacked the back of her hand.

The passage opened, revealing one of the wide roadways of the underground, lit by bioluminescent moss that cast a faint blue shine to light the way. She closed her eyes, letting her eyes adjust to the low quality of light. Strange how a few days in the Above had destroyed the conditioning of years underground. Sounds reached her ears: the low whistle of the air currents cycling through various cracks and offshoots, the drip of water from above, and the murmur of rushing water. There was an underground river nearby. Azzy breathed out and opened her eyes.

The near darkness looked strange, the moss somehow brighter and more vibrant than she remembered it, illuminating the tunnel like starlight. Faint shimmering veins ran through the walls. She frowned, running her fingers along the wall. What was she seeing? The stone was warm to the touch and buzzed beneath her fingers. The combination of the two light sources was dazzling, as if she was brushing her fingers along the ceiling of the night sky.

You'll see more than the surface. That was what Safiya had told her. She touched the corner of her colorless eye, swallowing hard.

As Above, so below, the path stretched before her, threaded by the same glittering veins that ran through the walls. This was the path that would lead her to her family, to Armin and Brixby. She slid the sharpened bone from the cloth sheath at her waist. The makeshift weapon was a small comfort; she tapped it against her thigh to the rhythm of her steps until her thoughts drifted. There were many challenges ahead of her. If she found Armin and Brixby, how would she free them? How long would the journey take? What if the Snatchers reached their destination before she caught up? And the great fear that overshadowed the rest: what humanity would Armin have left when she found him?

The thought made her grit her teeth. She remembered the eel woman's face at the gift of her bracelet. There were ways of bringing him back, all she had to do was find them. She shied away from dwelling on the uncertainty of her future, stumbling into unbidden memories of her mother, spurred by her interactions with Safiya.

There were many details buried deep in her mind that continued to float to the surface. Neat little rows of jars, swirling with memories and regrets, like ink-stained smoke. Her childhood home had been filled with them. How her mother had avoided Elder Prast's attention for so long was a mystery. Or had he not looked on purpose, not until he considered her a real threat?

Her mother hadn't fought Prast's men when they came for her. She'd begged Brixby to watch over her children and allowed them to lead her to the burning room. Safiya had told her witches did not fall ill to the taint of magic. Had her mother known this? Why had she let them take her? Azzy tightened her grip on the bone knife. There were too many unanswered questions in her past, too many holes— and now she wondered whether this was because her mother had meddled with her memories. She'd promised to give them back, but now Azzy wasn't certain what all she had taken. Such a promise would've held more weight if Azzy didn't know the dangerous love parents had for their children. Nell's love for her lost ones had laid the Rot over the entire Heap. Azzy hadn't forgotten the wretched look on the woman's face when she'd betrayed them to the Snatchers.

The ground rumbled beneath her feet.

Azzy went still, dropping to a crouch. She held her breath as small pebbles jumped and shuddered around her. A grimwerm passed beneath her, gnawing through dirt and rock on the hunt for its next meal. A familiar danger, one she knew how to avoid. She waited, keeping her hand braced flat against the ground to feel its proximity.

Compared to the myriad of dangers lurking in the Above, the grimwerms were mild. They had no eyes, relying on a poor sense of smell and vibrations through the ground to sense prey. Without the element of surprise, their great fat lumbering bodies were easy to evade and outmaneuver. They were more scavengers than hunters. She waited until the pebbles stopped shuddering before standing. The witch had promised her a safer route, but Azzy doubted that included protection against anything that wandered by.

She continued on the shimmering path, tuned to the hushed atmosphere of the underground. Would the path lead her through another city? She'd never been so far from the Heap, only having heard stories from the Foragers about other settlements. The next closest human settlement was Caletum, a city even more secluded than the Heap which often turned the Foragers away unless absolutely necessary; when the need was too great for scavenged ingredients and materials that the inhabitants could not procure on their own. The name was all she knew of the place. She prayed the path didn't cut through it, uncertain she could gain entrance through its gates.

Familiar wails and clicks floated from a dark hole to her left. Azzy skirted it, her steps skipping over themselves. The light caught on the bones littering the cave floor, drawing her unwilling eye. She stayed on the path, staring into the hole, listening to the natters. Too familiar a sight— no matter where she went, Azzy found herself surrounded by death. She darted away, trying to outrun the thought. If the wolf were here, he would have tucked his great head against her, comforting her.

But she'd left him behind.

Azzy slowed. The still-healing wound in her thigh twinged, reminding her how deep the puncture ran. She could feel the pain throb through her femur, as if the Bone Eater's scythe-like protrusion were still tapping against it. The wolf had healed a great deal of the damage, but the body didn't easily forgive such a grievous injury.

The pain only deepened as she continued, dragging into a limp as her breath hitched with each step. She stopped at a crossroads, resting against a freestanding boulder to wait out the pinch in her lungs. The wound shouldn't have stirred like this. If a short trot reduced her to this, how would she run from predators? She massaged the muscle, her traitorous thoughts returning to the wolf. He was not here to lean on now. It was all on her to keep moving forward. The fact that she'd begun to depend on him during their brief time together was dangerous. He was a wild animal of the Above—

Azzy stared at the ground, chiding herself. She had to stop thinking of him as such. A simple animal wouldn't have come for her in the Bone Eater's den or followed her into a river when it couldn't swim. It certainly wouldn't have cooked her fish or protected her so fiercely. She'd seen him as a man, driven by pain and magic, trapped in rage. He wasn't one or the other. But it did not matter now what he was. She'd left him behind, gone on without him. She wondered what her choice might have been if the drive to save her brother wasn't pulling her forward.

Sounds bounced through the open air of the crossroads, funneling into human voices. Azzy's eyes went wide. She stood, wobbly on her bad leg, and was opening her mouth to call out when the whispering voice in her mind erupted into a howl. Azzy clapped her hands over her ears, nearly dropping her bone knife. She scuttled back against the rock as her nerves crawled and snapped from the overwhelming sense of danger. She gasped for air, stumbling behind the boulder and out of sight. She moved one hand to her mouth to keep from screaming, overwhelmed by the intensity of her reaction as the voices drew closer, becoming distinct, gruff and coarse. Her other hand squeezed the bone knife until her fingers bled.

Azzy flattened herself against the rock, her body quaking as the men drew near, accompanied by the heavy clap and grind of cartwheels. The Foragers. The recognition did nothing to lessen the sharp vise on her nerves. The whispers in her head continued their harsh warning, keeping her pinned to the rock as the Foragers passed by, joking among themselves. Her body finally relaxed once their collective noises had faded into the distance.

Azzy drew in deep, quivering breaths. What was happening to her? The witch had sworn she wasn't tainted, but the whispering voices in her mind had never before been so insistent, so overwhelming she couldn't resist them. For that matter, why had they gone off in the presence of the Foragers and not for the grimwerm traveling beneath her feet? She winced as her fingers loosened their grip on the bone knife, blood pooling within the cuts. She opened her pack, intent on using the salvaged cloth as a makeshift bandage.

She stared at the contents. Piled neatly on top of her remaining supplies were carefully cut strips of clean cloth, a small jar, a pouch wafting the sweet smell of dried fruit, and a densely folded bundle. Safiya had even moved the silver scissors and ink bottle to the top of her pack. Azzy picked up the jar, uncorking an herbal salve which she gingerly spread over her cuts until they tingled. She wrapped her hand, pondering the witch's choice rearrangement of her pack.

Her vision wavered, turning the bloodstains on her fingers black. Ink dripped from her fingertips, falling, falling slowly through the air.

The drop of ink splashed to the ground, sending motes of dust into the air. The stain vanished from her fingertips. The ground shook. Another grimwerm? She stilled, tracking its progress as it moved under her, shooting down the tunnel from which the Foragers had emerged. Moving faster than the last one—or was it the same one? They tended to run a wide territory. It must have sensed some unwitting helpless creature. Otherwise, the scent of her blood might have slowed it down.

The grimwerm had barely passed her when she heard it, a sound that didn't belong underground.

"No." She used the rock to pull herself up as another yipping howl echoed down the tunnel, away from the witch's path. Azzy didn't hesitate, launching herself forward. Energy bloomed through her veins, pushing her forward, muting the pain in her leg as she raced the grimwerm to its prey.

A wild animal wouldn't have followed her here.

She dug her toes into the dirt as she ran, shoving against the ground. The bounding steps landed hard on her wounded leg. Azzy would pay for it later, would willingly pay for it, if it meant she reached him first. The whispers kicked up as she ran, a warning song that beat in time to her pulse. It didn't reach the incapacitating volume from before, prickling along her nerves instead. She overtook the grimwerm—an advantage of traveling above the ground rather than through it.

The light here was dimmer, the walls cold and dark with only the feeble strain of the moss to light her path. It was enough. She saw the tumbled rocks where he must have shoved his way through from the Above.

Why had he followed her? Why couldn't he have remained safe?

Something massive thrashed in the shadows, claws scrabbling over rock. Azzy could feel the movement through her own boots. The grimwerm would feel it too. She threw her body forward around the pile of stone, ducking as teeth snapped the air overhead, and threw her arms around the panicking wolf. He trembled in her arms.

"Why did you come?" she said in a choked sob as she surveyed the situation. His entrance wasn't a stable one. The rock had collapsed around him as he'd squeezed through, pinning his lower body. The angles were off, his legs partially crushed. His thrashing only made the stones pinch his hind legs in a tighter vise. The pebbles began to dance around them.

Azzy grabbed his scruff, forcing the wolf to look her in the eye. "You must be still," she hissed, rolling away from him. She kicked at the stones around them, punting a few several feet away. The vibrations from their landing would confuse the grimwerm of the wolf's location, but it was a chance gambit. She stomped the ground, moving in deliberate circles to imitate a thrashing animal. The wolf watched her, whimpering. She held her breath, the bone dagger clutched to her chest.

"Please follow me." She watched the hopping pebbles, counting the seconds beneath her breath. The whispers in her head grew louder, signaling the moment—the grimwerm broke through the dirt beneath her feet.

Azzy danced away, slashing out with the bone knife. The sharpened edge sunk into the pus white flesh of the grimwerm. Muddy fluid sprayed the ground as the creature gave an inaudible roar that hummed through her skin. Azzy flicked her wrist, slashing in an upward arc that left a wide gash in the pale pulpy flesh. The grimwerm slumped forward, black-green blood gushing from its wounds. Its body pulsed and writhed, wounded but far from defeated. It began to retreat into the soil, the spiny carapace of its mouth open and closing in hard clicks.

The damn beasts were simple to avoid but impossible to kill and she'd provoked this one. The wound might have bled freely, but against the bulk of its corpulent body, her blade had barely nicked it. They had a few minutes before it attacked again. Azzy stumbled back to the rocks, shoving all her weight against them.

"Come on, come on, come on," she muttered, straining, but they wouldn't budge. The wolf nudged his head against her hip, pushing her away. She dropped in front of him, covered in werm blood, panting, and shaking. The wolf was calm in comparison, despite the impending threat of the grimwerm. She couldn't leave him like this. Azzy ripped her pack from her back, digging through the contents. Her fingers brushed the bundle on top.

The ink bottle fell free, hitting the ground with a dull clack as it rolled in a slow circle by her knee.

Azzy drew out the bundle, unwrapping one of the Snatcher's inverted spiked collars. The wolf snarled, clawing at the dirt. Her eyes met his. As a man he'd been large, but the size difference between the two forms was a notable one. The sudden loss of his mass would cause the rocks to brace upon one another, creating enough give to pull him free.

She remembered the pain on his face, the madness in his eyes when forced to wear such a wretched object. Her thoughts whispered to her, tuned to the sound of glass scrolling over stone. Azzy looked down.

The bottle of ink still spun in a lazy circle on the ground.

She threw the collar against the wall, tilting her head as the whispers grew deeper and more defined. She swore she could almost hear words.

She drew a strip of cloth from the bag, uncapping the inkwell. Black ink spilled over her fingertips, staining the rock. The runes were carved into her memory, and she painted them blind, listening hard to the whispers. She was missing something.

The ink seeped across the fabric, spreading into a muddled mess. Azzy smacked her hand against the ground. Her eyes stung with her frustration. The ground began to tremble once again, heralding the return of the grimwerm. She looked into the wolf's eyes. They were beautiful, a smoky golden brown that pulled her in, a sanctuary from the cruel reality of the moment.

She could have saved him if only she'd listened harder.

Or if she could see more.

Azzy covered her good eye.

Through the colorless iris, the world appeared in indistinct shades of gray, sight without practice, unformed. She blinked, trying to focus. A spark of metal caught her eye. The handle of the silver scissors protruded from her pack. She reached for them as the bindings of her hair came undone, falling across her shoulders. She understood now, an exchange was required.

She grabbed the scissors, snipping a length of hair. Azzy braided it with the ink-stained cloth, ignoring the nearing vibrations. At first, nothing happened, not until she tied off the ends of the braided cord. The ink shrank back on itself, revealing the runes in sharp focus as if they were branded onto the cloth. There was no time to question it, no time to wonder what spell she wove. The rocks shook. The wolf gave a yip.

Azzy scrambled back as the grimwerm dove up from beneath her, its hard beak snagging the cloth of her shirt as it snapped at her. She held tight to her creation and kicked at the dirt-encrusted wound on the creature's side. The wolf snarled, grazing the grimwerm's other flank with his teeth. Between the two of them, they harried the beast back into the earth. She had no time. Grimwerms were too stubborn to give up on even a troublesome meal—fresh meat was simply too scarce. The only option open to them was to outmaneuver their food.

Azzy crawled to the wolf and wrapped the braided cord around his neck. The transition was abrupt. Fur melted to feverish skin beneath her touch. She could hear the sudden shift in his bones, catching him as he fell against her, the wolf's howl of pain ending in a man's cry.

She held him through it, gritting her teeth, as the shift finished in seconds. The transformation overtaxed his body and he slumped against her, unconscious.

"No, no, no, you must move," Azzy sobbed. The grimwerm would strike at any moment and she'd made him all the more vulnerable as a man. Breathing hard, she shifted, pulling his dead weight as she went. The rocks refused to release him without one last payment of flesh, scraping the skin of his bare thighs as she yanked him free. She kept shuffling backward, straining beneath his weight as she dragged him back to the narrow crevice he'd broken through from the Above. It was their best chance to wait out the grimwerm. The muscles of her arms burned. Her leg wobbled, threatening to give out on her.

"A little further," she whispered. The passage was so narrow it was a wonder the wolf had managed to shove his way through. The walls nipped and scratched at her shoulders as she wedged them into the narrow cavern. She managed to cram them both into the passage as the grimwerm returned, smashing into the wall. Its rage rumbled through the ground, realizing its prey was beyond its reach, the rocky nook too narrow and solid to squeeze through from beneath. Still, it tried to use its bulk to knock them loose, thrashing against the tunnel wall.

Azzy watched its struggle, cradling the wolf's human body to her chest. There wasn't a stitch on him except the ink-covered cord, which seemed to glow against his dusky skin. She shifted her weak limbs, determined to give him some form of modesty until she could reverse the transformation. She managed to retrieve the bundle of cloth Safiya had wrapped around the collar from her bag, unrolling it to reveal clothing. Clothing far too large to fit her frame.

A bitter laugh choked her throat. Had the witch foreseen this too? Her hands shook as she draped the cloth over his front, exhaustion dragging through in her veins.

Azzy tucked his head against her shoulder and kept vigil as the grimwerm continued to bash against the rock face, determined to wait until the creature gave up and moved on. She prayed the wolf could forgive her.

Bound

❧

The grimwerm beat itself bloody, snapping at the open crevice as the minutes crawled by. Azzy feared it would destroy itself against the rock, blocking them in with its ruined carcass. When it finally dragged its injured body back into the earth, she felt the vise on her muscles unwind. Her attention focused on the being cradled in her arms.

Her previous glimpse of his human side was a fractured one. Fear and adrenaline had twisted his snarling visage over hers into a nightmare. Now, his features at rest, she could see the smooth clean lines of his jaw and broad nose. The face of a man who appeared far younger than the feral creature that had chased her down in the woods.

He shivered, lips parting on a stilted breath to reveal his teeth, sharper than normal, the canines more prominent. The wolf wasn't completely buried inside the body of the man. She remembered his eyes were the same in either form.

Scars traced a life of violence on his skin, some she recognized from their first encounter in the winnowrook's web. For a creature whose saliva possessed healing proper- ties, the scars were telling of fights he'd barely scraped through, too injured to treat himself. She frowned at a massive puckered mound of scar tissue on his right shoul- der, absently tracing it with her fingers.

He was moving before her mind registered it, a blur of limbs in the enclosed space. In a blink he had her by the throat, pinning her to the ground with his much larger body as he glared down at her.

"What have you done?"

Azzy could hear the wolf in his voice, a low grating rumble that bore down on her. She tried to swallow. His grip loosened a fraction. Her mouth was full of dust, making her words hoarse and strained.

"I couldn't move you," she said, pulling at his wrist. The expression in his eyes was frantic, strained by the same feral energy she'd seen in the woods moments before she'd removed the spiked collar from his neck. She watched it deepen, feeling his panic thrum against her skin. Despite the aggression in his tone, he was quaking over her.

He leaned closer, his raspy voice feathering over her cheek. "Release me."

Azzy stilled, a riot of emotions and thoughts warring in her skull. He couldn't follow her deep into the earth as a wolf. Why had he come? Why had she left the path to save him? She hadn't hesitated—even with a clear route to Armin before her, she'd run headlong into danger for the wolf once again. The woven braid hung loosely around his neck, the white cloth and blonde strand of her hair stark against his dark skin. It would be the work of a moment to snip it off, and then what? She would find the path and face its dangers alone? He would return to the wilds of the Above?

"Why did you follow me?" she breathed. A tear tracked

from her good eye and fell to his hand. He jerked away from her, the panic in his eyes melting away to distress. His fingers slid off her throat. He shifted off her, leaning back against the rock wall. The space was so narrow his knees brushed the opposite wall. Azzy cautiously lifted herself up on her elbows, watching him.

"I—I don't know," he said. He stared at the grooves in the rock, frowning; one hand absently ran over the braid around his neck.

Azzy wondered why he didn't simply rip it off. It couldn't have the same insidious hold over him as the metal collar. She'd created it in a mindless haze, driven by instinct and adrenaline. From what she understood of magic, it shouldn't have worked, none of it should have worked. His reaction to her was more worrisome. As if her tear had scalded him. "What will you do when I free you?"

Another long pause, his expression unfocused. One hand clenched until its knuckles burned white, resting on his knee.

"I don't know," he said.

The bewilderment in his voice made her throat tight. Had she done this to him? She shifted, feeling the sting of torn skin along her shoulders. The rocks must have cut deeper than she realized in her haste to evade the grimw-erm. He tensed on an inhale, his gaze sliding to her.

"You're injured."

"It's nothing," she said truthfully; a few scrapes were negligible. Though she did notice the scrapes on his legs from where she had pulled him free were already closed over. He healed much faster than she did. He looked away from her, clearly agitated.

"Why did you come back for me?" He stared out into the cave passage as he spoke.

"How could I not?" The answer was out of her mouth

before she thought of it, but the words rang true. After all they had been through, all she had lost, there was nothing else she could have done but go after him. It was who she was.

He turned back at her words, the moment suspended, full of the unspoken and undefined connections between them.

"We can't stay here," he said, his voice quiet and rife with uncertainty.

He moved sideways, exiting the crevice for the tunnel, dragging the witch's clothes with him. Azzy stayed where she was, listening to the pounding rhythm of her pulse. What had just passed between them? Would he demand his release again? She had not relished her descent back into the earth alone. In this form, in his presence, she wondered if she could bear to do it again. She listened to the muffled sounds of his movement, his human movements—familiar ones—and felt a pang in her chest. Her family was within her grasp, and if she had to, she would walk the whole of the world alone. If she had to.

"I'm decent, you can come out." His voice startled her. Wearing clothes was a human gesture, as was decency. What was he thinking? She shuffled forward, emerging into the ill-lit tunnel. Blood-stained rocks and disturbed dirt were the only signs of the grimwerm, but Azzy stopped, listening for it.

"It's not here."

She looked at him, the simple wool-spun garments stretched tight over his large frame. He had the same height as Brixby but far more muscle mass, and the clothing did little to conceal the hints of wildness about him. He folded his arms over his chest, drawing her eyes to the braided cord visible under the neckline of his shirt. She thought of the witch's bargain, the shard of sky now hanging round Safiya's neck. Her mother and Safiya were purveyors of bargains and desires.

Jars of dreams, vials of memories, all in a row. Payments for services rendered, but more than that. The bargains were devices of manipulation, a means to dangle what a person thought they wanted in front of them while the witch got what they were truly after. She was under no illusions—Safiya had taken far more from Azzy than she had given in their bargain—it was how they operated. Could she dangle the promise of freedom before the wolf in exchange for his companionship through the earth?

The scars from the Snatchers' collar were still healing, pockmarks of shiny pink flesh encircling his neck. She swallowed hard, digging her nails into her palm. No, she couldn't.

"Do you have a name?" Azzy was stalling. She could feel the constantly tilting balance of emotions in her heart and the uncertain churn of her thoughts.

He frowned at her. "Of course I do." As if that answer would suffice. The silence remained between them, and when it became apparent that she waited for an answer he would not give, he repeated the request she dreaded. "Release me."

It was a soft-spoken plea. She'd put him into this shape, though she did not quite understand how she did it. She nodded, reaching between them to grasp the braid. Azzy began to pull. The whispers kicked up in her head, an abrupt shriek of warning that filled her ears.

Her head spun. A trickle of warmth spilled over her lips. The wolf snatched at her fingers. His free hand gripped her chin, forcing her to look up into his eyes, full of fear.

"What have you done?" he rasped, breaking her grip on the cord without pulling it free.

She blinked in confusion. He'd asked her the very same

question when he first woke, panicked by his new shape, but now his focus was shifted. A trickle of blood ran off her chin onto his hand.

Her nose was bleeding, or had bled. When she touched the cord. *The runes are meant to only unlock upon death.* Safiya's words echoed in her thoughts. She'd created a bastardization of the Snatchers' foul collar, but the runes were the same, tied to her through the inclusion of her hair. In her desperate rush to save him, she'd bound her life to his human form.

River of Stars

He followed her, a silent sentry, as Azzy led them through the underground. To her great relief, Safiya's path had not vanished when she'd deviated to save her irate companion. It was the single part of this journey that hadn't backfired, unlike the problem soundlessly trailing behind her. She flinched at the thought, shame pooling in her stomach, leaving an acrid aftertaste at the back of her throat. The betrayal and pain in his eyes ate at her, the guilt of her actions drilling deep as she replayed the course of events over and over as she walked.

"I'll find a way to undo this. I won't leave you like this."

"How can you undo it when you don't know what you did?"

That he continued to follow her was incomprehensible. She didn't understand why he didn't run back to the witch. She didn't understand him. But the distance between her and Armin was finally closing; she couldn't dwell on anything else. There were only so many hours in a day one could bear such emotional weight before it exhausted them completely, and unlike the wolf, Azzy had not slept or rested since leaving the witch's home. Little aches gnawed at her, from her scraped shoulders to her healing leg and everywhere between, dragging at her steps. She pressed on, as determined to make up for the time she'd lost as she was to outrun her mistakes.

He tugged on the back of her shirt.

"You're limping." It was a toneless statement. She turned, trying to read him like she would her brother or Brixby, but his expressions were foreign words on a page, their meaning beyond her comprehension. He was still the wolf in her eyes, unable to reconcile with the man.

"We can keep going," she said, but his grip on the hem of her shirt remained.

"You need to rest. Your leg hasn't healed, not completely, and your stubbornness will prolong the injury."

Azzy stared at him. For a man who had spent the majority of the time she'd known him as an animal, the cultured quality of his words threw her. He still denied her his name. Her internal whispers remained silent in his presence.

"I also wish to see the state of your arms." His nostrils flared as he spoke, the muted glow of the cave casting a silvery sheen on his eyes.

She tapped the offending thigh, glancing down the path. "Just a bit longer," she said, pulling herself free. His sigh caused a bloom of heat along the back of her neck. Azzy kept her eyes forward, refusing to let him see how skittish he made her feel.

It had been better when he was a wolf.

She shook her head, tossing that thought in the pit of her mind where it belonged. No, it had simply been easier when he'd protected her with claws and teeth, when she hadn't made a mess attempting something beyond her reach and understanding. It had been easier when he hadn't looked at her with the same expression of contempt she'd seen on her neighbors' faces in the Heap. She unconsciously rubbed her thigh, wincing at the bone-deep ache that shivered up her leg. Azzy knew he was right; she had to stop soon.

Her nerves hummed, a sudden raucous jangle of whispers rushing between her ears. She froze, her senses tuned to the discordant murmur. The sounds of the underground amplified: the shifting scrape of settling rock, the drip of moisture from hanging stalactites, the hushed flow of the nearby river, and the echo of approaching voices. The same gruff voices she'd heard before were coming to circle her path again.

The whispers grew louder into shrieks that made her skin prickle. A high scream tolled in her mind, like a broken nail scraping along her spine. Azzy spun, grabbing the wolf's hand.

"We have to hide," she rasped, her head full of screams pitched so high she was amazed her ears didn't bleed. Her muscles twitched as she tried to decipher their warning. He frowned at her, though he gave little resistance as she pulled him off the path until he saw where she was leading him.

"What—"

"Come on," she whispered, her movements gaining a frantic edge as the shrieks scratched at her mind. He dug his heels in, a dubious expression clouding his face.

"I can't swim," he said. His pupils dilated, giving away his fear.

She wrapped both hands around his wrist, one foot already in the water. "Come. I won't let you drown." Resignation set in, he let her pull them both into the cave river.

The water immediately grew deep, the ground beneath their feet cut into smooth ribbons and whorls by the endless press of the river. In five steps, they sank up to their shoulders, causing the wolf to return the tight grip on her wrist. The water flushed around them like tepid bathwater, warmed by the earth to spite the ice and snow of the Above. At its very center Azzy was forced to rise to the tips of her toes, but she managed to maneuver them behind a spiky ledge of stalagmites, the wolf trawling behind her, muscles rigid as he vaulted from the deepest part of the river.

Not a moment too soon, she thought, as the echo of voices joined the stilted footsteps emerging around a bend in the path. The Foragers, the same group as before, plodded parallel to the river. Confusion creased the wolf's brow at the sight of them. He opened his mouth to protest, to question, but Azzy couldn't speak as the riot of noise in her head made her clench her jaw, cupping her palm over his lips. He stilled beneath her hand, searching her face as the Foragers drew closer. A shudder hit her, cascading through her as the internal voices dropped to low-pitched cries, broken pleas and moans of mindless terror. What was happening?

The wolf tensed, nostrils flaring. He moved forward, pressing Azzy against the shelf of rock so close she could feel the tightened planes of his body caging her in. He tucked them completely out of sight as the Foragers rumbled past. Neither moved nor spoke until the group passed out of sight round the next bend, the voices in her head finally dropping to tolerable levels. Azzy let out a shaky breath, putting her palm against the wolf's chest.

"It's safe now."

"How did you know?" His proximity caused his breath to stir the damp hair at her temples.

Azzy swallowed, unwilling to reveal this part of herself. Before, she'd never spoken of the whispered warnings to anyone; not even Armin fully understood them. Brixby and her brother had never forced the issue.

"I just knew," she said. Her excuse was not accepted, but he didn't press her, peering off to where the Foragers had disappeared. She wondered if they would circle around again. Why were they circling around at all? "What did you sense?"

It was his reaction that justified the intensity of her own to the strange group of men. Their shared fear resonated between them. His gaze flitted to her for a moment.

"Their scent. They reeked of Snatchers."

The implications of his words drained the last of her energy. She dropped her head back against the rock.

"We need to make camp for the night, somewhere off the path in case they circle back," she said. A relentless fist pounded against her temples, compounding the aches riddling her body.

He nodded over his shoulder. "There is a narrow shoal on the opposite bank. We should be mostly out of sight from the main path."

They made for shore, crawling up the steep banks to a rock shelf, cupped between wall and river—their shelter for the night. Azzy's sodden clothes clung to her skin. The chill air seeped into her until her teeth clicked together. The wolf appeared unfazed by the cold, settling back against the wall, one leg stretched out while he propped an arm on his bent knee. His entire posture was relaxed, at odds with her tight ball of shaking limbs. Her exhaustion wasn't enough to ignore the cooling gel of moisture encasing her.

"It looks like stars."

Azzy glanced at him through her chattering teeth and forgot the cold. He stared up at the cave ceiling, a look of genuine wonder on his face. She joined his upward gaze, peering at the familiar constellations of luminescent moss, glow worms, and light bugs scattered among the dripping stalactites—a living mosaic of winking lights. It was a sight she'd seen most of her life, nothing compared to the jeweled night sky of the Above. Her eyes fell back to the wolf. Neither view compared to flecks of light captured in her companion's reverent gaze.

"It is beautiful," said Azzy, hugging her arms around her body. She nodded to the river. "Look down."

His sigh of awe brought a small smile to her lips. It was a sight to behold, the rippling reflection of the light-drenched ceiling scattered along the surface of the river.

She closed her eyes, trying to will herself unconscious. Her body so badly needed rest.

"Will you tell me what happened before those men appeared?"

Azzy didn't bother to open her eyes. "Will you tell me your name?" Another sigh at her deflection. There was a long beat of silence. She found herself drifting off despite the nagging chill and cushion of bedrock.

"It's Kai."

"It suits you," she said, cradling her knees as she drifted. On the precipice of sleep, she felt warmth envelope her side. Her teeth finally ceased chattering.

She dreamed of Armin.

He stood with his back to her, on an empty plain of shale. The sky swirled with black clouds, heavy with the portent of a storm. A fragrant scent teased the air, similar to the witch's flowering trees, spoiled by the tang of copper and rotting meat. Azzy walked forward, anticipation humming in her veins at the sight of her brother. She'd found him. She'd always find him.

A crunch drew her eyes to the ground. Shards of bone crackled beneath her feet. She could see them now, through the gloom, the dull gloss of old bones surrounding them.

Unease played a shrill melody along her taut nerves. Azzy broke into a run. Armin gained sharper focus as she approached. Twin slits ran along his shoulder blades, identical in length and size, leaving a lace-like trail of blood along his spine. Fine lines covered his bare skin, some deeper than others. Cracks. She ran harder, calling his name.

He turned his head at the sound of her voice, revealing the profile of his face. Scars lined his lips. Azzy's steps faltered, her mind ringing with the high-pitched shriek of danger.

Armin opened his mouth.

She yelled into the palm covering her lips. Kai kept his hand firmly in place, pinning her down as he spoke in her ear.

"They're back, do you hear me, Azure, those men are back."

Those Who Wander

Kai's words echoed on the backwash of the screams in her head, the same jarring prelude of warning that had plagued her each time these men appeared. But now it was muted, as if their current proximity overloaded her senses or the warning came too late. Or—

No, please no. Don't do this.

The short hairs at the nape of her neck rose as the whispers condensed into a single voice, that of a young woman whose words entwined through her thoughts. Her muscles seized as the cries continued, desperate pleas ending in sobs. What was this? What was she hearing? She must have made a noise because Kai dug his fingers into her cheek. His other arm held her across the waist, pressing her back against his chest as he tucked them both into the inadequate shadows around them. Her eyes caught sight of the Foragers on the opposite bank of the river, her first true sight of them: the grizzled shape of their bearded faces, threadbare garments and boots that creaked as they walked.

The cart rolled between them, uneven on damaged wheels. It was pulled by a golem of a man, black beard streaked with ash from the pipe clenched between his teeth. It was a fine piece of scrollwork, hand-carved. The pipe Armin had once traded for the more exotic stock in Brixby's cabinets. Recognition confused the whispered warnings. She knew these men, had known them for most of her life—they visited the Heap every month or so to trade supplies. Azzy thought it had been their carcasses she'd stumbled over in the deadly hole of the wailing natters. She knew there were a few groups that roamed the tunnels, but no one had seen Windham's crew in months. She swore it was their bodies she found in the nattering tunnels. Where had they been?

The cart wobbled to a stop, a puff of smoke clouding the air around the man's head as he glanced around. Windham's craggy features were unchanged from the last time she'd seen him, though there was now a gaunt cast to them, to all of the men. She could see it in their stillness as they halted with their leader, the sharpness of hunger shaded in their features. Azzy watched them, trying to decipher the meaning of the whimpering female in her mind as questions tripped over themselves. She felt Kai's chest press into her shoulder blades with a quick intake of breath the moment Windham turned their way. The man squinted, reminding Azzy of the change in her vision. To her, the cave was still awash in light; the stone sparkled and glinted beneath the Foragers' feet, illuminating their lean faces.

"Hello?" Windham's low baritone rolled through the tunnel.

No, please no...

The woman's voice trailed off, swallowed by a murmur that beat in time to her pulse. Azzy tapped Kai's hand over her lips, turning her face toward him, her movement casting shadows in the dark for Windham's searching eyes.

"Oi, Rodney, give me your torch."

She had only seconds. Azzy pressed her mouth to Kai's ear. "Say nothing. Close your eyes. Act unconscious." She felt his confusion in the tensing of his muscles, but he obeyed as a weak light splashed over them, casting their shadows up the wall. A fully formed instruction from the inner voice broke through her panic. *Convince them.*

She gave a startled cry, shielding her eyes as the Foragers gave a couple hoarse shouts. Between her fingers she could see them on the far bank of the river. Windham held their lantern high. She didn't have to feign the fear in her voice, letting it waver and catch as she spoke.

"Help us, please," she said. Windham's eyes widened as they mapped her features.

"Azure?" He thrust the light at one of his men, turning to rummage in the cart. "Hold on, girl," he called, fetching a coil of rope, the weighted end tipped in copper. Windham shoved his way through the others, casting the rope across the water to them.

Azzy grabbed it, wrapping it around herself and Kai without hesitation. His eyes cracked open, peering down at her as she knotted the rope between them. "Close them," she said for his ears alone. It was important, this one detail. Beneath the roil of confusion and questions, she clung to the whispered hymn that rode the current of her thoughts. *Hide him, hide the eyes, hide them.*

Azzy gave the rope a tug, signaling for them to be pulled across. She tucked Kai's head into her shoulder, keeping their faces above water until the Foragers hauled them ashore. Kai went limp the moment his body hit the ground. Azzy faced him away from the curious gazes of the men as

Windham knelt beside her. The men spoke over their heads. She kept her eyes downcast. Her colorless iris was odd but mostly obscured by the dim light. If they saw Kai's eyes, they would know he wasn't human. The taint caused physical change, though Azzy wasn't sure Kai *was* tainted.

"What are they doing so close to Caletum?"

"His feet are bare."

"Do you suppose she knows the city—"

"Enough," said Windham, his expression unreadable as he examined the two of them. "What are you doing out here, Azure? Where are Oswin and Armin?"

What excuse could she give him to believe? The truth hovered on her tongue.

No, please no. She swallowed Armin's name. Azzy needed a half-truth, one that would distract from their scrutiny.

"We were out of supplies," she said, the crack in her voice lending emotional weight to her words. "The Rot hit us, it hit everyone. They needed help. Caletum was the closest—" she broke off, not trusting herself to go further with the lie. The men exchanged uneasy glances over her head. Windham chewed on the stem of his pipe, noting the bloodstains on her clothes.

"Ran into a bit of trouble, did you?"

She nodded, sniffling. "We've been gone for weeks. Never made it to the city."

Another shared glance between the men as Windham's features softened. "Wouldn't do you any good if you had, child."

A chill swept through her, exaggerated by the wet clothes clinging to her skin. She shivered under Windham's stare. "Rodney, fetch her a blanket. What happened to your man here?"

Azzy struggled to collect herself. "Grimwerm. A falling rock caught him."

"When?"

"Last night," said Azzy. This question she understood from many nights aiding Brixby, bringing down fevers and watching over concussed patients. There was a delicate time frame to being unconscious. She expected them to tell her to leave him behind. Windham surprised her, reaching down to run his fingers over Kai's skull. She froze, terrified the ruse would fall apart, but his eyes remained shut.

"No apparent bumps or bruising. He's a bit warm to the touch."

Azzy gave a curt nod. She startled as Rodney settled a coarse blanket around her shoulders and managed a shaky "thanks" before returning her attention to Windham. The man was staring at her, his expression thoughtful as he drew from his pipe.

"We'll camp here for the night, lads," he said, initiating a flurry of activity. The men groused about, unpacking necessities from the cart. Rations were passed around, to Azzy too, who accepted a portion of hardtack with a murmur of gratitude. It was harsh food, the meal of weary men who kept long hours on the road. The grain-rich bread was akin to chewing gravel, but it had the nutrients that kept the men moving. Normally, the Foragers would supplement such a meal with traded items like dried meat. Eyeing their hollowed faces, she wondered how long they'd existed on the bread alone.

It didn't add up. From Azzy's vantage point, the Foragers' cart appeared full of items for trade; it was overflowing. Had Caletum refused them entry? Why had they avoided the Heap?

The men remained mostly silent through their sparse meal, keeping their chatter to light topics as Windham kept her company. She itched to question them, to extract any sort of answer to the growing list of unknown variables—

but that voice, the sobbing woman, stopped her each time. The more insistent it became, the more her desire for the truth faded. Azzy knew she and Kai had to slip away as soon as the opportunity arose.

The hours crawled by under Windham's watchful eye. The men settled into a loose cluster, many braced against the cart to doze off while the rest stood guard.

Windham packed his pipe from a pouch of shredded leaves in his pocket. The flare of the match left dots in her vision as he lit up. "Why don't you catch a bit of shut eye, Azure? We shall see how your friend is doing in a few hours."

She felt it, slithering in among his well-meaning words, like oil dripping down her skin. Windham was lying to her. A wan smile touched her lips. "Thank you for your kindness," she said. The platitude soured in her mouth. Azzy laid down next to Kai, curling against his side, close without touching. She let her breath out even as her mind listened for the Foragers, to every phlegm-filled cough and light snore. Time danced on a razor's edge, pressing along her nerves as she waited for the moment. It didn't take long before their words invaded the quiet and sucked the warmth from her skin.

"What do you think we'll get for her?"

Windham grunted. "Not much. Odds are she's already tainted."

Another man *tch*ed through his teeth. "Shame, Bragos pays good money for the pure ones."

"Looks pure enough for the flesh markets."

Azzy hugged her elbows, tensing as the sobbing voice swelled in her mind, the woman's voice ringing out clear, as if she spoke directly into Azzy's ear.

No, please no. Don't do this. You're human. Why would you do this? We're human!

Kai had told her they reeked of Snatchers.

"What about the male?"

"He's not waking up. Kill him," said Windham shifting to his feet. Footsteps approached her. Azzy cursed herself for not tucking her blade into her hand before lying down. She was hoping she had enough strength to throw the man off balance when Kai's eyes snapped open, flaring in the light of the torch. He rolled away from her.

"What the—"

"His eyes! He's tainted!"

Azzy scrambled up at the first scream, digging into her pack for her weapon. She ignored the chorus of shouting and swearing as the Foragers contended with a wolf in human skin. She had the sharpened bone in her grip when Windham reached her.

She slashed outward. The blade bit into his outstretched palms. He bellowed in pain.

"Wretched bitch," he snarled, kicking her in the side. Azzy rolled with the blow, ignoring the dull ache as she braced her feet. Windham stalked after her, blood dripping along the shining path. Azzy crouched, waiting for him. Kai was a blur in the corner of her eye, moving much faster than she or the bewildered men could follow. She focused on the one approaching her, lit up with rage and grim purpose.

Windham paused as Rodney toppled in front of him, the man's neck bent at an unnatural angle.

"What have you brought into our midst?"

Azzy didn't answer, watching for the moment when he snapped forward.

Even though she braced for it, he slammed her off her feet. She drove her blade into his gut and let his weight work against him. She felt the drag of the bone knife rip through him. A gush of warmth wet her hands. She fought not to vomit. She breathed hard through her nose, struggling to shove his bulk off her.

Windham groaned, still alive. She jerked, looking into his eyes. His bloodied lips stretched in a grimace.

"Foolish girl," he said, the words choked and broken. He rolled off her, sagging onto the ground. His arms were clasped over the grisly wound in his stomach. She didn't look to see how deeply she'd cut him.

"You sold humans to Snatchers," she said, unable to put venom into her words. Had Windham found her brother before she did? She had wondered how the Snatchers had found him so quickly. "Did you give them Armin?" The sob in her voice was genuine, causing her hands to shake.

Windham gave her a slow blink, his reactions fading as death seeped through his system. His voice was low, the last tumble of gravel down a deep well. "We haven't left these tunnels since Caletum fell."

Fell? Azzy gaped at him, unable to process his words. "The Rot?"

The man's smile was a reaper's mask. "There are worse things down here than the Rot." The smile didn't leave his face, not until his muscles went slack. Azzy stumbled away, making it almost three feet before she threw up.

She remained heaving on her hands and knees until Kai smoothed her hair off her sweaty forehead. Azzy didn't fight him as he lifted her up, carrying her to the river.

They were not interrupted. Windham's men had been silenced by the same hands which gently scrubbed the blood from her skin. It should have bothered her, the breathtaking violence he'd performed while she'd squared off against one man, but it didn't. Windham meant to kill Kai, and he would have sold her to the Snatchers and a fate worse than death, but that knowledge did not erase the guilt she felt taking his life.

"I've never killed another human before," she said. The whispers were silent in her mind, neither justifying nor admonishing her actions. The woman's voice was gone.

Kai took her hands, stroking his thumbs across her palms. "They weren't human, not anymore."

City of Echoes and Dust

Windham charged, spewing sparks and smoke as he picked up speed. Her vision tunneled, focused on his face and the two gaping pits in place of his eyes. No longer human, a body without a soul. The man who sold other humans to the monsters of the Above. She braced her feet apart, her knife clasped in both hands, pointed outward. The impact rattled her teeth, jarring her bones. She felt the gush of warm blood over her fingers, the metallic scent of it flooding her nostrils, mingling with the musky smell of pipe weed on his breath. Azzy swallowed hard as the blood pooled at her feet, seeping into her clothes, staining her skin like ink. She looked up into the black pits of Windham's eyes only to find them restored, human, staring at her in shock and fear as his life poured onto the dirt between them.

For a moment she saw him, the man who would bring her special trinkets he'd acquired for her: ribbons for her hair, tiny carved figurines, dried flowers. The man who used to flirt with her mother when she was still alive, had ruffled Armin's hair each time he stopped at the Heap. That man stared down at her, the accusation in his eyes fading as they clouded over in death. She'd killed him. She'd had to. Windham fell at her feet. The blood covered her, creeping up her body, staining her soul. The knife clattered against the stones as she opened her mouth to scream. Her voice failed to emerge, though it echoed in her mind, knocking around her skull.

Warmth surrounded her, lulled her away from blood-slicked hands and silent screams. It encircled her, like the warm glow of a fire chasing away the dark.

Azzy opened her eyes.

Kai was folded around her. Her cheek rested on his side, his legs tucked behind her back. He was still asleep, head on the crook of his elbow, features relaxed. She glanced down to where his other hand held hers.

"You wouldn't stop sobbing," he said, lids still closed.

She could feel the ache behind her eyes, the faint crust of salt on her cheeks. Exhaustion had hummed through her after they'd spent hours putting distance between them and the caravan of dead men. Windham and his crew were left for the scavenging grimwerms. A stinging heat of fresh tears pricked her. Kai opened one golden brown orb, his expression unreadable as he looked at her.

"Rest. We haven't been here long."

Any time felt too long when the path continued to stretch and stretch before her. The urgency to find Armin was still there, though there was now another strain that ate away at her.

"Rest," said Kai, reinforcing her body's insistence. Azzy closed her eyes, her fingers tightening around his. This time she slept without dreams of blood on her hands.

They'd spent another day in the tunnels, pausing for the rumble of grimwerms, before the path spat them out before the gates of Caletum.

The glimmer of power beneath her feet continued into the city, reminding Azzy that while the witch had promised her a safer path, danger was relative. She eyed the gates, slightly ajar, barely wide enough for a man to pass through the gap.

They shouldn't have been open at all.

She listened for the murmur of voices, or the sounds of common activity, but there was nothing. Had anyone survived the fall of the city? The whispers kicked up as she approached the gates, a hum of apprehension to match her nerves as she slipped through the opening. Azzy took a few steps and stopped, staring down the main avenue of the city.

Not a soul could be seen, nor were there bodies of the fallen citizens. Over everything was a thick layer of dust. Skidded footsteps marked where the Foragers had passed through. The steps were undisturbed and looked fresh, as if they had happened hours before rather than days.

Kai paused beside her, scanning the empty streets and darkened houses. "We shouldn't be here."

She agreed with him, but the path continued through the city, a faint but steady spark beneath the dust, so she followed.

The whispers didn't escalate above a low hum, encouraging Azzy to set a brisk pace. The faster they passed through, the safer they would be, though the mystery of Caletum unnerved her. What had happened here? If the citizens had perished suddenly, as had been Windham's ominous implication, where were the bodies? If the city had been abandoned, why leave behind their personal belong-ings? There were some signs of arrested activity—a child's sewn leather ball resting in the street, tools laid out beside workstations, the front doors of dwellings open to the street.

There wasn't a pall of death to the air, but staleness, as if the people had simply vanished. That emptiness permeated the air with the musty smell of enclosed spaces. The further into the city proper they traveled, the more overpowering that sense of emptiness became until it scraped along her spine. The lack of sound was worse, the sort of heavy silence that crouched on her shoulders, breathing down her neck, so impenetrable she could feel the unnaturalness of it in every step.

Her steps, which made no sound.

Azzy stopped, staring at her feet. She stomped her boot against the cobblestones. Nothing. Her awareness crackled, yet the whispers remained unruffled. The danger wasn't immediate, but it was there, surrounding them. She swallowed, remembering the last time she had encountered this same absence of noise in the fallen city above the Heap.

A door swung inward with a creak in a house near where she stood. The sound was muted, but it hit her like a shout in her ear, physically jolting her. She stared at the dark opening, frozen in place, waiting for something to emerge.

Kai jumped on her, hurling her aside as a massive slab of rock smashed into the ground where she had been standing, shattering on impact. His body shielded her from the worst of it. There wasn't a single sound from the colliding rock, only her gasp of shock, quickly swallowed by the silence. Azzy peered up at the faraway ceiling, waiting to see if another would fall as a grim realization rolled through her thoughts. She'd been baited to stand there. Kai shuddered. She looked at him, seeing the sheen of moisture on his forehead. A dark stain bloomed beneath his arm.

"I need to stop," he said, reaching over his shoulder. His hand came back, clutching a bloodied spike of stone, a shard that had impaled him while he'd covered her.

Azzy slid his good arm around her shoulders, helping him to the relative shelter between two houses. The malevolent silence pervaded, closing around them. She pushed aside the urgency to keep them moving, lifting Kai's blood-soaked shirt to survey the damage. The movement jostled his wound. He snarled, a vicious sound that made her hands jump. The silence paused and hovered.

She looked up, sensing the hesitation of the disembodied presence. Was it frightened of him? It didn't seem possible. Azzy released her held breath, looking over the deep puncture in his shoulder. The wound appeared to shrink as she watched.

She gently felt around it, making sure there were no other pieces of rock embedded in his skin. "It's already healing," she said. She swung her pack around, retrieving the last of the spare cloth to clean the area.

"I'll be able to move soon." His voice was sluggish, as if the act of healing drained him.

"We can rest a moment more," she said, eyeing their surroundings. The presence continued to leave them alone. Whatever haunted this city truly was wary of the wolf in human skin, though she doubted their reprieve would last long. The wound closed, a smooth seam of unmarked flesh. She marveled at it—at him—as she swiped away the blood, now the only mark of his injury. A wondrous yet imperfect process.

The evidence of his limitations was written in the scars marking him, like the nick on his ear from the winnowrook's web, where he'd almost severed it in his panic. Then there was a massive crater, the puckered skin that marked both sides of his shoulder as if something had impaled him. And there was a detail she'd missed before: four drag marks surrounding the exit scar on his back, like ridged petals of flesh. She traced one, causing his muscle to twitch beneath the pads of her fingers.

Kai sighed through his nose, reaching up to gently pry her fingers away from the area. He shrugged on the soiled shirt. Azzy couldn't bring herself to ask the question, the words hanging in the muted air.

"It's how the Snatchers catch their wolves," said Kai, rubbing the old wound. "You barely hear it whistling through the air, this great big spear trailing threads of iron. It pierces you, releasing the smaller barbs into your flesh before they reel you in, thrashing like a great big fish on a hook. The second they have you, they clamp their cursed collar round your neck, so they can break you." His voice was impartial, but she could see the tremor in his hands as he spoke. She curled her fingers into his, lending him any warmth she could give.

"We'll rest here a bit longer," she said, trying to bury her unease. Despite the unsettling atmosphere, the whispers remained at a constant low buzz. "Get some sleep while you can." It was a mark of his exhaustion that he slumped against the nearest wall.

Azzy wished she could do the same, if only to shut out the oppressive weight of the silence. She huddled beside him, staring out across the dust-laden streets.

Windham had told her there were worse things than the Rot. She ran a finger through the dust, examining the gray powder that clung to her skin. What had swallowed up Caletum?

Her breath fogged on the air. The cold was sudden, rolling over her as the whispers wobbled and snapped, leaving her alone in her head. The presence enveloped her, a vise around her body.

"Azure," whispered the dark.

Azzy clutched her knees, shivering as the dark called her name over and over. She kept her eyes on the patch of dirt before her, determined not to answer. The cold sank its teeth into her as the presence pressed against her with its unnatural quiet. She couldn't hear her own breaths, only the internal frantic pulse as her heart battered itself against her ribs.

The silence in her head scared her more. Where were the guiding whispers?

People surrounded her. Dust-covered feet and legs created a circle around her that drove Azzy up off the ground. They appeared in the space of a blink, their faces blurred. Panic caused her to take a step back—a mistake, as the shadowy figures flowed into the open space, cutting her off from Kai.

Should she call out to him? Would he hear her? Azzy opened her mouth as the nearest figure snapped into focus, causing her voice to dry up in her throat.

Armin, his face caked in the unending gray dust, stood an arm's length from her. So close, she reached for him, the desperation to save him rising to the fore of her thoughts, clouding her senses.

His eyes snapped open. Azzy's hand halted between them, shaking as she stared into the empty pits in his skull. His lips moved, the words slinking into her mind, coiling there like a venomous snake.

You brought me to those tunnels to die, he said. *Selfish, sister mine.*

Azzy snatched her hand back, pulling her limbs in tight as the other blurry faces around her solidified, revealing the dust-covered visages of Brixby, Nell, Elder Prast, and Windham. She whipped around. The skin around her eyes grew tighter at the sight of them.

You let the corruption in, said Elder Prast, his empty eye sockets snapping open. *Brought it to our very door.*

Turned on your own kind, said Windham.

My children could have lived. Nell tilted her head at Azzy, her face twisted by rage. *You waited and waited to act.*

"That wasn't my fault," Azzy whispered, holding her arms.

She shied away as Nell snapped forward. *You acted immediately to save those fools from the Rot. Destroyed your own brother for those cowards.*

Armin leaned in, his eyeless face seared into her memory. *You knew bringing me there would tip me over the edge.*

Her breath caught in her throat, unable to deny it. She had ignored the whispers, allowed him to come to her.

It was your fault they cast me out.

To the Snatchers, said Nell.

Your fault I was taken, said Brixby, the dust crumbling off his lips. *I followed you to my doom. Captured while you ran. Coward.*

Murderer.

Selfish.

"No," said Azzy, her voice choked, the word a barb that scratched her lips.

Another figure solidified, the familiar features delivering a punch to her gut, driving the wind from her lungs. Her mother's empty face stared at her.

I died for you, to save you. Look what you've done. You destroyed our family.

Azzy covered her mouth with her hands to muffle the sob, taking a step back. She wanted to scream, to rail against them, but the guilt wormed through her, eating her alive. Hollowing her out.

You killed me, said Windham.

Left me to die, said Brixby.

Left all of Haven to die, sneered Elder Prast, spitting shadows at her face.

Kai's face materialized with the rest, the pits of his eyes boring into her as he lifted the braided cord off his neck *You trapped me, tricked me.*

Abandoned me, whispered Armin, as he appeared beside her.

Her mother's dust-coated fingers stroked the side of Azzy's face. They left her skin numb. *Everyone around you suffers.*

Their vitriol continued, expounding her guilt until it flowed like poisonous sludge in her veins, squeezing her heart. She turned from them, trying to block them out, trying to run away. She took a step forward, into nothing...

An arm hooked around her waist and yanked her away from the edge. The figures closed in, clawing at her, leaving streaks of dust that stole the sensation from her skin. She screamed, thrashing, her eyes wide as Armin hissed in her face.

It should have been you.

Hands clapped over ears.

The figures vanished. Azzy stared out over an abyss, tottering on the edge where the ground came to an abrupt halt. She would have toppled over if not for Kai's hands on her ears, his arms braced up beneath hers, easing her back. The minute she stopped fighting, Kai swept her further from the edge, turning her toward him as they collapsed together on their knees.

Both were breathing hard. Kai hadn't relinquished his hold on her, grasping her shoulders as he looked her over. She couldn't meet his eyes, staring at the braided cord she'd placed on him. *Trapped him, tricked him.*

He deserved to be free of it, of her. She deserved to die for it. Her fingers reached for it.

"Azure," Kai snapped, shaking her. He grabbed her chin, forcing her to look at him. "Azure, please!" His amber eyes were wide, brimming with panic and fear.

Fear for her.

The strange influence on her cracked wide open. The whispers slammed back into her mind, screeching for her attention, and blew the coating of dust from her thoughts.

Azzy pressed her forehead against Kai's, tears running down her chin. His sigh of relief washed over her. He pulled back, searching her face.

"What happened to you?"

She swallowed the lump in her throat, looking at the sheer drop beside them. Azzy could feel the waiting hunger down there—vile, ancient, and evil, squatting in the dark. "The same thing that happened to the people of Caletum."

The perception of it hummed at the edges of her senses, tugging at her defenses, still trying to worm its way in. She couldn't begin to fathom what was its true form, but it had led the entire city to their deaths. She remembered her and Brixby's long run through the empty levels of Haven. A similar presence had hovered over her home, far weaker than this one. How long before it grew, before it spread into the city below?

It didn't matter now. *Left all of Haven to die.* Azzy knew the truth of those words. Haven would never be her home again.

"We need to go," she said. Kai pulled her to her feet.

She guided them back to the path and set a brutal pace. Another breathless run, but Azzy couldn't put distance between her and the pit fast enough. He held her hand the entire time.

They followed the path through one of the many crevices between buildings, emerging into the tunnels once again. Neither wished to stop until Caletum fell far behind.

Ruins

Kai slowed when the path spat them out in the Above. The strain finally left his face, smoothing the crease of his brow. His whole posture relaxed despite the light sleet. Azzy couldn't imagine how the icy ground felt to his bare feet but his relief at being out of the tunnels outweighed his discomfort. The unpleasant weather didn't appear to affect him, for all he wore was a threadbare shirt and pants. The atmosphere began to nip at her the moment snow crunched beneath her boot, a far more bracing cold than what they had encountered below. Here, the cold breathed in and out with the wind, almost like a living thing. As dangerous as it was, Azzy could feel the difference. Caletum, the tunnels, even Haven were all steeped in death and decay. The Above teemed with life. Were the dangers of the Above truly worse than below? She used to think so, but now, it appeared to be a matter of adjustment. Perhaps, when she found Armin, she could make a home like Safiya, carving a niche for them in the wilderness. Would Kai stay with her?

The question stole into her thoughts. Her eyes fell to

their entwined hands. He wasn't here by choice. He wasn't even human by choice. She'd thrust that upon him, binding their lives together without a thought to what it would do to him. What would have happened to him if she had dove into Caletum's pit? Would the binding have been undone? Or would it have snuffed him out as well? The uncertainty left an icy pit in her stomach.

Kai peered at the sky. "We should camp. It's going to be fully dark soon," he said.

"We shouldn't leave the path again," said Azzy. For something so invasive as the Foragers, this plan wouldn't have worked, but most of the wildlife seemed to avoid the path. Or they didn't notice it.

Kai frowned, sniffing the air. "That might be alright."

There appeared to be no immediate danger, though Azzy couldn't dismiss her own feeling of unease at being so exposed. A solution presented itself as they rounded a curve, the woods broken by the remains of a large crumbling structure, threaded through with tree trunks. Her lips parted as she took it in, realizing what it must have been.

A man-made building, so old it was gutted down to scraps of its former self, overgrown and receding back into the landscape. The shell was still recognizable and intact enough to provide them cover from the elements. The path cut directly through it.

Azzy approached the crumbling structure, the whispers quiet in her skull. A glimpse into a bygone era, it was larger than any dwelling in Haven, stretching outward in either direction, comprised of stone, rotting wood and corroded metals. Something crunched beneath her feet. She toed off the top layer of snow, revealing a material that trapped the fading light. Azzy stared down at her reflection in a shard of glass.

Kai ducked through the tilted entrance, leaving her to

stare into the glass at her mirrored self, her features fuzzing out as the world sank into an overcast twilight. Built by man, it was nothing but a rotting ruin left from before magic had crept over the world. The shell reminded her of pictures in her mother's ancient books of the massive factories, a means of mass production, churning out hundreds of objects a day. She could barely imagine such a feat, though from the scale of the ruins, it seemed possible. Another advantage humans had lost when they'd fallen.

"It's safe for the night," said Kai, interrupting her thoughts. She followed him in, leaving the girl in the glass behind. The insides had long been exposed to the elements, the contents withered down to formless lumps and shreds of material. Her fingers traced the seams between the stones as she wondered what this place had once contained. They'd found temporary safety on a piece of land lost from time. Kai settled in among the bracken, finding a somewhat dry spot on the ground, free of snow. She joined him, leaning against his shoulder. It felt natural to share their warmth.

"Can you tell me what really happened to you now?"

Azzy closed her eyes. Why hide it from him? He had shared his pain with her. "It lured me to the edge. I would have walked right off if you hadn't stopped me."

He peered hard at her, a frown twitching between his brows. He seemed to frown at her often, not certain what to make of her. "Why didn't you fight its influence?"

Because she was weak. "I couldn't," she said. Wouldn't. Why fight something she knew to be true? She sat beside someone she'd wronged, and the knowledge was a constant weight on her shoulders.

He was silent for a moment. "What did my shadow say to you?"

Azzy's eyes widened. "You saw them?" She'd believed the dust-coated shades were for her eyes only. Kai nodded.

"Saw them, but couldn't hear them," he said, cocking his head at her.

She swallowed twice, three times, unable to adopt the same toneless voice he had used to describe old wounds. The guilt was too fresh. "That I tricked you, trapped you like this," she said, the words tumbling over themselves, sitting heavy between them. Kai didn't speak for several minutes before he slipped his arm around her with a sigh, resting his chin on the top of her head.

"It doesn't matter," he said. He didn't say more, simply holding her tight against his side as her mind mulled over his words.

He hadn't denied her fault, but he didn't lay the blame at her feet. It almost seemed as if he didn't care about his predicament. After a while her mind couldn't process anymore, letting her sink into dreams.

She dreamed of the bone field. The hollow crunch of brittle skeletons filled her ears as she walked. So much death, no matter where she turned her gaze. The bones stretched on without end, as if Armin had finished off the world, human and monster alike. The plain of death seemed almost...peaceful.

She found him eventually, following a rush of wings. He walked toward her from the opposite direction, trailing feathers as pale as spider's silk in his wake. They stopped a few feet from each other. Azzy drank in the details of his face. Strange—there were marks that were not there before. A small scar over the bridge of his nose. Another through his eyebrow, almost identical to her own. The marks around his lips were healed over, faint indents around the smoothness of his mouth. His storm-filled eyes gave her the same treatment, distress flickering at the changes her journey had wrought.

When he opened his mouth, she waited, holding her breath.

"You've come so far, sister mine," he said, a sad smile tugging at the corner of his mouth. His hoarse voice held the slightest echo, a far cry from the howling voices.

"So have you," she said.

He nodded to her side. "Who's this?"

Azzy jerked, looking at the hazy figure beside her. A double image, man and animal existing in the same space. Her gaze traveled down, seeing their clasped hands for the first time. He was massive, standing next to her, phantom claws and teeth enshrouding the man within. Dark and dangerous, but Azzy felt safe.

She didn't know how to answer her brother, but when she looked up, he wasn't alone either. A figure stood behind him, shrouded in fog, out of focus except for the eyes— silver-cast irises that stared at her brother with dark intent.

"Who is that?"

Armin glanced back. A flicker of fear coursed through his features. "My future."

What did that mean?

A sound echoed over the bone field. Something whistled as it flew through the air. Armin turned back with a glare across the field, tracking the sound. The look he gave her was filled with worry.

"You need to wake, sister mine," he said. His gaze flickered between Azzy and her companion. "Trust your choices."

Her eyes opened. She blinked at the ground, rubbing at the ache in her chest.

"Armin," she said. He had seemed so real, so different. It was still early, the daylight weak through the constant cloud cover. She was thinking about settling back for a bit more rest when the whispers rose to a scream.

Kai bolted to his feet. His amber eyes flared in the filtered light as he snapped his head left and right, senses on full alert. His skin paled, anxiety rolling off him as he caught a scent. A feral growl ripped from his throat.

"Snatchers."

Trust

Kai spun in place, his irises shimmering in the wisps of early morning light. The tendons along his neck and shoulders were taut, a visual representation of the tension thrumming through him. If he had worn the wolf's shape, his hackles would have been raised.

Azzy slid her hand down his forearm, gently uncurling his fingers to weave them through her own. His grip was painful before his gaze slid to her and he forced himself to loosen.

"We need to stay as close to the path as we can," said Azzy, nudging him toward the crumbling hole in the back wall. She let him guide them out, trying to keep her emotions level, for both their sakes. The proximity of the Snatchers was as alarming as it was exciting.

What if this was the group that had her brother? If so, she had to find a way to get close, to risk capture if she had to. She studied her companion as he led her from the building to the nearest cluster of rocks and trees, peering through the surrounding wilds for any movement from the Snatchers.

She could feel the tremor in his limbs through their clasped hands. He was holding on by a thread, fighting off his panic to guide her. How could she get closer to the Snatchers when Kai was so intent to flee them? Would he follow her again if she broke off? The notion sat ill with her. She clenched her jaw. When she'd separated from him before, he'd been a wolf. She thought he would be safer in the Above than underground. She'd left with certainty that her decision was in his best interest.

Now his human hand held hers and the idea felt selfish. What if the Snatchers captured him again because of her? She couldn't forget the hollow madness in his eyes before she'd removed the collar from his neck, or the grisly scar that marred his shoulder.

Armin might be with them—and Brixby—her family so close. She glanced over her shoulder, torn between the hope of finding those she had lost and keeping Kai safe from further harm. Her heels dragged without thought, causing him to look at her.

"What is it?" His voice was hoarse, strained by his panic. The struggle was so evident. She couldn't risk him.

Azzy shook her head, not trusting herself to speak. All the while, the whispers murmured and shrieked in her skull, echoing her indecision. She mentally ran through the possibilities as Kai kept them moving. Could he catch her brother's scent amid the Snatchers? Or tell if they held human captives? She waited until they were in the rotted-out hollow of a large tree before she dared broach the subject.

"Are there any others with them?" She didn't specify Armin, unable to give voice to her desperate hope. Kai swallowed, his glance darting to their surroundings.

"They have other wolves," he said, the last word cracking as it left his lips. Other slaves, made insane by spikes of metal drilled into their flesh, forced into a human shape.

He caught her expression and pushed her up against the moldering wood as he framed her face in his hands. "What are you thinking, Azure?"

"Is the scent of the wolves all you can pick up?" She turned away, unwilling to face him as she peered out through the trees. Was that a flash of movement amid the thick trunks? The Snatchers were closer than she thought.

"Azure?"

"Can you smell—" she stopped, the words dying on her lips. Would Armin smell human anymore? What about Brixby? If he was still alive. Her lips trembled, anguish and frustration taking their toll. The answers were tantalizingly close, hovering just out of reach.

Kai's thumb brushed her mouth, distracting her. "Your family?"

She nodded, clamping down hard on the swell of emotion. His expression was unreadable, though she caught the subtle lift of his head as he inhaled.

"I can't catch anything beyond the musk of wolves and the stink of Snatchers," he said, hesitating, the words pulled from him. He watched her face as he spoke. "What do your instincts tell you?"

Azzy swallowed, forcing herself to focus on the internal murmur, to push aside the overwhelming desire to see her brother's face again. *Run, run, run.* She glanced down at the path, still aglow in her vision. It continued. It didn't stop here. The image of Armin's scarred visage rose in her thoughts. *Trust your choices.*

"Run," she breathed.

The word broke the moment between them. Kai seized her hand, pulling her into a pace she struggled to keep up with. He cut alongside the path, forcing them through thick clusters of undergrowth and icy streams. The wintry air burned in her lungs. It froze the moisture in her mouth and nostrils and chilled the sweat running down her back. They broke through the woods, running along the edge of a sheer drop. Azzy glanced over the cliff and lost her footing, dragging them to a stop in the snow. Her breath left her like the rush of impact, eyes blinking in disbelief at the endless expanse of water below.

It was the color of storms, a dark glimmering gray like her brother's eyes, rushing and rolling in white-tipped fury. She could hear it beating against the rocks and the shore, a rhythmic beautiful sound caught between a roar and a song. She was mindless of the cold snow seeping through her clothes, numbing her hands, of the danger still behind them. The whispers bowed to the entrancing call of the water, her gaze locked on her first sight of the sea, captivated until Kai's hands yanked at her waist and pulled her onto her feet.

"We need to keep moving," he said, frowning at her dazed expression.

"I've never seen the sea," she said.

"You can look later," he said, tugging at her attention. His eyes flickered with unease, being so close to water. She remembered he could not swim. She nodded, shaking off the clinging fog of reverie. The waters kept capturing her attention, stretching beyond the horizon, where the swirling waves lapped at the belly of the sky.

The whispers rose through the crash of waves on rocks, forcing her eyes to focus on what dangled directly before her.

Azzy blinked through her wavering vision, staring at a knobby stick spinning on a string from a branch. She frowned, reaching for it. The string stuck fast to her fingers as the spinning stick slowed. Her eyes widened. Not a stick —a bone, still bearing bits of dried flesh.

"Kai wait," she hissed, planting her feet in the snow. How could he not smell them? She caught the first tease of the winnowrook's syrupy sweet scent as she looked up. The surrounding trees were choked with webs. They were surrounded, caught between a cluster of winnowrook nests and the drop off to the sea.

Kai turned to her, eyes over-bright, skin dripping with sweat. He gasped in great gulps, chest heaving, as if he couldn't get air. A whimper escaped his throat at the sight of the strand of web stuck to her fingers. She scraped it free on the branch, and was alarmed when he released her hand. He clawed at his head, leaving bloody furrows along his scalp.

"What is wrong with you?" She reached for him, brushing his hot skin. He jerked away, crouching in an unmistakable position. He was going to bolt. "Kai, don't," she whispered.

Click clack.

The bones were stirring. *No, not now.* Kai emitted a high-pitched keening sob. His eyes turned glassy and blank as she watched. The whispers gave her the split-second warning she needed as he moved, mindless, diving straight for a swath of web. She threw herself at him, tackling his legs. He slammed into the ground, thrashing. Azzy ducked a wild swing that cracked the trunk of the tree by her head.

The click of dangling bones increased to a buzzing rattle, the vibration spreading to the trees until the branches throbbed with the movement of the winnowrooks descending on them. She counted the shapes scuttling through the branches above them. There had to be a dozen.

"Kai, I need to you come back to me or we're going to die," she said, her voice somehow calm as death stared down at them from a multitude of obsidian orbs. The back of her throat burned from their overpowering sweet odor, stinging her eyes. What was it doing to him? He yelled and nearly bucked her off. Azzy grimly held on. He rolled them against the tree, the bark scraping the skin off her knuckles.

Blood dripped between her fingers.

The winnowrooks surged forward in a frenzy. Azzy shoved her bleeding fingers against Kai's lips, directly beneath his nose.

"Ritual," she whispered. He stilled on a sharp inhale. His pupils contracted, and his bright amber eyes focused solely on her.

Kai surged upward, lifting her in his arms as he tore through the grove of webbed trees. A horde of nightmares followed in their wake, fast, gaining on them.

We can't outrun them. The thought rolled through her with finality. The whispers spun in her mind, seeking a way out. The webs stretched on and on, no clear escape visible as they ran parallel to the cliff. The crash of the surf bellowed in her ears until it was all she could hear. The sea...

"Jump," she said, speaking in Kai's ear. He stumbled, gritting his teeth as he put on a burst of speed. The winnowrooks continued to gain on them. "We have to jump."

"We'll drown," he snarled, his expression determined. But he was flagging. She tucked her face against his throat, listening to his pulse. It sounded like the song of the surf.

"You need to trust me," she said. His arms tightened around her. Her ribs creaked in protest. He pivoted for the cliff. The winnowrooks screeched, a sound that knifed her eardrums. The world rushed past her as Kai approached the edge, took one breathless pause as his legs flexed, and pushed them into the air. The screeches followed them down, a few of the creatures unable to halt their momentum, winnowrook bodies hurtling after them.

The air rushed past them, a roar to match the approaching water. She felt Kai's heartbeat thundering beneath her palms flattened against his back, fear singing in his veins.

I won't let you drown.

They veered close to the rock wall.

"Kick," she screamed. Kai acted fast, shoved them out and away. He pushed them toward the deeper waters as the winnowrooks continued a straight drop to the rocks below.

Azzy took a deep breath as Kai tucked his head against her shoulder. She felt the stinging impact as they punched through the surface, the murky water rushing over her, so cold it numbed her through and through as the sea swallowed them down.

It was peaceful. Azzy floated down through the dark, vaguely aware her limbs were still wrapped around Kai. The icy waters stole sensation, but somehow, she felt warm. Tired. Her lungs gave a weak protesting pinch, searching for a breath. She could rest here forever, floating, weightless in the arms of the sea. The world went mute, the whispers a hushed chorus in her head, distant strains of words she could barely hear.

Pressure increased around her ribs and waist—tight, tighter. The water churned as limbs flailed. She opened her eyes, adjusting to the faint faraway light of the surface as they continued to sink.

Kai was drowning.

A jolt sizzled through her nerves as her senses snapped back to life. Azzy kicked for the surface, dragging Kai with her. His struggles were lessening, the hold he had on her relaxing. She doubled her efforts, her eyes focused on the shimmering surface above her.

She broke through, gasping and choking on salty water. Kai floated beside her, unconscious. Azzy made for the shore, one arm clutching him to her as she swam. The seconds wove around her as she fought exhaustion and the sucking frigidity of the water. She pushed through the strain, her legs wobbling when they finally touched the shore. She dug into the pebbled sand, fighting against the fresh drag of gravity as she crawled onto the beach, her waterlogged clothes another anchor weighing her down. The water might have given him buoyancy, but on land Kai was dead weight. The retreating waves attempted to reclaim him.

A final yank, muscles screaming, and she hauled him out of the water, collapsing onto the wet sand. Black spots danced in her vision, threatening to pull her under. Azzy dug her fingers into the sand, drawing deep on the reserves of her strength. Kai still wasn't breathing.

This wasn't like the times children or drunks had fallen into the underground rivers. Kai's skin was as icy as the surf that licked their feet. She tilted his head, parting his lips to breathe air down his throat while she pressed her stacked palms down on his chest, over and over.

"Come on, come on," she muttered, trying to force the water from him. His skin had paled, leaving a purplish-blue tinge to his mouth. Azzy breathed for him again, though the world fuzzed from her efforts. She paused, struggling to regain her breath. She couldn't stop now. He'd put his trust in her.

Azzy closed her eyes, grounding herself, listening to the whispers. *Bring him back.* She gritted her teeth, probing deeper. Nothing but the same message over and over. For the first time in her life, she addressed the whispered chorus in her head. *How?* The whispers paused, perceiving her as she perceived them.

Look.

She opened her colorless eye, peering through the filtered world at Kai's inert form. No, forms—two forms—man and wolf existing in the same space, not one or the other, but one in the same. At his center, his heart struggled to maintain a feeble beat, wrapped in the same shimmering essence as the witch's path. Magic, she realized—magic was keeping him alive, but not for long. It needed a spark, something to draw from. Her gaze fell on the corded braid round his neck. It glowed the moment her eyes lit upon it. A physical bond between them, forged by intent or accident. She could draw from it. She wrapped her fingers around it as she leaned in, breathing into his mouth once more. The whispers breathed with her.

She could feel the answering crackle in her veins. The air burned as it left her mouth and poured into him.

Kai coughed, choking up water. She gave a cry, helping him turn onto his side as he expelled the water from his lungs. His skin warmed beneath her touch, his ashen pallor faded as she watched. She collapsed beside him, staring up at the overcast sky, awash with relief despite the violent shiver in her limbs. Kai rolled, shifting over her, filling the field of her vision. His arms were braced on either side of her. Heat radiated from him. His eyes searched her face, lit by an intent she didn't recognize until his head bent down and his mouth took hers.

His lips scalded her. Her arms wound around his neck, submitting to an instinct as old as time. She arched up against him, relishing the ebb and flow of warmth between them.

He broke away with a gasp, resting his forehead against

hers, one arm wrapped beneath her, holding her up. His breath fanned her face.

"We need to get out of the water," he said, his voice hoarse and spare.

"I don't know if I can move," she admitted, though Kai was already lifting her. He carried her away from the hungering surf, seeking the shelter of the woods. Between his strong, even strides and the warmth of his chest, Azzy found herself lulled to sleep.

There were no dreams.

She woke surrounded by warmth. Kai held her in his lap, a fire of driftwood giving off red-tipped flames a few feet from them. Between the two, there wasn't a trace of chill in her body. She thought him asleep until she glanced up, catching his gaze as he stared at the flames, flickering a brilliant orange in his irises.

"A fire?" Her voice didn't startle him. He reached up, threading his fingers through her loose hair.

"We had to risk it. You were freezing," he murmured, still clearly lost in thought. His fingers sifted through her loose strands. Azzy sank against him, lost in the novelty of the sensation.

Her thoughts tumbled, struggling to catch up to her current situation. Was the path lost to her? It had to be. Between their flight from the winnowrooks and their dive into the sea, how could she possibly find it again? Azzy took a breath. She was alive, safe in Kai's hold. She would find her way again.

She tilted her face, studying Kai's closed expression.

"What happened to you up there?"

The muscles of his jaw twitched. He closed his eyes, but not before she caught a flash of shame.

"We all have our predators, Azzy, even my ilk."

Her lips parted as she understood. "That's how you were trapped the first time."

"Their scent...twists the senses. Makes us hallucinate, drives us to madness if we get too close." A flush crept over his cheeks.

She tapped his chin, forcing him to look at her. "In the city, I didn't fight against those shadows. I could have, if I'd tried, but I thought they were right. But you didn't have a choice."

The flush darkened in a flare of anger. She balked at him. "What?"

"If we were down there again, would you fight them?" He glared down at her. The intensity in his eyes reminded her of his taste, warm, and earthy, salted by the cold biting water of the sea. She swallowed, looking away.

"With everything I have."

"Good," he said. "They were wrong."

Azzy fidgeted. "You forgive me for trapping you as a human?"

His sigh sent stray strands of hair swirling along her face. "You didn't trap or trick me," he said.

"Would you choose to stay like this?" She cringed as the question left her mouth. There was nothing defined between them, no promises or vows exchanged like the women and men she'd known in the Heap. She peeked at him, his expression thoughtful.

"I don't know," he said. What did she expect when she herself couldn't voice the strength of the connection she felt with him?

They stared at the flames together, both lost in thought. Azzy shifted her gaze to the woods behind them, wondering if they could safely find a way back to the path, far around the winnowrooks. Surely, the Snatchers must be gone by now? Despite the peace of the moment, the pull to find her brother and Brixby was still there, spurring her on.

Kai rested his chin on the top of her head. "I will help you find the path again," he said, "Rest."

Azzy relaxed and let herself drift. On the verge of sleep, she heard a distant whistling sound cutting through the air.

⟡

K ai roused her some time later, the fire long burnt to ash. It was still light out, though she suspected she had slept through the night, the longest rest she'd had since setting out from the Heap.

Azzy swiftly braided her hair as Kai scattered the evidence of their fire, hiding their presence. She watched him, frowning.

"Are the Snatchers still in the area?"

"I'm not sure," he said. "All I can smell is salt and ashes. It's best to be cautious."

They picked their way through the forest, both warily eyeing the trees, though there was not a hint of web amid the evergreens. The air was warmer here, the snow patchier, revealing a carpet of fallen yellow needles littering the ground.

Azzy stopped, staring at the exposed ground at her feet. The path lit up beneath her. "It's here," she said.

"Are you sure? We 're nowhere close to where we were."

There was no mistaking it. She could follow it through the snow if she had to. Had it moved to accommodate them? It didn't matter. Azzy turned, a smile on her lips. Kai stared at her with an expression that bordered on wonder.

"What?" she said.

"Nothing. Shall we?" He followed her lead, his hand slipping into hers, the gesture natural between them.

Their mutual silence was companionable, dulling the endless urgency she felt to reunite with her family. She would find them again, but she was no longer alone in the process. Not anymore.

The whispers rose.

Azzy slowed, looking back over her shoulder with her altered eye. The witch had warned her she would see more. What she saw now was a terrible choice. She had seconds to make it.

It whistled through the air.

Kai stiffened beside her, sensing it, turning toward it. She gazed up at him, memorizing his face. *I wanted more time.*

A choice. Not a choice at all, not when Armin and Brixby were the only ones who occupied her heart. But that wasn't the case anymore. The path dissolved as she stepped in front of him.

Kai flinched when the blood hit his face.

Pain blossomed with such ferocity it froze her insides, blooming through her shoulder. She touched the end of the hook protruding from her chest. Kai stared down at her in horrified anguish, reaching for her. Barbs shot from the hook, biting into her. Blood slicked her fingers.

Ritual.

She understood what the word meant now, what the whispers told her from their first meeting. She knew how to unbind them. She wouldn't drag Kai down with her.

"I'm sorry," she whispered. The pull came from behind. She wrapped her bloodied hand around the braided cord and ripped it free as the Snatchers' hook reeled her away. Kai screamed. It warped to a howl as he fell to all fours.

The howl echoed in Azzy's ears as she flew backward, snapping branches in her wake. Her vision dimmed as pain ricocheted through her.

Trust your choices. Her eyes watered. She had imagined her journey would end when she found her brother. Not like this, not a split decision between herself and the wolf. He had survived it once, could have done so a second time, leaving her to forge on. Azzy closed her eyes. Not a choice at all. She would have done it again to save him.

I'm sorry Armin...

PART II

BONDS

The Weight of Dreams

He woke with a start, clutching his chest as his heart thumped against his ribs. Sweat stung his eyes as the sensation of sand creaked through his veins with slow-moving dread. His mouth was open to scream before instinct kicked in and he shoved his face into the coarse cloth of his bedding, biting hard on the blanket to keep the sound locked in his throat. He heard his bunkmate tense beside him.

"Armin?" Brixby rose from the tangle of blankets. The older man burst into a flurry of movement in the dark as Armin waited for his equilibrium to balance itself.

The bedding tasted like soiled cotton on his tongue, salted by his sweat. He spat it out, slumping forward as the pounding in his chest subsided. Details of the nightmare trickled back to him in flashes of sharp, visceral detail. The cloying sweet stench of winnowrooks, the icy sensation of endless water closing over his head, the heat of another—close, so close—and finally the starburst of pain, like a lightning strike through his torso before the sucking rush of darkness. He palmed his chest, wondering if the wound was truly a dream. His skin felt bruised to the touch and fever hot, but that was normal for him now.

Brixby knelt beside him, offering a bowl of watery paste, dark vivid green like cave moss. "Here," he whispered.

Armin seized the bowl from him, downing the contents without hesitation. His stomach muscles tightened the moment the bitter liquid hit the back of his throat. Poison. His belly clenched, attempting to expel what he'd put into it, but Armin was used to the reaction, gritting his teeth through it. Like swallowing acid, it nipped at his throat. He rode out the feeling until it dulled, finally trusting himself to speak.

"I had another dream," he rasped, a faint echo in his voice. He pushed himself up onto his forearms, staring at his splayed fingers until Brixby gently guided him into a sitting position.

"So close to the last?" Brixby frowned, tucking away the small pouches of herbs their jailers paid so little attention, a small freedom. He paused, studying one. "You look more distressed than usual. What did you see?"

Armin hesitated. His guardian had many theories about the dreams, but the one they dared not pin their deepest hopes on was his tenuous connection to Azzy. If there was shred of truth to that connection... A slight tremor ran through his hands. That pain and darkness, what did it mean for his lost sister? An ache rose in his chest. The memory of his last sight of her—wide-eyed, fleeing the Snatchers' bestial trackers—flashed through his thoughts. His fingernails dug into his palms until they bled.

His guardian watched him, understanding drawing a sober expression on his face. The older man's throat worked as he tucked his hands into the loose sleeves of his tunic. "Is she alive?"

"I don't know," Armin admitted, staring at his palms as the crescent cuts slowly knit back together.

Brixby dropped his gaze, staring at the thin tarp they slept on. He couldn't seem to find the words to comfort his charge, the only indication of his hidden grief in the tightness of his jaw.

"She's—" said Armin, driven by the urge to banish those chilling thoughts from his head.

"Nothing is known for certain," Brixby mumbled.

Armin nodded, swallowing hard. Denial was necessary to survive.

The Snatchers would come for them soon, rousing them for another long march toward their destination. Just yesterday, from the peak of the mountain crossing, they caught their first glimpse of the shining city.

He'd never seen anything like it—those spires of metal and glass flashing gold in the last hints of evening sunlight. He'd never wanted to see anything like it. It was with bitter irony that he longed for the dim recesses of the Heap.

The sun still stung his eyes despite the near constant exposure to it. As they drew closer to their destination, winter's clutch on the land receded, leaving the sun to glare down on them like a baleful fiery eye. It scalded his skin, until he felt boiled from the inside out, leaving his flesh red by the day's end, healing through the night until it settled into a dusky tan hue. Brixby's dark complexion underwent a similar transformation, though the sun did not pain him as it did his ward. A deeper shadow rose outside the tent's canvas wall.

The entrance flap lifted, revealing Gorgath's misshapen face. "Time to move, dregs."

The two men rose, securing their bedclothes. The Snatcher kept an eye on them long enough to ensure swift obedience of his orders before diverting his attention to the caravan's female cargo. Brixby waited until their jailer's gruff bellows moved away before he grabbed Armin's arm.

"Whatever you saw, you need to put it out of your mind," he said, his green eyes boring into his charge. "Bury your emotions deep."

Armin's throat felt tight, the sour paste like a lead weight in his gut. Brixby didn't need to remind him of the danger. He could feel the itching beneath the surface of his skin. The near scream this morning was too close a call. He dragged his thumb along the smooth bumps lining his lips, a painful reminder for the necessity of his silence. The very thought of his sister's uncertain fate made the muscles between his shoulder blades writhe.

Brixby gave his arm another squeeze. "My supply of hemlock is almost gone."

A jolt of panic shot through Armin. His guardian released him, worry creasing his brow.

"I might be able to convince Gorgath to acquire more," Brixby said. He glanced through the tent flap as the Snatcher in question lumbered back towards them, scratching his lumpy forehead.

The two of them stepped from the tent as the jailer halted before them.

"Your talents are required, Apothecary," Gorgath rumbled, clapping a massive hand on Brixby's shoulder. "The female worsened during the night."

The trio flinched as a wail rent the air, steeped in a misery so acute it chilled the blood. Brixby nodded as he dug through the belt of supply pouches the Snatchers allowed him. "I fear some of my supplies have dwindled, sir," said Brixby, his green eyes calm as they stared up at Gorgath's craggy features.

The Snatcher studied the man with a calculating expression. Armin tried not to think of what rode on this moment. Gorgath was the reason Brixby continued to breathe. Fitting, as he'd saved the Snatcher's life. Their jailer held a begrudging modicum of trust for the Apothecary. After a moment, he nodded, rubbing a hand along his slouching jawline.

"I'll get your ingredients," growled the Snatcher. He thrust a large pair of metal mesh gloves in Brixby's hands. "Take these. Her skin's begun to crack."

The Snatcher sauntered off toward the supply wagon. Armin waited until he was out of earshot.

"Do you need my help?" The itching increased beneath his skin.

Brixby shook his head, staring down at the chain mail gloves with a carefully blank expression. "You don't need to see this, Armin," he said, his voice soft. Another shriek rose above the noise of the camp, accompanied by a chorus of swears from the attending Snatchers and the rattle of chains. Brixby walked toward the chaos.

Armin stood where he was, frozen in place by the deep-seated fear he strove so hard to hide. He watched his guardian enter her tent. The flap rose, giving him a brief flash of the writhing figure inside.

Nell.

He jerked his eyes away from the sight as nausea rose. Awareness tingled through his nerves. How much longer before he looked like that? Brixby upped the dosage of his concoction every day. The poison kept him human, for now. But it was only a matter of time before the monster scratching under his skin clawed its way out.

Into Avergard I: The Muddied Road

T he screams fell silent not long after Brixby entered the tent. It was a mark of his skill the Snatchers couldn't deny. Without the Apothecary, their captured cargo wouldn't have made it this far. It was only Brixby's skill that kept them alive. His fate hung like a sword over his neck, prepared to fall on a whim if he no longer proved useful to their jailers. Armin couldn't dwell on the situation, as it caused his anger to build on a slow simmer. He couldn't think of his sister. That burned more than the poison in his belly.

Instead he forced his thoughts to drift, a sailing ship in the quiet pool his mind needed to be. He went through the mechanical motions of breaking down the camp.

"Faster, wretch," a patrolling Snatcher snarled, swatting the side of Armin's face as he passed. He sucked in a breath against the numbing sting, the only reaction he allowed himself as he tucked their bedrolls and tent into the supply wagon.

Don't react and keep your head down.

His guardian's advice slid through his thoughts on

repeat. He used them to keep himself sane as his fingers inevitably found their way to the collar round his throat.

It was a slimmer version of the one the Snatchers forced on their bleak-eyed hounds, without the garish spikes. This version was an elegant choker, adorning the necks of all their acquisitions. It had a darker trick in store for any who earned the Snatcher's wrath, through behavior or attempted escape. He'd seen them in action—a metallic noose that slowly strangled the wearer. Only the Snatchers could loosen it again, which meant the further one fled, the tighter the collar grew. He'd felt the squeeze on his windpipe more than once, but only as a mere warning to force his compliance.

Not so for one of the other boys, several years younger than Armin, his blank eyes proof he'd been dead inside long before he'd broken into his final desperate flight. The memory whispered through Armin's mind before he could stop it.

⁂

The boy took off in broad daylight, running straight into the woods away from the Snatchers' wagon. The brutes watched him go, casually conversing with one another.

"How much of a loss?" said one.

"Not pure, but his taint is weak. He won't sell high," said Gorgath, elbowing the first in the ribs. "Five coins he falls in fifty paces."

The other considered the proposition, leering at the other acquisitions. "Forty paces."

Gorgath sucked on his fat lip, eyeing the group to see if any would attempt to follow. The urge gripped Armin tight. The ghost of freedom crooked its finger at him, beckoning him forth, but a sharp nod from Brixby kept him in place. He watched with the others, sick from the knot of hot anger roiling in his gut at their inaction. They all watched the boy, eyes on his staggering figure right to the very moment he pitched forward, clawing at his throat.

The boy fell to his knees, gasping for a breath that wouldn't come, at exactly forty paces.

"Bloody cheat, you are," Gorgath grumbled as he paid the other Snatcher.

Armin stared at the dead boy as the Snatchers forced them to continue on, watching until he could no longer see the body. They had left him there, carrion for the wilds. Armin had felt acid on his tongue, burning with the heat of his anger. The scars lining his lips had filled with fire.

A pulse of warmth went through them now. Armin braced himself against the slats of the wagon, breathing hard through his nose. He could feel his heartbeat in his bruising cheek, the beat quickening at his notice. Sweat beaded over his face. Something thrashed inside his chest, like a caged bird beating its wings against his ribs.

All it would take was a word, one word, and he would be free of them.

He eyed the cluster of carousing Snatchers enjoying their morning meal. So blissfully unaware of how dangerous Armin truly was. One word. It would end them. It would end all of them—Snatcher, slave, it did not matter.

His lips parted.

Not like this.

Armin froze, swallowing hard as he clamped his lips shut. He could almost feel his sister's presence, her quiet strength surrounding him. He shut his eyes, picturing her face, pleading for him to keep the terrible voices inside. A tear slipped down his cheek. It was harder and harder to resist the pull of the voices, even dulled by Brixby's administered poison. How long would he rely on his absent sister to steady him?

That last sight of her...

Armin shook himself, burying the threats of memory and dream deeply until the inviting warmth in his scars seeped away.

Brixby appeared beside him, calm green eyes seeing what Armin couldn't put into words. "The effectiveness is wearing off already," he said.

Armin gave a slight nod in answer, unwilling to admit to the man who had risked so much for him how close he'd come to slaughter and mayhem. Instead he focused on the roll and bowl of mush his guardian offered, eating with single-minded purpose. Brixby absently nibbled at his own roll, eyeing their surroundings.

"We're about three days out from Avergard now," he remarked. Armin stopped eating to stare at him.

It wasn't the first hint Brixby had dropped about the city, though he didn't elaborate how he'd obtained such knowledge of the area. Their guardian had always had secrets, many only their mother was privy to, secrets Armin couldn't fathom in his limited knowledge. Discussing such matters out in the open was too dangerous, and the exhaustion at the end of the day's long march sapped his will to ask questions. Most nights he was simply too tired to corner his guardian on the matter. Brixby remained awake long into the night.

"Move out!"

The other captives fell in line around the wagon, their features blurring together through their shared hollow expressions as they began the long march of the day. Did he look like that? Brixby didn't, ever calm and clear-eyed as he walked beside Armin. The Snatchers mostly left them alone since the Apothecary continued to prove his worth. When one of them moved close enough to swat at Armin, Brixby would shift his body between their captor and his ward, still protecting him despite their situation. Always protecting him. Everyone protected him.

Armin watched the ground beneath their feet. They traveled along the muddy furrows of the main road. He was spattered from head to toe in wet earth. It dried like clay on his skin at night, adding another layer of dust to his pale ghostly self. At least his downcast gaze muted the persistent sting of the sun in his eyes. He spent hours watching the swell of mud framing each step he took, a brief memento of the journey, dashed by the other broken wretches trailing behind him.

There were ten others, their names as fleeting in his memory as his muddy footprints in the road, a mix of male and female, two with skin darker than Brixby's. What they all shared was the same bitter truth, the horrific secret of what humans did to each other.

Elder Prast hadn't simply cast Armin and Nell to the Above. He'd handed them off for a fee. The greatest myth of the Snatchers had dissolved with the thrust of coins into the Elder's sweaty fist. He'd yet to tell Brixby, fearing his guardian was already privy to such knowledge and did nothing to stop it. Did Azzy know?

No, she would have gutted the Elder for it.

The drudging march came suddenly to a halt. What was happening?

Shouts filled the air. The Snatchers were excited about something. Armin looked up with a frown. The forest to their left was swathed in webs.

"Winnowrooks," Armin breathed. He'd only seen them

dead or in pieces, but Azzy often told him stories from her trips to the Above.

"Good fortune, lads," said the tallest Snatcher, a great behemoth of a man the others referred to as Mordock. He grabbed a small barrel from the wagon, rubbing the clear yellowish contents on his face and arms. Two others followed suit before the trio charged into the nest. The webs slid free from their coated skin as half a dozen winnowrooks emerged from the high branches with enraged hisses.

Armin felt his chest tighten at the sight of them. These were the creatures his sister had faced? They outnumbered the Snatchers two to one.

He watched in fascinated horror as Mordock and the others seized the frenzied monsters in their meaty fists, wringing the winnowrooks' necks until those scrabbling legs fell limp. The Snatchers returned to the wagon, opening one of their many empty barrels. Mordock popped off the first winnowrook's head, draining the body over the barrel as the air filled with the smell of burnt sucrose. The dead monster's head landed at Armin's feet.

Its numerous milky eyes stared up at him.

The scars lining his mouth burned hot as he fought down the urge to scream and scream.

Into Avergard II: Guardian

Brixby's calloused palm slid over Armin's eyes and blocked the monstrous severed head from his sight. He fell back against the warmth of his guardian's chest, listening to the plaintive words Brixby murmured in his ear.

"Don't look, son. Don't think of it. It can't hurt you," he said. Brixby's words seeped into the tensed muscles of Armin's shoulders, held in place beneath the gentle shield of his hand.

The Snatchers laughed and bantered as they ripped the winnowrook to pieces. The sharp crack of its limbs, the wet tearing of flesh—a contrast of sounds both slick and brittle. Armin flinched. Brixby turned him away from it all, moving his hands to the side of the boy's head. Armin opened his eyes, staring at his guardian's dark throat, watching the steady pulse beneath his skin. He could hear his own heart racing, the beat amplified within the muffled space in his head. Brixby's never wavered, never rose, the pulse of a man who'd seen greater horrors.

Brixby removed his hands and peered down at Armin,

worry evident in his dark green eyes. "We're getting ready to move."

Armin nodded, not trusting himself to speak without screaming. Part of him wanted to ask Brixby how he could be so calm, why it didn't bother him. All the great unknowns of his childhood were rising to the fore. He caught glimpses of the others around him, all clearly shaken and disturbed by what they saw. Brixby gently pressed him forward as the caravan started moving. Shock slowed the others, causing the ever-watchful Snatchers to encourage them with a hard cuff against the back of the head.

Armin glanced back. There was nothing left of the winnowrooks but a black stain seeping into the mud.

"Keep your eyes forward," said Brixby.

It wasn't a hard order to obey.

The long drag of the march soon siphoned the darker memories from the forefront of his thoughts. Armin struggled through the sucking mud to keep on his feet. He fell once and caught himself on the cart.

The surface contents shifted. A slender arm reached for him through the slats, blackened nails stroking across his knuckles before he snatched his hand away.

He forgot himself, looking up into dark glittering eyes that froze him in place. There was a promise there that sent a flood of heat through his lower body. Armin sucked in a surprised breath. A low chuckle came from the concealed person in the cart before Brixby plucked him off the ground.

"Don't look her in the eye," said his guardian, giving the extended hand a light smack.

"That was—"

Brixby put a silencing finger to his lips. "She doesn't know that name anymore."

Nell.

He had seen little of her since the taint took her hard some days ago. The Snatchers kept her heavily concealed between cart and tents, burying her in canvas and burlap. It was safer for everyone. Brixby was tasked with her general sedation and delaying the taint's effects on her body and mind. It was a losing battle.

Armin quaked inside. She represented everything he feared about the magic building in him. The alterations of the body, the rapid decay of the mind. His worst fear was the loss of self. To forget his mother, and his guardian.

To forget Azzy.

The quaking grew worse.

As if she sensed his fear, he heard another cruel chuckle from within the cart.

⚜

They may have been cast out together, but there was no ally to be found in Nell. She was already too far gone when they emerged in the Above.

"This is your bitch sister's fault," Nell sobbed. She clung to Armin for comfort all the same. Her too-thin frame felt akin to holding a bird with a broken wing, a fair comparison when he looked into her drawn, tear-stained face. The shadows were heavy beneath her eyes, around her mouth, hollowed and bruised, her inner self laid bare. This was the same Nell he'd seen holding her last lifeless babe in her arms. Her pain had poisoned the entire Heap, the catalyst for their current predicament.

But Armin couldn't hate her. He held her small frame tight against him. Touch was all he could offer. His mouth burned from the thread laced through his flesh. The horrifying moment they'd brought the needle to his lips was still fresh in his mind. His skin felt too tight, as if he would burst at the seams any moment.

The Elder sold them like chattel, without a backward glance as he and his men left back through the tunnels. The Snatchers circled them, eyeing their newest acquisitions. Armin considered running, fleeing into the wild and all its hidden dangers, but the haggard men chained to the cart posts watched him intently. Their eyes swam with madness.

A cluster of sad-looking people cowered in the snow nearby, their faces a further testament to the hopelessness of his new situation.

"Let's see what we have here," said one of the Snatchers, a great brute, his features mashed onto his lopsided skull. He pried Nell away, grinning at her terrified shriek. "Get it all out now, sweet, we have a fair-weather tolerance for the noisy ones." She fell silent as he pawed her, tearing at her dress to inspect her fully.

The Snatcher spat on the ground. "A sickly one?" He held her up by the nape of her neck, her body dangling limp as he swung her out to the chained men. They surged forward, snarling and snapping, more animal than human. The reaction shifted the Snatcher's disappointment to calculation. A collar was snapped around her neck and a rope tied around her waist.

They placed her atop the cart, her expression vacant. The Snatcher grabbed him next, forcing his chin up to observe the stitches sealing his mouth.

"Hell of a job there," muttered the brute, frowning at him. Armin received the same examination. The Snatcher thrust him toward the chained men. There was no snarling now. The men cowered, shrinking away from him. The rank smell of urine filled the air. The reaction scared Armin more than it did the Snatchers.

The brute dropped him to grip his chin tight, peering

into Armin's face. "This one's troublesome," he said. Even he sounded worried.

Armin felt something fracture inside of him as they coiled wire around his wrists, tossing him in beside Nell. He sagged to his knees. This was his fate? To become a monster who scared monsters?

The wild men strained against their chains, desperate to be away from him. Their eyes flashed like a predator's in the dim predawn light.

"We leave after sunrise, lads!"

The gradual light stung his eyes. Nell moved only to feverishly scratch her skin.

And then her head snapped up, mouth opening for an inhuman scream. "Theeeeerrreeee!" She pointed into the trees.

Armin followed her gaze. His heart dropped at the sight of his sister and guardian. They'd come for him. They'd come to die with him.

"Fresh meat, boys! I smell female!" The brute slammed the posts holding the chained men, unleashing two of them.

He tried to scream, the voices lashing him, building in his throat. Blood pooled in his mouth as he strained at the coarse stitches. He would kill them all. He would drop them with a single word. The desire to destroy rode him, a fever that built until he felt he would immolate inside the inadequate vessel of his body. The thread held.

Brixby's gaze met his, dropping through the black swirl of Armin's thoughts like an anchor grounding him in place. His guardian turned and shouted at Azzy.

"Run!"

Armin watched his sister disappear, pursued by one of the chained men. Another fell on their guardian and drove him to the snow-covered ground until the brute peeled off his attack dog, yanking his chain hard enough to make the wild man yelp. Armin froze as the Snatcher hauled Brixby to his feet.

"What sort of stray do we have here?" He looked Brixby over, his unimpressed sneer charging the air with ominous energy.

Would they kill him? If Armin had to watch his guardian —the only parent he had left—die before his eyes, the fragile tether to his sanity would snap. Brixby's cool green eyes slid to look at him, somehow calm and serene.

"I could be useful to you," he said, his voice hoarse from the Snatcher's hold on his neck.

"Useful?" The brute barked with a laugh. "You hear that boys—"

The brute staggered. Blood erupted from his mouth, nose, and ears, splattering the snow with blood so dark it was almost black. Armin had gaped at him. The other Snatchers circled in alarm. The second the chain went slack, the wild man lunged for freedom. Another Snatcher hammered his fist down onto the fleeing man's skull, splitting it like overripe fruit. The remaining two wild men fell back, subdued and silent, as they stared at their fallen fellow. Armin couldn't spare them the attention as the Snatchers rounded on Brixby.

"What have you done?" one roared, drawing back a fist. Armin surged to his feet, desperate to somehow stop the blow, but it never fell.

"I did nothing, but I can help him. Do you wish for me to save him or not?" Brixby slipped a small pouch from his belt, lifting it for the Snatcher to see. The fist stopped as this one considered him.

"Your life for Gorgath's, Apothecary," he said, sneering at the word as if it left a foul taste in his mouth.

E very morning, it was harder to rise.
"You need to eat something," Brixby insisted.
Armin didn't know how he could stomach the Snatcher's
gruel. It sat, congealed beyond all appeal in the shallow
bowl on his lap. When it was apparent his charge couldn't
be persuaded, Brixby drew a hunk of bread from one of his
many pouches.

Armin accepted it with a frown. He knew refusal would
only hurt his guardian more. It was Brixby's unwavering
care and protection that had helped Armin last this long.
He felt the familiar stab of guilt as he nibbled on the taste-
less crust.

"Why didn't you run?" It had been the first question out
of his mouth when Brixby had removed the stitches. He'd
whispered, the voices simmering within his own. A true
flash of pain passed through Brixby's features, a shade of
regret and grief that made Armin's heartache.

"You needed me more."

He was the one protected while his sister was left to the
brutality of the Above. That was the way it had always
been. His mother, Brixby, even Azzy herself had always
shielded him. They had all placed themselves at risk for
him. Sacrificed for him. When he'd forced his company on
Azzy into the tunnels, he'd destroyed their lives. His last
sight of her was fleeing into the wild, chased down like prey,
her fate unknown. What had happened to her? Had she
survived all this time? She was so much stronger than him.
She had to be alive. She had to be.

The bread was so terribly dry in his mouth, little better
than ash.

Brixby placed a hand between his shoulder blades. "You
are doing it again."

Armin shook himself, forcing himself to swallow the

mouthful. It settled in his stomach like a stone. A thousand worries weighed on his thoughts. He sought a distraction.

"How are you so calm through all of this?"

Brixby's gaze flicked to the half-open tent flap, watching to see how close their jailers were. After a pregnant pause, he set down his own half-eaten bowl of gruel and folded his hands in his lap.

"I was born in the Above," he said.

"Where do you come from?" Armin stared at him, unable to comprehend their guardian being brought up in this dangerous world. He'd long believed Brixby hailed from a neighboring city like the Heap.

Brixby's expression turned distant, his eyes peering at something far, far from their present place. "Beyond the white-capped mountains, beyond the clutch of winter. The world was lush and green, with sulfurous swamps and poisonous vines, and brimming with life."

It sounded both dangerous and wondrous. Here, the trees, like the road, were a muddied brown. "Why did you leave?"

The distance faded from his guardian's gaze, leaving a shadow in its wake. "I was forced out," he said, a grim smile hinting at what wasn't said. "I did not adhere to the strictures of the community. And I held no magic in my blood. So, I sought a place where I would be needed for what skills I had."

The words sank in, the implications causing his eyes to widen. Armin released a breath. "Your people had magic? They controlled magic?"

Brixby hedged. "It is different, Armin. Their magic is cultivated through careful breeding and exposure over generations." He didn't take his eyes off his calloused hands. "They are not tainted and twisted."

He ignored the churning in the pit of his stomach at Brixby's words. "What about Avergard?"

"That is a different creature entirely," said Brixby. Armin fidgeted, unsatisfied with such a sparse answer.

"What will happen to us when we reach the city?"

Another stretch of silence, so long that the accumulated exhaustion of their journey threatened to drag him under.

"We shall either be snapped up in the outer markets or taken to the auctions within the city proper. If our fortunes are good, we will be sold to a genteel house as servants."

"What if they aren't?"

Brixby closed his eyes. Without their brightness, Armin could see the weight of age on his guardian's face. "It is better not to know, Armin. Rest while you can. Perhaps you will connect with your sister again in dreams."

It was a brush-off, but Armin could not protest, not when sleep called to him like a persistent siren. He lay down on his bedroll, his mind quiet despite the hints of disastrous knowledge drifting through his thoughts. Sleep pulled him into its cloying embrace. On the shifting edge between waking and slumber, he thought he heard a low chuckle.

It was not his sister who slithered through his dreams.

Into Avergard III: Wounding

❧

His sister sat on the stool next to him, beside their
mother's work table. The scarred wood was scattered with shreds of strong-smelling herbs and
dark stains of dried blood. Their mother hummed as she
worked, crushing a handful of flowers in her mortar and
pestle. Flowers were a rare sight in the Heap, especially
ones so bright. He imagined their tufts were made of pure
sunlight. He twirled one between his fingers, the fringe of
yellow petals glowing faintly at his touch. Azzy was carefully
wrapping a string around the index finger of his other hand,
tying a knot that made his finger red and numb. She did the
same with her own hand, holding up the connected string
between them. They were younger, and her smile was easier,
without the tightness around her eyes she thought he
couldn't see.

"There, we're connected," she said, giggling. Her whole
face lit up. Her glow rivaled the flower in his hand.

"Always," said their mother, her gray eyes watching her
children. The smile on her face was sad. She set down the
pestle, picking up a small knife as she gestured for his hand.

Armin offered her the one holding the flower. She gently plucked it free from his hold and pricked his finger with her knife. His blood fell away into the mortar, combining with the mashed flowers in dark liquid swirls. His sister was next, twice the amount. Strange, how even her blood seemed brighter than his. Their mother continued to mix, muttering to herself.

On the shelf behind her, bottles of liquid memories began to slosh as she spoke, their contents spinning to the power in her voice. He could feel the rhythm of the liquid pounding against him, synced to the beat of his heart. Their mother scooped out a portion of the mixture. She leaned across the table.

"Take your medicine," she said, waiting for him to open his mouth. He hated it but took it anyway. He always took the medicine mother gave him, no matter how foul the taste. The paste sat on his tongue, bitter, stinging his taste buds. He swallowed it quickly, feeling it all the way down to the pit of his stomach. The flower his mother set on the table stopped glowing.

The medicine made his guts clench and cramp for hours after. Azzy would stay with him through the worst of it, running her fingers through his hair and telling him stories. Afterwards, their mother took Azzy into another room to draw strands of shimmering memory from her temples.

"Why must she forget?" Armin would ask his mother each time.

"She must," said his mother. "She cannot bear the weight of them now."

This time it hurt worse than before, causing him to whimper. Armin stared down at their tied hands. Azzy held his other hand, the blood still drying on their fingers.

"It'll be okay, Armin. I'll protect you," she said.

Something slithered along the floor. He jerked his head, distracted. This hadn't happened. This was wrong.

He looked down, trying to make sense of the shape that crawled toward him. It pulled itself forward with hands that ended in claws, black and wickedly sharp. A ragged curtain of dark hair hung over its face, obscuring the features. A woman? A flicker of recognition spiked through him. He tightened his grip on his sister's hand, fear squeezing him like a vise.

"Armin?" Azzy could sense his fear, her blue eyes wide.

The crawling woman dragged herself closer.

There was something terribly wrong with her legs. Deformed, misshapen. Armin was petrified, unable to move. He bit back a cry as his mother's hand gripped his shoulder.

"I know it hurts," her eyes passed over the crawling woman as if she wasn't there, looking at her daughter. "But it will keep you human a little longer."

The woman slid across their stone floor, a dry scraping sound that made him flinch. She was almost close enough to reach him.

His mother took his chin in her hand, forcing him to look away from that terrible sight. Her gray eyes were distant, not seeing him at all, though she looked right at him. "Whatever happens, you must not scream."

Claws sank into his leg.

Armin opened his mouth to find Azzy's hands against his lips.

"Not like this," she said, her eyes pleading. They were surrounded by Prast's men, the accusatory glow of the Rustic Oracle casting a golden sheen on their frightened faces. Frightened of him, of the voices that poured from his mouth. The scene shifted, blurred.

"Perish." This time, the word fell from his lips. Prast

dropped to his knees as blood poured from his mouth, his ears, his nose. Bloody tears leaked from his eyes as he stared up at Armin in horror, choking on unspoken words. His men fell around him in the same state. Their blood pooled at his feet.

Armin shrank from it. No, this wasn't what he wanted. He wanted to protect Azzy, to save her. Brixby fell to the ground, his eyes filled with blood. Armin covered his own mouth, disgusted and terrified of himself, emotions that warred with a perverse dark pleasure at what he'd wrought.

He ended them, like insects crushed beneath his thumb.

"Not like this," Azzy whispered. Armin looked up at his sister. A tear fell down his face at the sadness in her eyes, so like their mother.

Was this what their mother saw when she looked at him?

Azzy reached up, wiping away the tear. A knotted string still adorned her finger. A trickle of blood ran from her nose.

"No!" Armin reached for her, holding her tight against him. He didn't pull back to look at her, afraid of what he would see.

The crawling woman slid through the dead men toward them. A low chuckle fell from her unseen lips.

The voices built in his throat, begged for release. His dream shifted from nightmare to a fractured memory.

Nell's human skin had begun to crack and peel away days after their capture. He remembered his last sight of her before the Snatchers secluded her.

She had collapsed to the ground, the other prisoners scuttling away from her as an inhuman hiss fell from her lips. Her fingers had dug into the mud, as if she sought to anchor herself to the earth. Fractures like scorch marks had marred her skin. They'd grabbed her, carted her away. Not now, now he had to watch it all.

"Don't look." Brixby had pulled him away, a hint of true fear breaking through his guardian's stoic mask. Whatever had happened, the pain was obvious, casting an unearthly sheen on her pale skin, her mouth an open hollow as screams poured out of her. Her spine had twisted back at an unnatural angle as Armin watched, unable to look away. How could he have looked away? Her cries hadn't covered the sharp splintering sound of her bones.

Now, sweat broke down his back. He felt something writhing beneath his own skin, responding to her suffering. Her head swung to the side, cocked at an impossible angle. Her gaze found his, her eyes altered, alien. She smiled with a mouth full of too-sharp teeth.

The woman that was Nell was gone, shed like molted skin.

In her place, the monster began to crawl towards him. Armin fell back, prostrate on the ground. His body refused to cooperate, leaving him paralyzed and vulnerable. She grabbed his ankles, her claws biting into his skin as she scaled up his body. Her lambent gaze held his through the fall of her ragged hair. Her movements were jerky, unfinished, a creature half-formed. She reached his torso, hovering over him. Their gazes locked as something rose behind her, brittle and barbed, a living dagger that beaded with poison at the tip.

"Give in," she purred, raising her barbed tail high to strike.

Brixby gripped his forearms, fingers digging into his skin. Armin looked up at his guardian's panicked face. Brixby shouted his name.

Armin blinked, the world shifting as the dream broke, revealing the very real Nell hovering above him as Brixby tried to pull him free. Armin bit down hard on his tongue to keep from screaming. His blood tasted like bitter poison.

The tent ripped off them, the Snatchers drawn to Brixby's shouts. Gorgath grabbed at Nell, dodging as she hissed and whipped her tail around. The stinger narrowly missed the Snatcher's face. Her claws sank in Armin's sides, causing him to gasp. His breath shuddered as the Snatchers circled them. A stalemate.

"Don't do this," said Brixby, his voice calm despite the tension in his muscles. She looked at the Apothecary, her expression conflicted for a second before the smile slipped back into place. She reached up, her bloodied claws stroking Armin's face.

"Can't you feel his power?" She grinned down at him. "You will make them suffer."

The Snatchers took advantage of her distraction, diving forward to grab her waist.

It happened in a single moment. Armin felt her weight lift off him. Brixby seized him, attempting to drag him clear. They were too close, everyone was too close. Nell shrieked and thrashed. Her tail shot forward, a lightning strike, the barb burying itself in Armin's shoulder.

He couldn't stop the scream, not completely. A strangled cry ripped free from his lips, a swarm of voices blasting them all. The Snatchers and Nell rolled away, their hands clapped onto their bleeding ears. Brixby shuddered, slumping to his knees but he didn't let go, carefully lowering his charge to the ground.

Armin couldn't get air. The wound pulsed. This wasn't like the poison Brixby dosed him with. It was a venom that shredded his veins, eating him alive. He wanted to scream again as the pain intensified, tearing and chewing through every nerve. Brixby held him, grounding him. The contact kept his mouth closed. He gritted his teeth until his jaw creaked in protest.

The monster fluttered beneath the surface of his skin, scratching at him from the inside. It was too tight—his skin was too tight. He was going to crack wide open. He looked up, meeting Brixby's gaze.

His guardian's green eyes were filled with sadness.

Interlude I: Tethered

❦

Kai's thoughts fuzzed, broken, a riot of impulses and sensation. Her blood still stung his nose despite the miles he'd put between himself and that moment...

The hook protruding through her chest. Tears on her face. Reaching for him. Bloody fingers. She yanked the braided cord off him.

His legs tangled, confused by the forced shifting of forms, from man to wolf. He crashed hard through the underbrush, branches and vines snagging on his fur. He gazed at the stars overhead, unfocused and dizzy, still trying to look at things like a man. He wasn't a man, nor a beast, but some pitiful creature locked in between.

Her lips against his, the sweetness of her, the taste, the electric connection between them. Belonging.

"I'm sorry."

Her choked words. Blood hitting his face, her blood. No, no, no!

He felt himself falling all over again. The urge to retch rose and died, unable to carry the signals through his changed anatomy. He couldn't scream with a canine tongue, his teeth too sharp, meant to tear and snap. It felt wrong, all wrong. He lay on his side, eyes staring, unable to make sense of his world.

His pain wasn't physical, but he felt it, sharp and keen in every nerve.

"I'm sorry."

The coppery smell of blood coated him, drowning him, warm and slick, not like the cold black depths from which she'd pulled him.

"Trust me."

Kai yipped, rolling up on his legs, imbalanced as a toddler. His padded feet covered the long miles, numbed by the snow. He followed a trail embedded in instinct, chasing a half-remembered scent across the whited-out world. He ran until his body collapsed in a heap, panting and exposed like an open wound. He licked the snow for precious water, resting long enough to recover his breath before he pressed on.

She stepped in front of him.

Blood on his face.

His lips moving on hers. So sweet.

The scent of her blood was sweet. Too sweet. He knew it then, could taste it on his tongue. The scent of her magic. Unlike any he'd encountered before.

Too much, the sensations of her were too much.

She was magic.

Anger fizzed through his veins. He had stood there, simply stood there, shocked, his human limbs too slow to grab her, to save her.

Her limbs had hung limp as she flew back, the world tilting, the wolf rising, swallowing him up.

Kai lifted his face to the cold stars above and howled his misery. He could still feel the man, seething beneath the surface, two forms out of sync with each other, both yearning for her.

He'd failed her.

It was all he could do not to lie down on the ground until the snow buried him. A wolf could not cry like a human, couldn't weep tears of sorrow. They mourned through their voice.

He shook himself, forcing his tired legs to run further, longer, until the tender pads of his feet were bloodied. He ran until a hint of spring wove through the scents of winter, causing him to sneeze. He was close.

The woods drew in thicker around him. Something was different now—the scent of rot stronger through the heavy floral aromas in the air. He hit the barrier not far from the hollowed tree—a tangled mass of briers, thorns wickedly sharp and nearly two inches long. Kai didn't hesitate, plowing through the thicket.

The thorns snagged on his fur, bit into his skin, and gouged him as he passed. He put his head down, protecting his eyes until he'd muscled his way clear.

The witch's hollowed tree gave him pause. The area looked ransacked, pots and dried plants were strewn everywhere, skins torn and scattered. The grass and plant life surrounding the trunk were a brittle brown, dead. His ears pricked forward. He could hear a heartbeat within the hollow trunk. Kai crept forward, nudging the skin hanging over the entrance with a soft whine. When he heard no answer, he pushed his way inside, the space too small for his bulk. He peered through an animal's eyes at the listless figure curled on the bed of furs.

The inside of the abode was also in disarray. Only the rack of jars and vials was untouched, still glimmering. The witch stared at him. The blue circle of glass was clutched in her hand, so tight her knuckles paled. He had wondered, then, why the witch had demanded such a payment. There was a connection that formed when a person gave over a piece of themselves. A price paid by both parties. The witch would feel everything that happened to the former owner. He had tried to ask her why the morning after, a frustrating conversation when he could not speak. The witch had eyed him with amusement. *"She is a witch's daughter. I will watch her."* It was a connection he didn't truly understand, but it was why he returned to the witch. Now, the glass looked wrong, darkened.

Her eyes were stark, the molten amber dulled to a pale brown, as if a spark had gone out. The witch's other hand rested on her chest, in the exact spot the Snatcher's hook had pierced...

A growl rose in his chest.

The witch closed her eyes at the sound and a tear tracked down her face. She sat up, her dark red hair tumbling around her face. With a hoarse shriek she grabbed a jug beside her bed and hurled it at the wall beside his head.

"You abandoned her!" She hurled the words at him, verbal barbs that drove far deeper than her wall of thorns. "How could you leave her to those monsters?"

His ears lay flat at the accusation, dropping his nose to the ground. The witch must know why he hadn't followed, why he couldn't follow. She knew what an involuntary shift took from his kind, the weakness, the confusion, and loss of their senses. He heard her sigh and slide from the bed to sit beside him.

She drew up her knees, cradling the blue glass oval to her breasts. For a moment he thought he saw a faint pulse of light deep within.

"That wasn't fair," she said. She placed a warm hand on his head and swallowed hard. "I am the coward here." He did not understand the admission, but their shared grief and regret allowed them a moment to lean on one another.

The witch's hesitant voice breached the silence between them. "Can you...can you sense her?"

Kai whined his confusion, his senses still rioting for control. It was a miracle he'd found his way here. Frustration choked him. He missed the ease of communication in his other form, unable to convey the limitations of his current form to the witch.

She looked at him, peering into his eyes. Whatever she saw there surprised her. "She didn't just make you human, did she? She touched the man in you." Her fingers wrapped around his snout, forced him to look up as her eyes caught fire, burning into his. "The bond is there, forged in blood. Look deep, find the tether between you."

Kai tore out of her grasp before he snapped at her. The rhythm of his heart turned erratic as the implications of her words sank in. He lay on the ground and closed his eyes, trying to shut out the overwhelming stream of scents and sounds.

He sank within himself, chasing down the essence of Azure.

Kai thrashed in the winnowrook's web, hastening his death in blind panic. His mind was all animal, unable to rationalize, to tap into the extra instincts that gave him an edge over so many creatures of the Above. Not the winnowrooks. Their scent drove the man from his mind.

He was going to die here. Alone. The web cut into his flesh, growing tighter the harder he fought.

Hands on him, a heart pounding beside his. A grain of sanity rose at her touch. Cutting him free. His fight with the winnowrook was a blur of scents and bursts of color. Those blue eyes stared at him —so frightened, so brave.

Her bloodied fingers slicked along his jaw, marking him,

imparting a piece of her essence to him. He should have felt her power then. Forged in blood.

There...

He followed the bond, sinking deeper and deeper.

Kai felt the faint beat of her heart.

Into Avergard IV: Fever

Light speared Armin's eyes and scalded his retinas, an opening note to the scale of agony moving through him in a tortuous crescendo. His mouth felt gummy and grainy. He tried to swallow but his throat was shredded. His blood was acid in his veins, a pulsing burn with each beat of his heart. He waited for his vision to focus, not recognizing the slanted roof slats above him, but the pain was a reminder of who he was. He was grateful to wake up alive.

Everything hurt, to the tips of his eyelashes. Fire blazed beneath the thin membrane of his skin. He sucked the rank air into his pinched lungs. The faint taste of metal and refuse touched his senses, a far cry from the bracing air of the wilderness. The room around him was closed in, suffocating and stuffy, a ramshackle construction of weathered wood and worn metal. A single window was positioned on the far wall, spilling light like dirty water across the unswept floor.

He appeared to be on a low bed, the threadbare

mattress filmy and damp from his sweat. Armin attempted to roll off it and met resistance.

Leather straps spread across his chest and circled his wrists and ankles, securing him to the metal frame of the bed. He tried to quell the panic stirring in his gut, wondering what had happened. He strained to recall, the memory a crusted scab he tentatively scratched. Digging made his head ache.

Where was Brixby? What had happened? What—

Claws crawled up his body, sinking into his sides. Nell's low chuckle echoed in his mind. The wound in his shoulder throbbed, a pulse that made him gasp. He strained to look down at himself, noticing the clean, stiff bandages in contrast with the general filth that clung to him. The simple act made his head swim. His temples pounded as spots danced in front of his eyes.

A gush of air brushed his damp face. Light the color of weak tea spilled into the room as the door opened. Armin couldn't see who it was, his vision blurred to uselessness. He turned his head away from that awful light, gritting his teeth.

A calloused hand settled on his forehead, cool compared to the inferno blazing inside. He peered up at the familiar outline of his guardian, trying to whisper, to ask him what was happening. Nothing emerged but a hacking cough that jostled his pain-wracked body. A metal cup touched his lips, cool water spilling over his lips. The liquid was bitter, infused with herbs, but it was the best thing he'd ever tasted. He guzzled it down, feeling a moment's relief until it hit his stomach.

His body seized, bucking off the bed. Armin couldn't control himself as he thrashed against the restraints, the leather rubbing his skin raw. He felt something forced into his mouth, another leather strip that kept him from breaking his teeth and biting through his tongue. His spine cracked and popped as he twisted.

Brixby held him down by his forehead. He could hear his guardian murmuring to him, the words slowly sinking through the fog of pain to reach him.

"Hang on, son, it will pass." The hands that cradled his face shook ever so slightly. Armin held onto that voice, a tether he used to pull himself back to the present. He blinked, focusing on Brixby's face above him.

His guardian's eyes were closed, exhaustion etched at the corners of his eyes and mouth. He whispered the words like a prayer.

Armin tried to speak, his throat still sore but manageable. "Brixby?" He need not have bothered with a whisper. There was no endless echo, no sound at all but a breathy rasp, little more than a half-formed shape between them.

Brixby pulled back to look at him, his bloodshot eyes tinting his irises an effervescent green, sharp as the blades of grass they'd passed along the road, like small flags of life amid the endless mud. His guardian released a short puff air as his hands tilted Armin's face left and right, examining him.

"You're still you," he said, the relief in his voice easing the tight knot in Armin's chest. Brixby was here, no matter where here was. His guardian was always with him.

Brixby moved alongside him, unbuckling the straps before he gently levered Armin into an upright position. He seemed to know what would happen next, guiding Armin forward to the waiting basin as he retched. There was little to throw up except a swallow of water and bile, but his stomach wrung out every last drop. Armin's arms trembled as he clutched the sides of the basin. He would have collapsed again without Brixby holding him up. He managed to wipe his mouth on the grubby fabric of his sleeve, pulling it up along his arm. He froze, staring at his bare skin.

His veins looked scorched, the blackened brownish color of charred meat, streaking just beneath the surface. It was happening. Wide-eyed, he looked at Brixby, unable to ask any of the dozens of questions vying for attention, except one.

"Where?" he whispered. Brixby's eyes darted to the open door. Armin followed his gaze.

Buildings rose up farther than his eyes could follow, massive constructs of metal and glass. There was more glass in a single building than he'd seen in the entirety of the Heap. They were ablaze in the sunlight, tinted into a metallic shining beacon for all to see from miles away. The streets were evenly laid cobblestones filled with carts pulled by all manner of creatures, as well as smooth metal boxy contraptions that sputtered smoke and moved without the aid of beast or man. Pedestrians crowded the street, a mix of monstrous and seemingly normal beings until Armin's gaze focused on them. Women with glittering eyes and skirts who moved with unseen appendages. Men with mouths that stretched too wide. A group of children ran past; one stopped, curious, blinking at Armin and Brixby with six jewel-like eyes.

Brixby shooed her away with a flick of his fingers.

"Welcome to Avergard," said Brixby.

Armin watched the moving crowd, morbidly fascinated by the monsters dressed in genteel garments. They wore finery he'd only seen Elder Prast and the wealthier merchants wear on festival days. Brixby rose from the bunk, exiting the shed. He returned within moments, bearing a fresh basin of water and a washcloth. Armin didn't protest as his guardian gently swabbed the dirty raw skin of his wrists.

"They will bring you fresh clothes soon," said Brixby, continuing his ministrations. "We are to be auction-ready this evening."

The tone of his voice pulled Armin's attention away from the street to look at his guardian's face. Brixby's throat worked and his eyes were too wet. A small shock ran through Armin at the sight. He couldn't remember Brixby ever weeping, not even for their mother, his closest friend. He'd held them close, unyielding when Elder Prast screamed at their mother, sentencing her to death. Brixby had turned their faces away from the gathered crowd and covered their ears as they led her into the burning room. Through all of it, his face had remained a mask that concealed his private pain. He was their stalwart protector, the unwavering pillar who'd supported them through every trial and hardship.

Brixby sighed, pulling Armin's head to his shoulder. "I won't be able to protect you there. I can't protect you from anything in this place."

He wanted to tell Brixby he'd done the best he possibly could. Instead Armin clutched the man's forearm like a lifeline. It wasn't until he felt tears dripping off his chin that Armin realized he was weeping.

"You don't have much longer," said Brixby, his voice tight with restrained emotion. "Your body is changing. Nell's poison merely accelerated it." His hold tightened, as if he could keep Armin from slipping away.

"I don't want to forget," Armin sobbed, his voice a broken thing.

"Then don't," said Brixby. "Bury yourself deep inside

your mind, put yourself in an unbreakable cage that can't be touched by madness or magic. You can do this."

Armin silently repeated the words to himself over and over as they waited for the Snatchers to come for them, grateful for such a beautiful lie to comfort him to the very end.

Into Avergard V: Auction

꧁꧂

Gorgath's shadow stretched across the floor, blotting out the light. He wasn't alone. The Snatcher ambled aside, gesturing forward the two beings who followed in his wake.

"Have at them," said the Snatcher. Armin stared up at them, feeling a tremor start deep in his bones.

These two were several inches taller than the brutish Snatcher, but built like waifs. Long fingers cupped bowls of steaming water, which the creatures set at Brixby and Armin's feet. They knelt before them, their long robes pooling around them like crumpled white blossoms. Armin sat, mesmerized, as they dropped a porous sponge to soak in each bowl. Their ears were pointed, the tips pierced with silver rings to match their luminescent skin tone, which glowed like moonlight. Both were beautiful, living pieces of art, their opalescent features accented by their glittering onyx eyes. No emotions were discernible in their marble-like faces.

He jerked when his attendant grabbed his ankle. The glowing creature scrubbed away the filth of the road from his feet with brisk precision. Those long fingers possessed surprising strength. A strand of ivory-colored hair came loose, falling across the attendant's black eyes. Armin reached out, gently tucking it behind one tipped ear. The creature looked up and pinned Armin with its gleaming stare.

Why had he touched it? His shaking grew worse. The creature smiled at him, revealing sharp, crimson teeth.

"They'll like this one." The voice was feminine. Her hand came up and tucked under Armin's chin. She forced him to look up, left, then right as she examined him.

Her ivory claws pressed along his jaw.

"Pretty under all that filth," she said, clicking her teeth together as she noted the appearance of his veins. "But deeply tainted."

She pulled his chin down. "Open your mouth boy."

It was a command, one that terrified him. His gaze darted around the room, from the bored-looking Gorgath to the other half-interested attendant cleaning Brixby.

"Do as she says," his guardian whispered.

Armin held his breath and opened his mouth. The attendant's black eyes widened in a flash of surprise. Her gaze turned calculating. She nudged the one next to her, pointing to Armin's mouth.

The other attendant peered at him for a moment, then returned to her task as she spoke to the Snatcher over her shoulder. "Inquire with the Registrar if Lord Vashon will be in attendance this evening."

"Oh yes," said Armin's attendant, her voice a sensuous purr. "You will entice a high bid, boy."

The shaking grew worse.

The attendants bathed them, washed their hair, cleaned their teeth, and trimmed their nails. The daylight faded as they worked. Near dark, a fresh attendant arrived with an armful of faded white clothing. Perched on top of the bundle were coils of silver chains and shackles.

Amid the chains was another odd-looking contraption Armin did not recognize, not until his attendant lifted it up. His heartbeat redoubled at the sight of the elaborately cast silver muzzle, fashioned as a closed mouth, etched with symbols. They were going to bind his mouth.

Armin shot a panicked look at his guardian, afraid to speak as the urge to scream rose. His body begged him to fight, to lash out with the voices squatting in his throat, awaiting release. Brixby wouldn't look at him, but he had to be watching. A slight shake of the man's head stopped the building frenzy that clawed beneath Armin's skin. His guardian could not protect him now.

Armin tried to cease trembling as his attendant dressed him. Every shaky breath he took deepened the gleam in her dark eyes. He couldn't stop a sharp inhale as she settled the muzzle over his face. The interior curve of the metal comprised of pin-sized spikes that pressed against his lips, providing pain to deter him from opening his mouth. He breathed hard through his nose, trying not to jostle the muzzle as the pins dug into his skin.

The attendant snapped the cuffs onto his wrists and ankles, wrapping the attached length of chain around the palm of her hand. She leaned forward, tucking an errant strand of hair behind Armin's ear. Her thumb brushed across the lips of the muzzle. He winced from the movement.

"Come along, pretty one," she said, as she led him toward the door. "The auction will begin soon."

Another spike of panic. Sweat slid along his spine and down his temples. She led him alone, without his guardian. Armin tried to look back at Brixby but the muzzle pricked a warning into his flesh. Unable to do anything else, he followed the attendant outside. A crowd of pedestrians still walked through the early evening streets—men and women dressed in genteel finery that did little to disguise the monsters within.

Walking made Armin's vision swim, but the attendant didn't slow and jerked him forward when his steps faltered. The pins drew blood. He could taste iron and salt on his tongue.

Pedestrians around him stopped walking. Their eyes settled on him. He could feel their hunger thrumming against his skin. His heart sputtered in his chest, unable to maintain the rhythm of his fear. The attendant kept going, unconcerned by the attentions of the others as she led him to the auction house.

It was a massive structure of stone and glass, large squares of smoothly hewn rock cobbled up two tall stories above the ground. If the height wasn't impressive enough, the building stretched far down the street, encompassing an entire block. There were several entrances from the street, including a gilded doorway where horseless carriages drove up to unload more men and women dressed in velvet and silk.

The doorway Armin approached possessed no such frills. It was a yawning mouth that swallowed him up and spat him out into a cavernous room lit from high overhead. He peered up, shocked by the flickering orbs of glass on strings hung from the ceiling. They hummed and crackled, glowing brighter as he walked beneath them. The attendant led him down a long corridor, the stone cold beneath his bare feet. Dozens of doors lined the hall, carved with numbers that descended as they passed.

Something slammed against the other side of one door. Armin startled. His lips burned as the pins pierced deep.

Muffled howls seeped through the thick wood. Unseen claws scrabbled from behind the door.

"Don't worry, boy, they can't reach you," said the attendant, continuing without pause. Armin followed, bracing himself for the next one. The first prisoner seemed to have set off a chain reaction because a riot of sounds followed their progress. The sounds scourged his nerves raw, but the moment they turned the corner at the hall's end, silence fell like a hammer strike.

The attendant opened a nondescript wooden door. The bustle and smells of the auction house wafted over the threshold, entangling his senses. A man's voice called out numbers in a harsh staccato. The murmurs of the crowd rose and fell with the thwack of wood on metal. Oil, sweat, blood, and an overarching sweetness that blanketed everything else teased his nose.

Armin could hear the soft sobs of the others as the attendant pulled him forward through a channel of silky black drapes. They emerged at a holding pen, filled with dozens of men, women, and children in the same gauzy white outfit Armin wore. They were a dead-eyed group, their resistance broken. Some wept, but most stood silent, their faces blank. His chest tightened.

Where was Brixby?

The few humans who were self-aware cowered from the gate as the attendant unlocked it, gesturing Armin inside. He entered, earning more than one fear-laced stare. Where the others could stand unbound, the attendant attached the chain of his cuffs to a portion of the linked metal fence.

She grinned her ruby-tinted smile at the collective group. "Sit tight, pretty ones."

Armin watched her saunter away, his eyes on the door. They had to bring Brixby in next. They had to. He clung to that hope, aware his fragile calm hung by a thread. The heavy thwack sounded, an unseen signal. He felt it in his bones, in the marrow. His skin itched.

The curtain lifted to the side, giving them a brief glimpse of the raucous audience, bedecked in flashing jewels and colorful silks, their appearance a cruel mirror to the humans led on stage.

A hulking Snatcher filled the space, bigger than any Armin had seen. He towered over the pen, scanning the quivering humans before he reached over to pluck up a screaming girl in one meaty fist. The Snatcher caught Armin's eye as he watched, horrified. The brute winked at him and carried the girl away, dangling by the scruff of her neck.

A soundless roar filled Armin's ears. Fire threaded through his veins, rising from the base of his spine.

He wanted to kill them, all of them.

Thwack!

The sound jolted across his sensitive nerves. The girl's screams rose, high and desperate, shearing the thread of Armin's control. He sank to his knees, breathing hard through the mask. His lips throbbed. He ground his teeth and sank his nails into the meat of his thigh, struggling to focus. The others shrank from him, huddling in the corner as far away from Armin as their narrow confinement would allow. He grew mindless of them with each passing moment. They would die too, more fodder to feed the dark creature rising inside him.

The Snatcher came and went, snapping up a mewling boy.

Armin should have killed Elder Prast, killed him and his lackeys. He could have taken Azzy and Brixby and vanished from the Heap, far from the Elder's petty cruelty. He could have killed anyone who got in their way, brought them down with a single word. He—

The far door opened.

The attendant emerged, leading Brixby straight past the holding pen. Headed directly to the stage. Armin slammed against the fence, ignoring the flash of pain in his mouth as he clung to the braided wires, imploring his guardian look at him.

The man stood stoic, still as stone, his gaze set straight ahead. Why would they lead him out separately? The wires of the fence cut into Armin's fingers.

Thwack!

He couldn't help the whimper, caught in his throat, as the curtain peeled back.

Brixby turned. He smiled at his ward. His guardian's green eyes seared into him, steeped in a sadness so deep it pierced the pulsating violence surrounding Armin. He drew in a deep breath as the attendant lead Brixby onto the stage. The curtain swung shut.

Armin leaned against the barrier. His eyes stung with tears. He strained to hear the calls of the auctioneer, the gruff male voice speaking at a rapid clip muffled by the heavy curtain.

Thwack!

Armin closed his eyes. He hung from the fence, waiting as the Snatcher returned to drag another human from the pen. Their number dwindled until Armin was the only one left.

Thwack! The curtain swung open. The behemoth Snatcher gingerly detached his chain from the fence, his movements stilted and gentle. As if Armin were made of spun glass. The very idea frayed the edges of his mind. He squinted as the Snatcher led him into the brilliance of the stage amid murmurs and laughter. The stage reeked of urine and blood from the other humans. Rusted smears still soiled the floor.

A massive chandelier of cut crystal loomed from the ceiling. Hundreds of glass bulbs flickered as he walked across the stage. The light wavered, intensified.

The audience drew a collective breath.

"Ah, ladies and gentlemen, may I present number 156, tonight's prime selection."

Armin swung around to look at the auctioneer, one of the same milky white beings as the attendants, his frame thicker than the females'. He stood behind a podium, a gavel dangling from his long fingers.

"The pit is now open for anyone who wishes a closer inspection before we start the bidding."

Armin stiffened as a dozen patrons rose from their seats and entered the open area before the stage. His muscles grew rigid, the weight of their eyes on him, examining every inch of him without touch. So close, yet their faces blurred out of focus. Armin looked past them, searching the remaining audience for a hint of his guardian. Somewhere. Anywhere.

Nothing. Brixby had vanished.

He clenched his hands to hide the fear shaking his limbs, continuing to scan the crowd. He passed over a man once. A mental tug swiveled his gaze back. The man's finery was dull in comparison to the colorful creatures around him, a low-key gray as plain as the rock slabs of the outside wall. He hadn't approached Armin like the others clamoring at the foot of the stage, but his mercurial gaze was the most intense of the lot. His continued stare remained uninter-rupted as the pit cleared.

"Let's open the bidding at 500. Do I hear 500?" The auctioneer's voice rang out, his gavel swinging between casual signals from the patrons. The bids pushed higher in seconds, and left Armin bewildered.

500 what? In the Heap, they'd used copper and silver coins. What currency did Avergard tender?

The itch grew beneath his skin as the number rose. Men and women with hungry eyes leaned forward, anticipation in their lean faces. One woman licked her lips, her skirts shifting with unusual movement as she flipped her hand up for the auctioneer.

The man in gray did nothing. He continued to stare at Armin as the bidding drew to a close.

"3,500. Going once..." The auctioneer raised his gavel, a lustrous gleam in his onyx eyes. "Twice..."

"20,000," said the man in gray. There was no great volume to his voice, but it rolled over the room. The other patrons averted their eyes. No one bid against him. The air fizzed with tension, an aura that stemmed straight from the silent gentleman with silver eyes.

The auctioneer recovered first.

"Sold to Lord Vashon."

Thwack!

Interlude II: Witch and Wolf

❦

The witch knelt before the thorny barrier surrounding the hollowed tree. Her dark hands kneaded the earth as she mumbled a breathy string of words that buzzed and numbed his ears. He heard a tinkling tumble of glass.

Kai sneezed. The scent of magic hijacked his senses, coiling and writhing through the air, invisible but tangible as a blur of rising heat. He sensed the moment the magic peaked, when it broke and shuddered, shredding the briers. The witch stood and wiped her hands on her soiled skirts. She strode forward, barefoot over the scattered thorns. He picked his way through to avoid piercing the pads of his feet.

In his mind, he listened to a distant heartbeat.

His thoughts were ordered and clear, a reversal from the chaotic frayed knots of emotion and memory that had choked his mind when he'd arrived. Azure was alive. He could feel her through the tenuous tether between them. The fire within, kindled by the continued existence of his bond, was tempered by the witch's presence. He did not trust Safiya's intentions, nor the faint smell of death that persistently clung to her dusky skin. Misgivings or not, he trailed after her, eyeing the blue circle she clutched tightly in one hand.

A shard of sky. An inner light pulsed deep within the glass, feeble and flickering.

A piece of Azure's essence, one the witch had used to observe them. To watch but not to intervene. She had watched the hook pierce Azure's fragile form and had done nothing. He could hate the witch for this alone, for the audacity of peering through Azure's eyes, but there was another force at play here. The agony etched on the witch's face was not a farce, but a true pain. Why feel such pain for a woman she barely knew?

It echoed what he felt for her, his little waif. His heart ached, remembering her sacrifice for his sake. No one had protected him before in all the long days of his life.

"All Snatchers bring their catch to the same destination. There is a swifter passage to Avergard than the road, but it's dangerous," said the witch, intruding on his thoughts. She headed for the river, coaxing more memories that stung him with each step. "Not like the hidden path I set you on. We'll be exposed to any and all predators who wish us harm."

He huffed. Witch and wolf, formidable alone but too dangerous together for all but the most desperate predator to bother. She looked over her shoulder at him, her gimlet gaze eyeing him from ear tip to claw.

"The creatures we'll encounter will not fear us," she muttered, reaching the shore. A tied-off skiff waited them. He understood now. They weren't merely following the winding path of the river. The witch intended for them to travel by water.

He dubiously eyed the shallow-bottomed boat, far more

secure than the raft he'd used to travel on this river before. He looked at the witch, who watched him in turn, arms crossed, waiting for him to make the first move. Kai whined.

"It's the fastest way. Granted, it would be less cumbersome if you could assume your human form," said the witch.

He snarled at her, clambering onto the skiff. His legs wobbled as the wooden boards creaked and bucked, slowly settling beneath him. The witch was far more graceful, transferring herself to the boat with the lightest bob upon the water.

She pushed them off from the shore with a long pole, letting the drag of the river current grab them. The same stick steered their course round obstacles but only the ones they could see. He felt the hum of danger bristling beneath his fur the moment they graced the deep waters—a mild sensation for now, but he remained wary and watchful.

The river was perhaps more dangerous than the land, but vital. Every manner of beast chanced a drink at the shoreline. Kai spotted more than one pyguara, like the one he had tangled with earlier, lazing on the shore. A herd of massive shaggy creatures drank together, dipping long tongues into the water to keep their necks away from unseen teeth. For a time, the witch was quiet, perhaps observing the wildlife with him.

"You can't find your human half."

He stiffened. The words were not a question. He rolled an eye in her direction to find her umber eyes watching him. She tumbled the blue stone end over end in her hand, casting a distracting flash across her face each time it caught the light. They stared at one another, refusing to give ground, until the witch sighed and looked down at the churning water that buffeted the sides of the skiff.

"It's rare, that hidden power, deep in the marrow.

Hidden from all the world. I wondered, you see, why a witch would choose to burn, even for her children," she said as she steered them around an outcropping of jagged rock. "That girl was so certain she could bring her brother's humanity to the fore. Such vital confidence when a normal person would abandon a tainted human as a lost cause."

Kai grew still, listening to the steady pulse of his heart. The witch was driving at something, a thought hovering just out of reach.

The witch's fingers trailed along his ruff. He whirled, snapping his teeth, but she was exactly where she'd been all along, calmly steering the skiff. He could still feel the sensation of her fingers running through his fur. His hackles rose, a low growl rising from his chest. Unperturbed, she tilted her head, staring at him.

"How did she do it? Peel away this form like rind on fruit? I both saw it and did not. It frothed up inside her, bursting free, like instinct. That kind of power, well, I can understand why her mother would burn for her."

His mouth itched, words trapped on a tongue that could not form them. Kai knew what the witch spoke of. The cord of cloth and hair, half-forgotten while affixed round his neck, and so very different from the brutal pain of the Snatcher collars. How Azure's lifeblood had poured from her when she touched it. How she'd ripped it free from his neck when the Snatcher's hook tore her away. He shuddered. Questions spurned him, unable to pass his lips. The witch coveted information, traded in it. Of course, she would hold this over him too.

"It wasn't the cord alone that made you human," said the witch, her voice low. He heard it like a shout in his ear.

Kai looked around, tension teasing the base of his spine as he noticed the water.

The current continued to push them swiftly along, but

the surface of the water was mirror smooth and black as ink. The skiff made not a ripple as it passed.

A growl left his mouth, cracking the silence like a shot of thunder. The witch pressed a hand to his shoulder. This time he did not snap at her, sensing the warning in her touch. She was whispering again, words that echoed without volume, tangling in each other. Then she stopped speaking.

The silence strummed over his nerves. No animals, no insects, not a ripple in the water. He could not hear his own breathing.

It was a familiar silence, akin to the dead city below, but he could sense no lurking presence, no waiting hunger. Except there was something. An unnatural sensation he could not name.

The slight pressure on his shoulder vanished. Kai looked back to find the witch gone. Simply gone. The skiff stopped with a jolt. It had grounded on a small island in the middle of the river. The land mass hadn't been there a moment ago. Kai noticed the bank of fog as it rolled toward him over the water, swallowing the world until all that remained was the spit of land in front of him.

There was nothing on the shoal: no tree, nor cave, nor refuse of bones. Yet the pull was there. It was a clever trap.

Kai stepped from the skiff onto the lifeless ground.

His paws made no sound on the fine black sand. The beating of his heart, the draw of his breath, and the crackle of his nerves—all were consumed in the encompassing silence. This presence was familiar and unseen, the same undefinable entity that had created the empty city beneath the ground. Kai's ears twitched, trying to catch a hitch of breath or the scrape of claws, anything to give away what waited, watching, in that terrible silence.

The witch was nowhere to be seen.

Had she abandoned him? Sacrificed him to the creature that lurked here? Or had something happened to her? His back had been turned only for a moment, but there was no splash, no indication of how she's disappeared. Kai growled. He could feel the vibration of it in his chest, but no sound penetrated to the air. The unnatural void strangled his senses and sliced along his nerves like a jagged blade. He felt raw, exposed, hovering on a precipice of anticipation.

When it happened, he almost missed it. One moment, he was alone in the fog over black water. Then he was not. The figure stood, still as stone, draped in a gauzy shroud that hid her features, but he knew. He knew by the fine dirty blonde filaments of hair peeking from beneath the cloth at her crown. He knew by the lips, their shape taunting him beneath the veil with their haunting familiarity. Her name clawed at his inhuman throat, begging to be whispered, and he wanted to call for her, but in the same breath he could smell the lie. No scent of earth and salt and sweetness. This was not his woman, only a specter sent to torment him, like the specters that had driven the real Azure to dance along the edge of an abyss.

The veil stirred without wind, lifting in teasing glimpses of soft lips and mismatched eyes. Her lone blue eye was startlingly vibrant against the colorless wash of gray around them. It bore into him, pinning him to the sand. *Not real, not real.* The words rolled through his mind but the influence she held over him was hard to resist. The gauze slipped away, falling free of her form, dangling from her waist in a tantalizing offer of flesh. False flesh, too pale, and lacking the blush of life. He jerked his eyes away from her —*it,* or whatever this entity was—to find that the fog had closed around the isle. He could see nothing beyond it, not even where the black sand came to an end nor the boat that was supposedly behind him. A dangerous prospect, not being able to see where he needed to flee. He looked back to the specter.

She crouched in front of him, less than a foot away, reaching for him with pale fingers.

Kai froze.

Her touch graced his fur, as insubstantial as the surrounding fog, but he felt it through his entire being, sinking into him, tangling with his essence.

Brave wolf.

The words appeared in his thoughts, not spoken. His spine tingled as they poured into his skull.

Brave fool.

You left her there.

Broken and pierced.

In the hands of your enemies.

The specter drew closer until its lips brushed the tip of his ear.

"You left me to die." Azzy's voice, tinny and surreal, strained as if spoken from a great distance. A tremor set in his limbs at the suddenness of her voice in the void, piercing his defenses. He took a step back.

The witch erupted from the water and burst through the fog. She landed on the black sand beside Kai, dripping water, clutching the blue oval of glass in one hand and a short blade that dripped black gore in the other. She spun on the specter of Azure, thrusting the glass forward as she opened her mouth in a silent shriek that popped and sizzled in his ears.

The glass pulsed, flaring with blue light. The specter fell back in twisted angles, joints bending in a fashion that turned the stomach. Her head twisted to an impossible degree, hissing and spitting at the advancing witch. The light flared brighter.

He caught the faint scent of earth and salt and sweetness. It surrounded him, wrapping him in invisible arms that burned the specter's influence away. Kai surged forward, snapping his teeth at the retreating figure that howled in the face of its diminished power. It continued its wending crawl backward, slipping off the spit of sand into the black water. The river closed over the creature until it was smooth as glass once more. Not a ripple marked its passage. His heartbeat thundered in his ears, sounds returning with visceral clarity, roaring into existence. The witch collapsed beside him, planting her stained knife in the sand as she clutched the dimming stone to her chest. Kai sniffed her, sneezing into her damp hair. The scent of Azzy was gone.

"Oh, don't look at me like that," said the witch, wiping an arm across her forehead. She left a smear of black fluid across her skin. "You didn't fare much better out here on your own. You let the blasted beastie destroy our craft." Kai jerked up. Their skiff floated in pieces at the lip of the island, ripped apart by unseen forces. He snarled, berating himself for allowing the phantom to distract him so. The witch's hand lay on his shoulder, firm, warm, and alive.

"No, don't. Its influence was on you before we touched shore," she said, balancing against him as she climbed to her feet. He tasted iron and mud, whining as he nudged at her sodden skirts. The witch winced and shooed him off her. She gritted her teeth as she peeled the wet cloth from her shredded leg, her flesh torn in long bloody ribbons to the glistening bone beneath. She slid back to the ground, breathing hard, her face twisted in pain. Kai bent over her, catching her eye as he ran his tongue along her ravaged flesh. Safiya's eyes flared to a rich gold. She held still and silent beneath his ministrations until the tears began to close. She tore a strip from her skirts, covering the closing wounds as she studied Kai.

"Thank you," she said, and winced as she forced herself to stand. Kai huffed at her. The action merely opened her healing cuts, but the witch waved him off, limping to the water's edge. She'd reclaimed her knife from the sand, covered in grit and fluids which she wiped on her skirts. The knife winked as she slashed open her palm, letting her blood flow free, red drops swirling in the dark water of the river. Words left her lips, buzzing in his ears from the magic she poured into them. She staggered, falling to her knees and swaying from the effort. Kai stepped forward, leaning against her, holding her up as she clung to his neck for support.

"It won't take long," said the witch, her words more cryptic than clear. "Come. Help me build a fire to light the way." The remains of the skiff were close enough to grab without touching the water. Kai piled them and stepped back as the witch worked another small magic in lighting the damp wood aflame. Low and smoky, with a hint of sulfur, but the wood burned and gave enough heat for Kai to gratefully lie next to it. Safiya crouched on the other side, her hand roughly bandaged with another strip of her tattered skirts. She refused to let him heal the cut. Her expression was lost in the low flames.

There were questions of what had transpired, the weight of them dragging his muzzle into the sand, but the witch seemed to hear them without a word being spoken.

"It grabbed me a moment before it lured you," she said, flexing the fingers of her sliced-open hand. "They've grown bolder over the years."

Kai lifted his shaggy head, ears swiveled forward as he listened to the witch's words. She looked up at him, her eyes over-bright and feverish.

"It was a foolish man who opened the Gate. Lusting for power and dominion over all. He didn't know what was waiting. Magic is not a structured entity. It lives and breathes in beautiful, cruel chaos. It corrupts the living. And it breeds creatures of ceaseless appetite." The wood snapped and shrieked as she spoke. The witch lifted her distant gaze, peering out over the water. "The children of magic are the hungriest of all. Eventually, they will consume all that is left in the world." Her hand reached up and rubbed the blue stone hanging from her neck once more. Kai stared at it as well, wondering what force Safiya had channeled through it to repel the entity that had attacked them. Was that a child of magic? Is that what lurked in the empty city below? How had the witch escaped what dragged her under? He grumbled as he rested his head back on his forelegs, left with more questions than answers.

"Ah, here comes our ride."

Kai noticed the raft as Safiya pointed it out, speeding across the surface of the river against the current. He was on his feet by the time it bumped against the dark sand. A head popped out of the water on the opposite side of the raft. Kai sneezed in surprise.

The eel woman grinned at them through her pointed teeth, pulling herself up onto the raft to rest her arms on the planks. The stones of a handmade bracelet clinked on her wrist.

"Hello again, wolf."

۞

The raft was an assemblage of planks, hastily tied together with water-rotted twine. It shifted and groaned beneath his body, but it was a far better trade-off than the deadly sands of the isle they left behind. The witch was a counterbalance on the raft, her healing leg stretched between them as she watched the passing shore. She rubbed the blue stone between her fingers, the shard of sky, a faint light pulsing within as steady as a heartbeat. He couldn't take his eyes off it, wondering if it was *her* light.

He could almost feel Azzy's phantom limbs around him, shattering the shadows swallowing him up. Kai rested his chin on his forelegs, an empty ache in his chest. A human ache, a human yearning, but he could not dismiss it. It was part of him, same as the sinew, muscles, and wolf skin that bound him to this form. Two as one, one and the same, since his first bleating cry into this world.

The early years were easier to bear as a wolf. Wolves were strong, less fragile, and able to survive sooner on their own. His kind were quickly schooled in the varying cruelties of the world. The humans, in their deep cities, rejected the wildness of the wolf, while the monstrous lords of the Above wished to harness it, conscripted thugs for the vicious infighting amongst the city nobility. They were soldiers, mercenaries, attack dogs—but collared and chained, no better than slaves. Two forms and no place to belong. In time, that knowledge had broken him, like it had so many other wolves. He'd lost the control to become one over the other, forced by wicked collars until a cord of cloth and pale hair, like silk, wrapped around his neck.

The memory of their kiss haunted him, her mismatched eyes staring at him, truly seeing him for what he was.

A rap on the wooden slats distracted him, pulling him from the painful cycle of his thoughts. The witch bent over the back of the raft as the eel woman's face broke through the surface, whispering in her ear before sinking underneath the water.

"She is tucking us against the shore for the night. We all need to rest and recover our strength," said Safiya, wincing as she bent her leg. Her cuts had sealed to shiny pink scars, still puffy and new. She frowned, studying him from beneath her lashes. The faint moonlight silvered her skin like dark iron and made the tawny umber of her irises all the more striking. Whatever thoughts she had regarding the rapid healing of her wounds due to his ministrations, she thankfully kept to herself. It let Kai sink into the wolf, easing the ache of his heart as his human half submerged deep. He drifted on instinct, resting until the raft bumped against a rocky inlet—one of many along the cliff-lined shore—and clambered onto solid ground.

The witch followed, slow and stiff, turning to the eel woman in the water. "Thank you, Corrine, for answering the call. Your debt to me is paid."

The wolf lifted his head at the name. The significance of it was important enough to rouse the human, resistant as he was to wake. The eel woman's slit pupil eyes were on him.

"I shall hunt and rest. I will return for you in the morning." Her gaze swiveled up to the witch. "There is another debt I owe." Kai stared after the eel woman as she sank back into the river.

"She remembered her name a few days after you left," said Safiya, answering another unspoken question. "Said she remembered it bit by bit every time she traced her fingers along the stones of that bracelet—another humble gift from our lost friend. Do you know what I felt when I examined it, wolf?"

Kai looked at her, wondering what truth she would reveal to him. She held up her hands, open and lax.

"Nothing," she said, "not even the faintest hum of magic. But I knew it was there, it had to be." She caressed the blue stone hanging from her neck. "I bet you couldn't feel that cord round your neck, forgot it was there half the time. Not like the collars of those beastly Snatchers, was it?"

Kai sighed through his nose. He settled on the damp

shore, wishing to drift into a mindless slumber. But the witch had other intentions.

"Do you know what the strongest form of magic is, wolf?" Safiya ripped two thin strips of cloth from her shredded skirts as she spoke. "It's not the wild power that flows through your veins, though you are a strong specimen of it. Nor is it the smoky dark magic of the monstrous lords who rule Avergard." She palmed her blade, slicing a curling length of her dark red hair. "The witches use the magic of life and death, the swirling energies of the natural world, but there is another energy we can draw on. It's the strongest I know." Her fingers worked, swiftly braiding the cloth and hair into a familiar looking cord. "If I do this right, I might be able to create what she did."

Kai's attention locked on her, unable to look away as the words slowly sank in. His body was exhausted, but the temptation was too great. The witch untied the bandage on her sliced palm, hissing as she reopened the crusted wound. Fresh blood dripped onto the cloth, fat drops blooming like the poppies that grew in the Avergard gardens. Safiya murmured words that made the air throb. The bloodstains twisted, shrinking and writhing into a line of symbols. Sweat beaded the witch's brow, her eyes burning over-bright as she crawled on her knees to him.

She smelled of wildflowers, charcoal, and the faintest hint of bittersweet Rot—a scent of old death that clung to her skin, a murderer's scent. Kai forced himself not to move as she tied the cord around his neck, and didn't until the pain began.

The witch fell back at the first snarl, eyes wide as his pelt writhed. His bones snapped and shattered, reforming along shredding muscles and peeling skin. Horror in her eyes, she moved forward to take the cord off him. Kai held up a half-formed hand.

Safiya covered her mouth with shaking hands as she watched the transformation. Kai's howling cries gave way to hoarse screams. He fell back on the sand, gasping for air in lungs that didn't feel fully shifted, staring up at the cold stars pinned to the night sky—glittering, motionless witnesses. He lifted a human hand, studying it in his wavering vision. The witch had ripped the man from the inside out. Blood dotted his skin. Pain wracked his insides. The braided cord sat heavy on his chest and neck like a blade. This was too similar to the transformation of the Snatchers' collar, the agony of being ripped apart and pieced back together again.

It was not the instantaneous shimmer from one form to the next that Azure had created when she'd slipped the pale cord round his neck. The cord that made her bleed when she touched it.

"I tried," said the witch. He struggled to look at her, shivering against the chill night air. Safiya was shaken. The cut on her palm left a smear of blood across her lips. She looked down at her wounded hand. Within minutes she swayed, pale and sweating. The glassy sheen of her eyes darkened a moment before she coughed and spat up blood. The air pressed down on them both, squeezing his bones together until he gasped at the fresh hell the witch had trapped him in.

"Take it off," he pleaded through his teeth.

The witch shook her head, a trickle of blood running from the corner of her mouth. "Too soon, it could kill you."

"If you don't, it will kill us both," he gasped back. He couldn't draw a full breath. It felt like drowning again, like the cold depths of the ocean were closing over him. Water sloshed as his vision grayed and blurred. Something slid toward him along the shore, long and sinuous, moving with a predatory grace. A shadow fell over him, blotting out the watching silent stars. Drops of water hit his face. Tears? No, too cold, his mind reasoned, distant and unfocused, trying to process the little details as his body failed him. A cold wet hand clasped the cord around his neck and tore it free.

His mind protected him this time, blacking out through the change. The blissful cushion of unconsciousness did not last long, his instincts bristling from the proximity of a predator, forcing his body to wake. Kai whimpered. The cool hand gently stroked his head between his ears. He rested against slick gray flesh. The eel woman held him, whispering comfort to him until it penetrated the fog of fear and pain.

"Easy, wolf, easy," she hushed his whining growls, running her webbed fingers down through the fur of his ruff. Corrine, the witch called her Corrine. She was the one who had ripped the cord free. Across from them, the witch braced herself on hands and knees, scowling at the eel woman through bloodied teeth.

"You dare interfere—"

"You're a damn fool, witch," Corrine snapped. "Powerful as you are, you forget your limits."

Safiya slumped, the anger left her in a rush. "I had to try. I had to see if I could," said the witch. She sat back on her haunches, wiping the blood from her mouth. Her expression was one of wounded pride and remorse. "I'm sorry, wolf. I cannot give you what she did. I cannot fix you." Kai gave a soft whine, struggling to stay awake. Safiya looked at her hands, crestfallen, rubbing her bloodied fingers together.

"What was that?" Corrine kept her comforting hands on him, lending a strange sensation of safety even though she was as dangerous to him as any winnowrook.

Azure had trusted her. Kai forced his instincts to settle in the eel woman's presence.

"Blood magic," Safiya murmured, more to herself than her companions. "It is the strongest magic that exists, and the most taxing to use. It requires the essence of self, a price most cannot pay. It can bring down entire cities. The power of it is in the sacrifice. Those who use it usually don't live long."

Kai's heart squeezed at the thought. His memory stirred. He'd been half out of his mind, pinned beneath rock with death circling beneath the ground, but he remembered Azzy's frantic fingers braiding the cord, stained with ink. She hadn't used blood to draw the symbols like the witch. He wondered what would have happened if she had.

Safiya's gaze found his, a flicker of fear and excitement in the burning gold of her eyes. "That is not what Azure does. She created that spell from nothing, wove it into being from just a thought and untried instinct. There was no sacrifice—not truly. It was something else, something deeper that tied your essence to hers."

The eel woman's hand stilled. "She doesn't use blood magic?"

Safiya grasped the blue oval hanging from her neck, leaving rust-colored fingerprints. "No, I don't think she does."

The Theater of Flowers and Bone

ord Vashon parted the finely dressed crowd like a blade through a pool of petals; the brightly dressed patrons shied away from him as if afraid of his touch. The Snatcher shuffled uneasily at the man's approach, leaving Armin with a burgeoning sense of dread. What manner of being would all these gathered monsters fear? It was a surreal scene, since Lord Vashon possessed the most human appearance in the room. His height was average, his skin and hair muted natural tones compared to the complexions around him. No hint of other appendages or features to mark him as a predator, though he moved like one.

Camouflage, thought Armin.

The flaw was in his eyes—a mercurial gaze that radiated power like the press of a steel blade to the throat.

This was the lord who'd purchased him for a staggering amount of coin. One of the pale attendants slid beside Armin with a bow, holding up her hands while keeping her face turned down and away. The lord placed a neatly-tied ream of colored paper in her open palms. She slipped away as fast as she had appeared, leaving him reeling. Paper, Armin's life was worth nothing but slips of illustrated paper.

A hysterical thread of laughter stole up his throat, held at bay by the ever-present silver pins digging into his lips. Lord Vashon's shadow fell over him, blotting out the lights of the stage. Armin looked up into liquid silver.

"Come. Don't stray." The lord turned, not bothering to see if Armin followed his command. He soon found out why. The tug resonated through his whole body, wired into each vein and blood vessel. Armin's legs moved of their own volition, his movements jerky as invisible strings pulled him through the crowd. The other patrons made way for Lord Vashon once more. None met the lord's gaze, but their dispassionate eyes followed Armin—a collection of silent, appraising stares that made his skin crawl. Why were they silent? Why look at him and not at Lord Vashon?

They emerged into the bustle of the city proper, where the crowds continued to part without Lord Vashon speaking so much as a word. Armin could feel the weight of his power now, a fluid shimmering influence that slipped over his skin cool as silk. His footsteps smoothed out, mirroring the lord's in a perfected pantomime.

Where was the lord taking him? What did he mean to do to him?

A blonde head of hair winked through the pedestrian crowd, a minnow flashing through a stream. Armin jerked, his eyes tracking the movement. The blonde had her back to him, walking away, the set of her shoulders so familiar his chest ached.

"Azzy," he whispered. Armin thrashed and stumbled. The lord's invisible puppet strings were severed.

He didn't stop to think, chasing after the retreating figure that called to him with a siren song. *Follow her, follow her, find her, save her.* The last thought jolted through him, ringing false. Azzy never needed saving. How could she possibly be here? He remembered his last dream of her, the agony and awful silence of it. His steps faltered. The figure stopped, as if sensing his sudden hesitation. She peered over her shoulder. A chill crept over him. *Not your sister. Not your sister.*

The female smiled at him, beckoning him to her with too-long fingers. Her eyes were hungry black pits in her face. Her smile faltered as a hand fell on his shoulder. Armin watched the feverish hunger in her face twist to fear before she melted into the crowd. The urge to chase her faded to a whisper as the presence at his back swept over him. The hand on his shoulder spun him around to stare up into the silvery gaze of his new owner.

"Did I not tell you, don't stray? Follow the hollow-eyed ladies, lad—" he said, his voice even and without anger, "—and they will eat you alive, literally." He stared at where the blonde woman had vanished, his expression thoughtful. "She wouldn't have caught your eye at all unless she had a way in."

It was the longest sentence the lord had spoken since taking Armin off the auction block. His voice possessed a lyrical cadence that made passing pedestrians sway on their feet. The crowd skimmed around them, giving them a wide berth. The lord studied his acquisition for another long moment, the sensation of silk threads winding around Armin until he flinched. Whatever Lord Vashon was beneath his subdued gray silk and velvet disguise, it was as monstrous as everyone else in this wretched city.

As monstrous as Armin was going to become.

The thought lacked the urgency it had possessed before, ever since he entered Lord Vashon's presence. Armin didn't know if that was for good or ill as the lord led him to a boxy vehicle parked at the far end of the auction house. Armin stared at the contraption, wrought of sleek metal in a curving shape smoother than any cart he'd seen, with mirrored squares of glass that concealed the interior compartment. There were no visible reins or hookups to pull the metallic box, and its shape certainly didn't indicate how it moved. He was still puzzling over it when the lord pulled the latch and a portion of the metal side swung open on a soundless hinge.

The interior was nothing like a cart, comprised of cushioned benches coated with the buttery leather of some unknown beast. Lord Vashon slid inside, tugging Armin along after him. The panel slammed shut behind them with a hollow clap, enclosing them in the plush interior. Armin fidgeted in his seat as the lord knocked on a glass partition behind his head.

He jumped as some unseen creature rumbled beneath him.

"Easy, boy. It's merely the engine," said the lord, though nothing could ease Armin's nerves as the vehicle started forward, gliding through the crowds, a metallic dragon on the prowl. His fingers dug into the seat as he watched the scenery scroll by faster and faster.

"Let's have a look, shall we?"

Armin froze when Lord Vashon reached forward and unclasped the muzzle. Both winced as he peeled it away. The pins were embedded in his skin from his tumultuous experience in the auction house, leaving his mouth a bruised and bloody mess.

"Fools," Lord Vashon muttered, retrieving a handkerchief from his breast pocket to dab at Armin's bleeding lips. "Such a brutish device wouldn't have stopped you."

He peered up at the silver-eyed lord. What did he mean? The muzzle had stopped him when he would have destroyed the auction house to nothing but ashes. He would have screamed and screamed until everyone fell at his feet, innocent or monstrous.

A smile twitched the lord's wide mouth. "And yet, you kept yourself from doing just that. Not one to kill...innocents, are you boy?"

As if he had reached in and plucked the thought from Armin's mind with his gloved fingers. Armin shuddered away from his touch. Lord Vashon wasn't offended by the reaction and continued to gently dab at his wounds.

"I wonder," said the lord, "what temptation the hollow-eyed woman dangled to lure you. Strong enough to disrupt my hold. A lost love perhaps?" The lord sat back, removing his hat to smooth a hand through his close-cropped dark hair, as neatly trimmed as his beard. His eyes seemed to glimmer in the passing street lights.

"No, not a lover. I doubt you are old enough to understand love. A far deeper bond. A sibling."

"Stop it," Armin rasped through his torn lips. The layered echo was still present in his voice, but weak from forced disuse. Would the lord perish if Armin told him to?

"I'm afraid your ability is muted at present. It will not work."

"Get out of my head," said Armin. He forced his gaze away from the unsettling lord. The man said nothing until Armin's eyes inexorably found their way to him once more, unable to look away for long.

"If you wish me out of your head, then keep me out."

Armin didn't know what to say to such a statement. In a way, the lord reminded him of Azzy with her uncanny ability to see the intentions of others. Her face and name popped into his mind before he thought better of it. He paled at the spark of interest in Lord Vashon's silver eyes.

"A sister?"

Armin launched from the seat, tearing at the lord's shirt

as he seized him. "You will not speak of her," he hissed. He banished her from his thoughts, refusing to give the lord anything else. His interest merely intensified at Armin's reaction.

"Release me," said the lord. Armin grunted as invisible strings yanked him back, pinning him to the seat. Lord Vashon perched on the edge of his seat, peering hard into Armin's face. His silver irises began to glow. "Tell me more about this sister."

Armin clicked his teeth together, turning his head as the lord's silken influence wormed its way through his skull. Velvety fingers dug into his mind.

"NO." The word erupted from his mouth, strained and hoarse, but it was enough. Lord Vashon eased back against the seat, stroking his chin. He appeared thoughtful rather than irritated by Armin's resistance.

"You're closer to the change than I thought," he said. The words made the itch flare beneath Armin's skin. "Excellent. From what I've observed so far, you may prove to be a useful tool for my pet project after all."

Their transport came to a halt.

Armin peered out the window at a street of neatly spaced homes, a far cry from the crowded ramshackle clusters of the Heap. The homes themselves were as spectacular as the transport that carried them there: tall elegant structures of stone and metal. But when Lord Vashon opened the hatch to their ride, the air felt heavy and stale. The shadows were deeper. The splendor reminded him of the abandoned city above the Heap. Death resided here.

"This way," said the lord, giving him a wink on the last word, a reminder of his purchase. Armin felt the same inescapable tug as before, forcing him forward, dragging him from the transport and down the lined walkway.

Lord Vashon's residence possessed the same hollow feel

as the street, surrounded by vibrant plant life that dripped over the high fences attempting to contain it. Despite the concentration of so much green, Armin couldn't tear his gaze away from the massive windows of glass—dark gaping portals watching their approach. There were no lights, no movements within. The transport pulled away from the mouth of the path. Armin never saw what propelled it or who—if anyone—drove it. The door before them swung open. He dug his heels into the ground, but Lord Vashon's grip was tighter than before, shackles of invisible silk stronger than the iron that bound his wrists. He wanted to scream but his mouth refused to open.

The lord dragged him over the threshold. The door slammed shut, casting them into darkness.

Armin's heart pounded in his chest. They were not alone. He could hear the whisper of cloth, of soft steps moving around him. Lord Vashon kept him bound in place as unseen beings surrounded them.

"Lights," the lord commanded. There a soft click followed by the flicker of lights overhead; the electricity made Armin's molars tingle. The abruptness of the light blinded him, his vision slowly clearing to reveal the night-mares he was expecting to see.

He pressed back against the door, warily eyeing the loose circle of monstrous beings surrounding them. Their servant uniforms didn't register until Lord Vashon handed his torn coat and hat to a tall woman, her skirts writhing in odd places. She bowed to her lord, the hinge of her hips in the wrong location. Two of her eight eyes peered at Armin with quiet curiosity. The other servants shared similar oddi-ties. One little boy, younger than Armin himself, shimmered like a ghost, intangible from one moment to the next.

"Hello, my loves, I've brought home a new toy," said Lord Vashon, his tone cold and detached. The head woman turned all her glittering eyes on him. The imprint of an hourglass peeked out from beneath her bangs.

"Is this the one?" the little boy spoke as he darted in between the others. He studied Armin with measured disdain.

"There is excellent potential," said Lord Vashon.

The boy sneered. "He barely looks like he'll survive the fever, never mind the Gate—"

"Hush. Shall we bathe him, master?" said the woman. There was a lisp to her words, as if the contents of her mouth didn't quite fit behind her lips.

"Not quite yet, Adele. Emory, how close is he?"

One of the other women approached him, her appearance normal but for the seam of skin that ran down the middle of her face, disappearing beneath her collar. She stood in front of Armin, studying him with two lustrous brown eyes, holding his gaze until the seam began to split open like a red wet maw...

Armin blinked. The girl, Emory, stood before him, normal as before, the seam closed as if it had never opened. He felt moisture tracking down his cheek. He raised his hand, brushing away a bloody tear.

Emory turned to the others, none of them fazed by whatever had just taken place. Armin pressed harder into the door, wishing he could sink through it.

"He's hovering on the edge, my lord," she said in a discordant tone, like two voices speaking at once.

"Hmm, bring him to the theater," said Lord Vashon, stalking away from the group. The moment the lord was out of sight, his influence shattered.

Fever swept through Armin. The lord's presence had truly halted what was happening to him. Now he swayed on his feet. His vision blurred as his temperature spiked. He couldn't fight off the servants if he tried.

Emory laid a hand on his forehead, her skin like ice against his fevered heat. "Best hurry. Not long now."

The others surged forward, half carrying, half dragging him down shadowed corridors and winding stone steps. Armin couldn't track his surroundings, not until the end when the group deposited him in a round pit of a room. He fell to his hands and knees on top of crumbling bones, scrambling back to the circular stone walls as he recognized the remains of long dead humans. And they *were* human—not misshapen or altered by the twisting magic that hummed beneath his skin.

Why were they left here to rot?

"Because they did not change," came Lord Vashon's voice, high and cold, echoing from above him. Armin looked up to see stars. A perfect circle of them pinned to a swatch of night sky. Lord Vashon was nowhere to be seen but he knew the man watched him.

"Time to see if my investment was worthwhile. To see if you survive."

Armin ignored him as the fever increased, his blood steaming in his veins. His breathing grew shallow and uneven. An unbearable itch settled between his shoulders, and if the fever hadn't sapped his energy, he would have clawed off his skin. His eyes focused for a moment, meeting the empty sockets of a yellowed skull. Long dead, beyond the reach of the world's poisonous magic.

Which of them was the more fortunate?

His fingers curled in the dirt floor beneath him. *Not long now.* Emory's words rolled through him, drawing a sob as their truth sank in. He stared up at the distant stars. His last sight as a human.

"What trouble have you found yourself in, brother-mine?"

He couldn't bear to look. He knew she wasn't real, wasn't with him, no matter how fiercely he wished for it.

The hallucination of his sister persisted, hovering beside him, close enough to touch, but neither reached for the other, maintaining the illusion.

The ground began to glow, tugging his gaze from the stars above to the flowers that pushed their way through the dirt, a field of sun-like stars beneath him, their tufted heads flaring open as he watched. Dandelions, the Rustic Oracle, the heralds of magic. Armin whimpered.

"I'm here, Armin, I'm here," whispered Azzy. *"To the end."*

Cracking

He followed her through the dark. The dancing flame of his lantern brought out the filaments of gold in Azzy's fine hair, carelessly braided down her back. So careless, his sister-mine, everything about her pieces of a puzzle that didn't quite fit. She never fit. Tossed together and selfless as a saint; she was too good for anyone in the Heap. His heart ached at the idea of his sister trapped in shadows and dust for the rest of her life. Yet here she was, risking her life for the people who despised her...

Armin tensed. The chittering of the wailing natters echoed in the hollowed dark. He remembered this place. This was where they'd found the supply wagon. He stumbled. His foot plunged through the ripped-open torso of the lost Forager, the rotting flesh giving way beneath his boot, sinking him further in the foul mess of tissue, brackish blood staining his pants. The shattered ribs scratched along his shin until they bit down—jagged teeth that pierced him. He felt the flare of fire in his veins, venom threading through his system...

He fell forward, gasping for air. The lantern rolled from his fingers, sputtering and flickering as it struggled to stay lit.

The maw of ribs held fast, pinning him to the ground as heat crept through him, sweeping beneath the surface of his skin. This was different than before. Something was wrong, something had changed. Wildfire. Azzy spun, the gold filaments of her hair sparking in the low light. Was this a dream? She fell to her knees, crawling toward him as the wailing natters swooped overhead, growing bolder and bolder as the flame sputtered. He watched the outline of her face, her worry, her determination to save him.

The flame died but they were not plunged into darkness. The Rustic Oracle bloomed around them, its golden glow too bright to look at. He watched Azzy instead, her eyes wide with panic.

She drew up short, staggering as she rose to her knees. Blood seeped from an unseen wound in her chest. No, it gushed—it poured down her front, pooling on the earthen floor. Too much, too much blood.

"Azzy." He reached for her as the monster of bone and rot pumped its necrotic venom into his leg. She pressed her hands to the bloody fabric of her shirt, trying to stem the flow. Her face was too pale. What had happened to her?

Her body vanished, ripped away into the dark.

"No!" Armin screamed. The voices rose and erupted out of him as the cave melted away, revealing the theater, filled with yellowed bones and the swelling tufts of the Rustic Oracle. The dandelion heads tickled his forearms, teasing his nose with a hint of clean air and sunlight. He stared at the glowing flowers, trying to burn out the image of Azzy's body being torn away like a lifeless doll. His lips were alarmingly dry, cracking open when he screamed. He tried to lick them but found not a drop of moisture in his mouth. He doubled over with a dry hacking cough.

It vibrated through his body.

Something was wrong, something...fire in his veins.

The memory became reality, the flip of an invisible switch. Armin rolled, clutching his head as he screamed himself hoarse. Acid ate him away from inside, bubbling beneath the skin, dissolving bone and tissue until he was nothing but raw nerves on fire. His voice broke, his screams soundless as he twisted, spine popping, disjointed, turning beyond its former limits. He could feel them, he could feel them growing from his spine, slithering beneath his skin, scratching away at the thin membrane. Armin bucked, hugging his torso, feeling the inferno blazing inside him, baking him from the inside out. He was dying.

Cool hands slipped around his head, lifting him into a familiar lap. He glanced up through fevered eyes at his sister's face. Altered. The eyes that peered down at him were two different colors, one pale colorless iris peering straight through him. There were fresh scars, but it was her. Her cool hand stroked his forehead, her expression one of sadness. She wasn't bleeding now, was whole and intact and here by his side. She smoothed his hair from his eyes, cradled his face between her palms.

"Remember," she murmured, her smile sad and serene.

His mind blanked as the fever took him.

৩৯৩

It wasn't his first unnatural fever. He was much younger at the time, but the memory came to him with a fierce clarity. He lay on a pallet in his mother's workshop. Bottles of liquid sloshed in painstakingly labeled rows, the memories and regrets of their neighbors. His body was wracked with dry coughs that brought blood bubbling to his lips. Heat and more heat beneath his skin. Dying. His mother's hands trembled as she wrung a cloth in water, pressing it to his forehead. Her lips kissed the damp cloth as she whispered to him, imploring him to stay, to survive. He remembered rain on his face, cooler than the heat within, splashing against his cheek and the bridge of his nose. He hadn't realized, at the time, that it was her tears.

Azzy burst through the shop door, dragging Brixby through, her other arm brimming with bundles of herbs.

"I brought him, I brought him." She dropped her burden on the work table, half crawling to Armin's side, blue eyes wide. He imagined he could see the summer sky when he looked in her eyes, could float away into the endless blue. Another dry cough seized him. Azzy's fingers grasped his, anchoring him to the earth.

Their mother cupped Azzy's face, kissing her cheek before she rose. "Watch him." A plea, her face strained by fear. She joined Brixby's side as the two began frantic work at the table.

"You mean to poison him again?" Brixby's admonishment was sharp.

"What would you have me do? Let them banish my son to the Above?" Their mother's hands shook so hard she dropped the herbs, bracing herself on the table until Brixby slid his hand over hers. "He's just a boy. My boy." Her whisper was a rasp, her hands gripping the table until her knuckles burned white. "I can't save my boy."

Brixby's mien softened, his dark skin stark against hers: shadow and snow. He dragged her hands off the table, tucking her against his chest as he stroked her copper fire curls. "We'll bring him back. We'll—"

The floor of the shop gave an audible crack as the Rustic Oracle thrust up through the floorboards, rearing its tufted head toward the siblings. Azzy's fingers tightened around Armin's as he watched the golden glow, mesmerized.

His mother darted forward with a cry, ripping it up, shredding it between her shaking fingers. "The windows," she said, her eyes wild. Brixby had already shut them, stuffing rags into the cracks, leaving the room stuffy and closed.

"We are running out of time, Lia," Brixby pulled their mother back to the work table.

"What if the potion doesn't work? What if we can't suppress it anymore?" She wrung her hands, unable to tear her eyes away from her children.

Brixby tucked his fingers beneath her chin, forcing her to look at him. "Then we find something else."

Armin felt the shift in their concentration, the two immersing themselves in the work, leaving him to Azzy. His sister stretched beside him, pulling him tight against her. She didn't tremble like their mother. There were no tears, but her grip was fierce, tightening when his body seized with coughs. He blazed in her grip, certain his skin would scald her, but Azzy remained with him, stoic and strong. Always so strong.

"I'm scared, sister-mine," he confessed to her. He felt her stiffen before she pulled back, her hands on either side of his face. Her blue eyes bore into him, stripping away the haze that clouded his mind.

"I'll save you," she whispered, pressing her forehead to his, flinching at the heat of his skin. "I'll find you." He frowned at her words. He was right here. He didn't understand the promise until he focused on her eyes, blank and glassy. Staring beyond him. Her mouth continued to move with unspoken words.

"Azzy?"

Her pocket knife appeared in her hand. He watched,

unable to look away as she sliced a long thick strand of her hair free. She sat up, her mouth continuing to move, the words silent. He couldn't understand them. His sister nodded as if listening to someone, pulling apart the hair into three even strips she braided together. The shining cord grew as he watched her. He never realized how golden her hair was—it looked so pale in the feeble streetlights of the Heap.

Azzy tilted her head. Armin jumped as the knife flashed across her palm. Blood spilled over her pale skin. He could hear the drops fall against the shop floor. It was the only sound in his ears. Her pupils dilated as her hands moved faster, dipping and drawing symbols on the braided cord, moving so fast they blurred. The blood moved, solidifying, stark as ink before the symbols disappeared. Azzy leaned over him, tying the braided cord round his neck.

Electricity—a white-hot bolt of lightning—struck his spine before he numbed. The coolness spread through him, a fluid sensation like melting snow. Azzy lay back next to him, her palm still bleeding freely as her good hand wrapped his. Her eyes were blank when they met his, but he could feel the bond between them, the power of her blood twisting around him, smothering and stamping the magic that threatened to burst out of him. He felt the cool chain of her influence wrapping around whatever was inside him, weighing it down, burying it deep. The fever evaporated.

Armin released a breath, exhausted.

"I will always find you," Azzy whispered. Her eyes closed as she slept. The cord sat heavy on his skin, leeching the heat from him. Their mother squawked, rushing over, Brixby on her heels.

"What has she done?" Her fingers brushed the cord round Armin's neck, and she startled as it disintegrated into ash, gray powder coating her fingers. Her eyes widened as her other hand laid on his forehead. "His fever...it's gone."

"Have you ever seen anything like this?" Brixby's voice was filled with awe and the smallest sliver of fear.

Their mother shook her head, her expression unreadable as she stared at her children. "Never." The adults startled at the pounding on the front door. The shouts were muffled but the color leeched from his mother's face. She grabbed Brixby's wrist. "Give me as much time as you can."

He answered with a nod, leaving them as their mother pressed her fingers to Azzy's temples, drawing a silvery thread of memory. It was the last memory she took. This was Armin's last memory before the Elder carted his mother away to the burning room.

He turned his head, peering at his unconscious sister. Her hand never released his.

I will always find you.

🕉️

The scream tore from his lips before he was fully awake. Armin rolled onto his knees, away from the phantom presence of his sister. His back bowed on a breathless gasp. The skin began to split, hot rivulets of blood dripping down his sides. He heard each drop as it hit the ground, echoing in his ears. They slid from him, these new limbs, blood-coated like a newborn, stretching up to the observing stars overhead. A bloodied feather drifted down, landing sticky and wet, on the back of his hand. He stared at it, shaking hard.

The yellowed skull began to clack, jawing up and down as more dandelions burst into being through the floor, pushing up between his splayed fingers, through the empty eye sockets of the skull. Their golden glow seemed to sink into his skin, lighting up his veins. No, his veins were truly aflame, burning. His skin cracked like overheated glass.

Pain like nothing he'd ever felt flooded through him. Blood dripped from his gasping lips as his insides tore apart. He could feel his very self—his soul—peeling away. Memories faded, flaking away like ash. The change was on him, devouring the person he once was to spit out something dark, twisted, and new. Armin screamed and screamed, thrashing against the pain, against the horrible sensation of loss that coiled around him, squeezing tighter and tighter, determined to make him disappear. He was losing himself.

Pale hands slid over his, framed by a curtain of pale hair threaded in gold. Armin struggled to look up into Azzy's eyes.

She smelled like how he used to imagine sunshine— bright and hot—the light he'd spent his entire life chasing, sheltered by it. Protected. There for each small wound, each skinned knee and childish tear. There when the fever gripped him in its inexorable grip, wrenching him free through sheer will. Not even their mother had managed such a feat. Their mother...Azzy had been there for that too, pressing his face against her shoulder. She'd held him nestled between her and Brixby as their mother turned to ash and smoke in the burning room. Her sunshine scent had filled his nose, banishing the scent of burnt hair and meat that choked the air, her whispering voice blocking the taunts of the others and their mother's broken cries.

It was Azzy who had shielded him from thrown stones and cruel words. Who had held him through every nightmare, through the long months when the voices ravaged his throat, pouring out of him? She had anchored him through each one, perhaps in more ways than he'd known. He could still feel the cord around his neck, an invisible symbol, binding them together.

She was there, in the nattering cave when the magic finally broke free. Somehow, she was here now. He felt it, knew it by instinct. It was Azzy, truly here. A sob broke from his lips.

Here to the end.

"Armin," she said, forcing his gaze to meet hers through the pain. "Remember."

Remember what? The words wouldn't leave his lips. Another bloodied feather floated to the ground, speckled black and gray. His gaze flicked to it as a shiver went through him. His fingertips were blackening, the color spreading up his arms. Something snapped within his rib cage. He bellowed, trying to curl into himself. Azzy didn't release his hands.

"Remember."

His gaze snapped up to her mismatched eyes. Brixby had warned him about this: the fever, the forgetting...

Who was Brixby?

His breath came in short pants, his nails digging into the dirt floor as he tried to gain purchase. Pieces of him were slipping away, dissolving, blown away by a breath. He looked down at Azzy's hands on his and gasped, his panic mounting as her skin blackened where it met his, cracking and flaking away at his poisonous touch. His sister was burning away.

"No, please, no," he sobbed, shifting his hands to clasp hers. The blackening spread, flaking up her arms, her chest —to her face in a blink. But her eyes never left his.

"Remember," she said. A tear left her blue eye, tracking down her cracked ashen face. Her hair withered as he watched, gold to gray, pieces breaking and falling to the earthen floor. A cry choked in his mouth. He wanted to beg her to stay, to never leave him, even as the rest of him flaked away. Her hand slid out of his own. For a breathless moment, he thought she was going to blow away into ashes, but her blackened fingers traced his neck in a looping circle until they rested against his frantic heart, pounding in his chest.

"Here," she said, her voice a distant echo but strong, etching into his fading memory. She pressed her hand against his heart. "I'm here Armin. Remember, I will always find you."

She shattered, black and gray ashes sifting through his fingers, joining the bloodied feathers to swirl around him. He rose to his knees, lifting his face to the endless stars, new limbs stretching wide from his spine. The dandelions faded, the tufts bursting to feathery shreds that floated, dull and lifeless around him.

Who was Armin?

PART III
WOVEN

Linens and Scars

Azzy opened her eyes to sun-bleached canvas.

Her body was a collection of throbbing aches and sore muscles. One massive bruise that was skewered through and through. Each short breath hit her lungs like inhaling broken glass. Her limbs felt too heavy, encased in rock. She lay in a tent, muted light streaming through the canvas to warm her face, on a cot that sagged in the middle. The murmuring voices were a quiet hum at the back of her thoughts, like a stream trickling through the woods. *Where was she? What happened to her?* Armin's face flit across her fogged memory. Her fingertips tingled.

Moisture tracked and pooled on the right side of her face, clinging to her lashes and plastering her hair to her temple, now a sticky mess compared to the dry left side. She attempted to lift her hand and wipe the area. A chord of pain sang through her at the motion, drawing a startled cry that caught in her throat.

The front flap of the canvas lifted, the dazzling sunlight blotted by the misshapen figure that filled the entrance.

Azzy froze, eyes wide as the blurry image settled, revealing the uneven face of a Snatcher. The expression on his malformed face was impossible to read. He hunched over, squeezing his bulk into the confines of the tent. She squirmed, attempting to roll away from him, but her watery muscles could barely lift her limbs. She shrank in on herself as the hulking monster loomed over her. She closed her eyes as he reached for her.

A single gentle finger smoothed the damp hair off her face.

Azzy blinked, peering up at the Snatcher as his hands moved down her body in an impersonal perusal. Her skin was covered in bandages, the thickest of all round her chest. The center of the firestorm, obscured by swaths of stiff white cloth.

"Can you lift your arms over your head, little one?"

She looked up at a pair of lopsided brown eyes. Through the aches and pain, the inner voices stirred, familiar as her heartbeat, endless whispers. She focused on them, her head cocked to the side as she held his brown eyes with her own.

They radiated warmth.

Azzy swallowed and tried to lift her arms. A white-hot rod of pain pierced through her chest, blinding her. She bit down on her shriek and slumped forward. The strange Snatcher caught her, easing her back with a worried frown on his mashed-up face.

"I was afraid of that. Your healing is quite slow," he said, *tsk*ing to himself. He proceeded to shuffle around the tent, which dwarfed by his size. The confining space didn't faze him as he stripped the yellowed blanket covering her. Azzy had a brief, dizzying glimpse of her bruised and bandaged body before the Snatcher fetched a fresh one from somewhere behind him. He fluffed and fussed, tucking the blanket loosely around her with care. "I need to change your bandage. You need fresh salve and I want to make sure your wound isn't infected."

She opened her mouth to speak and erupted into hoarse coughs, a dreadful result, the pain so fierce she was gasping for air when the Snatcher lifted her head up and brought a cup to her lips.

"Drink little one," he said, clear concern in his craggy face. Confused and overwhelmed, she drank, the cool liquid tinged with bitter herbs—an immediate relief to her dry throat. Azzy sighed, feeling the tingling rush in her limbs as the herbs dulled the fiery pain. She recognized these effects. Her mystery Snatcher was an apothecary.

The relief unlocked the grip the pain had on her memories. Azzy drew a breath as the Snatcher bustled about. The frantic run along the cliffs, the dive into the frigid deep waters below, Kai's mouth on hers, and that final terrible choice played through her mind in flickering slow motion. She'd survived, somehow, she had survived.

The hook had pierced her, ripped her away, and torn her inside—the moment was fresh in her thoughts. Everything after was disjointed pieces of agony and blurred recollections. She couldn't remember stopping, though she remembered the ring of astonished misshapen faces looming over her, peering down at her. The strange Snatcher had been there, the closest of all, his features twisted in abject horror at the sight of her. He'd bent down, gingerly scooped her off the ground, cradled her against him with such care. It had been her last sight before darkness gripped her, pulling her down.

"Who are you?"

The Snatcher's movements halted, hovering over the rolls of bandages he'd set beside her. A flash of uncertainty and fear crossed his face. What did a Snatcher fear?

"I'm Morglint," he said, falling back into the familiarity

of his actions. "I need to undo your bandages." He braced a folded blanket against her lower back as he spoke. His massive paw-like hands moved with surprising precision as he undid the knotted bandage at her side. She obligingly leaned in and out for the motions, swallowing as the layers unwound, revealing a spreading dark stain that hadn't seeped through the top layer. She forced herself to look, to see what the bandages revealed as the last layer fell away.

A weeping mouth, sewn shut by black twine in an angry grimace, the flesh puckered and raw between the stitches. Azzy swallowed hard, staring at her ruined skin. The Snatcher caught her hand before she could touch it. She met his gaze, the compassion in his eyes almost too much for her.

"It's too soon for your touch, little one," he said, releasing her as he held up a bowl of paste, the astringent scent harsh to her nose. A fresh cloth covered his hand as he scooped the paste onto her wound. His movements were featherlight, but the sting of the herbs still made her hiss and grip the sides of her cot until her fingers were numb. "Not infected. It will scar, but it will be a clean scar, not like that mark on your leg."

Azzy had forgotten it, the memory of the bone eater piercing her thigh faded and buried by all that had happened after. She shifted the blanket down until it was visible, amid the deep bruising on her skin: a dent, a chunk missing from her thigh where the monster had stabbed her through and through. Unlike her chest, this wound was completely healed, the scar tissue white and smooth, as if it had happened years ago. Her fingers traced along the scar on her thigh as the Snatcher wrapped a fresh bandage around her torso. There was a fierce ache in her chest that had nothing to do with her wound.

Had he gotten away?

Morglint tied the ends of cloth off when the question left her lips. "Did you catch anything else after they reeled me in?" Her tone was light, but the Snatcher sighed, easing his bulk onto an empty cot beside her. His blunt fingers tapped an unspoken code atop her blanket as Morglint glanced out through the narrow gap of the tent. He nodded, leaning in close to her, his gravelly voice low as he spoke.

"They were a bit preoccupied by what they did catch to set up a fresh hook for a wolf," he said, watching her face as he spoke. Searching for her reaction. The internal whispers rose. Azzy stilled.

It was different. There were words now, the murmuring whispers sharper, clearer, filtering pieces of information. A clarity she'd never felt before. It went beyond the guiding push and pull of instinct that kept her alive. She knew Morglint, knew he was the one who had saved her life with skills the other Snatchers scoffed and reviled. Knew he continued to save her life by keeping the others from her tent, protecting her as he had protected countless humans before her, an outcast among his own. The knowledge was there, as if it had always been. It flared in her mind—dazzlingly clear for a single instant—and subsided, receding and fading until she could no longer grasp the specifics, only the feeling behind them. Morglint was a friend.

Azzy slipped her fingers over his, holding his gaze. "Thank you for saving me," she whispered. His eyes darted, his expression thick with anxious fear. "It's okay, no one's around. They can't hear me."

Morglint's expression relaxed into softer anxiety, the panic dispersing as he eyed her. "How do you know?"

She shrugged, immediately regretting the movement as her wound protested. "I just do."

The Snatcher continued to study her, until a light of understanding slowly lit his face. "It wasn't an accident they hooked a slip of a girl instead of a great wolf, was it, little one?"

Azzy shook her head, causing the Snatcher to scowl at her. "Then you're a fool, human. That hook should have shredded you to pieces. That you survived at all is a damn miracle."

"Only because you told the others you would dispose of me," she said, staring down at her scarred leg. It was the Snatcher's silence that made her look up.

"You were awake?" Shame tinged the Snatcher's skin a deep russet brown, deeper than his eyes. "I'm sorry, little one. My brethren, they don't...they don't place the same value on life. Especially those they feel wouldn't survive the journey to the Avergard markets. A mortally wounded untainted being would be a waste of time and resources."

Untainted. The word burned in her ears. Azzy shook herself, giving the tent another cursory glance. "This is your tent."

"They generally leave me alone here. Eventually they'll know you survived. This was the best place to hide you till then," he said, his skin darkening further. The Snatcher's embarrassment teased a small smile out of her.

Morglint's tent comprised of two cots, one for her and a slightly wider one for him. Stacks of boxes filled the surrounding space, overflowing with dried herbs, stoppered vials, and all manner of apothecary necessities that reminded her of her lost guardian. On top of a low box was an array of unfamiliar tools, gleaming metal instruments with cutting edges and a roll of black twine. The tools Morglint had used to save her life.

He noticed her attention on them and quickly covered them with a spare cloth.

"Is that why they stay away?" Azzy meant the words in jest but Morglint's expression fell.

"Never mind that little one," he said, placing a hand on her shoulder to ease her back. "You need to rest, to heal. There isn't much time before we break camp for the markets."

Azzy didn't need the Snatcher to tell her. She could feel the sucking exhaustion dragging at her, but his mention of the markets nearly had her sitting up again. "The markets?"

He didn't quite meet her eyes as he answered. "Yes, the night markets. In Avergard."

Her heart slammed against her ribs and the sudden jump in her pulse left her dizzy. She wasn't sure how, but she knew to her core that was where she must go. To Avergard, to Armin.

Morglint misread her paling face. He gripped her ankle, drawing her attention to him. "I won't let them sell you, not like this," he said, his tone low and sincere.

The Snatcher meant every word.

Azzy nodded, forcing herself to calm before her excitement made her pass out. "They'd sell me whether I am tainted or not?" She didn't miss the shudder in his massive shoulders at her question.

"It's usually worse for the pure ones. They sell fast, but unless they have viable skills they don't last long." said the Snatcher. Morglint's description left her cold.

"You're so sure I'm not tainted?"

He nodded, pulling a stoppered glass bottle from his array of boxes. He handed it to her, watching her fingers stiffly curl around it. "See? Pure human as they come, little one, though you must share with me sometime how you came to be on the other end of that hook. Now rest." He eased himself from the tent, leaving Azzy to stare at the bottle in her hand.

KRISTIN JACQUES

Crushed Rustic Oracle, the same damnable powder that had condemned her brother. She stared at the dull vial until she couldn't keep her eyes open. It didn't flicker once.

Outcast

Time blurred between moments of consciousness, a great internal pendulum between waking and sleep. She could feel it, whenever she fought to open her eyes—the inevitable passage of time, chased by a dread she couldn't define. As if her time had run out without her knowing. Azzy woke with her brother's name on her lips, tears gathering on the eyelashes of her good eye. Her left eye, the altered eye, remained dry and clear.

"That's the third time you've called his name in your sleep." Morglint rumbled from the cot beside her. She turned her head to find him lying down, watching her. Weak gray predawn light filtered through the canvas, casting deep shadows on his uneven features. It should have made him menacing, fearsome to behold, but Azzy felt no fear of the Snatcher. He shifted beneath a threadbare blanket, propping himself on one arm. "Is this Armin the reason you were wandering with wolves in the woods?"

Azzy eased the rest of her body onto her side, the pain in her chest a dull throb compared to its former sharpness. She lay parallel to Morglint, their conversation reminding her of the nights Armin would come find her, unable to sleep, stretching out beside her to talk until the street lamps were lit. An odd comparison, but one that felt right.

"Yes," she said, "They cast my brother out of our home because he was tainted. Right into the arms of the Snatchers."

Morglint sighed. "That clarifies a lot about you, little one. Was he all you had left?"

"No. We had a guardian, who loved us like his own. He followed me to the Above. The last time I saw him, he was in the grip of the same Snatchers who had my brother," she said. The admission made the muscles in her chest tighten, reminding her of her failure with Brixby. "He was an apothecary, like you."

Morglint chuckled. "Oh, I doubt that. He's likely far better than me."

"If he still lives." The words left her lips as a whisper, the fear she'd carried with her since her desperate run through the woods. She'd left him behind to save her own skin. The memory was a bitter sting in her weeping right eye. Morglint reached over, gently grasping her hand in his.

"Listen to me, little one," he said, his face somber. "If your guardian was a pure human like you, they would consider him too valuable to kill. If he had the skills of an apothecary on top of that, he would make them a fortune at the night auctions. They might threaten and bluster, but my brethren are motivated by greed. Your guardian is still alive."

"Thank you, Morglint," said Azzy, pressing a hand to her heart, inches from her healing wound. The two stared at one another as the sky lightened overhead. "You aren't motivated by greed."

The Snatcher scoffed, shifting. "So certain, are you?"

"Yes," said Azzy.

Morglint looked away. He still held her hand, caught in the act of comfort. His pulse jumped as she spoke. There it was—that inexplicable fear.

"Little one—"

"It's Azzy," she said. "You aren't greedy, Morglint. You are kind."

"I can't afford to be," he said softly, peering out through the narrow opening of the tent. "It's not acceptable for what I am. None of this is," he said, waving a careless hand at the overflowing boxes of instruments and herbs.

"Why not?"

Morglint's uneven brow twitched. "Tell me something, Azzy. Were there wealthy merchants and craftsmen where you came from?"

"There were those with coin and those without," she said, "and those who lorded what they had over those who didn't."

"That is something the Above and below have in common," said Morglint, releasing her hand to pick up one of his silvery metal instruments, an oddly shaped knife with a short flat blade at the end. He ran the sharp tip against his calloused fingertip. "Our class system might be more structured than yours. There are the lords, who rule the cities with an iron fist from their great houses. There are the merchants, the procurers, the auctioneers, and the slavers, who filter the wealth of the city through their fat fingers. Then come the skilled ones, the artisans, the apothecaries and smiths and all manner of craftsmen. Necessary, but not as esteemed as the mercantile lot. They all sit on the backs of everyone else—the servants, the slaves, the ones who sell their bodies for pittance."

Azzy eased herself onto her back. "We have no lords in the Heap. Only the Elders and they starve like the rest of us."

"Is it true...um, sorry never mind," Morglint muttered. She frowned at him.

"Is what true?"

The Snatcher fidgeted. "There's a rumor the humans eat their dead."

Azzy was quiet for a long moment. "It's not a rumor," she said. She felt the weight of the universe's cruel humor. She was not surprised when the Snatcher visibly blanched at her answer.

"Surely not?"

"It is not a practice taken lightly. Have you ever been hungry, Morglint? So hungry all you can think of is filling the yawning hole in your belly? Watching your body waste away as it consumes itself trying to stay alive?"

The Snatcher pondered her words. "No, I've missed meals before but never from lack of food." He made a face. "Still, do your people not realize the consequences? The sickness, the increased risk of taint?"

She wondered that herself—had the Heap continued to limp along or had the Rot returned to claim them all? "I think they do now."

Shouts broke the early morning silence, startling both of them. Morglint tumbled to his feet. "Stay here, little one," he said, ducking out of the tent.

Azzy struggled upright. The whispers in her head were rising in warning. Something was happening, her glaring vulnerability all the more obvious as she slowly sat up.

Morglint burst through the gap a moment later, clearly flustered as he dug through his boxes of tools and herbs.

"What is it?"

"One of the acquisitions started turning in the night. It's bad. I don't think she'll survive it."

Azzy swallowed, half listening to the whispers as

Morglint muttered to himself, slapping the side of a crate in frustration. "You're going to help her?"

He leveled a look at her, his brown eyes fierce. "If I can't ease her transition, they'll cull her." He swiped a hand over his face, a gesture so like Brixby it hurt to watch. "They might have put her down already."

She stilled, listening. Azzy could hear it now, what the whispers strained to say. The blanket twisted between her fingers. "Bring her in here. I'll help you."

Morglint frowned at her. "Even if you learned from your guardian, you can barely stand, little one. I won't put you in danger. I'll figure out something. I'll—"

"Morglint," said Azzy, the authority in her voice forcing him to meet her mismatched eyes. "Please bring her here." Whatever he saw in her face made him pull back with a frown. He left with a stilted nod. Azzy tapped out a silent rhythm against her scarred thigh as she waited for him to return. She knew he drew close when the vial of Rustic Oracle flared, bursting with radiant light. He stumbled into the tent, trying to keep the thrashing girl from slipping out of his arms.

The Snatcher laid her on his cot, loosely holding her down. "The fever has her," he said.

She was younger than Azzy expected, younger than Armin, her body still transitioning to womanhood from the narrow breadth of her hips. Her eyes were already altered— solid black pools that darted between the Snatcher and Azzy, brimming with fear and pain. Her muscles were taut and quivering, her body riddled with bloodied cracks. Something writhed beneath the surface of her skin, trying to force its way out. Azzy stared, horrified. Was this what was happening to her brother?

The girl bucked, spine curving as she violently retched. Black fluid dripped from her lips. She dissolved into hysterical laughter. Her eyes leaked the same fluid in inky tears that painted her face. The laughter faded into quick pants as she struggled to breathe.

Azzy slid from her cot, ignoring the jolt of pain in her chest as she crawled across the floor. Dandelions popped up around them, their glowing heads leering toward the girl. Azzy's head pounded as the whispers clamored. They told her things, details, offering her a scroll of information of a life about to be lost, burnt away by the transformation. The girl's pain and fear tickled at a half-forgotten memory of Armin seized by fever, thrashing about and cracking apart. *Or was it a dream?*

Please be a dream, Azzy thought as she pulled herself up. She reached around Morglint, ignoring the Snatcher's cry of protest as she grasped the girl's face between her hands.

"I'm here," she said. The whispers echoed through her voice. Morglint went still beside her.

The girl stopped thrashing. Her black eyes focused on Azzy's.

"A shard of sky," said the girl, awe clouding her wan face as her body relaxed. Morglint pulled away without a word.

Azzy didn't look at him, couldn't look at him, not when the girl needed her more. She stroked the girl's face, feeling the dreadful heat of her skin. The whispers swarmed inside her. Her hands tingled where they touched the girl, but she didn't pull away.

"Make it stop," the girl begged. Her tears ran over the back of Azzy's hands in stark black lines.

Azzy tilted her head as the whispers urged her on, her own thoughts blanking until they were all she heard. She released the girl's face and picked up the short blade from where Morglint had left it. The Snatcher inhaled a sharp breath but didn't interfere as Azzy dragged the blade across her own fingertips. The pain was distant, almost forgotten as the first droplets hit the girl's fevered skin. She gasped in surprise as Azzy traced a finger between her collarbones.

The air grew heavy, weighing down on them as Azzy's hand moved. The pressure was almost unbearable as she finished the mark. The moment her fingers lifted, the air shimmered and rippled, as if reality coiled in on itself. Morglint's glowing vial dimmed to a dull gray, ceding to the morning daylight. The dandelions folded in on themselves before bursting into silky white puffs.

"That's not possible," said Morglint.

"Thank you," the girl breathed. Her new limbs curled, sinuous and sleek as she sank into an exhausted sleep.

Azzy slumped, the whispers simmering back to an intelligible murmur. The symbol began to flake and peel away from the girl's collarbone, disappearing from existence. She ignored it, plucking one of the dandelions from the ground; the spherical head had the density of a cloud, dark at the center.

"I've never seen them do that," she said. At the gust of her breath, the sphere blew apart into tiny individual tufts, swirling through the air around her, each carrying a minuscule brown seed that slowly wound around her in a lazy circle.

"What are you?" Morglint's deep voice, hoarse with awe, broke the spell. The seeds drifted off, scattering to the ground.

Azzy stared at the naked stub, all that was left of the Rustic Oracle, withering between her fingers. She dropped it, swallowing as she looked up at the Snatcher.

"I don't know."

Morglint slid his bulk onto the ground beside her, staring at the sleeping girl. He gently pushed her barbed tail back onto the cot. "I've never seen anything like that. That symbol, it's already gone. What was that?"

"I just wanted to take her pain away," said Azzy. Already the symbol had faded from her memory, drifting out of her grasp. She picked up the vial of powdered Rustic Oracle, holding it out to Morglint. "They never glow for me, you know. I don't know why."

The Snatcher took it from her, staring at the dull powder within as if it would give him answers. "That didn't simply take away her pain, little one," he said, a tremble in his gravelly voice. "The change was seamless, like changing clothes. The fever, the shedding of her form, the forgetting —you bypassed all of it." He shot the sleeping girl a speculative glance. "I wonder—"

Azzy sat up, gripping the Snatcher's forearm. "Someone's coming."

Morglint scrambled to his feet, lifting Azzy as delicately as he could. The tent flap swung up, revealing the mismatched face of another Snatcher.

The newcomer sneered at Morglint, who froze with Azzy in his arms. She could feel the cruelty wafting off him in waves. The whispers continued their clamoring alarm, different than before, muted, allowing her to react instead of overwhelming her. She listened to their warning, her fingers wrapping around Morglint's thick forearm as the new Snatcher turned his sneer on the sleeping girl. Until he realized she was still breathing. His face twisted into an incredulous mask.

"Saved the little bitch after all? And the other one," he scowled at Azzy, snorting through his teeth. "How many bandages did you waste on that scrap? That's coming out of your wages."

He strode forward and scooped up the sleeping girl who woke with a drowsy yelp. Her scream was cut short when the Snatcher's brutish hand slammed over her mouth. He lifted up her tail and new legs, examining her with a critical eye. "Another bloody scorpioid woman. Better for little more than the pleasure markets." He hefted her up against his hip, pinning her tail against his side while his hand remained over her mouth despite her nails digging into the back of his hand. He nodded to Azzy. "Throw that one in the back of the wagon already, twit, we move out in an hour."

Morglint's grip on Azzy tightened before he set her down on the spare cot. His hands shook as he turned to face the other Snatcher. "She's not healed enough to be thrown in with the rest."

Azzy tensed as the Snatcher's eyes narrowed. "Then leave the runt behind to rot." Morglint flinched, his hands fisted behind his back.

"She's—she's untainted," he said.

The tension thickened. Azzy felt her jaw clench a moment before the Snatcher struck hard. Morglint staggered, sending the boxes of herbs and instruments tumbling over as he caught himself. Blood oozed from the corner of his mouth.

"You stupid fool," snarled the other Snatcher, his hand still curled in a mallet-like fist. "How much coin do you expect to get for a scrawny, half-dead female? She wouldn't last one round with a lord, if any would take her."

Azzy flinched with a sob as the Snatcher struck again, smashing Morglint's nose with an audible crunch.

"I'll carry her," Morglint wheezed.

"Along with your boxes of toys," the Snatcher jeered, kicking a fallen bundle of herbs that had rolled to his feet. The dried plants exploded into shreds. Azzy bit her tongue. She knew a single word would enrage the Snatcher further.

"I'll leave it behind," said Morglint, his voice pleading.

"Wretched bleeding-heart simpleton," the other spat, but his eyes slid to Azzy, his cold gaze calculating. "Then carry her. Perhaps she will take in a hefty bid at the flesh markets." His chuckle made her skin crawl, but the Snatcher finally took his leave, dragging the girl with him. Her terrified eyes met Azzy's one last time before the tent flap closed.

Azzy released her breath. She rose from the cot, her steps slow, each one jarring the wound in her chest. She braced herself on a fallen crate, sifting through the scattered contents until she found a clean bandage. She tore a length free and gently dabbed at Morglint's bleeding nose.

"I'm sorry. I should have hidden you sooner, I—" he said. Azzy wiped the blood from his mouth, silencing the apology.

She placed her hand flat against his cheek as she continued to tend his broken nose. "You are one of the bravest people I know."

Morglint snorted, his expression saddened as he looked over his scattered boxes. "Let's hope I'm also one of the smartest," he said.

Azzy frowned at him. "I'm certain you are, but why?"

"To plan," said Morglint, his jaw set. "I won't let them sell you to the flesh markets."

Interlude III: A String of Teeth

The witch was not one for prattling, but she grew more and more reserved the closer they drew to Avergard. Kai gauged her disquiet by the movements of her fingers, rubbing the shard round her neck as if it were a protective talisman. It could be; his understanding of the witch's magic was painfully lacking. His understanding of her motives, even more so.

He watched her often, attempting to glean what insights his senses could provide him. Her scent changed as they drew closer to the outer area of the city, tinged by the sharp tang of fear.

Safiya's face, however, remained smooth, belying no emotion, but her hands gave her away. He watched her hands as they stopped stroking and tugging on the oval shard, retrieving an object from her pockets. A string of dull ivory lumps, which she pulled through her fingers. He did not recognize them at first, too large to be from a human, but he knew them by scent—the scent of stale calcified bone and old blood.

The witch ran the string of teeth through her fingers.

She caught him watching her. Her fingers stilled. Their gazes held, each asking a question, wondering who would break first.

"Why do you carry a string of teeth?" Corrine's voice broke their stalemate. He often forgot she was there because of her silence, as she propelled them up the river. The thought shamed him; he could never repay the debt he now owed her for bringing them this far.

A small smile tugged at the corner of the witch's mouth, her brow raised as she nodded to Kai. The eel woman may have asked the question, but she knew he wondered as well.

"It's a relic of my past," said the witch. She might have left it at that if Corrine hadn't been there, her innocent expression prying the details from the reluctant woman. "I was born far south of here. I haven't seen my true home in a long time." Her umber eyes were distant, lit with a somber light, lost in memory.

"What happened?" Corrine nudged.

"What usually happens," said Safiya, her fingers tightening around the grisly memento. "The Snatchers, the great procurers of Avergard, invaded in the night. They brought mercenaries who ate through our defenses and killed our warriors. I watched them kill my mother, the only family I had." The flush of old fury colored her features, her hand so tight around the teeth Kai could hear the grind of her bones. "They brought me here. I became another cog in the overarching machine of Avergard, a servant for a powerful lord."

She ran her thumb over the lumps of teeth.

"He was a good master, far fairer than most," she murmured. "When I grew strong enough, I left his household. I walked through the gates of the city and found the camp of Snatchers who destroyed my home."

The string of teeth rattled in her grip, though Kai knew

there was no wind to send them chattering. He could easily picture the witch moving between tents of sleeping Snatchers, a wraith of wrath and vengeance, collecting the spoils of her dark victory. He could understand a vengeance like that. The scars around his neck still twinged whenever he thought of ripping out the throat of the next Snatcher he saw. Foul monsters, the lot of them...

Though the same could be said of wolves.

Kai sighed, lying on his forelegs as he stared up at the distant city walls. They weren't getting closer. Lifting his head, he looked back to find the eel woman gripping the edge of the raft, her features pale with worry. The witch frowned, noticing as he did.

"Corrine?"

"You killed them on city grounds?"

Safiya's face settled into a perfect mask. "What does it matter? It happened years ago—"

"They never forget those crimes," Corrine snapped, baring her teeth at the witch. "You're heading to your death."

The witch remained stoic and unreadable. "How would you know what they do and do not forget? You've spent years roaming the rivers."

Corrine's eyes flickered to the bracelet around her wrist. "I didn't always inhabit the rivers, and I did not always live beneath the ground, witch. Avergard is the in-between place for many of us. And the memory of the city is an old, long one. If they catch you, it's a murderer's fate. They will hang your body on the city walls to rot."

Safiya looked down at the string of teeth in her hands. "Perhaps it's time to face my fate."

The eel woman hissed at her, her expression mutinous. "I won't take you further, I won't—"

"Did you know one of the last human cities has fallen?"

Safiya looked up, her eyes flashing. "Nothing left but dust and ghosts. He's seen it," she said, nodding to Kai.

He stilled at the memory, the awful moment of Azzy teetering on the edge of the abyss. The expectant hunger below...

"And again, on the river, did you not feel the span of death that lurked there? The emptiness of it as you passed through?"

Corrine shivered. "What does that have to do with anything?"

"It is everything," said the witch, reaching down to touch the bracelet on Corrine's wrist. "I have to find her. The risk is worth it."

Kai stared at the witch. Through her cryptic words he saw the shadow of something vast and incomprehensible. A woman searching for her lost brother, he could understand. The eel woman paying the debt of returned memories, he could understand. Safiya's reasons, her motivations, for finding Azure, were far more complicated than his own, than anyone's, and he trusted her less than ever.

The raft began to move again. The three of them maintained their silence, their eyes fixed on the approaching city. Its buildings rose to catch the fading sunlight—tall glimmering structures of metal and glass, like the gleaming claws of a giant predator tearing into the sky. The structures grew shorter the further they were from the city center, dispersing into private residents and estates. A massive wall circled it but was unable to contain all within as the city spilled out through the gates in surrounding encampments and the outer market.

Even from the river, hints of the city teased Kai's nose. Corrine had called Avergard an in-between place. They'd all felt the stifling embrace of the city in some capacity. Kai had never fully experienced the city itself, but he'd spent a great of deal of time in the outer markets, chained to a post with a Snatcher collar gouging his neck. He recognized the smell of the encampment slums, the abrasive scent of food cooking mixed with raw sewage. The scent of hundreds of unwashed souls milling about, listless and desperate outside the city proper. He hoped Azzy didn't linger there. Though part of him felt he would be able to find her even in the chaos of the outer slums, picking her scent free from the flow of refuse. He would find her anywhere.

The raft carried on past the sprawling camps, following the path of the river as they cut beneath the wall. They avoided the gates altogether. Corrine slipped them deep inside the city via the sewers. They entered the cavernous stone tunnels, as massive as the buildings overhead and home to just as many denizens. He could scent them, slithering in the shadows, watching the peculiar passage of witch and wolf through the secret ways of the below. Their curious gazes didn't bother him. The low creatures would not trouble them; this was a hidden world beneath the city. Those who lived in hiding usually desired to remain so.

The raft bumped against a rock landing situated at the foot of a steep stair carved from the wall. It ascended upwards, no doubt leading to an unassuming exit into the city above.

"That leads into the slums," said Corrine, her slit pupils wide in the dim light of the sewer. She seemed immune to swimming in the filth. "At the end of the row stands the Nightingale Carnal house. Knock on its alley door. Ask for Rose. She will help you."

The name struck a faint chord of familiarity for Kai though he could not place it. The witch however, softened. "You found your daughter."

A shadow of sadness passed over Corrine's face. "Yes. What's left of her." She nodded to them. "Safe travels."

"Safe travels, Corrine," said the witch as she eased herself off the raft. She slipped the string of teeth back into her pocket. Kai lingered, feeling the weight of his debt to the eel woman and the weight of her pain. He ignored the sour stench of the water and gently nosed her shoulder.

Corrine lifted her hand, the bracelet clicking on her wrist as she ran her fingers through his ruff. She pressed her face to his. "Find our lady, wolf."

Kai gave an answering whine. She released him, holding the raft steady as he clambered off. A backward glance revealed the eel woman was already gone. The witch waited for him at the foot of the stair. The city waited above.

A Taming Hand

Morglint kept a steady pace on the muddy road. He dragged at the rear of the Snatcher's train with Azzy in a hastily fashioned sling across his chest, cradling her like a child as he tried to spare her the jar and jostle of the uneven terrain.

He made such a careful effort, she didn't have the heart to tell him that each step still knifed through her chest. She could feel the wear and tear on her stitches, the cooling warmth of blood that slowly saturated her bandages. Azzy kept her face buried against the Snatcher's shoulder, surprised by the leathery softness of his skin. Silent and still. Necessary under the vicious gaze of the others. She could feel their ire and dispassion surrounding them, an invisible noose ever tightening around Morglint's neck. He wasn't simply an outcast. They hated him with an irrationality so like Elder Prast and his ilk for the tainted that she worried for Morglint's safety. They muttered and cursed him at every turn, a corrosive hatred that grew with every mile that passed under their feet. Morglint the unnatural, with his plants and poultices. The girl she had helped and

Azzy herself made them uneasy. The nasty Snatcher who'd broken Morglint's nose kept looking back at them, a constant sneer twisting his lips.

Her whispers stirred each time he glanced at them.

Her fear for her friend gave her the strength to grit her teeth through the agonizing journey.

"We're stopping for a midday meal." Morglint's chest rumbled against her cheek. He eased her free of the sling and was taken aback as he set her on a nearby rock. "You're pale as bleached linen."

He winced as he examined her bandages. "I knew it was too soon to move you," he said, his brown eyes brimming with concern. "You're bleeding through. You must have torn a stitch."

Azzy clasped his hand before he could pull away. The whispers clamored in the back of her mind, tolling a warning that filled her with dread. "Don't," she said, pausing through a wave of nausea. "You can't stall them, Morglint."

He frowned at her, opening his mouth to argue.

"Please trust me," said Azzy. "Tie my bandages tighter. We'll handle it later."

A true healer, Morglint snorted in anger, but he reban-daged her with the utmost care, cinching them tight to staunch the bleeding. His pace grew slower as the caravan began to crawl forward once more. This time, the Snatcher held her aloft and away from his body, his extended arms providing a welcome relief from the impact of his steps. She could feel the tremble in his muscles when they finally halted close to dusk. Morglint set her down with the same care, groaning as his pack slid off his back.

He hastened to make camp, unpacking their tent. His supplies had been left behind except for a few spare bandages and necessities which he set aside as he worked.

In minutes they were sequestered away in their canvas shelter, out of sight of the other Snatchers as they gathered and groused for their evening meal.

"You should eat something," said Azzy, forcing herself to hold still as Morglint peeled away her bandages. She closed her eyes at his hiss.

"I have rations," he murmured. He sighed, setting her bloody bandages aside. "Azzy," he began, his voice hesitant.

"It's infected isn't it?" She didn't need him to confirm it; the fever was rising, blooming through her veins.

"If you'd let me treat you at midday—"

"Your brethren would have beaten you for slowing them down. Or worse," she said, tracing the scar on her thigh. There was a smattering of wolves with Morglint's caravan— gaunt, hollow-eyed men with collars digging into their necks, half-wild and broken. She'd briefly considered broaching the subject with Morglint about asking for their help. The thought had risen and died. What if the ability to heal was a gift unique to Kai? His name alone caused such pain in her chest it was hard to breathe. She couldn't bring herself to ask. What would the Snatchers do to the wolves if they knew? What would they do to Morglint if he asked? The whispers spoke to her of outcomes that made her shiver.

Morglint wrapped a blanket around her shoulders, her wound still bare to the air. He rubbed his chin, deep in thought.

"We are low on options, little one," he said, rolling his jaw. "What about healing yourself?"

Azzy blinked up at him, her vision fuzzing at the edges. "What do you mean?"

"That rune you painted on the girl," said Morglint, his gaze slanted at the narrow opening of the tent. "It reminded me of what the witch folk use. Except I've never seen a symbol like the one you drew." His gaze returned to her with a frown. "Where did you learn it?"

"Never learned it," said Azzy, another shiver rippling through her nerves. She pulled the blanket tighter around her shoulders, nothing but a strip of cloth across her breasts for the sake of modesty.

"Then how did you..." Morglint trailed off, considering her. He bent over, using his finger to trace in the dirt. "Witch folk use this rune to promote healing."

"How do you know what they use?" Azzy spoke through chattering teeth.

"I've cared for more than one witch in my time." Her friend shrugged, but his expression betrayed the sadness such knowledge cost him.

Azzy followed the path of his finger in the dirt. The shape of it felt wrong, incomplete. "This works for them?"

"It might keep you alive," said Morglint, a pleading note in his voice.

She nodded and raised a shaking hand to dab at the blood oozing from her wound, tracing the symbol on her skin. Wrong, it was wrong. The whispers rose as her fingers moved, slowing until she came to stand still. An incomplete mark, one she could fix. The whispers nudged her on, the path of her fingers diverging in fresh curves and angles. Morglint's eyes widened.

"Azzy..."

She felt the tug on her flesh, an itch that escalated to sharp pull. Azzy ignored it. The symbol was nearly complete, a little more, a little more. She stopped breathing.

Morglint grabbed her hand, gasping as if she'd shocked him. His other hand landed heavily on her shoulder, shaking her. "Azzy!" His voice was frantic. The cut at the corner of his mouth sealed and vanished.

A sharp pop broke her concentration. Azzy inhaled a breath, coughing at the sudden rush of air in her lungs. Her chest didn't so much as twinge. Morglint released her, brushing a hand across his face.

"What happened?"

"You fixed my nose," said Morglint, his voice muffled behind his massive hand. His eyes were filled with awe as he pointed at her. "I'm going to have to remove those stitches."

Azzy looked down. The scar on her chest was white and smooth, marred by black threads that jutted from her skin. Her hand shook as she touched it. No pain, only the barest twinge that accompanied a long-healed wound.

"It looks years old," whispered Morglint. The Snatcher's brown eyes matched her bewilderment. "That symbol, you changed it, you—"

Azzy gasped, pulling the blanket tight around her. "He's coming."

Morglint was on his feet in an instant, shoving her behind him as the cruel Snatcher from yesterday burst into the tent.

"Where have you been? We called your name over and over." The Snatcher's lopsided face twisted in a leer as he caught sight of Azzy. "Tending your human pet? Surprised she lasted the day—"

The Snatcher's eyes widened as the whispers screamed a warning. She didn't have time to react before he darted forward, batting Morglint aside as he grabbed her.

The end of her scar peeked above the blanket.

Azzy cried out as the Snatcher tore the cloth from her grip, exposing her healed wound, still peppered with damning black threads.

"What is this?" The Snatcher rounded on Morglint, shaking Azzy at him. "This isn't one of your tricks. You have no magics," he said, accusation dripping from his voice. His hand strayed to the knife hanging from his side. She knew the Snatcher would gut Morglint if he caught him in a lie, looking for an excuse to do violence on the healer. Azzy caught her friend's frightened gaze, wishing she could scream at him to say nothing. Her fingernails dug into the Snatcher's wrist. He held her aloft with his large hand wrapped around her throat, fat fingers curling over her shoulder, ready to snap her neck should it suit him.

The moment stretched, the tension thick and suffocating. Morglint stuttered, his words tripping over themselves. She felt the moment the cruel Snatcher's hand closed over the hilt of his knife. She opened her mouth to scream, to tell Morglint to run, when the whispers unfurled within her.

He's here, he's here.

Azzy went limp; she let herself go blank. The whispers continued in a sing-song chant, a chorus of childlike voices that wove around her.

Who's here? She asked the whispering voices.

Snippets and pieces came to her, too many voices speaking at once, the words blurring into one another until they meshed together, uttering the same words as one echoing voice.

The Lord of Seven Smiles.

Shouts rose from outside. Another unfamiliar Snatcher stuck his head through the tent flap.

"Oi, the lords are here," he said, severing the tension. The cruel Snatcher waved him off, his hand finally away from his blade.

"Line 'em up," he said and tossed Azzy at Morglint's feet. "You stay in here with this little dreg, hear me? I'll deal with you when we're done." Neither of them released a breath until he'd stormed from the tent.

"What does he mean, the lords are here?" Azzy rolled to her feet.

"The city lords sometimes ride out and intercept the caravans before they hit the outer markets, looking for choice selections," said Morglint, his hands opening and closing with the need for action. He seized and ripped the discarded blanket apart, helping her wrap it around her torso in a makeshift shirt. "You can't stay. You have to run now, before he comes back."

Azzy took one of his large hands with both of hers. "We need to run."

His brown eyes met hers, full of sadness and resignation. "I can't run, little one. I am too large, too noticeable. I would only hinder your escape."

Her fingers tightened on his, fear squeezing her chest. "No," she said, her voice breaking. "You can't stay. They'll kill you."

His expression didn't change. He knew. "I can get you out of the camp while they're distracted with the lords."

The whispers tugged at her. Nudging her. "Are all the lords so bad?"

"Most are vicious despots," said Morglint as he shoved a handful of his rations in a traveling pouch. "There are a few who have strange motives, but I don't know, little one. The whole lot of them are cold and aloof."

She wavered, wanting to ask more, but the urgency of the moment weighed on her. Morglint was about to spirit her away and resign himself to death. Her hands curled into fists. There had to be something she could do, something she could say to convince him to come with her. She couldn't leave another friend, another guardian, to his fate.

"Morglint," she said, but he lifted a finger to his mouth, asking for her silence as he peered out of the tent.

"We go now," he said, taking her hand and pulling her

along as they ducked outside. The Snatchers camp was a loose cluster of identical canvas tents circling their transport wagons. Morglint's tent was set up several yards away from the rest. From here, the camp looked empty, a wall of canvas blocking their view of the others as Morglint circled out, toward a dense grouping of trees. The only sign of the visiting lords were their mounts and transports—some vicious-looking creatures tied to thick tree trunks, and sleek metal contraptions she'd never seen before. There was no time to look her fill. She followed in the Snatcher's footsteps. Her friend moved with surprising grace and skill for someone of his bulk. They made it to the tree line without snapping a single twig underfoot. Morglint stopped just inside the lip of the forest.

"We have a problem," he whispered.

Azzy peeked around him, staring at the creature before them. It was beautiful and deadly, a seamless melding of reptilian and equine features, its powerful flanks hinting at the breathtaking speed it could reach. The beast stood even taller than Morglint and stared down its long face at them with intelligent eyes. A saddle sat on its back.

It was one of the lord's mounts, tied up further away from the rest. The reason was obvious when it unleashed an aggressive hiss at the Snatcher, rending the ground with its taloned feet. Its mouth was full of pointed teeth. Morglint stiffened, taking a step back as the beast took a step forward, crouching to attack.

"Get ready to run, little one," said Morglint reaching back to empty air. "Azzy?"

She moved around him, offering a piece of dried meat from Morglint's rations from a steady extended hand.

"Azzy!" He nearly yelped her name, reaching for her when the beast snarled at him. Azzy moved forward, undaunted, lifting both her hands.

"Easy," she said. The beast shifted, its threatening growl softening as she drew close. It tilted its head to look at her, dipping forward to sniff the offering she held. A forked tongue darted, licking at the strip of meat. She waited for it to take the food from her. It chewed on the treat before she took a final step forward and placed her hand against the side of its neck. The beast stilled, its slit pupil eyes rolling to look at her. She looked up, staring at the beast with her colorless eye. She could see the sparks of magic lingering beneath its skin, just as she had with Kai on the shore of the ocean.

Azzy ran her fingers along the beast's scaled hide, watching in silent wonder as the sparks were drawn to the tips of her fingers. The beast shuddered beneath her touch, closing its eyes as it leaned into her, nuzzling against her hair. She smiled and continued to stroke its warm skin until she heard a sharp intake of breath. Not behind her, but to the side, in the shadows of the trees. She could see the tip of polished boots in the corner of her vision.

"My-my lord," Morglint stuttered, dropping to his knees as he shook. Azzy glanced back at him, wide-eyed. She could feel her friend's terror. They'd been caught at the edge of the camp, away from the others. The beast shifted, sensing her own terror. The boots took a step toward them and the beast reacted, crouching in front of her, shielding her from view as it hissed a warning at its own master.

"Fascinating," whispered the lord. Azzy steeled herself and peeked at him around the beast's neck. The lord was a tall one, dressed in finery above anything she'd seen in the Heap, but the effect was spoiled by the wild growth of his beard and hair, a dark mane that gave him an untamed air to match the amused smirk on his lips. She thought his eyes black at first, as they looked between Morglint and the rebellious mount, until they caught her peeking gaze. A bril-

KRISTIN JACQUES

liant cobalt blue, deep and dark and full of secrets. The smile fell off his face when their eyes met. His lips parted in an expression akin to wonder. The whispers rose. Azzy put a comforting hand on the beast's neck, forcing herself to remain calm.

The lord took another step toward her, his hands slack at his sides.

"My lord, please," said Morglint, "Please, don't hurt her."

Azzy wanted to ease her friend's worry, to tell him the lord wouldn't harm her, but she didn't know how the man would react to her words.

He did react to the Snatcher's words, shaking himself from whatever spell had been cast between them. "No, of course not," he said, his eyes never quite leaving Azzy's. "Whatever price your caravan master asks for her. I'll double it."

Morglint's hands closed into fists against his knees. "She's not for sale."

This time, the lord did look away, frowning at the kneeling Snatcher. "Did you intend to flee with her? You wouldn't have gotten far."

"She might have," whispered Morglint. He peered up at the lord with a pleading expression. "Please, please let her go."

The lord paused, considering the Snatcher. He didn't shout for the others. He didn't lash out at them for resisting his offer. Azzy soothed the beast a second more and ducked beneath his neck, trying to keep herself calm as she faced the lord.

"Buy both of us," she said. She kept a reassuring hand on the beast's neck, as much to strengthen her as calm him.

"What?" Morglint looked at her, his brown eyes wide in confusion.

326

The lord smiled at her. Or at least, he partially smiled at her. Her colorless eye picked out the seam of skin nearly hidden by his facial hair. His mouth was much wider than it appeared. He spoke carefully, doing his best to hide it. "I don't know if you are aware, girl, but the Snatchers don't actually sell their own."

"Then request that he be given into your service," said Azzy, catching Morglint's eye.

"Little one, no," said the Snatcher, lifting a hand toward her. The lord noted the movement with a flicker of interest.

"I have no need for a procurer in my household," said the lord, his tone even as he watched her. It wasn't an outright denial. He had given her the opportunity to haggle with him.

"He's a skilled apothecary and healer," said Azzy. "He saved my life."

The lord tugged on his beard, considering her proposal. A show. He'd already decided to take them both, no matter what the cost. Azzy released her breath, leaning back against his mount. The lord noticed her relief, raising a curious brow.

"You seem rather confident I will make an offer for you both," he said, no accusation in his tone. Azzy looked up at him, sensing the quiet power he hid so thoroughly, a power she needed to help her find what she'd lost.

She nodded to him. "Yes, I am, Lord of Seven Smiles."

Bargaining Tactics

I t was meant to throw him, to disarm the casual smirk on the lord's face, but it was Morglint's reaction that worried her. He paled, shrinking against the ground as his uneven eyes darted to the lord's face.

"Lord Wallach," he murmured, gripping the ground. Azzy was certain he would dig a hole to climb into if given the chance. The lord himself was frowning at her. He took two steps toward her, pausing at his mount's low hiss.

"Come here, girl," he said with all the arrogance of his station. Azzy patted the beast's neck as she left its protection, resisting the urge to look over her shoulder at it.

In many ways, the creature reminded her of the thrashing wolf in the web, tied to a tree and surrounded by enemies. Her heart gave a twinge at the thought. She stopped an arm's length away from the lord, surprised by his height. Tall, though not as tall as Kai. She pushed thoughts of her lost wolf aside, focusing as Lord Wallach gently gripped her chin and lifted her face toward his. His cobalt irises were even more striking up close, rich and beautiful, but filled with wariness. He tilted her face to the side, studying her colorless pupil.

"You have the mark of other magics on you," he said softly, his thumb running along her cheekbone. "The mark of sacrifice." His gaze shifted to the scar on her brow, the mark she carried from the wailing natters. He continued the study of her face, lingering on her lips with an appraising look. "Even a touch of wild magics."

Azzy bit the inside of her lip, refusing to blush, while wondering what the lord saw. His eyes traveled back to meet her gaze. "All lingering shades of other magic and yet," he released her face, grasping her hand. "I would have thought you a pure human until you ran your hand along Iago's flank." He rubbed his thumb along her fingertips, his expression distant and thoughtful. "How did you know who I was when your...friend did not recognize me?" A small smile touched his lips at the mention of Morglint, as if the idea of the Snatcher's friendship was somehow amusing. The smile was a careful one, not stretching beyond the corners of his lips. Azzy lifted her free hand and traced a single fingertip along the seam of the lord's jaw.

"Why don't you smile with your whole mouth, Lord Wallach?" He froze at her touch, pupils dilating as her finger reached the end of its path. She dropped her hand, worried she'd offended him. Considering the shock on his face, it was as if she'd slapped him.

Morglint made a strangled noise behind them.

Lord Wallach swallowed, staring down at her. "Do you have any idea who I am, what I am?" His tone was too even, dull, as if he feared her answer.

And he did, she realized. The whispers were quietly percolating in her mind, no warnings. Whatever he was, he wasn't dangerous, not to her. It was her turn to study him, the wild lord with the too-wide mouth. Little things stuck out to her. The weather here was far warmer than the mountainous area she'd come from and his clothes were far too heavy for it. He was covered from the neck down in thick velvety fabric. The gloves were equally thick leather. Dulling his touch.

Tentatively, Azzy looked at the hand still holding hers and pressed her thumb against his gloved palm. There, beneath the thick leather, was another groove, another seam in the flesh. The Lord of Seven Smiles.

"Where else do you have them?"

He laughed at the question, the noise strained—but it eased some of the tension between them. His cobalt eyes crinkled. "You're not afraid of me?"

Azzy hesitated. Gauging Morglint's reaction, she felt she should be, but the whispers didn't so much as flinch at Lord Wallach's touch. "You feel safe," she said.

His mouth became a thin line at her words. He dropped her hand. "I'm not safe, girl. Never forget that," he said, tugging the ends of his vest as he regained his composure. "I find myself rather intrigued by you." His eyes shifted briefly to Morglint. "By both of you actually. I've never met a Snatcher with a compassionate bone in his body."

"I assure you, I am a rarity, my lord," Morglint wheezed.

The lord's lips twitched at that. "What are your names?"

"His name is Morglint," she said, ignoring the Snatcher's fluttering hands. "I'm Azzy."

The lord raised an eyebrow at her. "Well...Azzy, can you ride?"

She glanced at the beast. "Honestly, never ridden one of those before."

"You're about to get a quick lesson," he said. He stepped up to her, wrapping an arm around her waist. Her feet left the ground before her mind caught up, but the whispers remained at ease. Azzy forced herself calm as Lord Wallach carried her against his side with one arm, far stronger than he appeared. He threw her up across the saddle just as the cruel Snatcher shouted at them, appearing from around the spill of tents.

No, it wasn't them he shouted at. He'd spotted Morglint.

"What are you doing out here you bleeding mongrel? Didn't I tell you to keep your little bitch in the tent?"

Lord Wallach stiffened at the words. He helped Azzy sit upright in the saddle. The Snatcher completely missed his presence, his focus tunneled on Morglint. He had a hand raised to strike when the lord announced himself by clearing his throat.

The Snatcher spun on them and froze, paling to a pastier shade than Morglint. "Lord Wallach, my sincerest apologies, I didn't mean for you to bear witness to this unpleasantness." He bowed, all grease and charm. An eye twitched when he noticed Azzy on the back of the lord's mount.

Lord Wallach acknowledged the direction of his gaze, his gloved hand clamping on her thigh in a manner that suggested all the right things to the Snatcher's judgement.

"Ah, yes, about 'the little bitch'" said the lord, "what are you asking for her?"

The Snatcher flashed Morglint a vicious look before wheedling at the lord. "She's a pure one, my lord, I'm sure you've noticed. Hard-won and freshly caught. We haven't the chance to properly appraise her yet."

Lord Wallach released her thigh, lifting a lock of Azzy's hair. "Nor bathed," he remarked. He winked at her. The Snatcher hemmed and hawed, rubbing his hands together.

"We caught her only the other night," he lied. "Rescued the little lamb from the wolves."

Azzy clenched her teeth at that, resisting the urge to snarl at the devious Snatcher.

"How dreadful," said Lord Wallach. He stroked his beard, considering. "Does 20,000 sound reasonable?"

The wheedling expression froze on the Snatcher's face. He blinked rapidly, his hands rubbing together so fast she was surprised he didn't catch fire. "Twenty, you say?" The Snatcher slurred as Lord Wallach retrieved a thick folded leather pouch from inside his vest. He pulled out a handful of green paper slips and held them out to the Snatcher, who began to stumble forward. Lord Wallach's eyes slid to Morglint's cowering form. He made a show of withdrawing the handful of paper, tapping his chin.

"What about that one?"

The Snatcher staggered, his warped face incredulous as he glanced back at Morglint. "I apologize again, for his behavior, my lord. He will be dealt with after you depart." Azzy shivered at the promise of pain in the Snatcher's voice.

"I'll make it 30,000 if you give him to me," said Lord Wallach. For a moment, the Snatcher wavered, greed pouring off him in waves.

He drew back, appearing affronted by the proposition. "A tempting offer, my lord, but I must deal with him," he ground out, the words pulled from his lips on point-of-pride. Morglint's face never left the ground but she could feel his sinking resignation.

Lord Wallach had warned her they didn't sell their own, but his expression didn't waver. "30,000 and I'll take care of him for you," he said. For a brief moment, he let his smile stretch wide, just past his lips.

The greed drained from the Snatcher's face. He shot a wide-eyed look at Morglint and bowed his head. "Would my lord consider taking your leave down the side avenue?

Merely to avoid unwelcome questions, you see." His voice wavered.

Azzy closed her eyes to hide her relief.

Lord Wallach slipped the stack of papers in the Snatcher's hand. "I believe I can accommodate your request." He turned to Morglint. "Come."

The kneeling Snatcher flinched—whether for show or from true unease was unclear—as he dragged himself to his feet. He skated around his former caravan master, keeping his head low. He halted beside them.

"Good bye, Morglint," said the head Snatcher, treating Morglint to a final sneer before he left them, counting the green paper as he walked away.

Lord Wallach pursed his lips at the retreating Snatcher. "Greed and fear never fail."

He offered Morglint his hand, which, after a long tense moment, the Snatcher gingerly shook. "Are you good to walk?"

"Yes, my lord," said Morglint, clasping his hands in front of him to hide their shaking.

Azzy knew they were safe, as safe as they could be, but her friend still radiated fear. She began to swing off the saddle. "I can walk too."

Lord Wallach caught her before she could dismount. "No, you can't. You are the commodity. You must act as such." He sighed when she frowned. "Besides, it's a short walk to the gates. You'll want eyes up high. And he needs to get used to me," he added for her ears alone. He untied his mount from the tree, clicking his tongue to signal it forward.

Iago was happy enough to be moving again, threatening the Snatcher with a halfhearted snap as he allowed Lord Wallach to set the pace at a brisk walk. Morglint followed at a slight distance, leery of mount and master, but it was a far better fate than what the caravan master had certainly planned for him. When Azzy managed to catch his eye, he gave her a grateful nod. The three walked in silence for a few minutes when a turn in the road revealed what she'd only caught in glimpses.

Avergard stretched before them, a short muddy plain that erupted into a city of towers wrought from metal and glass. They blazed bright as torches with the last streaks of sunlight. It would be dark by the time they reached the city gates, but already, an unnatural phosphorescent glow rose from the low city streets.

Azzy stared up at the towers, absorbing it all. At last she'd reached the end of the path.

I'm here, Armin.

Interlude IV: Into the Dark

Safiya peered through the slats of the wooden grate,
the last barrier that stood between them and the
sprawling metropolis of Avergard. Kai shuffled close
behind her, his fur damp from the moisture of the underground. They'd crawled up the rough-hewn steps in
complete darkness for hours, cautiously placing their feet
with each step to keep from plunging over the edge. The
distant beacon gradually dissolved in the solid lines of weak
gray alley light. The witch hesitated at the opening, snaking
her fingers through the slats as she studied their surroundings through the largest crack.

"Maybe we should wait until nightfall," she said. Her
eyes slid to Kai as she spoke. She sighed, her fingers curling
around the splintering wood. "We didn't discuss it, but we
both know a wolf cannot walk these streets and I do not
have the power to shift your form. Are you willing to do
what is necessary?"

Dread slithered along his spine. He knew what she
spoke of. The scars along his neck tingled as the question
burned in his throat. He dropped his head with a soft

whine. Safiya nodded, reaching over to run an absent hand through his ruff.

"It's amazing what you can procure in a bawdy house," she muttered. Her burnt gold eyes rested on him, resigned to their course of action. "Wait here." With one good shove, the rotted wood splintered and fell away. Safiya eased herself out, casting one last glimpse over her shoulder before she sauntered away.

Kai curled himself tight against the broken teeth of the doorway, peering into the litter strewn alley. A riot of scents and sounds wove through his senses. He could hear the bellows and shouts from the auctions. The calls of the merchants and the hissing invitations of the street ladies. Stale cooking oil, rotting vegetation, sweat, and garbage mingled with the cloying scent of the blooming trees that lined the streets, chosen for their strong fragrance to drown the spoiling city in natural perfume. It was almost too much, buried as he was in the mouth of a back-alley gutter. Would he be able to stomach it at full force? If the witch came through, he wouldn't have to; a collar would dull his senses. There were other side effects, worse ones few knew about, but he accepted them.

Somewhere, in the city, she lived and breathed. The connection fizzed within him, an exposed wire that burned him if he concentrated on it too long. Could she sense him? Did she feel their proximity? Despite his prostrate position, his muscles were tensed, itching to run to her, to plow through the crowded streets until he found her again. He wanted nothing more than to run and run until he collapsed at her side. The minutes stretched, the scents and sounds falling away until all Kai could hear was the furious pounding of his heart. The light was fading to dusk when the witch reappeared, hurrying toward the broken grate, her arms full. A familiar object hung from her wrist. He bit down on the growl but couldn't stop his tail from puffing out at the sight of it.

The metal spikes held a polished sheen that taunted him in the low light.

Safiya crouched in front of him, her expression torn. "I cleaned it up best I could," she said. He could smell the iron taint of old blood soaked into the leather fasteners. If she'd gotten it from the brothel, it was acquired through violent means.

The witch inhaled, her features pinched tight as she held up the collar between them. "Are you ready for this?"

He bobbed his head, ignoring the tremble building in his limbs. Kai braced himself as the witch placed the collar round his neck, the ties still lose as she clenched her jaw and pierced her thumb on a spike, drawing the necessary symbol on a patch of smooth leather. Her blood soaked into the material. Kai felt the drag of magic on his veins. Safiya's features smoothed into an emotionless masque as she wrenched the fasteners tight, forcing the spikes into his skin.

He fell into her, the change taking him, pained yelps muffled by her hands on his face, seamlessly moving with the shift of his jaw to silence him. She held him to her tight as his body cracked and reformed. She became a wall of warmth he slumped against, panting as he stared up at the evening sky with human eyes.

The witch sighed, smoothing her hands down the trembling muscles of his back. "I'm sorry," she whispered.

She shuffled back, eyeing him critically as she offered him the other package she'd carried with her: a pile of clothes, plain and homespun. She turned away, giving him privacy as she kept an eye on the alley. Kai forced his shaking hands into the act of dressing, the outfit a bit tighter than he was used to, but it covered his frame. His body readapted to his human form quickly enough, but his mind was another matter. The spikes were a constant pain, searing his nerves as they began to slowly erode his senses. It was their main function, and the reason so many wolves went insane the longer they bore them.

"What now?" He rasped, planting a hand against the stone wall for support. The scents and sounds of the city no longer overwhelmed him, a small blessing against the exhausted tremor of his muscles.

The witch slid her arm around his waist, supporting him without a word. "She's waiting at the back door for us." There was an unspoken tension in her words. He wondered how well received they were by Corrine's daughter. The witch did not trust her.

"What was left of her?" Kai echoed the eel woman's words.

"Not much," replied the witch, her face grim as she helped him stumble along. He leaned heavily on her and hated it, but his legs wobbled like a newborn pup's with every step. They stopped twice for him to retch the contents of his stomach, merely adding another layer of filth beneath his bare feet.

Kai knew they had reached their destination when the witch propped him against the alley wall so she could pound on a door crisscrossed with iron brackets. They waited, him fidgeting and her still as stone, until the door opened a crack to reveal half a woman's face.

"Is he with you?"

He knew by her voice, before he even saw the emptiness in the eye that peered at them, her iris a faded gray like her dishwater blonde hair. Kai watched this pale shadow of a woman from the corner of his vision as she took him in. The sight of her made his throat tighten. The Nightingale Carnal house appealed to specific appetites, the appetites of those who wanted a woman pink and warm and pure. This was where the true humans bought at the city flesh auctions were sentenced to short violent lives.

Corrine's broken daughter reflected what could happen to Azzy.

He clenched his fists tight against the cool brick and mortar. No, she wouldn't land here, not in this vile place.

Rose's blank stare swung in his direction. "He stays in the basement," she said. "If the Madame catches him, she'll skin him alive."

Forced underground again. Kai closed his eyes. The effects of the collar increased in enclosed spaces, where he had nothing to distract him from the pain and suffocation of his senses. The witch's hand squeezed his shoulder.

"It's only until full dark," said Safiya.

Rose nodded, opening the door further to reveal a horror show. The right side of her face was gone, nothing left but a mass of twisted scar tissue that barely covered the bone beneath. Kai tore his gaze away, unwilling to make her uncomfortable.

"This way," she said. Moving away from the support of the door, her footsteps dissolved into an uneven shuffle, heavily favoring her right leg. Her scars went all the way down. The brothel door clicked loudly behind them, immediately imparting a sense of claustrophobia that grew worse as they moved along the narrow hallway. Rose paused at a nondescript wooden door, withdrawing an antique key from her pocket to unlock it.

The moment she opened it, his feeling of unease escalated. Something was off. The back of the door was a solid metal slab, riveted in place and scourged by fingernails. Rose said nothing, silent and blank as she held the door open. Kai slid a glance at Safiya, spooked by the flicker of apprehension in her golden eyes.

"Is this necessary?" The witch frowned at the foul-smelling hole.

"Yes," said Rose. The lack of inflection in her voice made it impossible to gauge the truth.

Kai placed a shaky leg on the first step, peering into the damp dark. His nerves were singing. He couldn't do this, be it for five minutes or five hours, he would not be locked in the dark. Not again.

It was the collar's fault. He caught the scent as he turned, realizing the trap far, far too late. Safiya met his wide-eyed look a moment before Rose's hand shot out, pushing against his sternum. Weak from the change and off-balance on the stairs, Kai failed to catch himself.

His arms flailed for purchase as he fell through empty air. The uniformed men closed in behind the witch, her screams muffled as they thrust a cloth bag over her head. Rose's empty eyes stared at him, emotionless, watching his body twist in free fall. He lost sight of them all as he hit the ground.

The impact brought the taste of blood to his mouth. The spikes pierced further into his neck, the pain blinding, overwhelming the snap of bone in his thigh. He released a breathless cry, clawing the ground in front of him for purchase. His blurred vision slowly settled, the open door so very far. The witch and guard were gone. Rose continued to stare at him, a broken doll; the only sign of emotion was the tension in her white-knuckled hand gripping the doorknob.

Kai took a shuddering breath, pulling himself toward the bottom of the stair. The pain was too great to cry out, he could only pant through it, gulping down each breath as he struggled to lift himself. He craned his face to look at Rose.

"You were to help us," he gasped out, coughing as the

blood flooded his mouth. Warmth trickled down his chin. "You were—"

Rose took a step back and closed the door.

"No," Kai screamed, his voice raw. "No, wait, please."

Over his cries he could hear the tumblers turn as she locked him in.

City of Monsters and Light

They made an odd trio passing through the camps that spilled from the edges of the city—the lord with muddied boots, the silent and humble Snatcher, and the saddleback girl with mismatched eyes. Eyes followed them, people pausing in their tasks to watch the procession pass. Azzy felt the weight of their curiosity. When their eyes slid to Lord Wallach their gazes dropped, heads bowed until they passed.

He ignored their reactions, an aloof expression on his face as he led them toward the city gates. Azzy's eyes were everywhere, trying to drink in everything at once. The differences between Avergard and the Heap left her reeling. The buildings, even the squat boxy houses, were comprised of stone, metal, and glass—finely constructed and sturdier than any building from her home. Many towered high overhead, reaching for the sky with glass fingertips. Long clouds of smoke rose from deeper in the city proper, winding through the buildings like fat black snakes. As the last strains of daylight faded, the towers were lit from within, shining beacons in the night that banished the smoky haze.

Her neck ached from tilting so far back, but she couldn't get enough of them, imagining what wonders they held within. It wasn't until they passed through the actual gates —a thirty-foot-tall arch with massive iron doors flung wide —that she was able to tear her eyes away.

At night, when the street lamps were snuffed, the Heap was silent as the grave and empty. Here, the night brought the city to life. The streets hummed and throbbed with energy, full of people. Merchants called from street stalls, touting their wares. Finely dressed ladies walked on the arms of refined gentlemen. Children darted through the streams of people, slipping their hands into unsuspecting pockets to be caught and scolded by the patrolling guards in sharp dark blue uniforms.

The street lamps flickered to life with a faint buzz. Azzy stared at one, wide-eyed, watching the coiled inner wire burn hotter and hotter until it blazed with white light. The image imprinted on her vision until she blinked it away. Lights appeared at even intervals along the crowded avenue, casting a brilliant luminescence that painted long shadows against the stone walls. The light captured the real differences between Avergard and the Heap.

The shadows revealed the truth of tails and misplaced limbs. The merchants displayed grisly wares: of pieces of creatures, skins and carved bones alongside common buckles and mugs. The street lamps caught and flickered in the eyes of the passing ladies and gentlemen in their frocks and finery, reflecting with a predatory sheen. The children who ran past laughed with mouths full of needle-like teeth.

Azzy's hands curled in her lap. Tall graceful beings with milk-white skin and ink-stained eyes led men and women in chains toward a long stone building that echoed with shouts and the hard, hollow smack of wood on wood. Hungry-eyed women lingered in the shadows between buildings, tempting the passersby with siren smiles and luring stares while their skirts billowed with unnatural movements. Lord Wallach didn't pause for anyone, the crowd parting around them as they moved. The people outside the gates bowed their heads—in the city proper they averted their eyes, even the children, expressions of pinched worry on their faces as they recognized him. The Lord of Seven Smiles was greatly feared. There were a handful who caught his eye with bold stares, nodding to him, men who wore the same quality of fine clothing—the other lords of the city.

She released a breath she didn't realize she was holding, slumping in the saddle. There was so much to take in, too much. She closed her eyes; the energy of the city pulsated against her skin. Shadows played against the back of her eyelids.

"I put you up there to observe," Lord Wallach murmured. His voice carried to her with perfect clarity over the cluttered noise of the street.

"It is an awful lot to observe," she said. She smiled and peeked at the world through her colorless eye. A gasp left her lips.

For an instant, she was the girl who spun beneath the stars again, staring up at a sea of flashing jewels suspended in the velvety pitch of the night sky, the distance between them insurmountable and vast. Now she moved among the stars, a sea of glittering flesh and blood that twirled around her in spectacular displays of flaring sparks. She glanced down at Lord Wallach, stars blazing beneath his skin as bright as the sun. The beast beneath her was a pattern of muted lights that fizzed wherever she touched it. She lifted her hands, watching as the lights floated off, a living constellation that shifted as she watched.

Azzy laughed, dazzled by the sight. She looked to Morglint, observing the concentration of lights that darted through his hands. She turned to find Lord Wallach staring up at her. Azzy smiled down at him, placing her hand on his, delighted when the sparks swirling in his hand began to swarm beneath her fingers.

"So much light." She grinned, opening both her eyes. The sea of glittering light faded until she stared down into Lord Wallach's dark blue eyes. They'd stopped in the middle of the street. The crowd continued to flow around them, though curious eyes darted to the island of Lord Wallach and his newest acquisitions. A few on the edges of the crowd, mostly children, stared at Azzy with wide eyes.

"Why are they staring?" Azzy nodded to them. The attention sent them darting away in a cloud of giggles.

Lord Wallach's expression remained stoic but for his eyes, creasing at the edges as he hid his smile. "A human woman who laughs at monsters and touches the Lord of Seven Smiles without fear. They've never seen anything like you." He gently slipped his hand from her touch, pointing down the street. "Another couple of blocks before we hit the Wallach estate. I am one of the few lords who live within the city proper."

A feeling stirred in her mind, a chorus of whispers that clamored for her attention. Azzy frowned, looking up over the crowd as a group of uniformed men rounded the corner, dragging a struggling woman between them. A coarse sack hid her face and muffled her cries but Azzy couldn't take her eyes off her. Dread wormed through her as she watched them work their way through the crowd. The denizens of Avergard didn't hold the same regard for the uniformed men as they did for Lord Wallach, not moving until they were shoved out of the guards' path. It made the cluster's progress slow. The woman screamed and jerked in their grip. Azzy's nerves prickled. The hooded woman's struggles caused the pendant around her neck to swing free. Azzy's gaze locked on the oval of glass, the color of the sky. The witch of the wood here? How? Why? She was not the only one to react to Safiya's presence. Lord Wallach shuddered, his composure disappearing as he whipped around. He inhaled sharply, his expression stricken.

"No, not here, not after all this time." His voice cracked. He dropped his mount's reins and took a step toward the knot of guards.

Azzy felt the air warm around them, the crackle of danger against her skin as the whispers tolled in her mind. She tumbled from the saddle, wrapping her arms around Lord Wallach. "You can't," she said. She could feel him through the thick cloth, scorching to the touch, but she didn't let go.

He wasn't listening. He took another step, mindless of her weight on his back.

"Wallach, you'll get her killed," Azzy hissed, but it was Morglint who stopped him, stepping in front of the lord to cut off his view.

"Listen to the girl," said the Snatcher. "We are attracting a crowd."

Lord Wallach stumbled, falling back into her hold. Azzy squeezed her eyes shut, holding him tight. She could feel the desperation in him, shocked by the connection between the witch of the wood and a lord of Avergard. What history lay between them?

"Why would they seize Safiya?" Azzy felt Lord Wallach twitch at her question. She released him as he rounded on her, his gloved hand seizing her chin in an almost painful grip.

"Explain your connection," Wallach ground out.

"She helped me in the woods," she said. His jaw flexed. The whispers recoiled within her. Azzy could feel eyes staring at them, unfriendly eyes watching from the shadows between the street lights. Morglint was aware of them too, placing his hand on Lord Wallach for the first time.

"My lord we cannot do this here," he said.

Lord Wallach sagged, releasing his grip. "I'm sorry, girl," he whispered, his conflicted gaze following the cluster of guards as they pulled out of sight.

"Do you know where they are taking her?"

He nodded, swallowing. "There is an old crime she must pay for. They will take her the city cells to await trial."

"Then we find a way to get her out," said Azzy.

Lord Wallach's gaze dropped to her, his cobalt eyes glinting in the street light. The longing in them was some-thing she could sympathize with. He sighed, seizing his mount's reins. "Come, we shall discuss this within the safety of my own walls."

The whispers continued to buzz and throb in her mind. Morglint was right. It was not safe to talk about Safiya out here, not safe for Lord Wallach to display his weakness for prying eyes. She fell in between the Snatcher and lord, frowning at the ground. Part of her itched to run, to flee them both and begin searching the city for Armin—but the sight of Safiya, bagged and dragged through the streets, anchored her to the lord's side. She couldn't leave the witch to her fate, no matter what reason brought her here. She would help Lord Wallach save her, and in the process, perhaps he could help her discover the fate of her brother. Maybe even help her find Brixby.

A feather wove through the crowd, kicked up above the debris of the street. It swirled on the wind of moving bodies until it rested against her leg, snagged in the fabric of her leggings. Azzy plucked it free, twirling it in her fingers. Free of the dirt from the street, it was glossy and soft, possibly the softest thing she'd ever touched. She spun it between her fingers, mesmerized by the mottled pattern of black spots over brown. It was a beautiful feather. She wondered what it belonged to.

Azzy searched for a hint of feathers among the monstrous citizens of the city. At first nothing stood out to her from the flowing skirts and dark suits, but then she caught sight of them—a flash of white through the mob of muted dark colors! Wings, actual wings, flexed tight but unmistakable in shape, shaded in ribbons of black, brown and tawny white. Beautiful!

Her gaze focused beyond the wings on the boy they were attached to, his long blonde hair tied back. He turned, offering her a glimpse of his profile.

Her breath caught in her throat. Her fingers tightened around the feather. The world fell away as she stared; the only sound she heard was her heart thumping against her ribs. He must have felt her stare on him. He paused, frowning as he looked for the source. His gaze finally met hers. Eyes the color of a storm-ridden sea, empty as they passed over her face.

The connection snapped. The winged boy disappeared into the crowd. Azzy stared at the spot where he'd been, her steps leaden. She stumbled to keep pace with Lord Wallach and Morglint even as her heart cracked like spun crystal in her chest.

She'd found Armin at last, and he did not recognize her.

Epilogue

⚜

The journey to Lord Wallach's house passed in a blur of shapeless sights and muddied faces. It wasn't until she stood in her new room that her thoughts began to process.

This room was much smaller than her bedroom in the Heap. It contained a bed, a chest, and a small table and chair. There was a single window, but it captured her attention as nothing else in the grand house had.

She hadn't noticed any other windows or had dismissed them out of hand. She had missed the marvel of them, the clarity. Clear, unblemished glass, a true portal to the outside world, like the shards of glass she'd seen in the ruins.

Azzy looked at the bed, but the tug of exhaustion was muted compared to the swirl of worries and questions clogging her thoughts. She pulled the chair up to the window and finally pulled the feather from her the folds of her clothes.

Ivory white, with brown specks and black ribbons. She twirled it in her fingers, studying it, teasing up the memory of her brother. Wings. Actual wings on his back.

What had Armin become?

She wiped at the tears streaming down her face.

He didn't remember her, but that had always been a possibility. She knew setting out on this journey that she might find him again like this, though it was a distant worry when she could barely grasp the hope of finding him at all. It was Kai who had made it possible. She closed her eyes at that, her hand pressing on the healed-over scar on her chest, nothing left but a thin white line and pockmarks where Morglint had pulled out the thread.

Was he safe?

Would she ever see him again? Or Brixby? Could she really save Safiya from whatever fate awaited her? Could she make her brother remember her again?

So many uncertain fates, the weight of them crushing, pressing down on her from all sides. Azzy leaned forward, pressing her forehead to the cool glass of the window. A list of tasks began to form in her mind. Rescue Safiya. Find Brixby. Save Armin. And when all those tasks were said and done, perhaps she could search for her wolf again.

She sighed, the glass fogging, clouded as her future. Always searching for another answer, facing another complex knot to unravel.

"One thing at a time, Azzy," she said, clutching the feather tight between her fingers. "One thing at a time."

Azzy Still Needs You

Did you enjoy Marrow Charm? Reviews keep books alive . . .

Azzy needs you now! Help her by leaving your review on either GoodReads or the digital storefront of your choosing.

Azzy thanks you!

Acknowledgments

You never, truly, write a book alone. Nevermind the long hours, punching words through the keyboard. There are the late night venting sessions. Brainstorming and brain drizzles with people who help you unravel the tangle of your thoughts. There are the people who lift you up and keep you from drowning on your worst days.

This book is nearly five years in the making, a journey well traveled with the Wattchicks (Darly, Debbie, Tammy, Leigh, Gaby, and Keri, love to you all, so much.) and with the diamonds I found, MB, Robyn, Lucy, and Candace, who pushed and pulled me over through many mires. I am forever grateful and filled with wonder for each and every one of you.

To the Coven of Parliament, Shayne, Chantal, and Amanda, for giving Marrow Charm a chance to shine and believing in the story as much as I did.

About the Author

Kristin Jacques is science fiction and fantasy author based out of New England. She holds a B.A. in Creative Writing from Wells College and has been published in numerous anthologies including *Outliers of Speculative Fiction, 13: Night Terrors, Vices & Virtues,* and the upcoming *Urban Legends* anthology.

On the digital writing platform Wattpad she was selected to be part of the Wattpad Stars program. She has written for Warner Bros and has participated in several contests. Her flash fiction *'Skirt'* was a winning entry in Hulu's *#myhandmaidstale,* selected by Margaret Atwood. Her stories, including *Marrow Charm,* won two consecutive Wattys in 2015 and 2016 for excellence in digital storytelling.

In 2016, she published *Zombies vs Aliens,* a humorous science fiction horror romp, which was picked up by Chapters Interactive Stories in 2018 to be released as an Interactive Story Game.

Her contemporary fantasy Ragnarök Unwound will be published with Sky Forest Press in the fall of 2018.

When not writing, she is juggling two rambunctious boys, spoiling her cats, and catching up on a massive TBR pile. She is currently working on a the sequel to Marrow Charm, and various other projects full of magic, mystery, and delight.

For more info:

Wattpad:https://www.wattpad.com/user/krazydiamond
Website: http://www.kristinjacques.com/

The Parliament House

THE PARLIAMENT HOUSE
WWW.PARLIAMENTHOUSEPRESS.COM

Want more from our amazing authors? Visit our website for trailers, exclusive blogs, additional content and more!

Become a Parliament Person and access secret bonus content...

JOIN US

CPSIA information can be obtained
at www.ICGtesting.com
Printed in the USA
LVHW031616071119
636673LV00003B/656/P

9 781691 022298